Oddly ★ Normal

WRITTEN & ILLUSTRATED
by OTIS FRAMPTON

IMAGE COMICS, INC.

Robert Kirkman – Chief Operating Officer
Erik Larsen – Chief Financial Officer
Todd McFarlane – President
Marc Silvestri – Chief Executive Officer
Jim Valentino – Vice-President

Eric Stephenson – Publisher
Corey Murphy – Director of Sales
Jeff Boison – Director of Publishing Planning & Book Trade Sales
Jeremy Sullivan – Director of Digital Sales
Kat Salazar – Director of PR & Marketing
Emily Miller – Director of Operations
Branwyn Bigglestone – Senior Accounts Manager
Sarah Mello – Accounts Manager
Drew Gill – Art Director
Jonathan Chan – Production Manager
Meredith Wallace – Print Manager
Briah Skelly – Publicity Assistant
Sasha Head – Sales & Marketing Production Designer
Randy Okamura – Digital Production Designer
David Brothers – Branding Manager
Ally Power – Content Manager
Addison Duke – Production Artist
Vincent Kukua – Production Artist
Tricia Ramos – Production Artist
Jeff Stang – Direct Market Sales Representative
Emilio Bautista – Digital Sales Associate
Leanna Caunter – Accounting Assistant
Chloe Ramos-Peterson – Administrative Assistant
IMAGECOMICS.COM

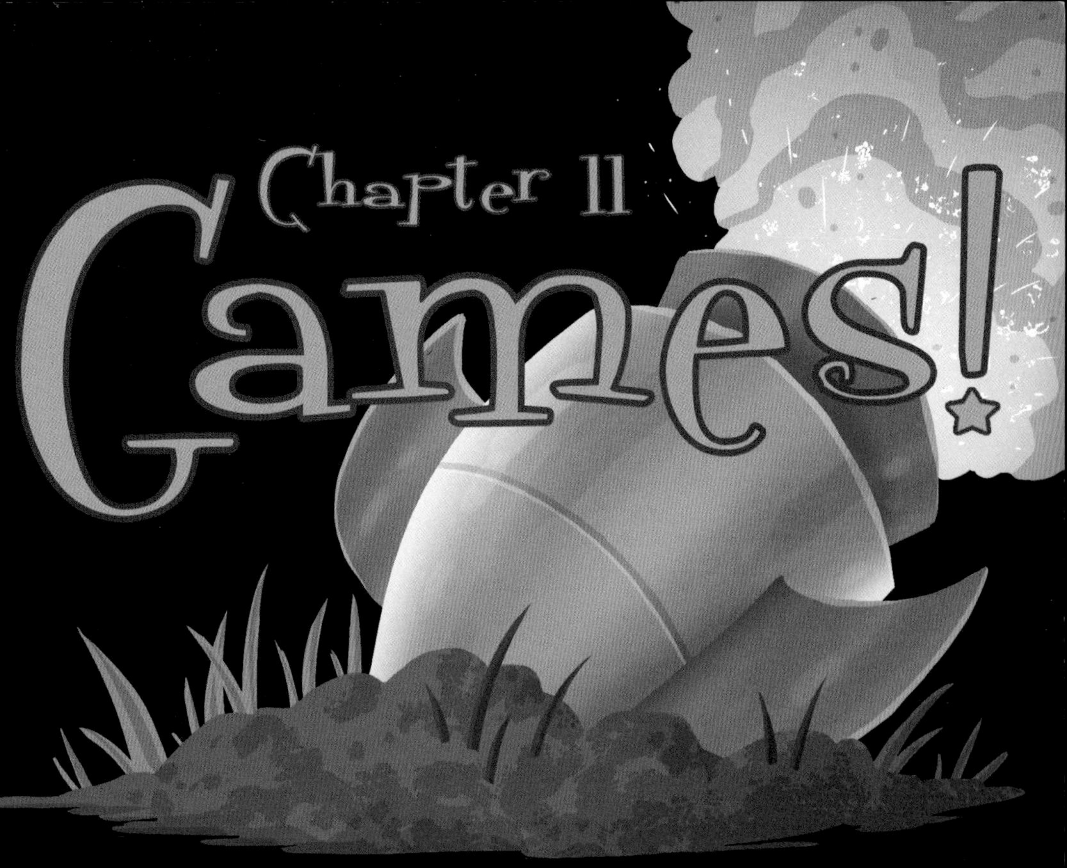
Chapter 11
Games!

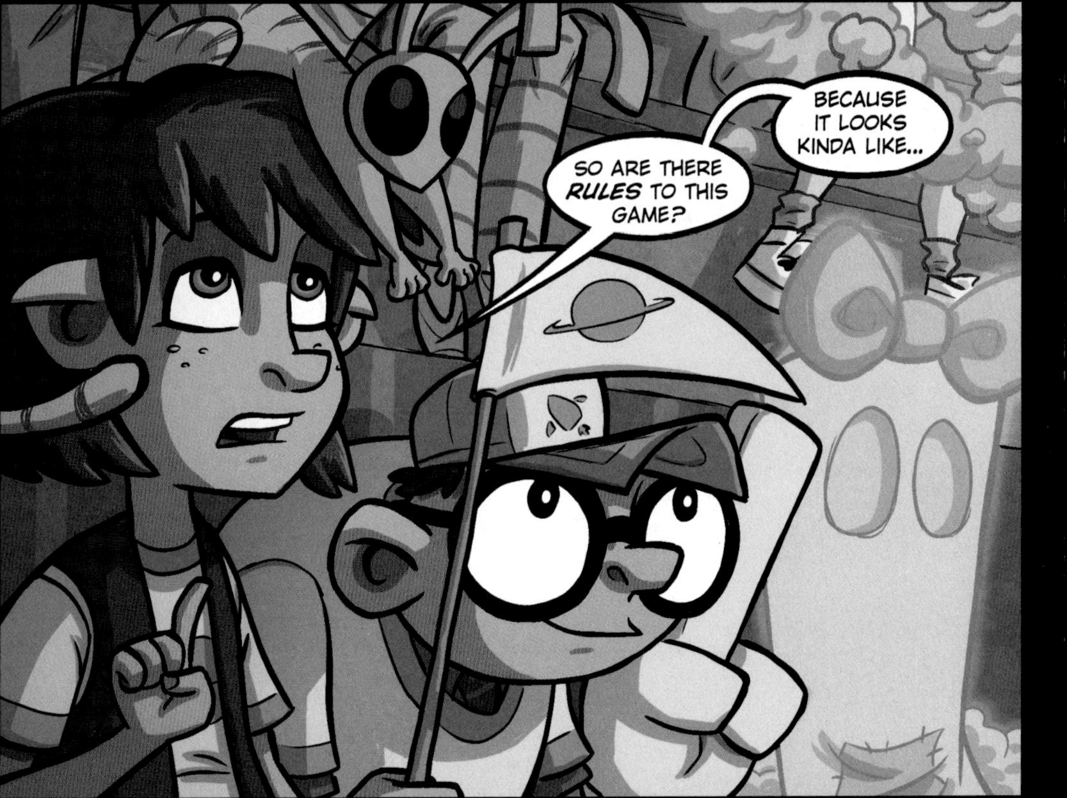
SO ARE THERE **RULES** TO THIS GAME?
BECAUSE IT LOOKS KINDA LIKE...

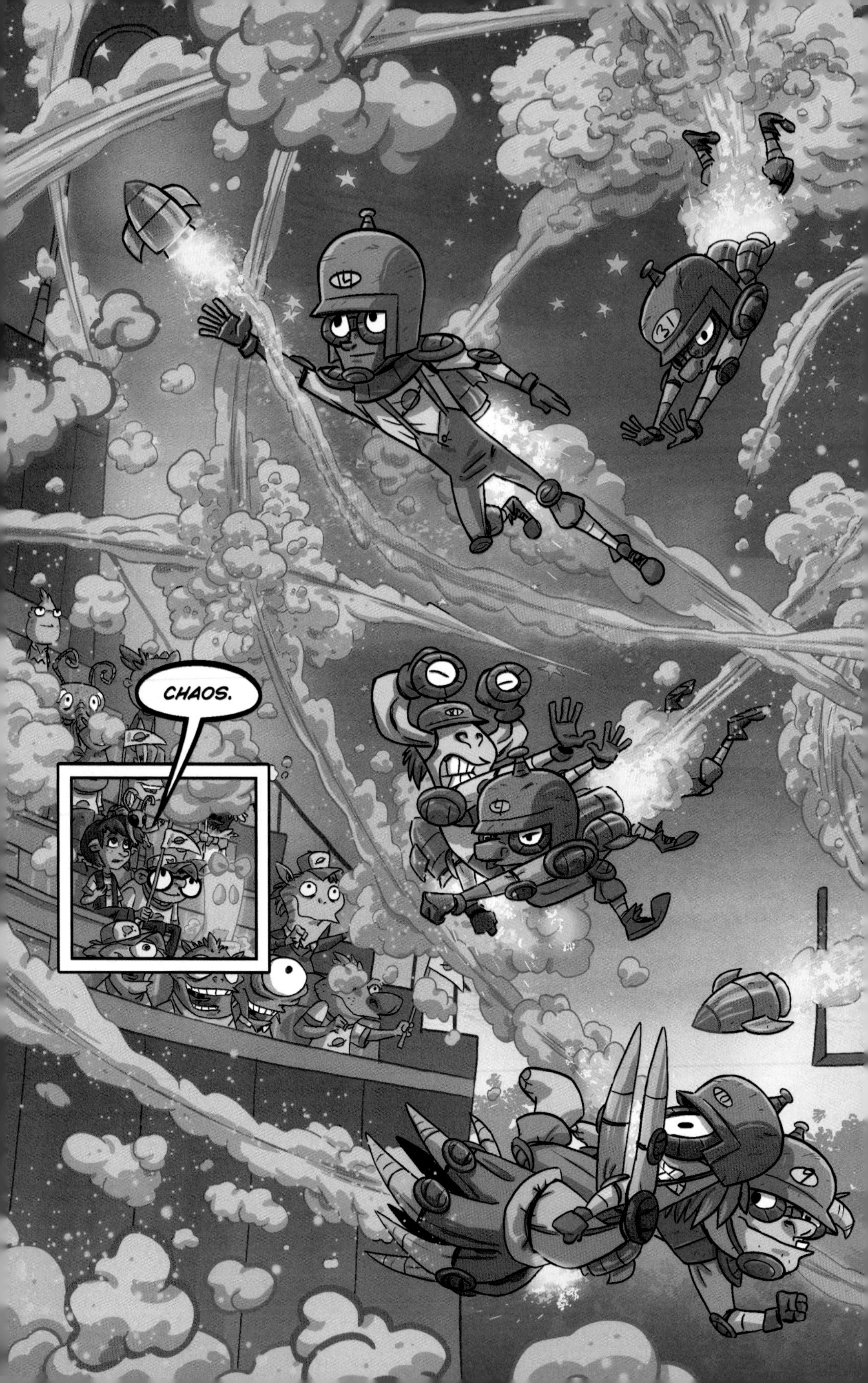
CHAOS.

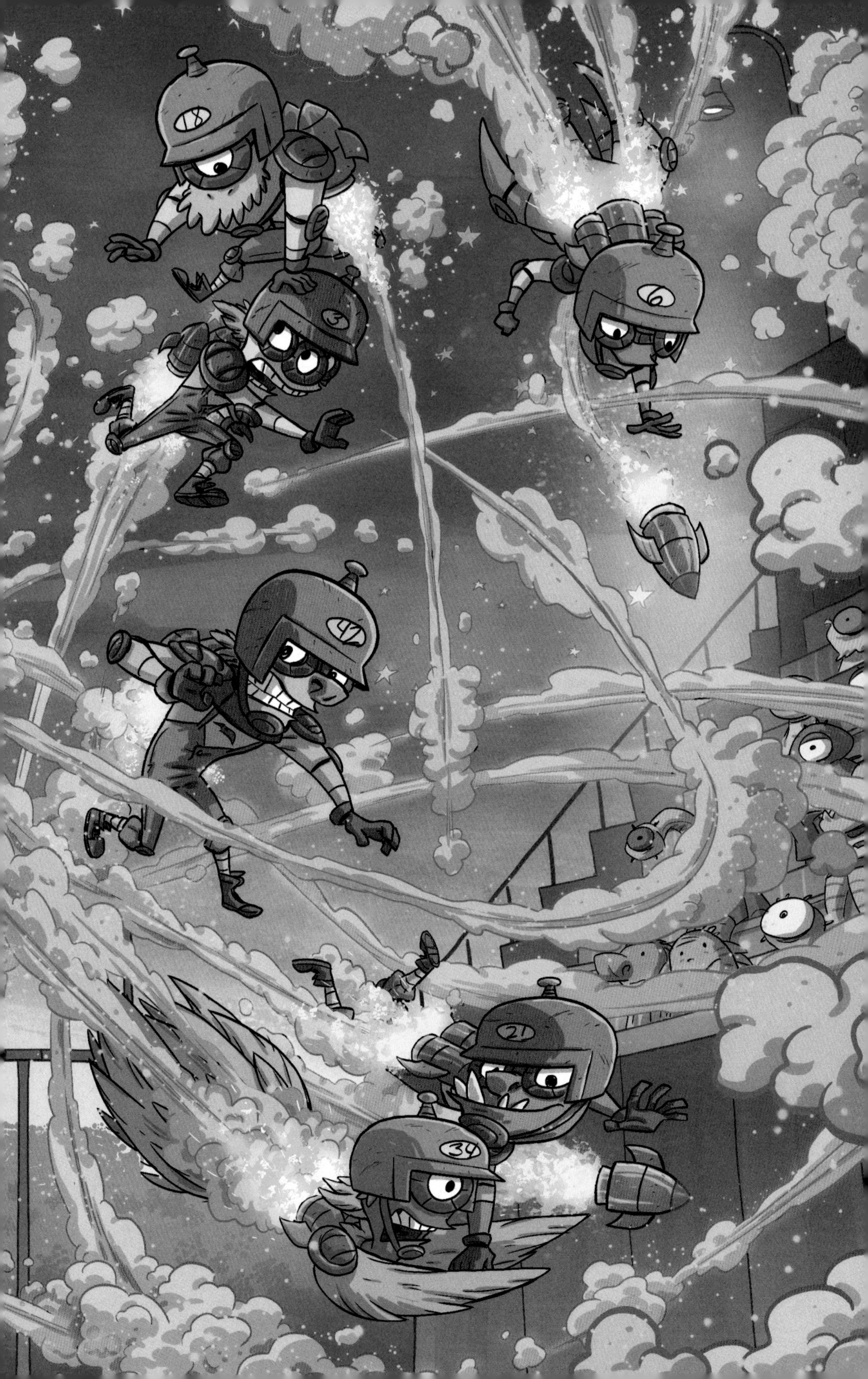
18
3
6
42
21
34

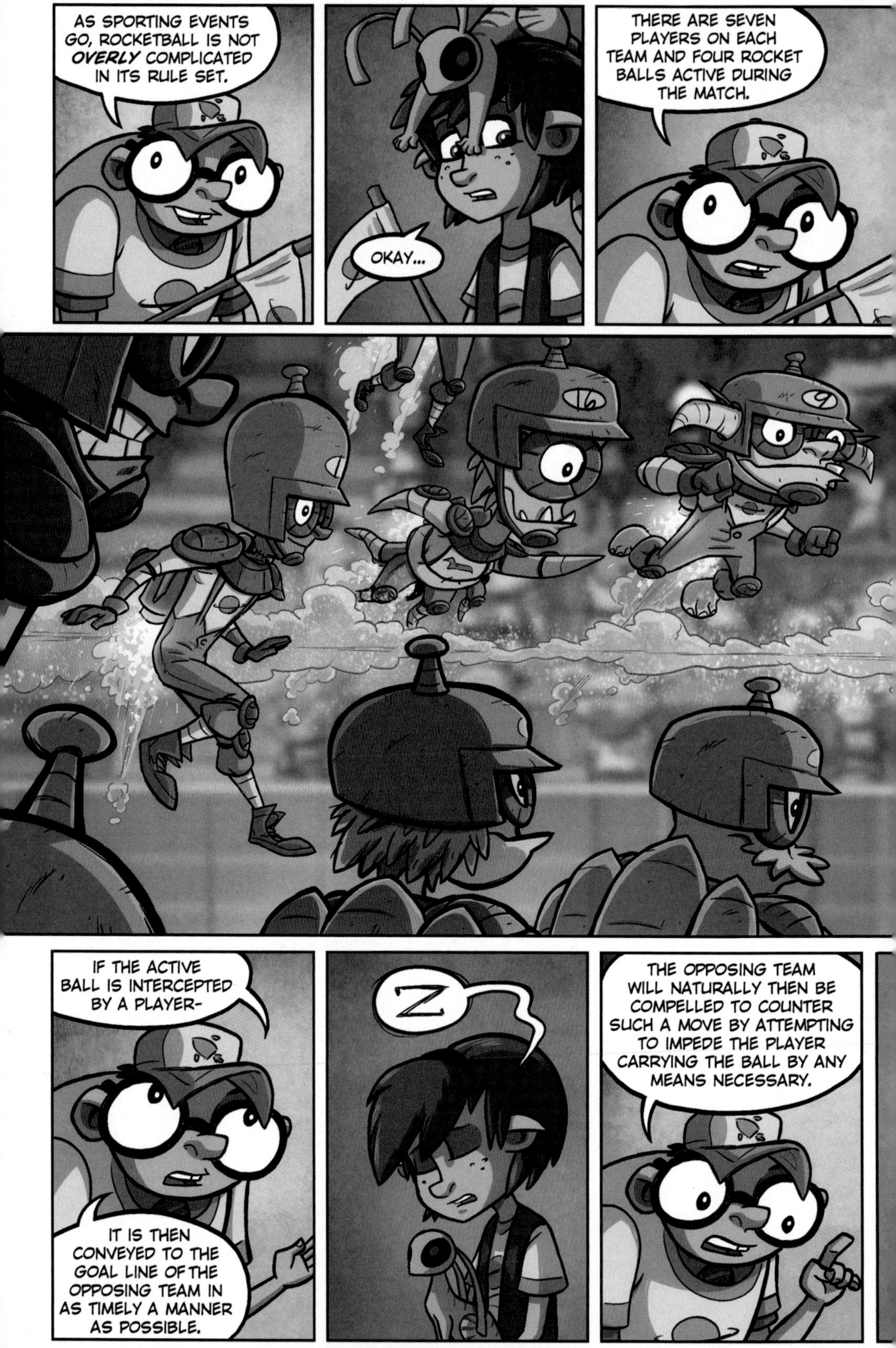
AS SPORTING EVENTS GO, ROCKETBALL IS NOT *OVERLY* COMPLICATED IN ITS RULE SET.
OKAY...
THERE ARE SEVEN PLAYERS ON EACH TEAM AND FOUR ROCKET BALLS ACTIVE DURING THE MATCH.
IF THE ACTIVE BALL IS INTERCEPTED BY A PLAYER-
IT IS THEN CONVEYED TO THE GOAL LINE OF THE OPPOSING TEAM IN AS TIMELY A MANNER AS POSSIBLE.
Z
THE OPPOSING TEAM WILL NATURALLY THEN BE COMPELLED TO COUNTER SUCH A MOVE BY ATTEMPTING TO IMPEDE THE PLAYER CARRYING THE BALL BY ANY MEANS NECESSARY.

UH-*HUH*...

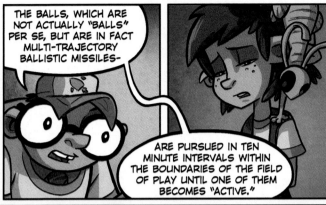

THE BALLS, WHICH ARE NOT ACTUALLY "BALLS" PER SE, BUT ARE IN FACT MULTI-TRAJECTORY BALLISTIC MISSILES—

ARE PURSUED IN TEN MINUTE INTERVALS WITHIN THE BOUNDARIES OF THE FIELD OF PLAY UNTIL ONE OF THEM BECOMES "ACTIVE."

BA-DEEP! BA-DEEP! BA-DEEP! BA-DEEP!

SNORT!!!

HUH?

OOPIE OOPIE!!

AND THOSE ARE THE BASIC RULES OF THE FIGNATION NATIONAL PASTTIME.

YEAH. OKAY.

THAT SOUNDS SIMPLE ENOUGH.

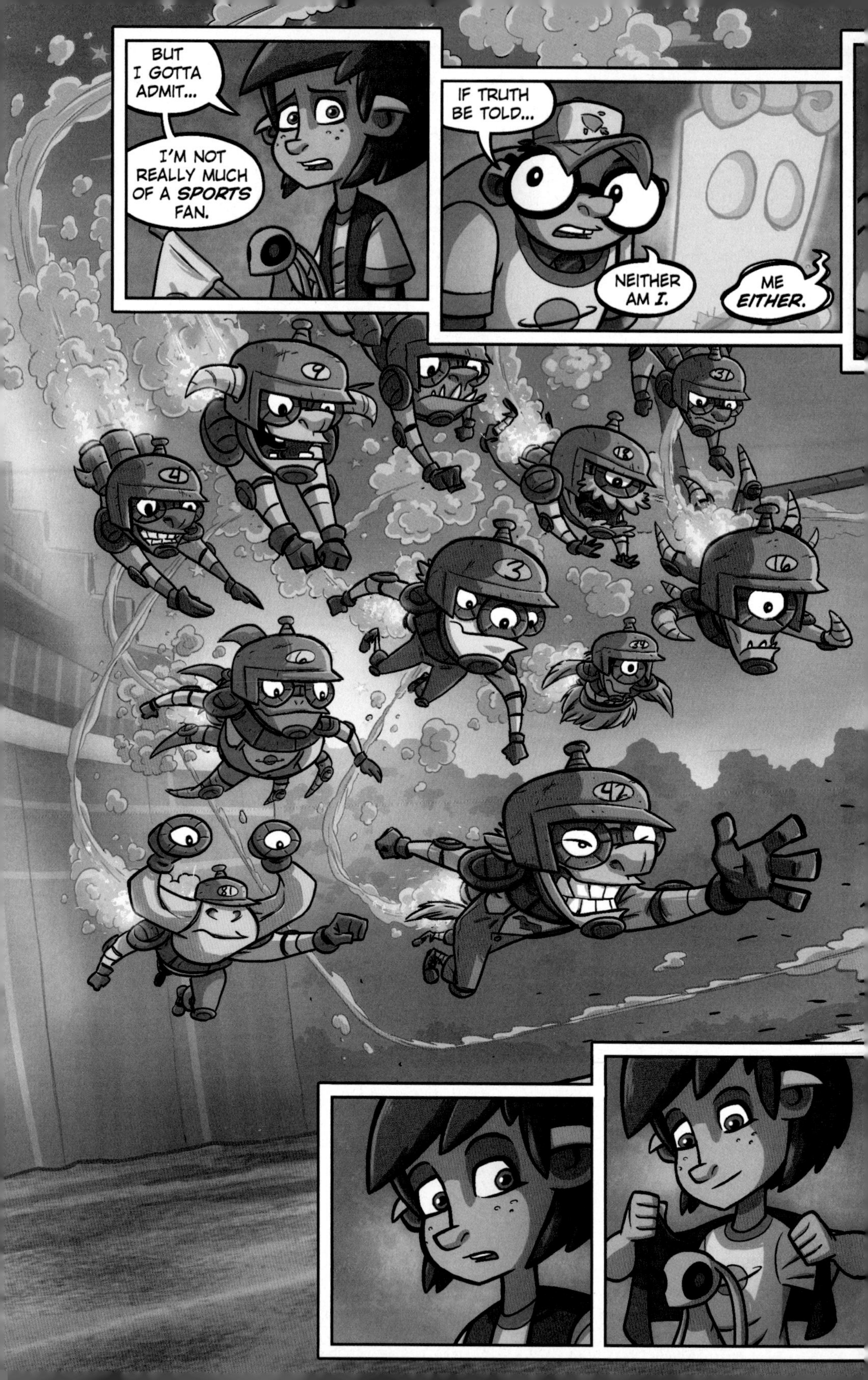
BUT I GOTTA ADMIT...
I'M NOT REALLY MUCH OF A *SPORTS* FAN.
IF TRUTH BE TOLD...
NEITHER AM *I*.
ME *EITHER*.

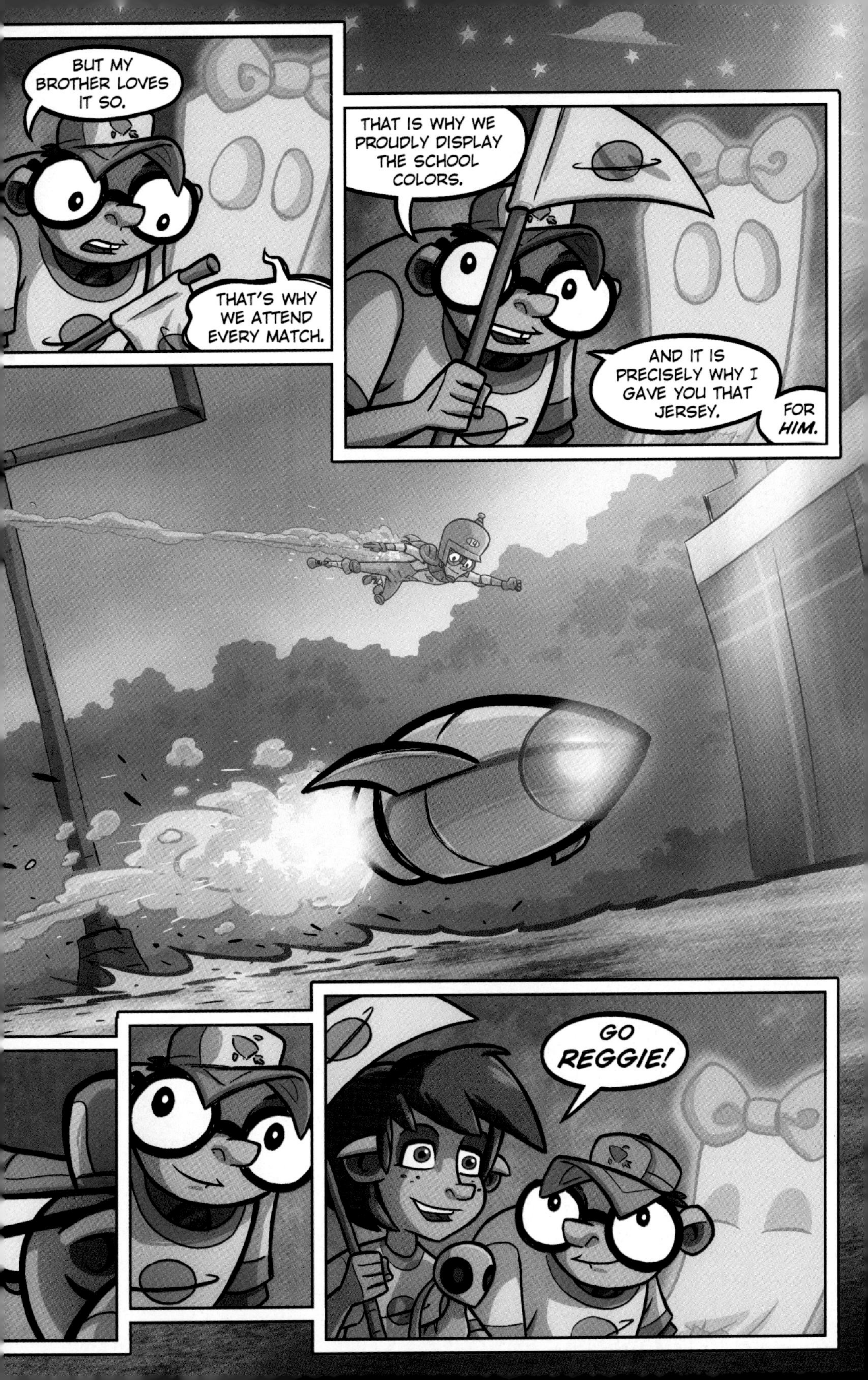
BUT MY BROTHER LOVES IT SO.
THAT'S WHY WE ATTEND EVERY MATCH.
THAT IS WHY WE PROUDLY DISPLAY THE SCHOOL COLORS.
AND IT IS PRECISELY WHY I GAVE YOU THAT JERSEY.
FOR HIM.
GO REGGIE!

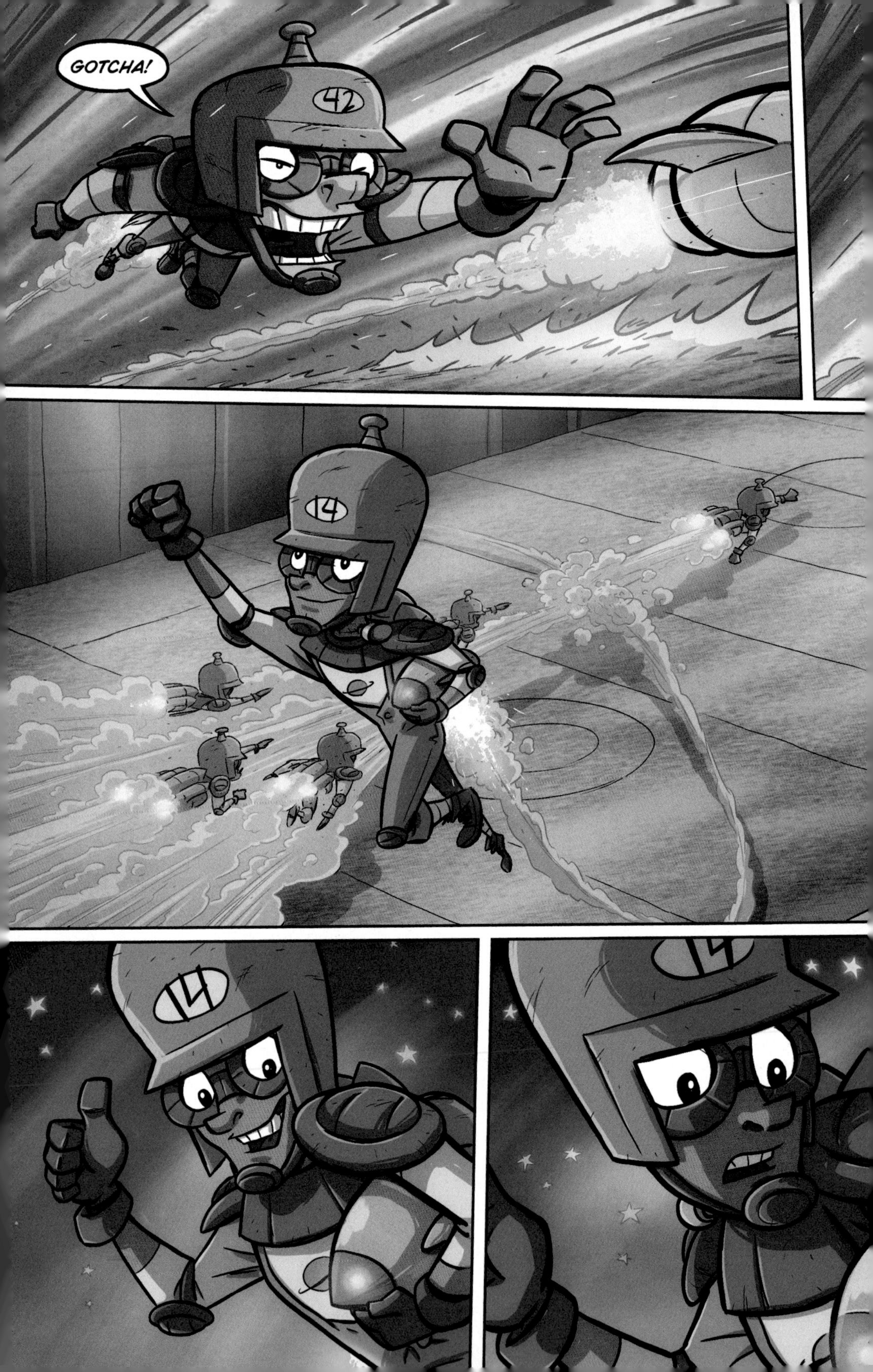
GOTCHA!

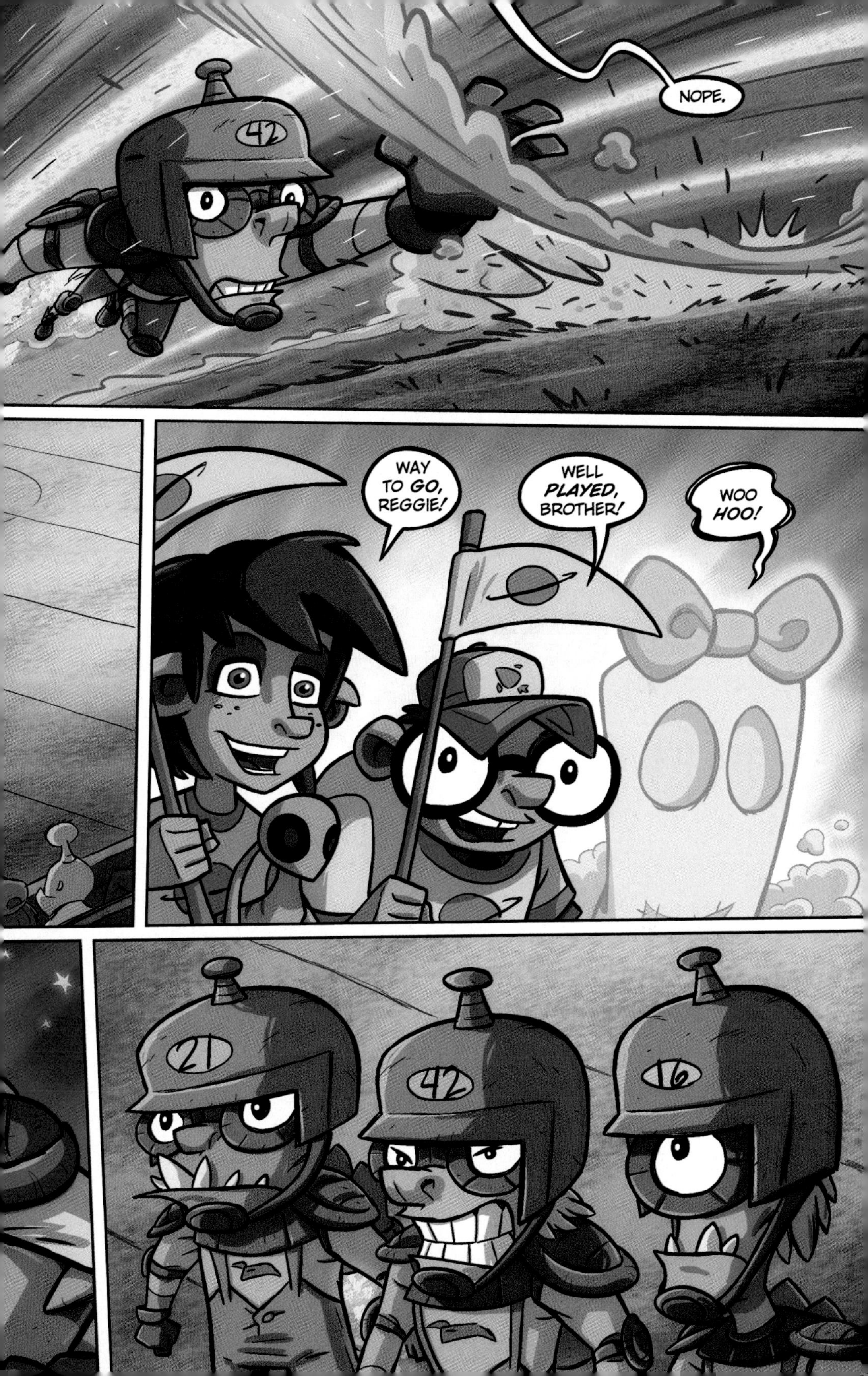
NOPE.
WAY TO GO, REGGIE!
WELL PLAYED, BROTHER!
WOO HOO!

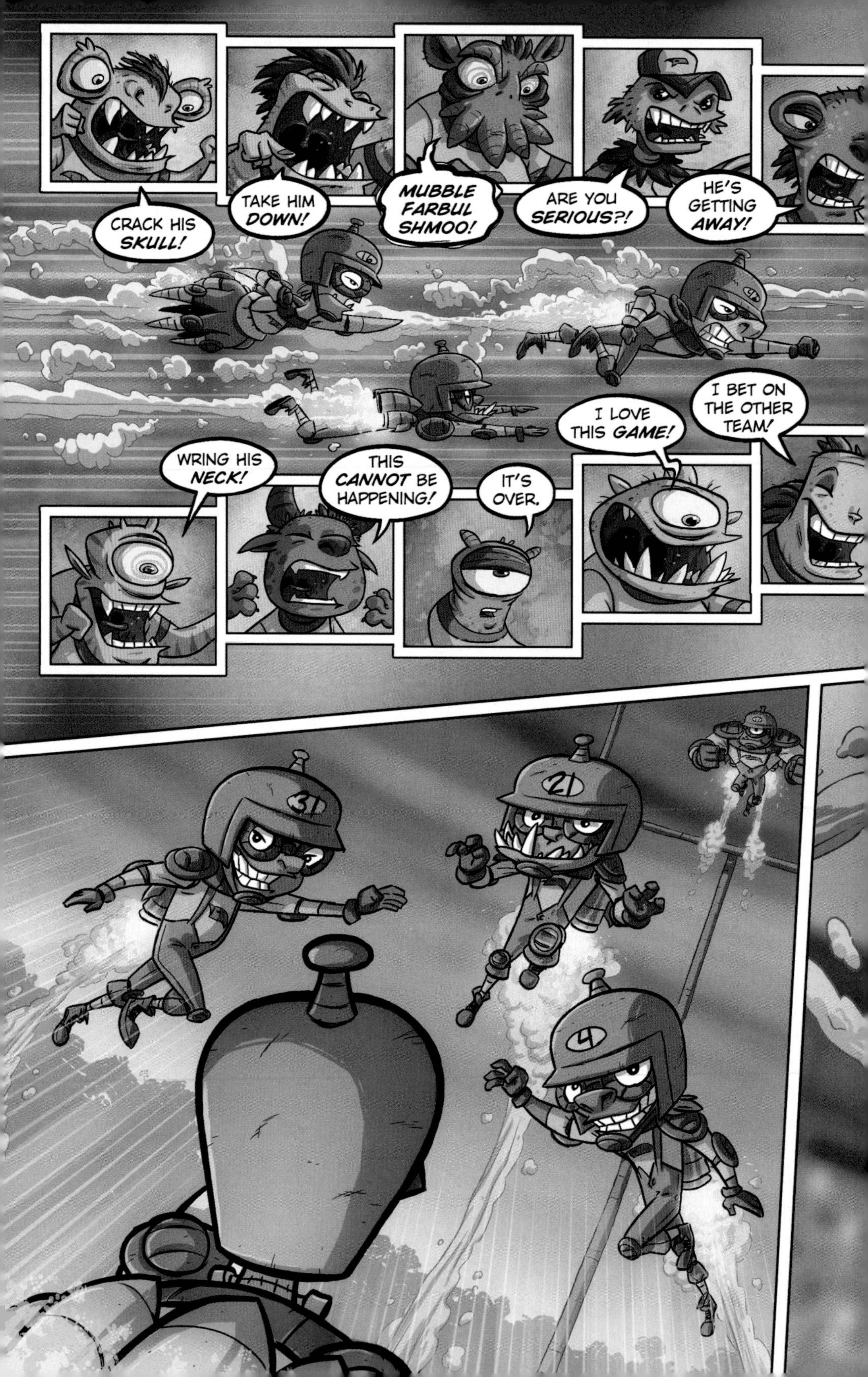
CRACK HIS SKULL!
TAKE HIM DOWN!
MUBBLE FARBUL SHMOO!
ARE YOU SERIOUS?!
HE'S GETTING AWAY!
I BET ON THE OTHER TEAM!
I LOVE THIS GAME!
WRING HIS NECK!
THIS CANNOT BE HAPPENING!
IT'S OVER.
31
21
4

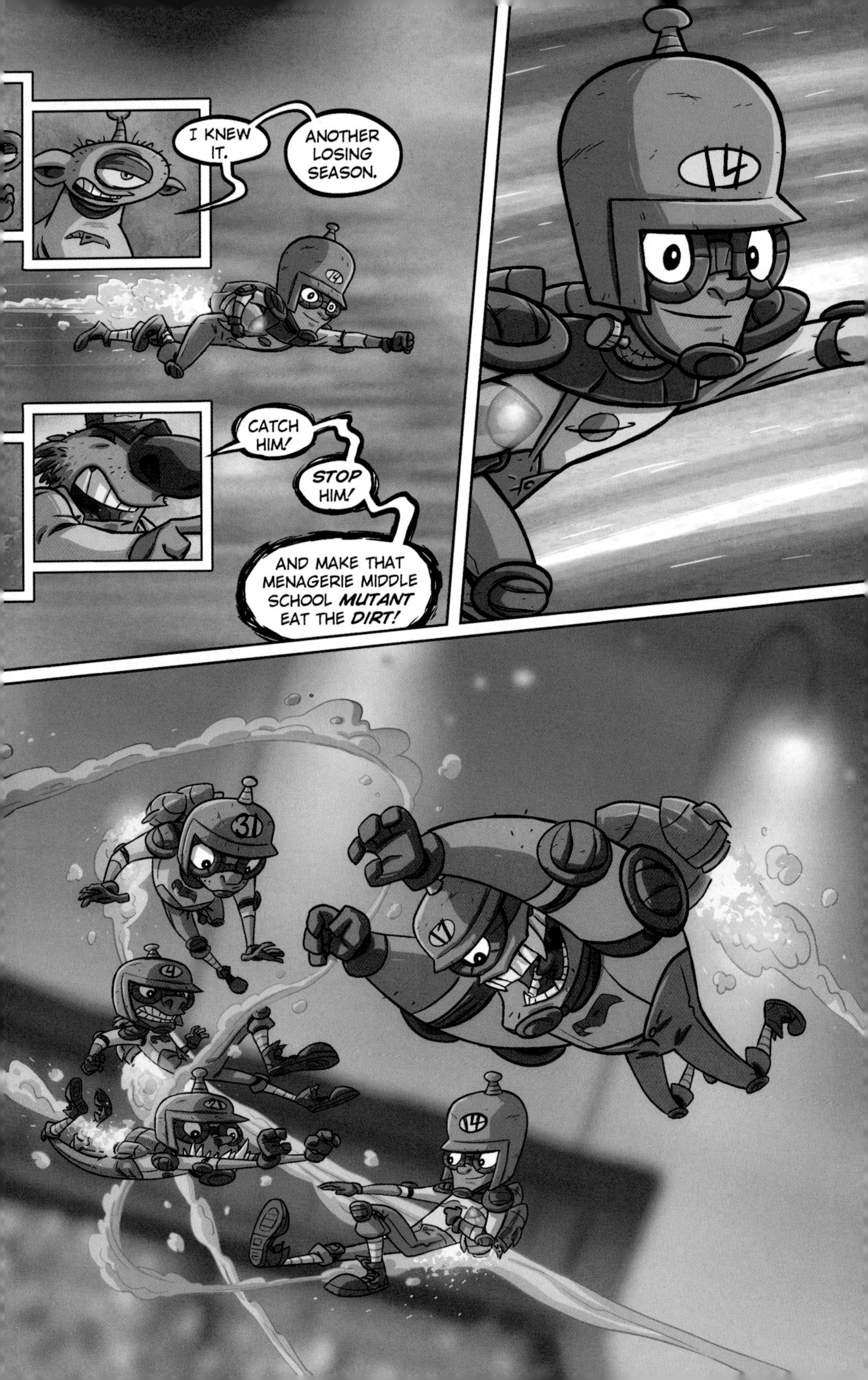
I KNEW IT.
ANOTHER LOSING SEASON.
CATCH HIM!
STOP HIM!
AND MAKE THAT MENAGERIE MIDDLE SCHOOL MUTANT EAT THE DIRT!

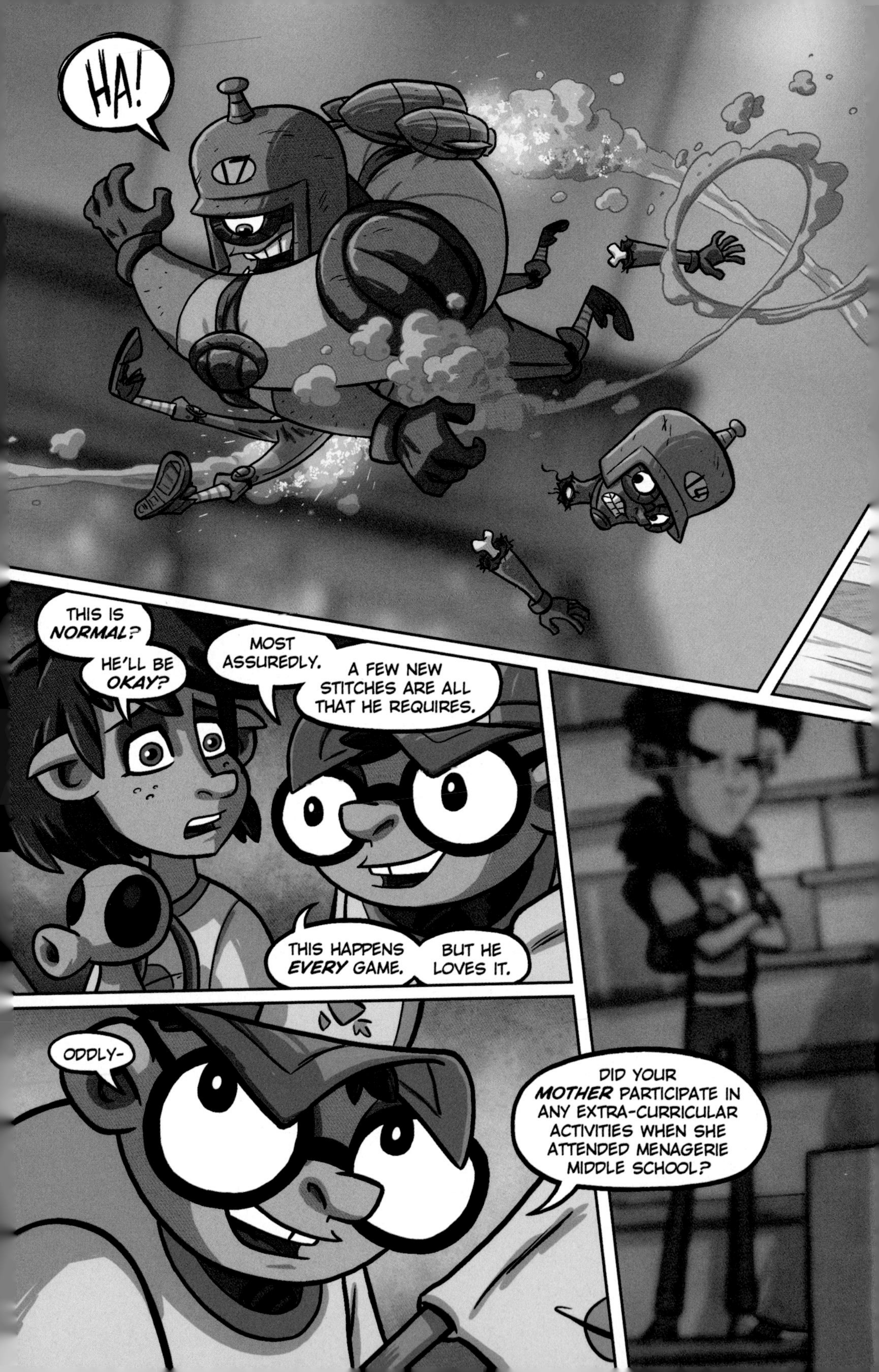
HA!
THIS IS NORMAL?
HE'LL BE OKAY?
MOST ASSUREDLY.
A FEW NEW STITCHES ARE ALL THAT HE REQUIRES.
THIS HAPPENS EVERY GAME.
BUT HE LOVES IT.
ODDLY-
DID YOUR MOTHER PARTICIPATE IN ANY EXTRA-CURRICULAR ACTIVITIES WHEN SHE ATTENDED MENAGERIE MIDDLE SCHOOL?

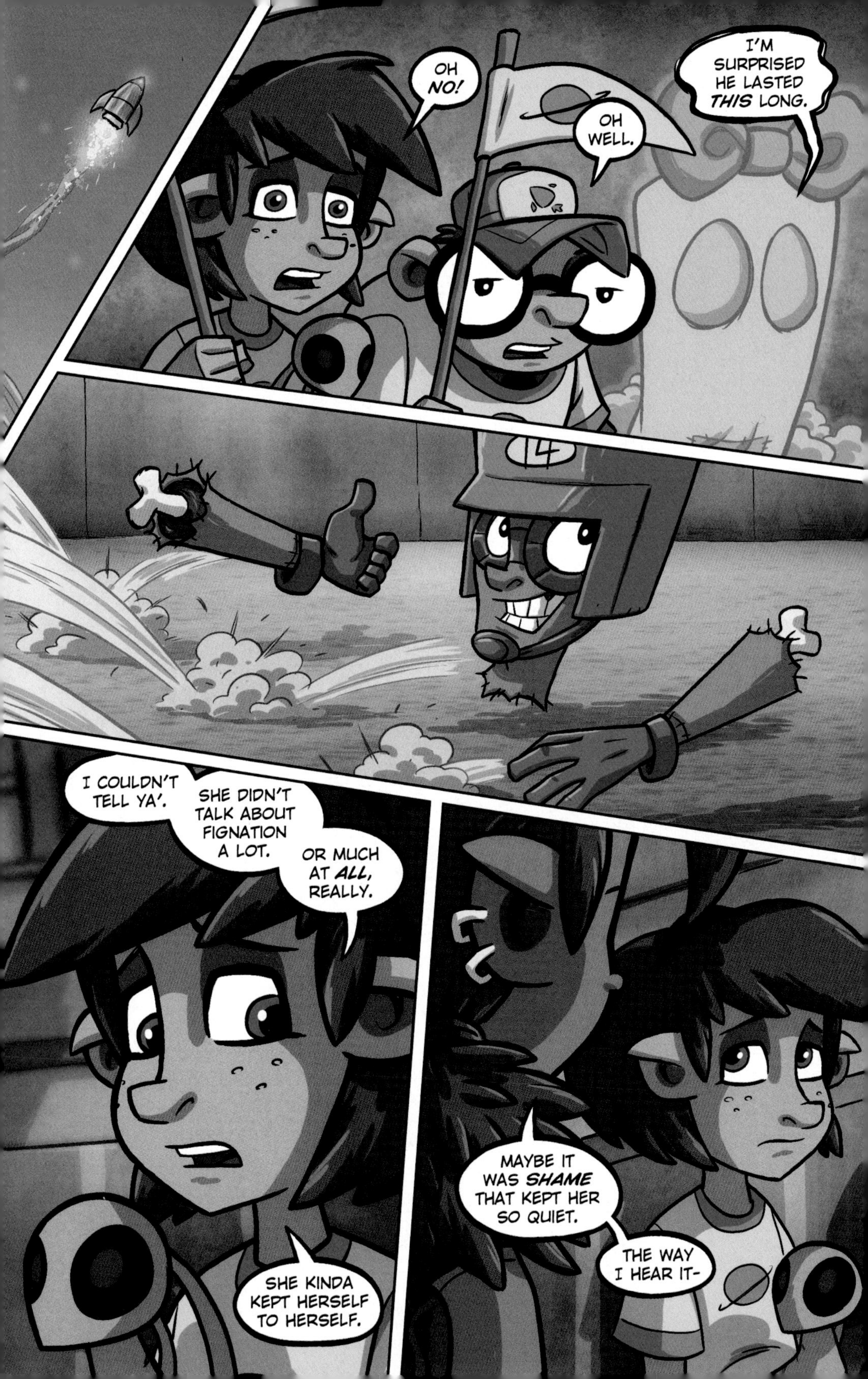

OH NO!
OH WELL.
I'M SURPRISED HE LASTED THIS LONG.
I COULDN'T TELL YA'.
SHE DIDN'T TALK ABOUT FIGNATION A LOT.
OR MUCH AT ALL, REALLY.
SHE KINDA KEPT HERSELF TO HERSELF.
MAYBE IT WAS SHAME THAT KEPT HER SO QUIET.
THE WAY I HEAR IT-

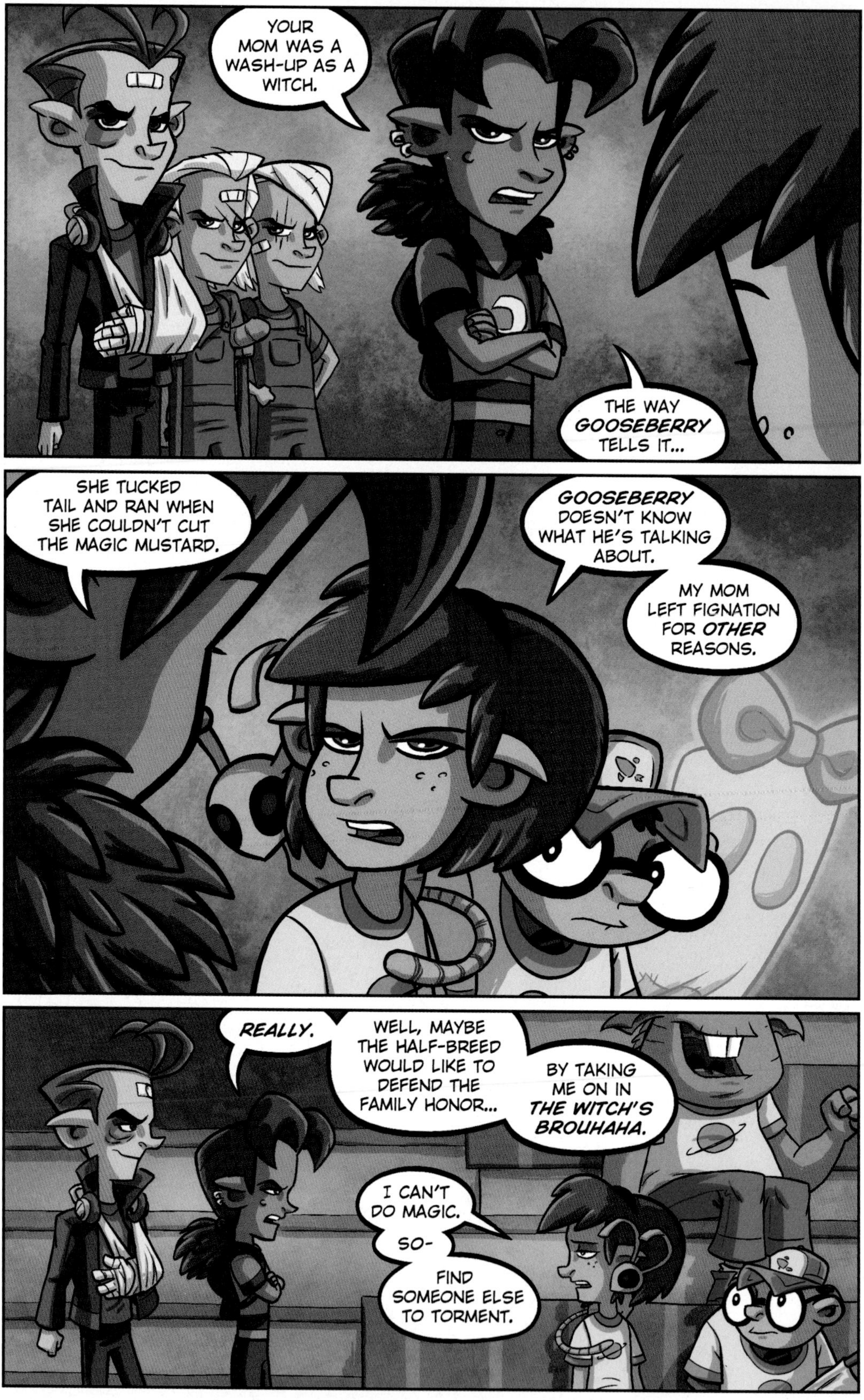
YOUR MOM WAS A WASH-UP AS A WITCH.
THE WAY GOOSEBERRY TELLS IT...
SHE TUCKED TAIL AND RAN WHEN SHE COULDN'T CUT THE MAGIC MUSTARD.
GOOSEBERRY DOESN'T KNOW WHAT HE'S TALKING ABOUT.
MY MOM LEFT FIGNATION FOR OTHER REASONS.
REALLY.
WELL, MAYBE THE HALF-BREED WOULD LIKE TO DEFEND THE FAMILY HONOR...
BY TAKING ME ON IN THE WITCH'S BROUHAHA.
I CAN'T DO MAGIC.
SO-
FIND SOMEONE ELSE TO TORMENT.

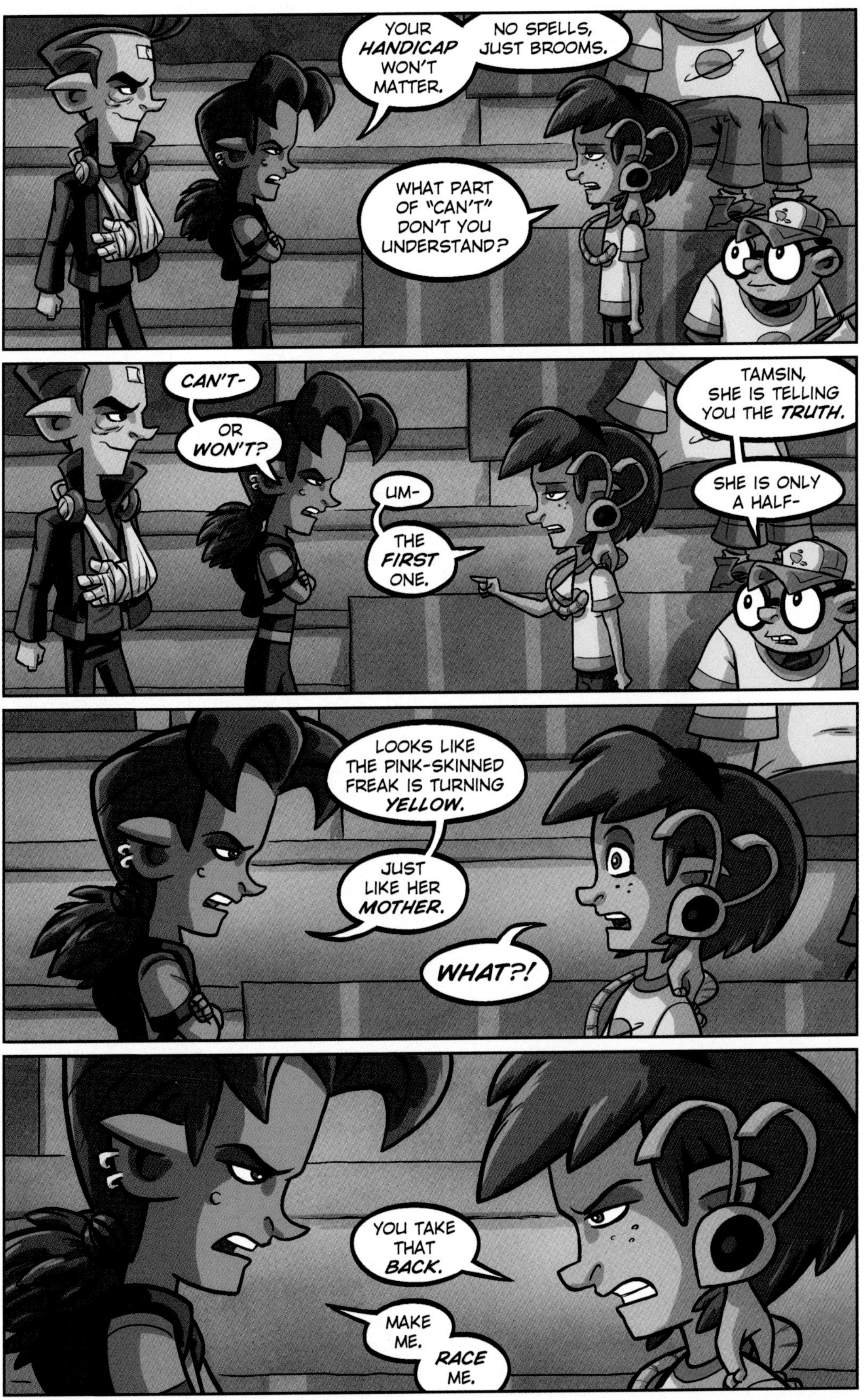

YOUR *HANDICAP* WON'T MATTER.
NO SPELLS, JUST BROOMS.
WHAT PART OF "CAN'T" DON'T YOU UNDERSTAND?
CAN'T-
OR *WON'T?*
UM-
THE *FIRST* ONE.
TAMSIN, SHE IS TELLING YOU THE *TRUTH.*
SHE IS ONLY A HALF-
LOOKS LIKE THE PINK-SKINNED FREAK IS TURNING *YELLOW.*
JUST LIKE HER *MOTHER.*
WHAT?!
YOU TAKE THAT *BACK.*
MAKE ME.
RACE ME.

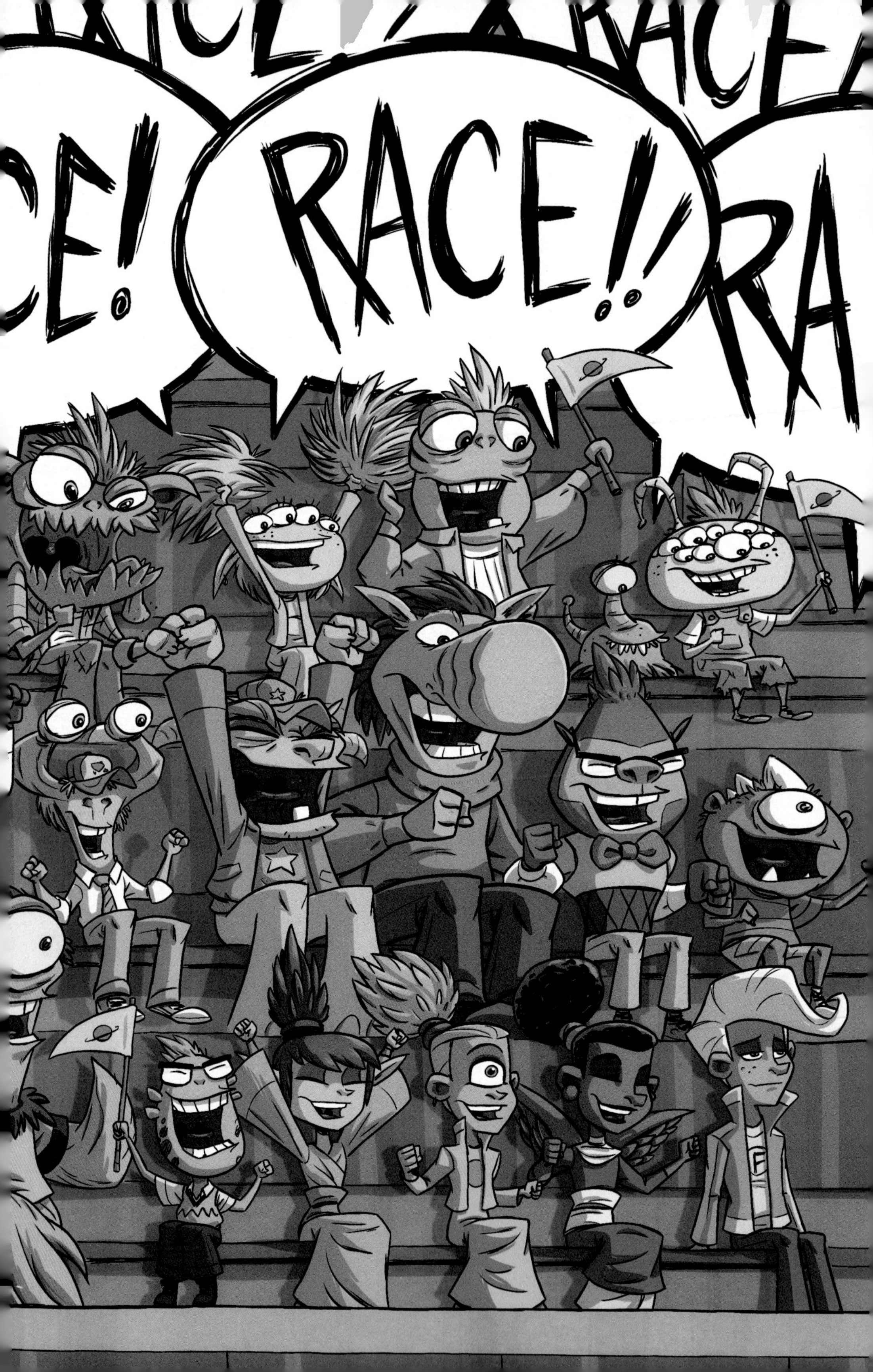
RACE!!

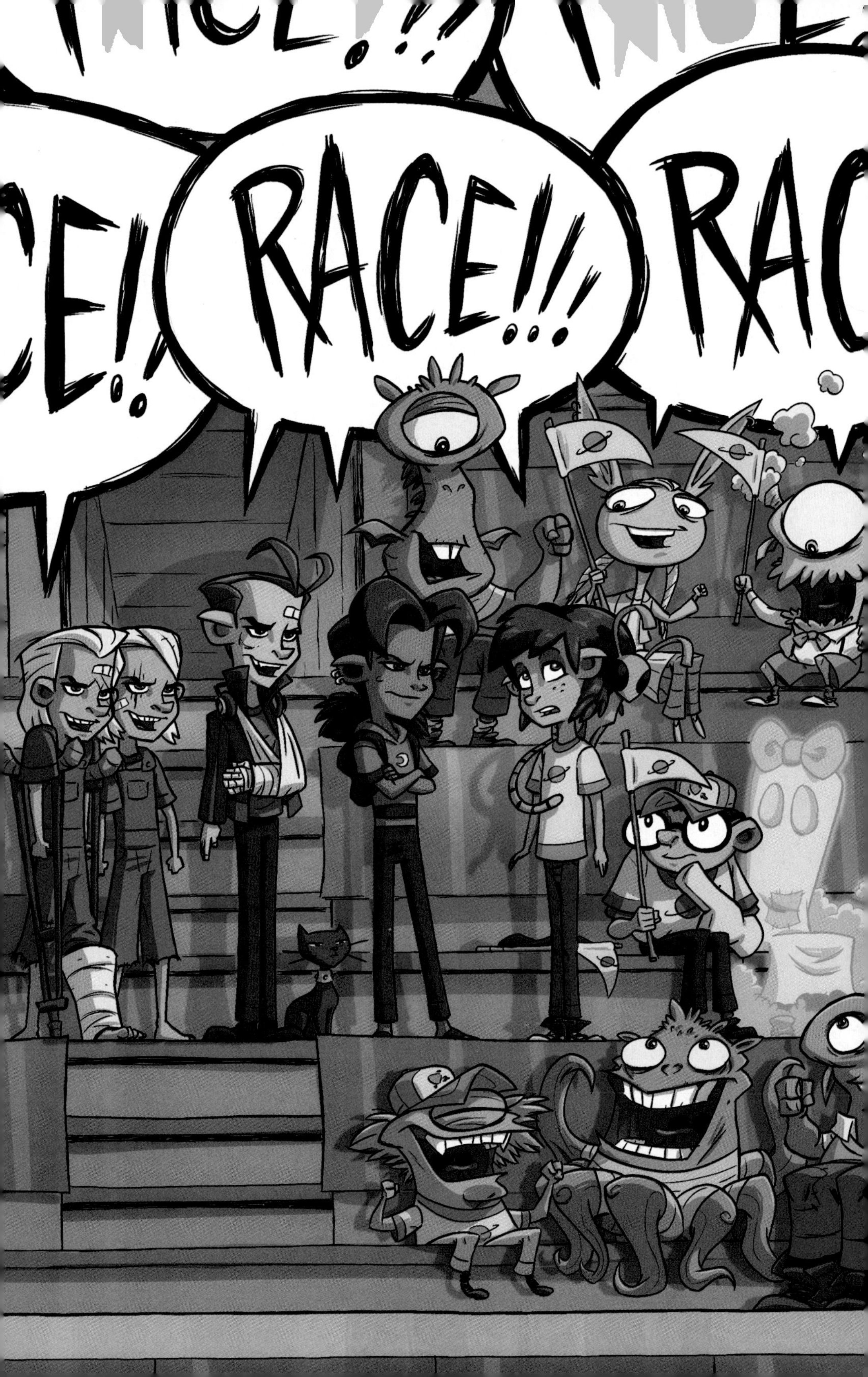
RACE!!!

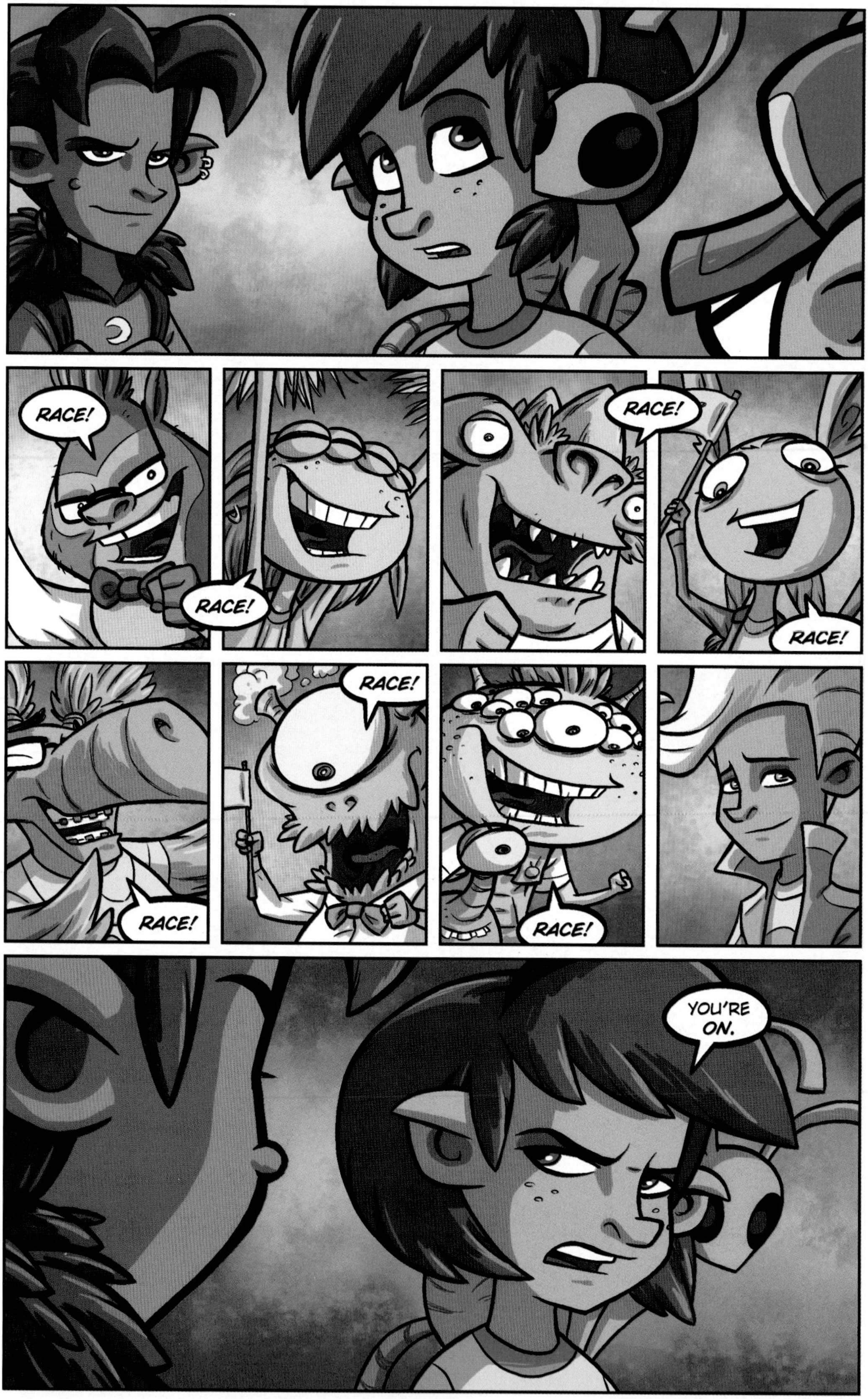
RACE!
RACE!
RACE!
RACE!
RACE!
RACE!
RACE!
YOU'RE ON.

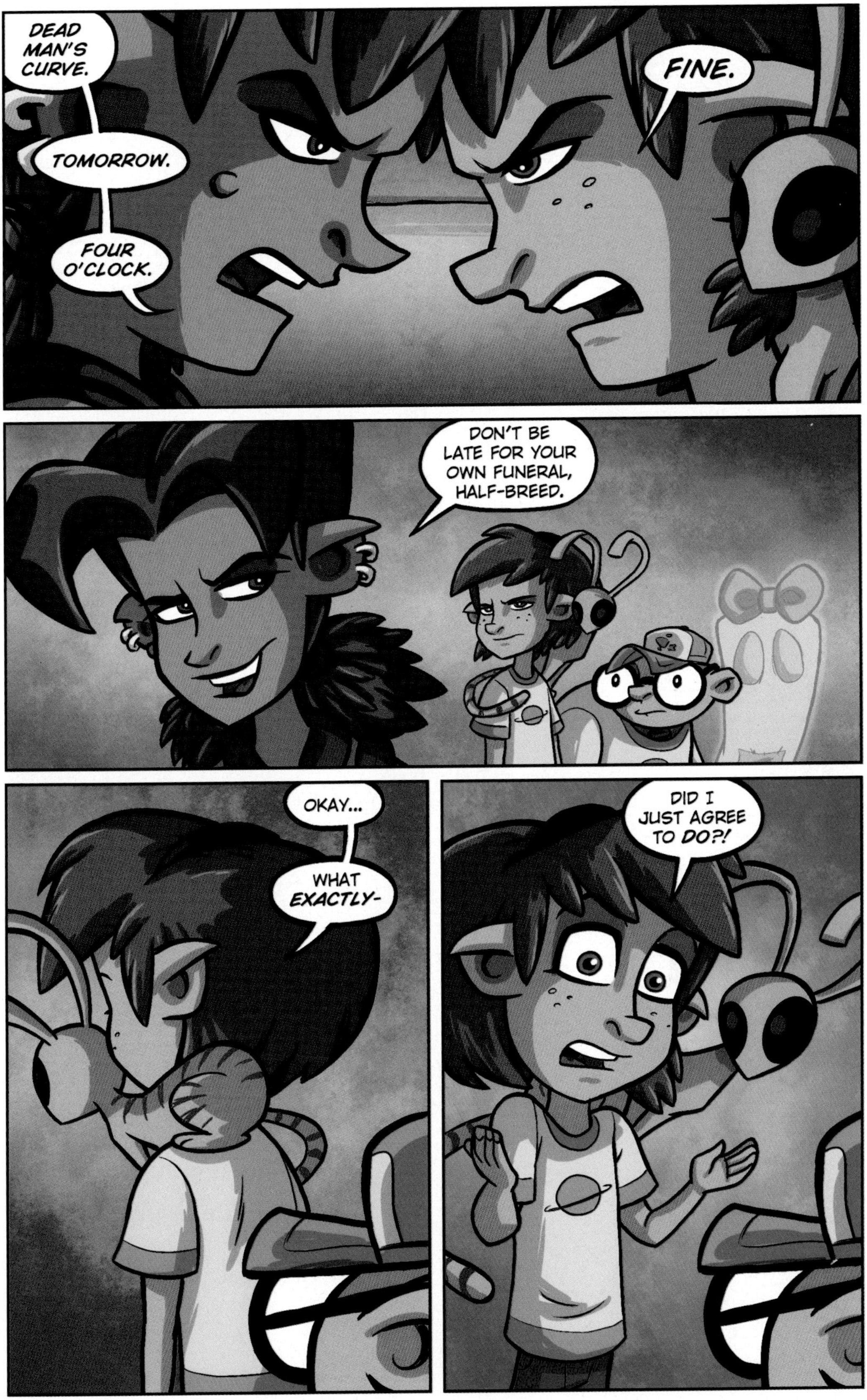
DEAD MAN'S CURVE.
TOMORROW.
FOUR O'CLOCK.
FINE.
DON'T BE LATE FOR YOUR OWN FUNERAL, HALF-BREED.
OKAY...
WHAT *EXACTLY*-
DID I JUST AGREE TO *DO*?!

AS I UNDERSTAND IT—

THE WITCH'S BROUHAHA IS A RITE OF PASSAGE FOR *EVERY* YOUNG WITCH.

IT'S A RACE THROUGH SNAKE-BITE CANYON, HIGH ABOVE A TWISTING RIVER FILLED WITH EVERY MANNER OF BEAST.

OH. OKAY. *GREAT.*

IS THAT *ALL?*

BECAUSE MY ONLY FEARS ARE—

HEIGHTS—

FLYING—

AND *WATER!*

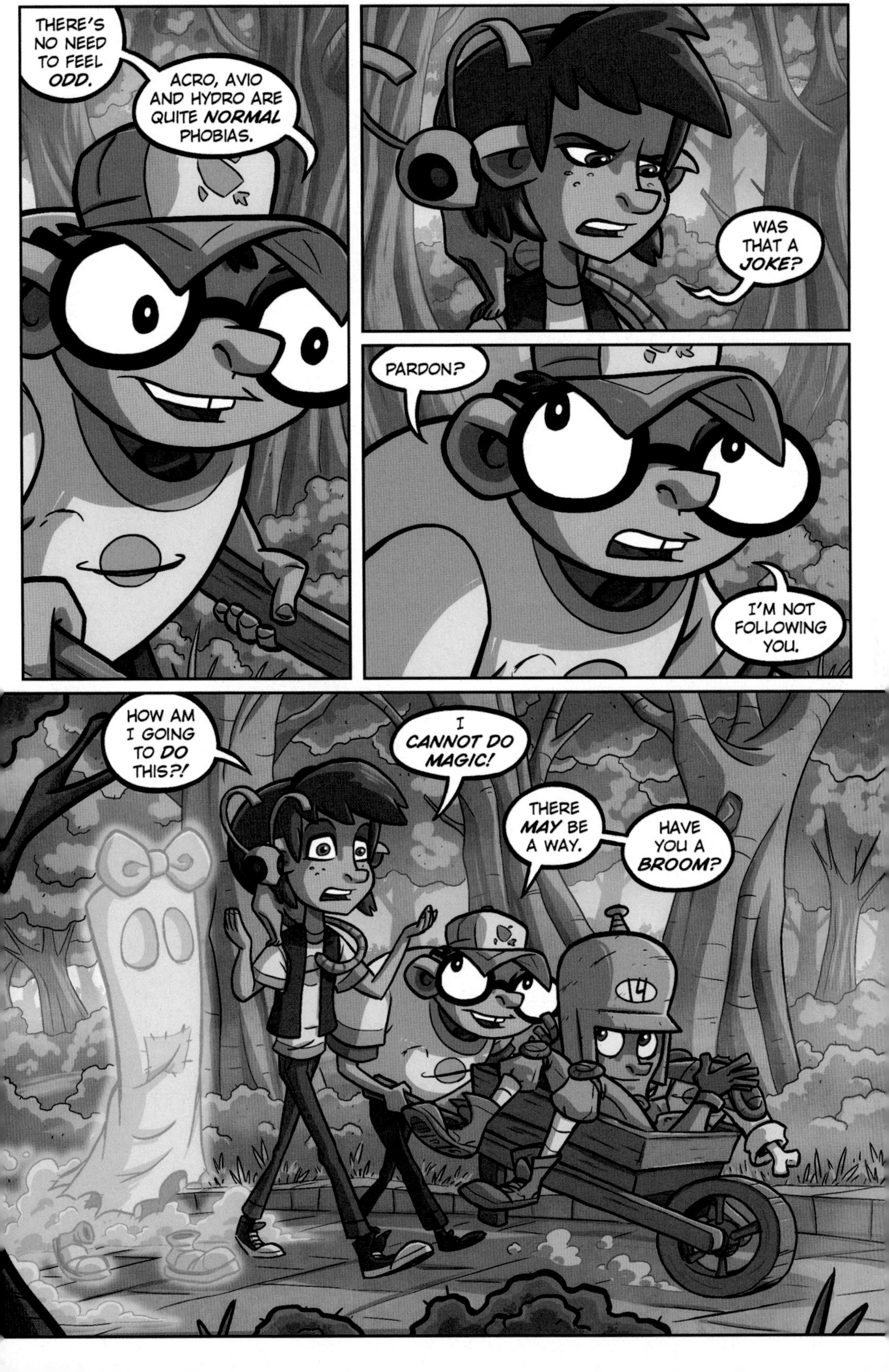
THERE'S NO NEED TO FEEL ODD.
ACRO, AVIO AND HYDRO ARE QUITE NORMAL PHOBIAS.
WAS THAT A JOKE?
PARDON?
I'M NOT FOLLOWING YOU.
HOW AM I GOING TO DO THIS?!
I CANNOT DO MAGIC!
THERE MAY BE A WAY.
HAVE YOU A BROOM?

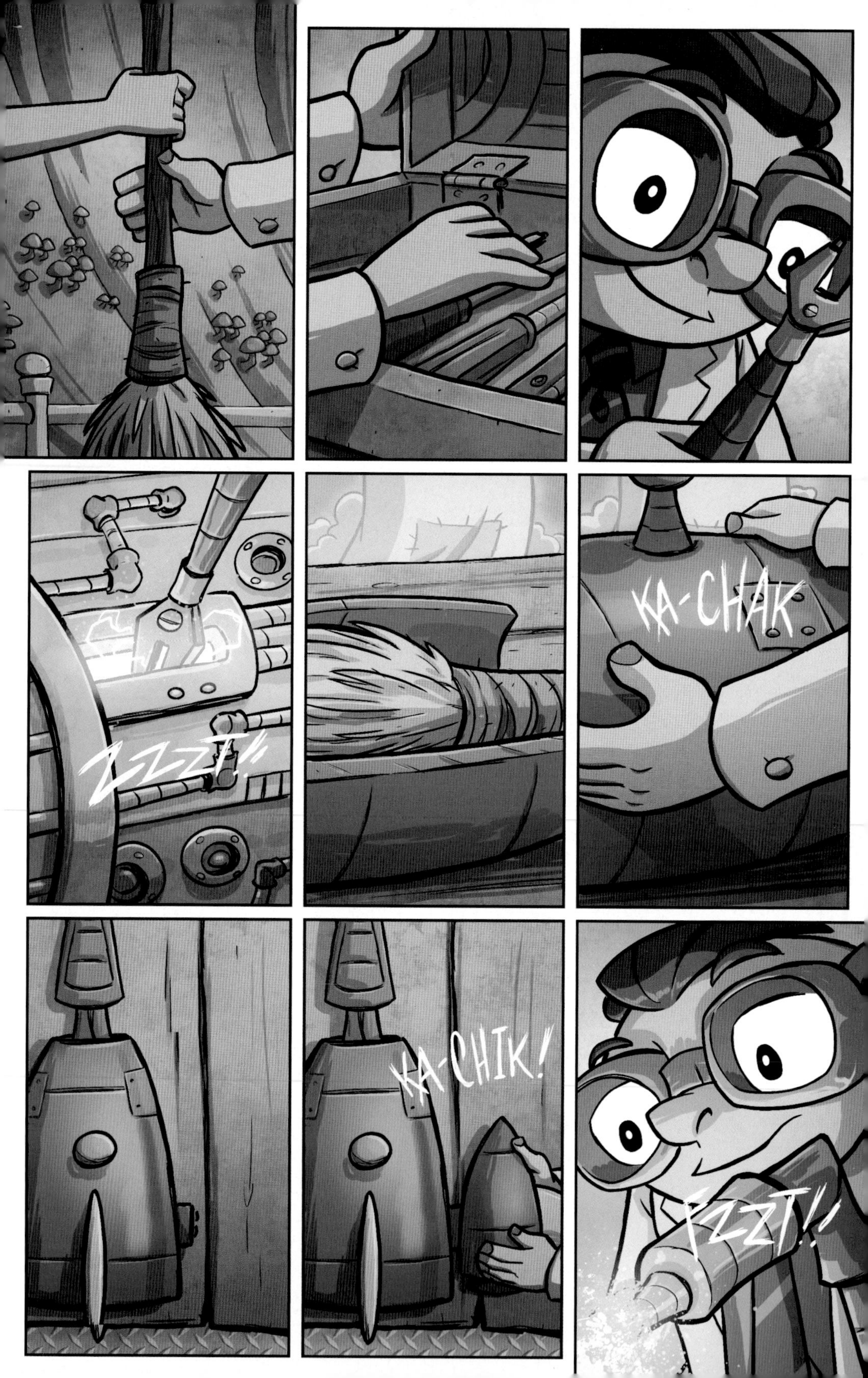
ZZZZT!!
KA-CHAK
KA-CHIK!
FZZZT!!

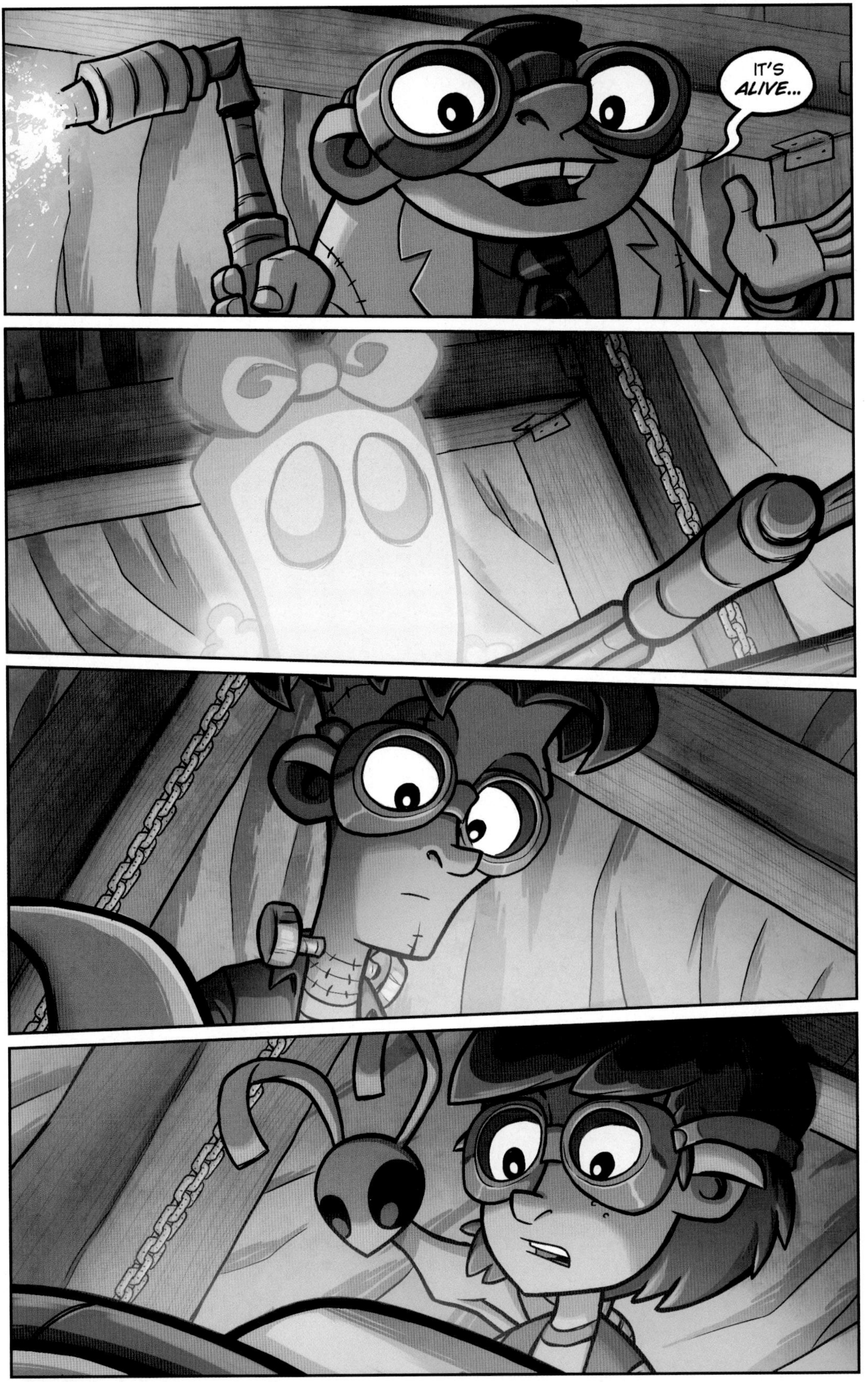
IT'S ALIVE...

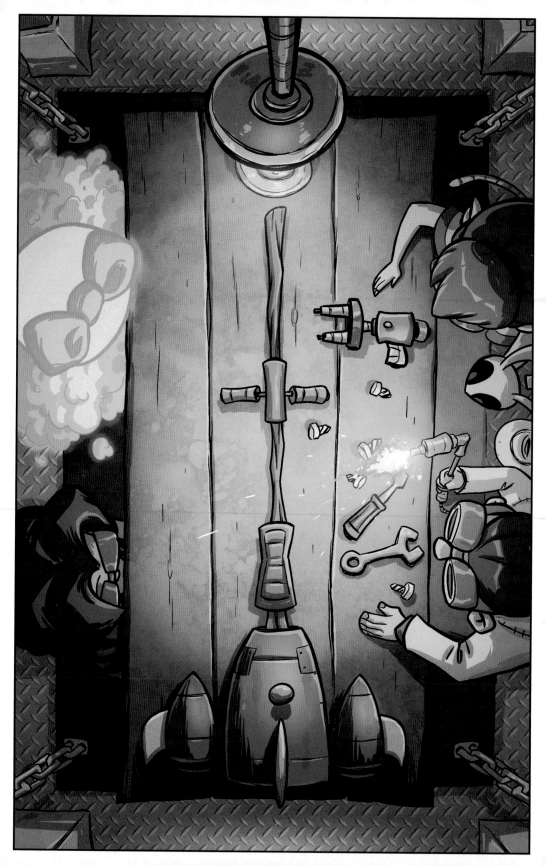

Chapter 12

Acro, Avio & Hydro

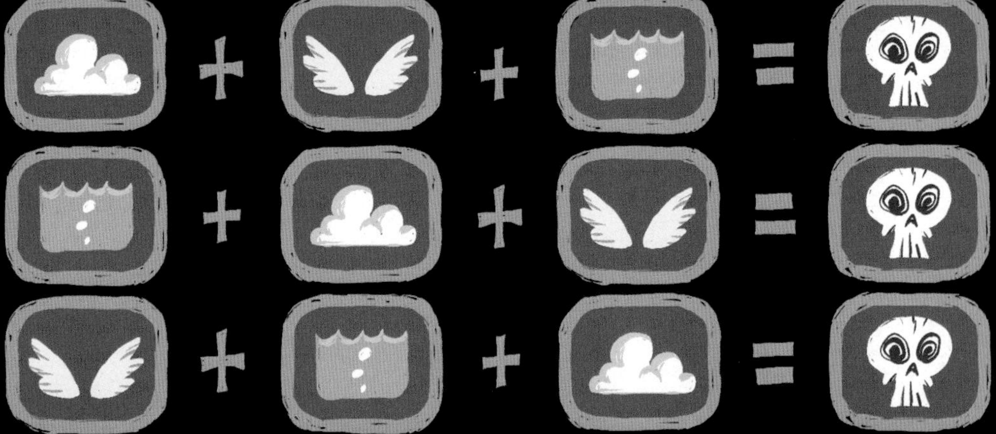

(Not Necessarily In That Order)

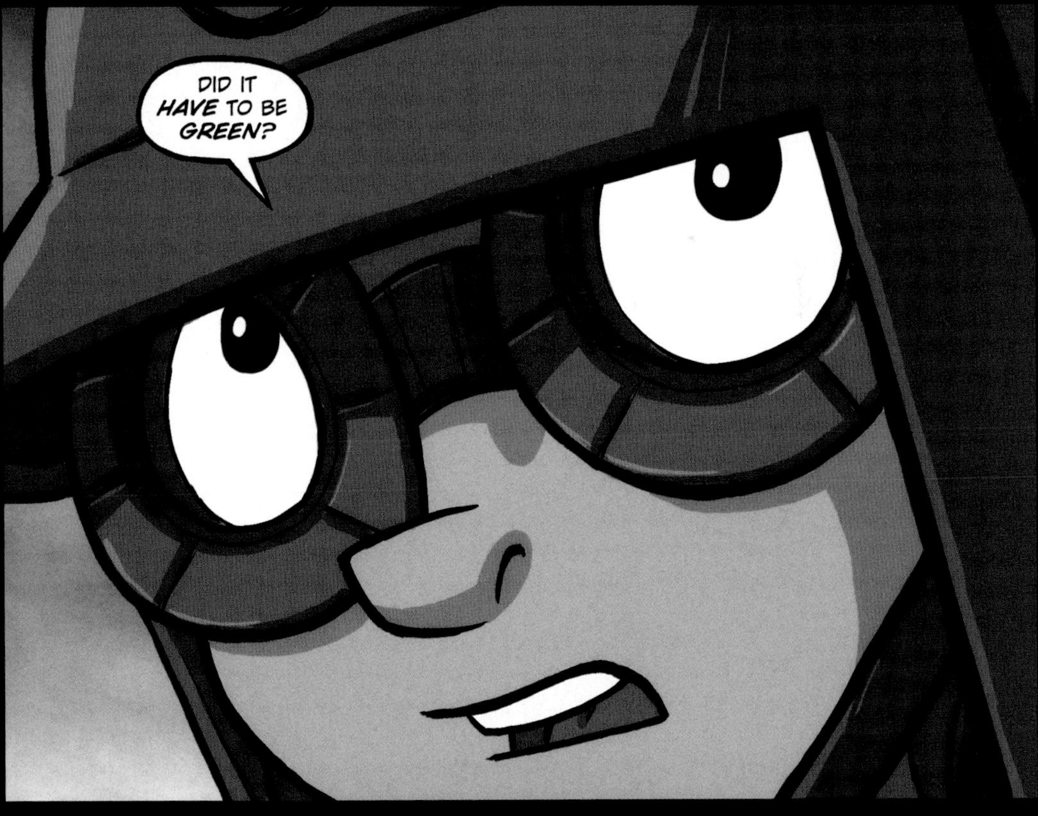
DID IT *HAVE* TO BE *GREEN?*

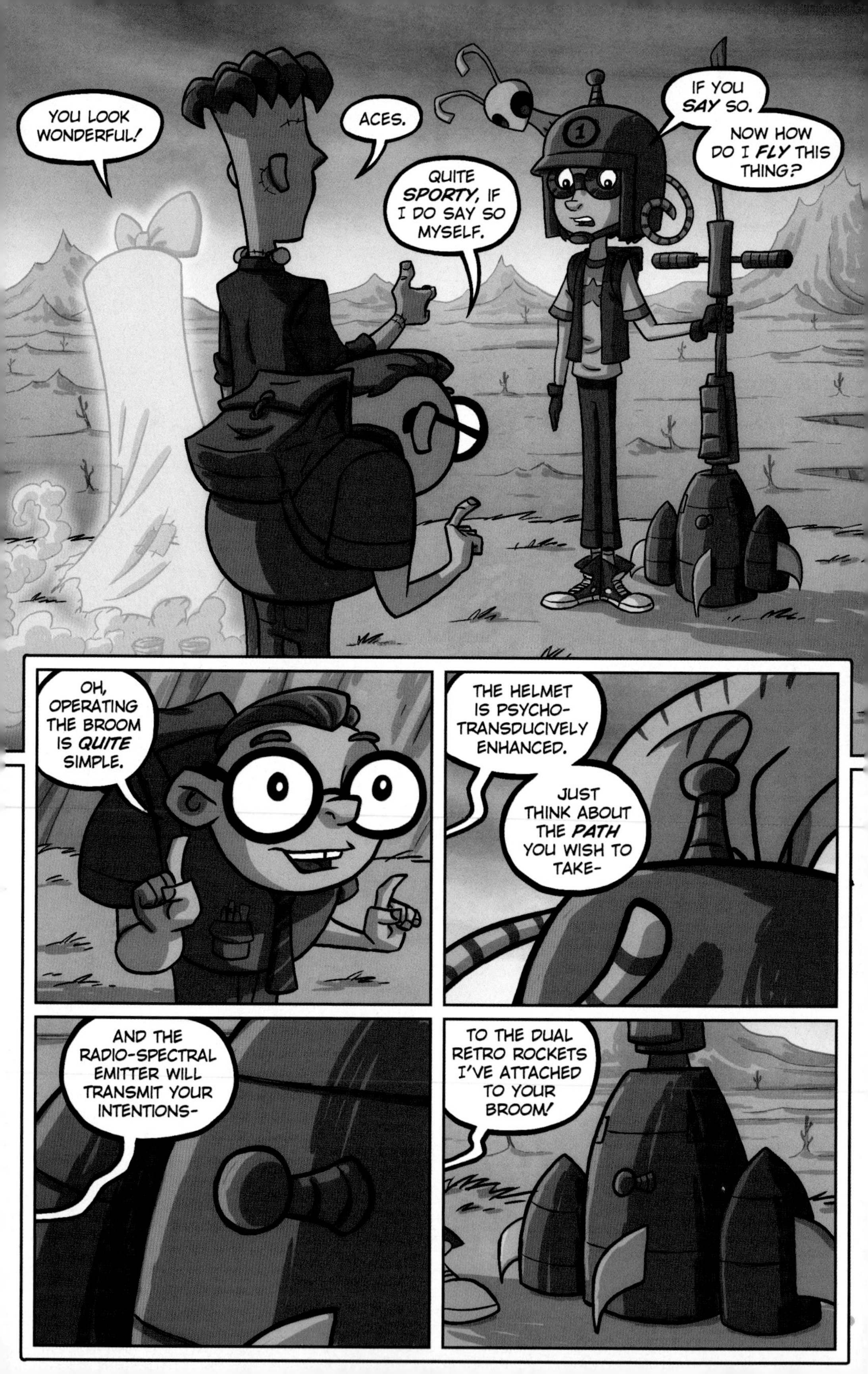
YOU LOOK WONDERFUL!
ACES.
QUITE SPORTY, IF I DO SAY SO MYSELF.
IF YOU SAY SO.
NOW HOW DO I FLY THIS THING?
OH, OPERATING THE BROOM IS QUITE SIMPLE.
THE HELMET IS PSYCHO-TRANSDUCIVELY ENHANCED.
JUST THINK ABOUT THE PATH YOU WISH TO TAKE-
AND THE RADIO-SPECTRAL EMITTER WILL TRANSMIT YOUR INTENTIONS-
TO THE DUAL RETRO ROCKETS I'VE ATTACHED TO YOUR BROOM!

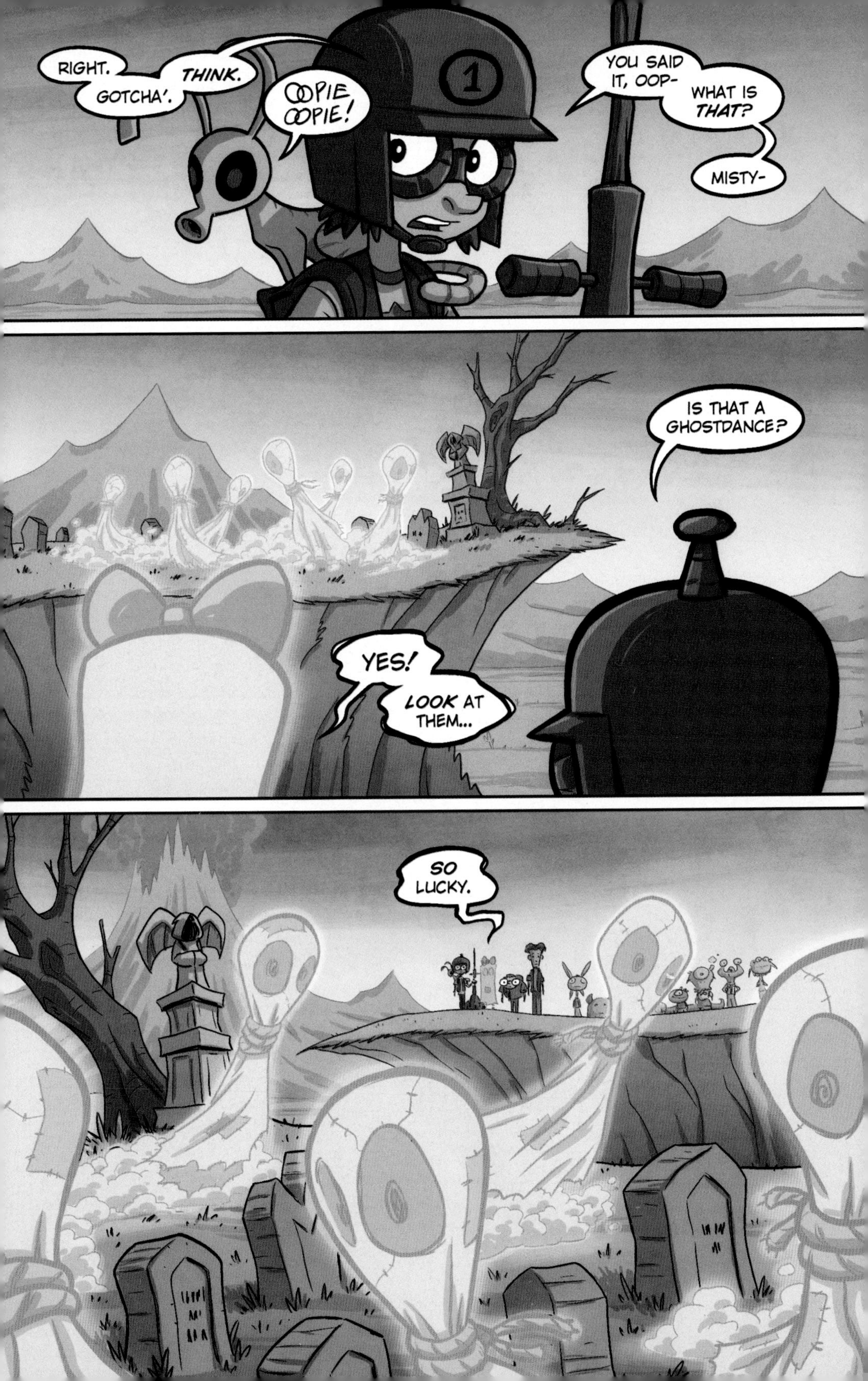
RIGHT.
GOTCHA'.
THINK.
OOPIE OOPIE!
YOU SAID IT, OOP-
WHAT IS THAT?
MISTY-
IS THAT A GHOSTDANCE?
YES!
LOOK AT THEM...
SO LUCKY.

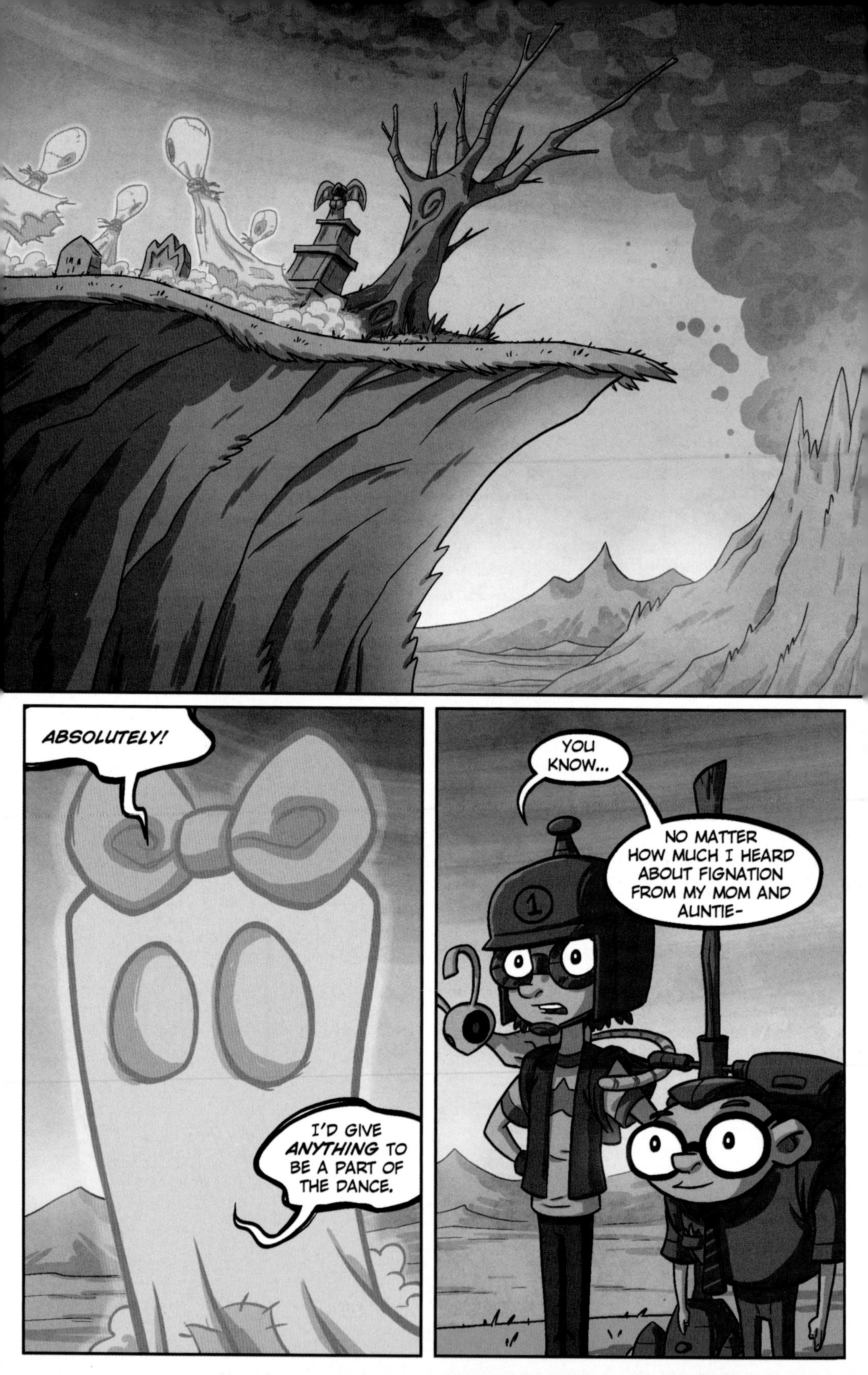
ABSOLUTELY!
I'D GIVE ANYTHING TO BE A PART OF THE DANCE.
YOU KNOW...
NO MATTER HOW MUCH I HEARD ABOUT FIGNATION FROM MY MOM AND AUNTIE-

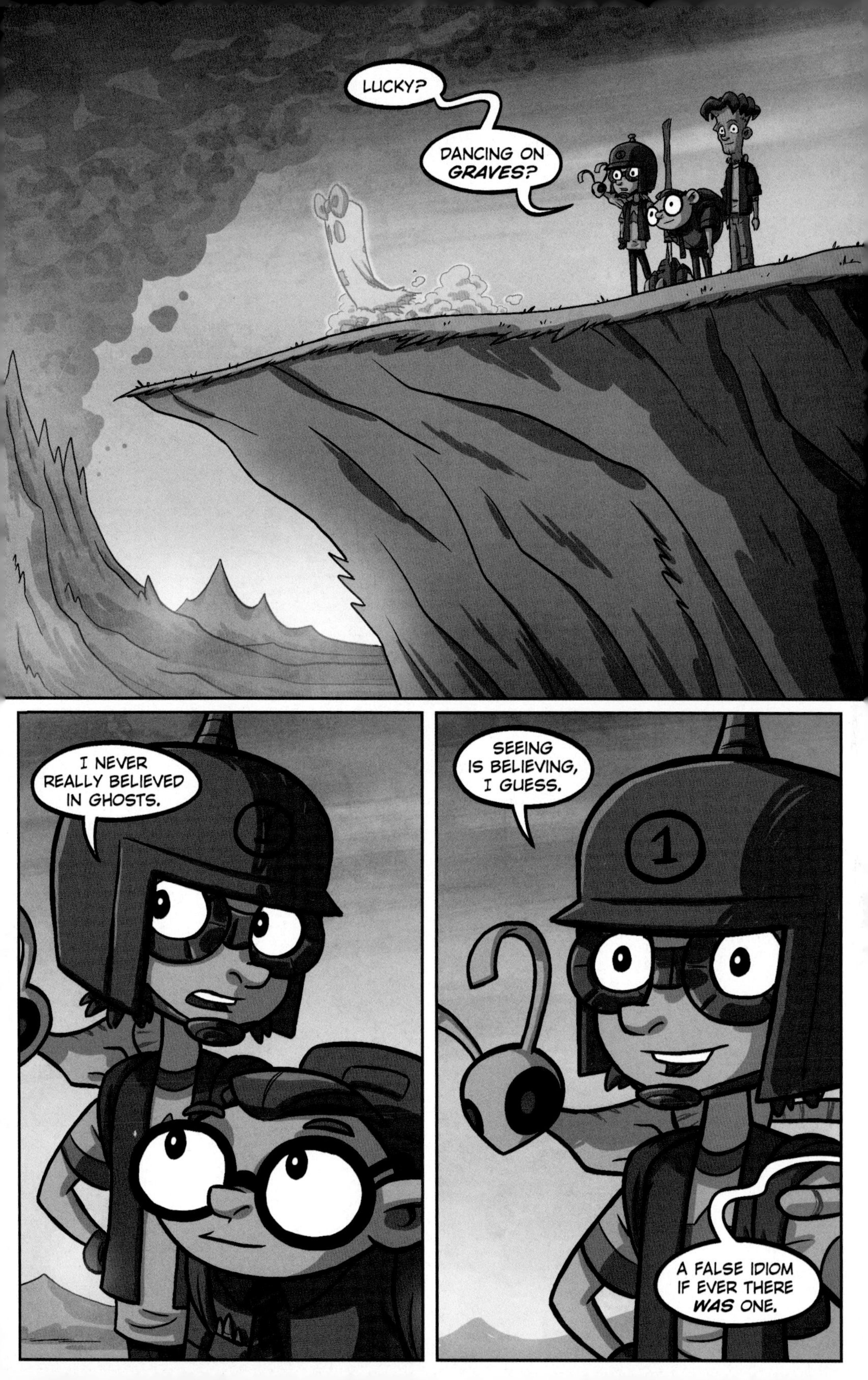
LUCKY?
DANCING ON GRAVES?
I NEVER REALLY BELIEVED IN GHOSTS.
SEEING IS BELIEVING, I GUESS.
A FALSE IDIOM IF EVER THERE WAS ONE.

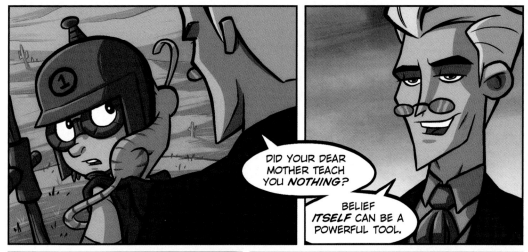

DID YOUR DEAR MOTHER TEACH YOU *NOTHING?*

BELIEF *ITSELF* CAN BE A POWERFUL TOOL.

BEST BE CAREFUL HOW YOU CHOOSE TO EMPLOY IT.

FOOD FOR THOUGHT, MY *DROLL DYNAMO.*

RIGHT.

SO—

MISTY—

THE WHOLE DANCING ON *GRAVES* THING...

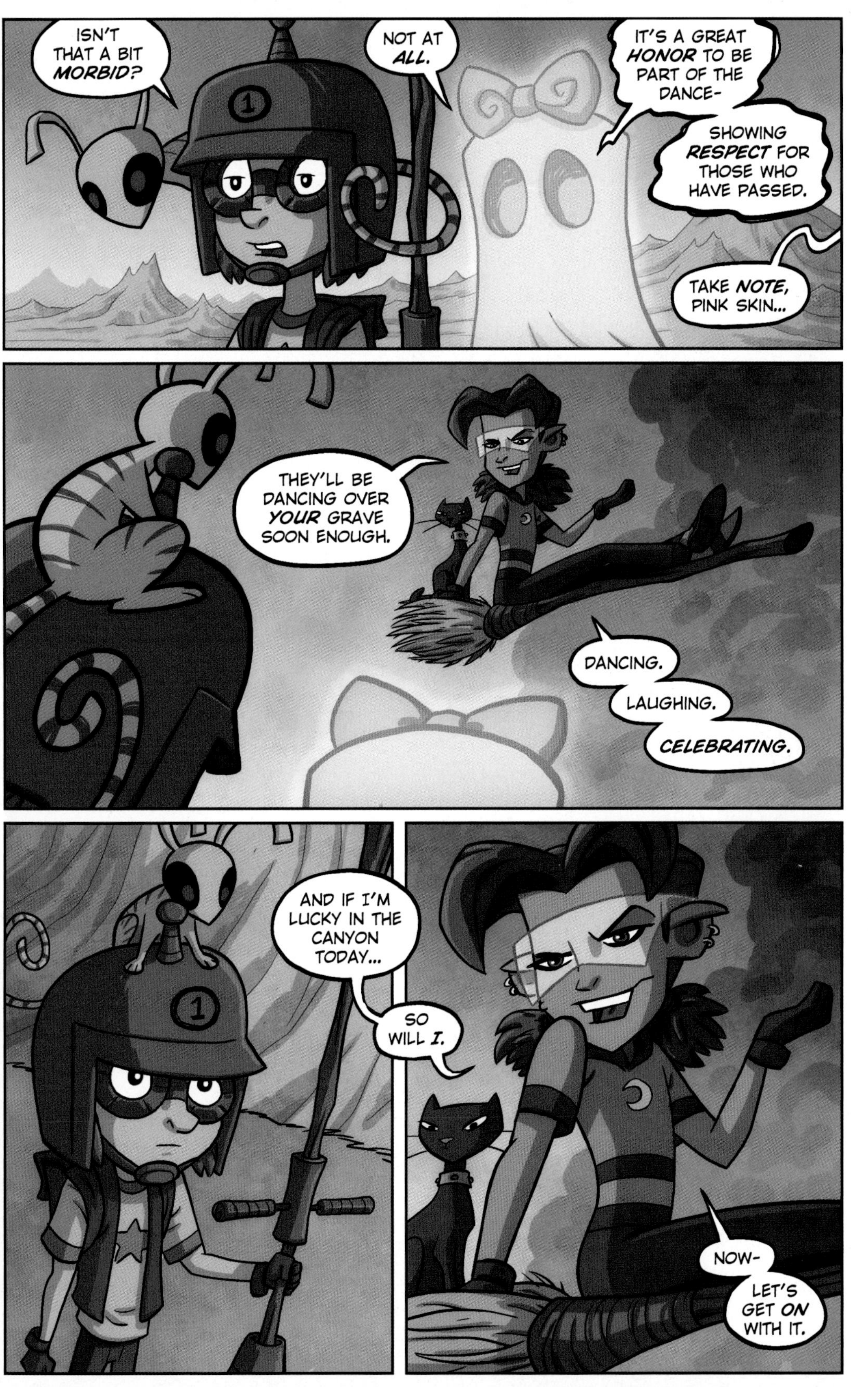
ISN'T THAT A BIT MORBID?
NOT AT ALL.
IT'S A GREAT HONOR TO BE PART OF THE DANCE-
SHOWING RESPECT FOR THOSE WHO HAVE PASSED.
TAKE NOTE, PINK SKIN...
THEY'LL BE DANCING OVER YOUR GRAVE SOON ENOUGH.
DANCING.
LAUGHING.
CELEBRATING.
AND IF I'M LUCKY IN THE CANYON TODAY...
SO WILL I.
NOW-
LET'S GET ON WITH IT.

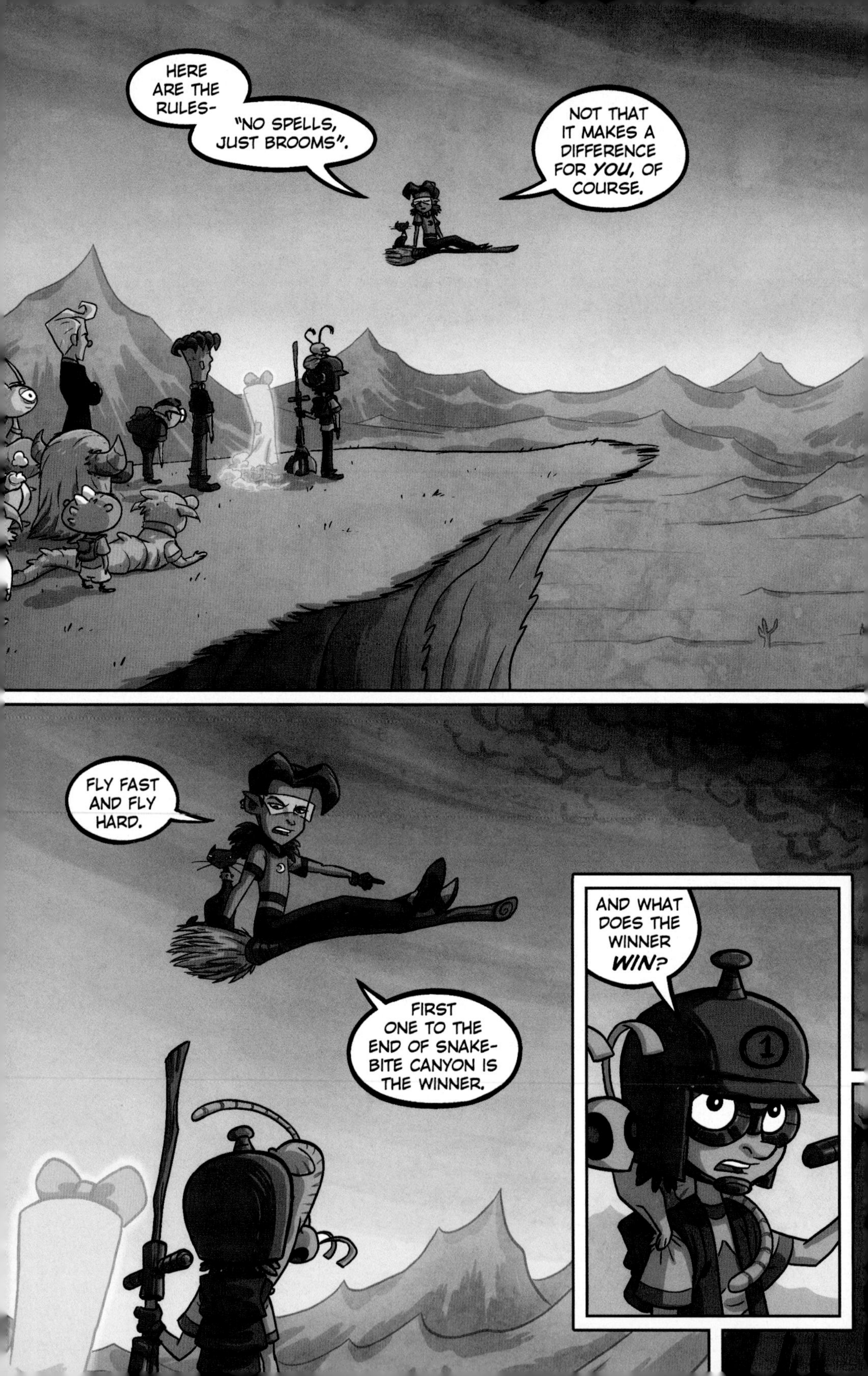
HERE ARE THE RULES-
"NO SPELLS, JUST BROOMS".
NOT THAT IT MAKES A DIFFERENCE FOR YOU, OF COURSE.
FLY FAST AND FLY HARD.
FIRST ONE TO THE END OF SNAKE-BITE CANYON IS THE WINNER.
AND WHAT DOES THE WINNER WIN?

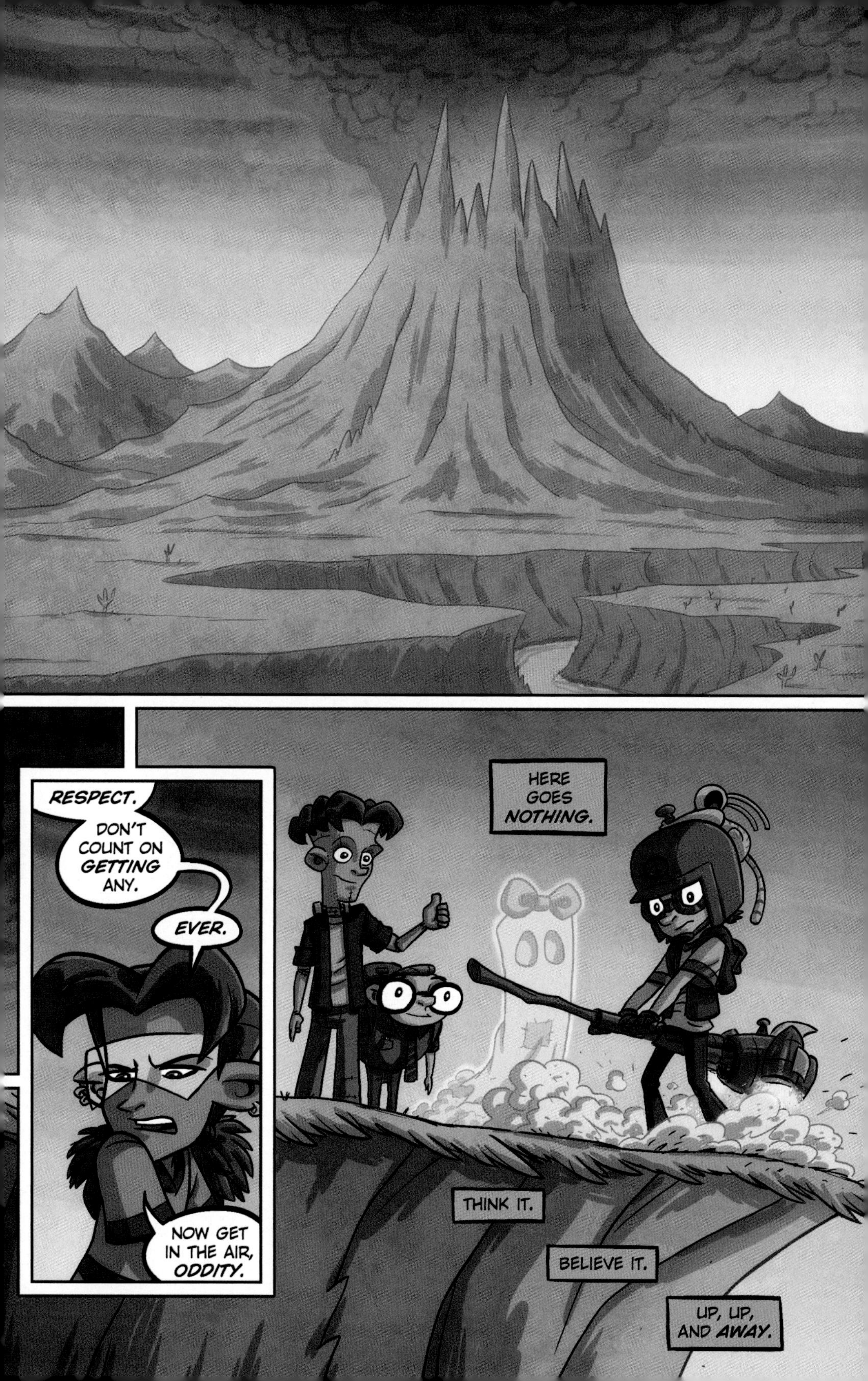
RESPECT.
DON'T COUNT ON GETTING ANY.
EVER.
NOW GET IN THE AIR, ODDITY.
HERE GOES NOTHING.
THINK IT.
BELIEVE IT.
UP, UP, AND AWAY.

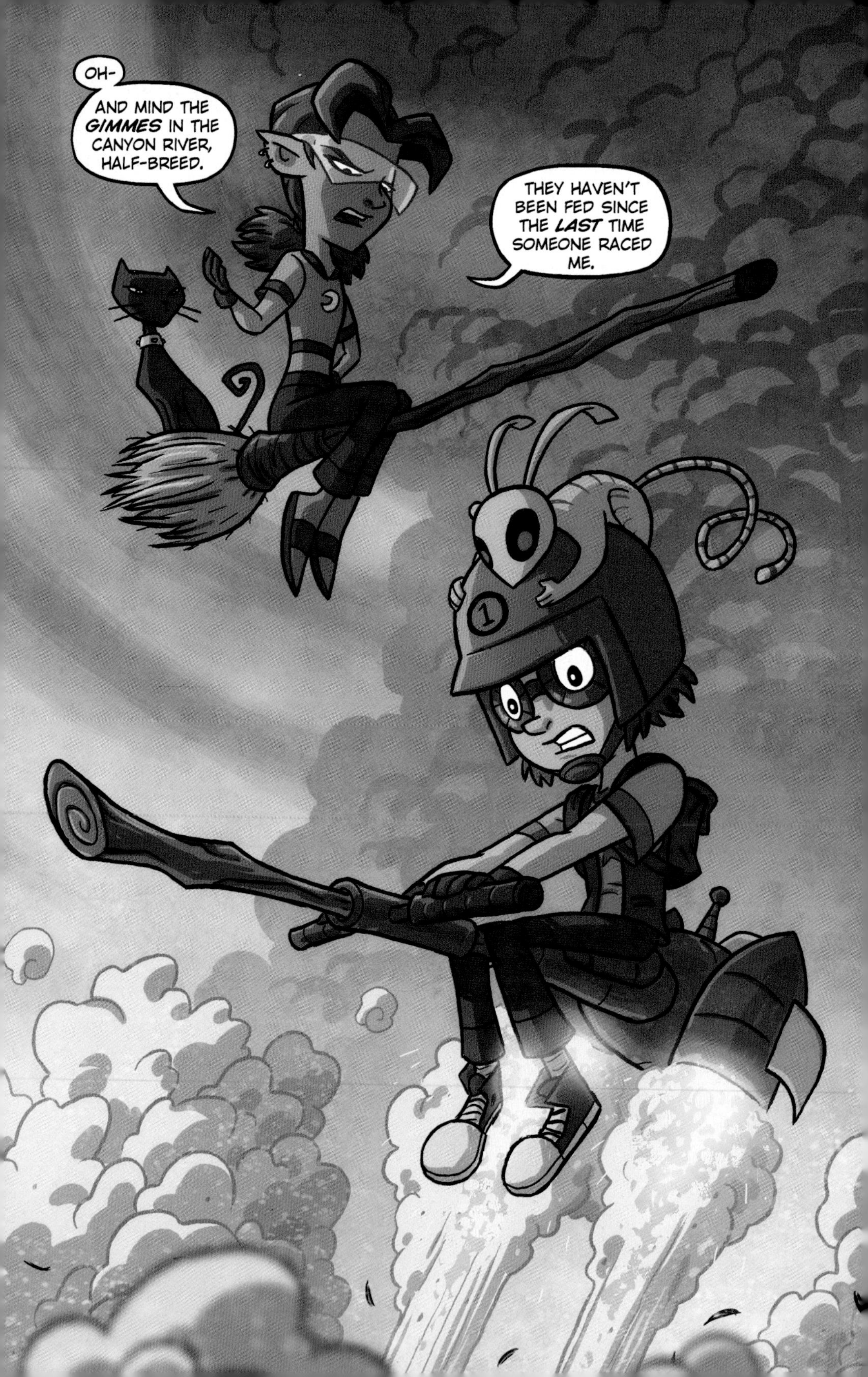
OH-
AND MIND THE GIMMES IN THE CANYON RIVER, HALF-BREED.
THEY HAVEN'T BEEN FED SINCE THE LAST TIME SOMEONE RACED ME.

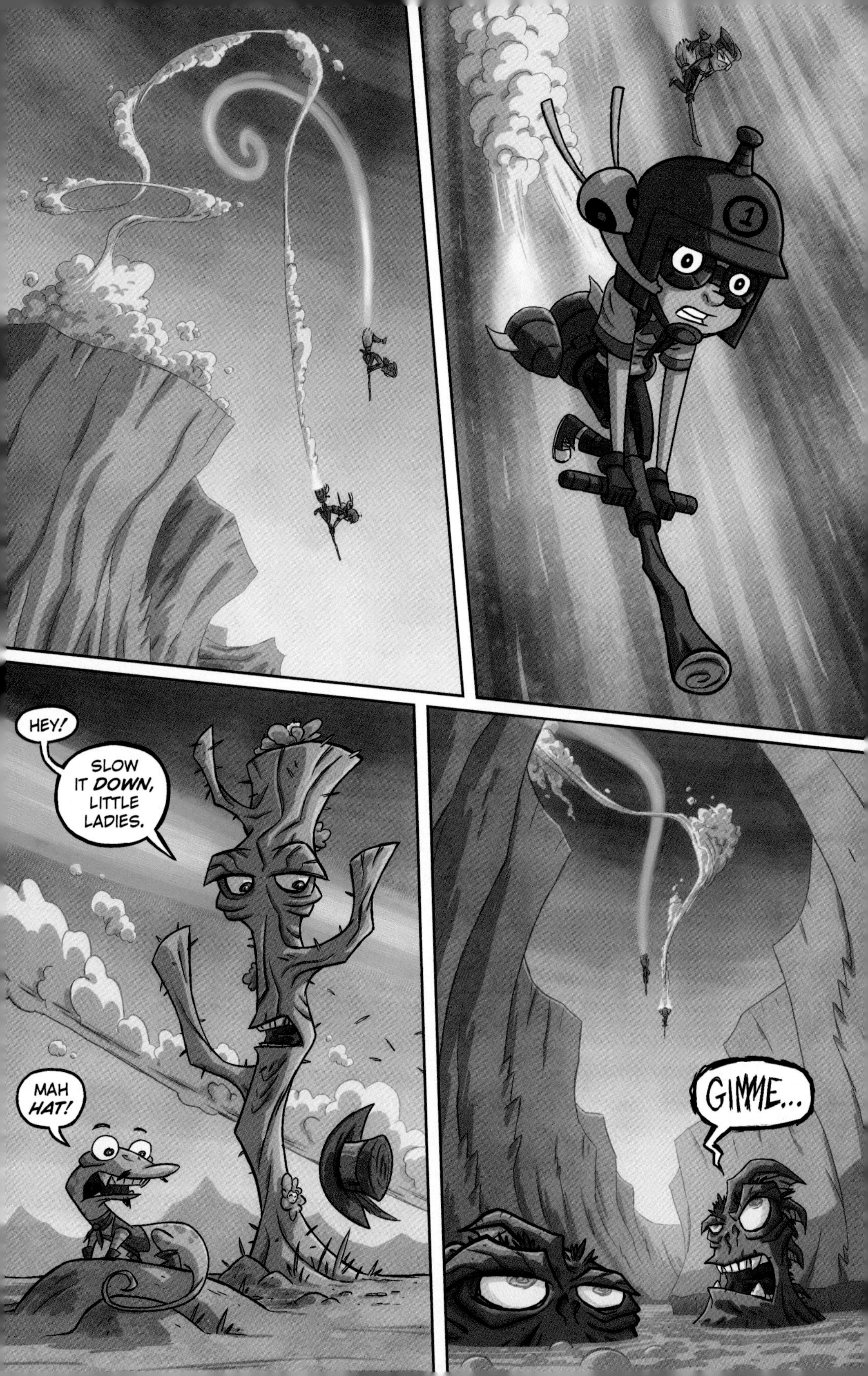
HEY!
SLOW IT DOWN, LITTLE LADIES.
MAH HAT!
GIMME...

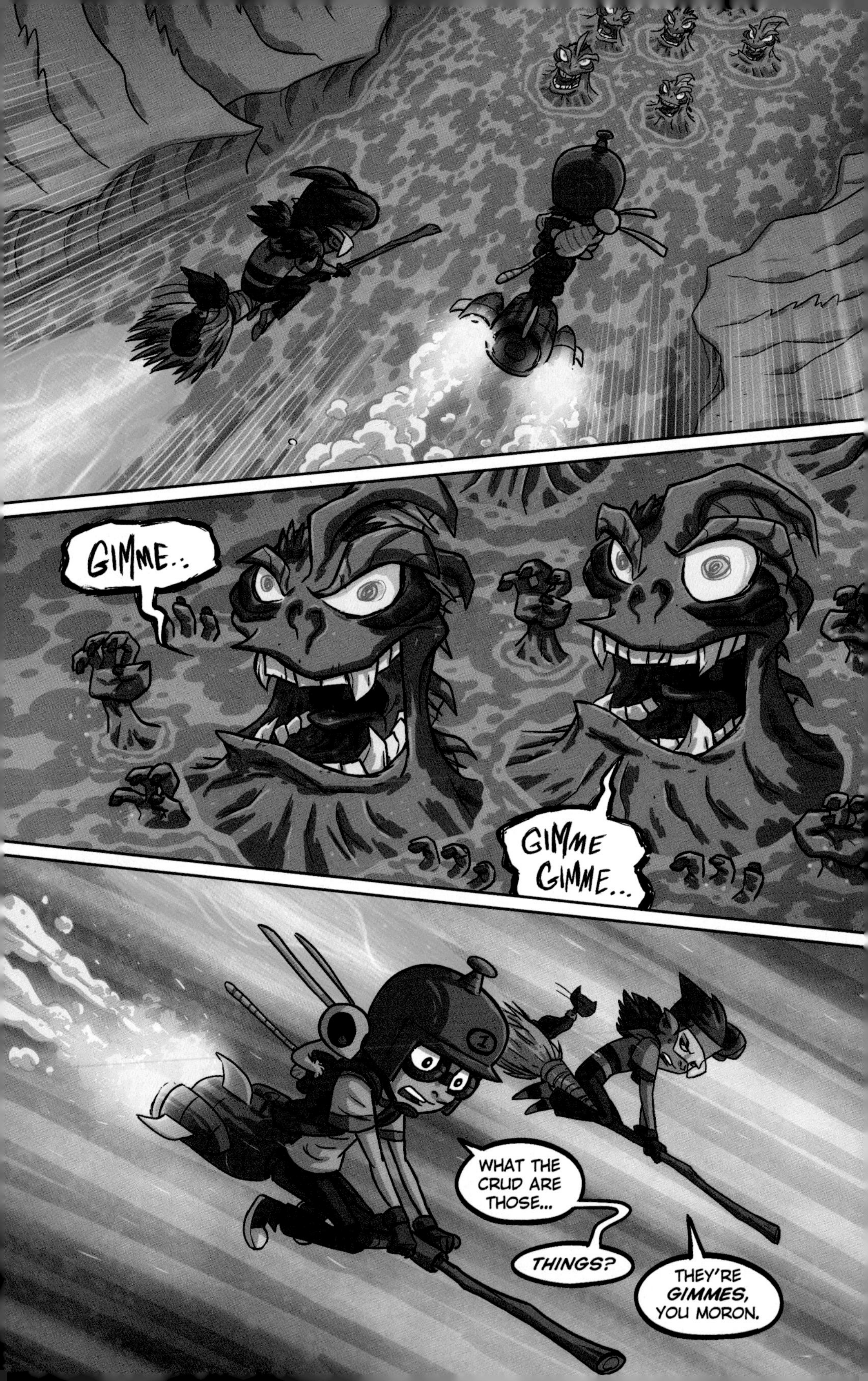
GIMME...
GIMME GIMME...
WHAT THE CRUD ARE THOSE...
THINGS?
THEY'RE GIMMES, YOU MORON.

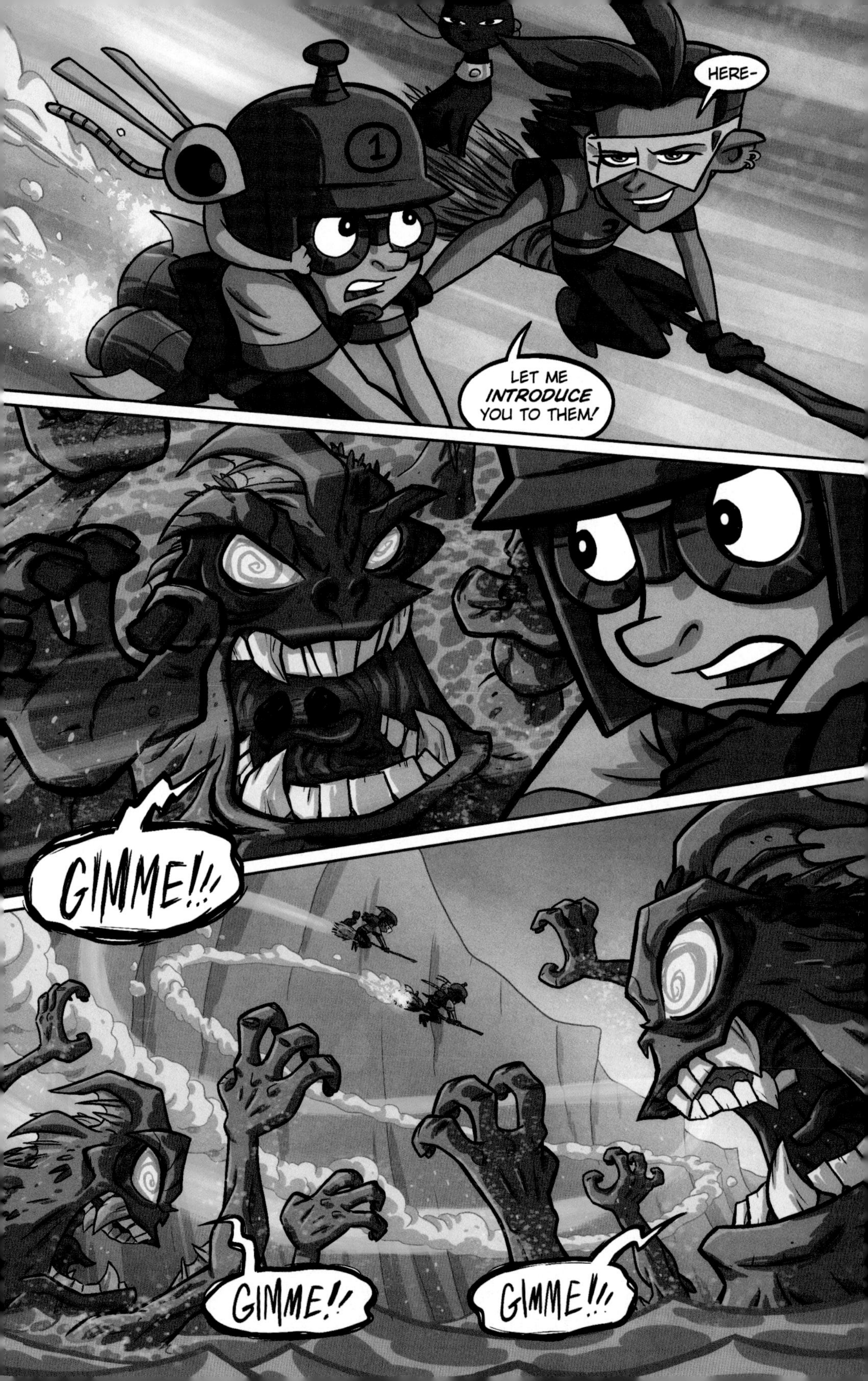
HERE-
LET ME *INTRODUCE* YOU TO THEM!
GIMME!!!
GIMME!!
GIMME!!!

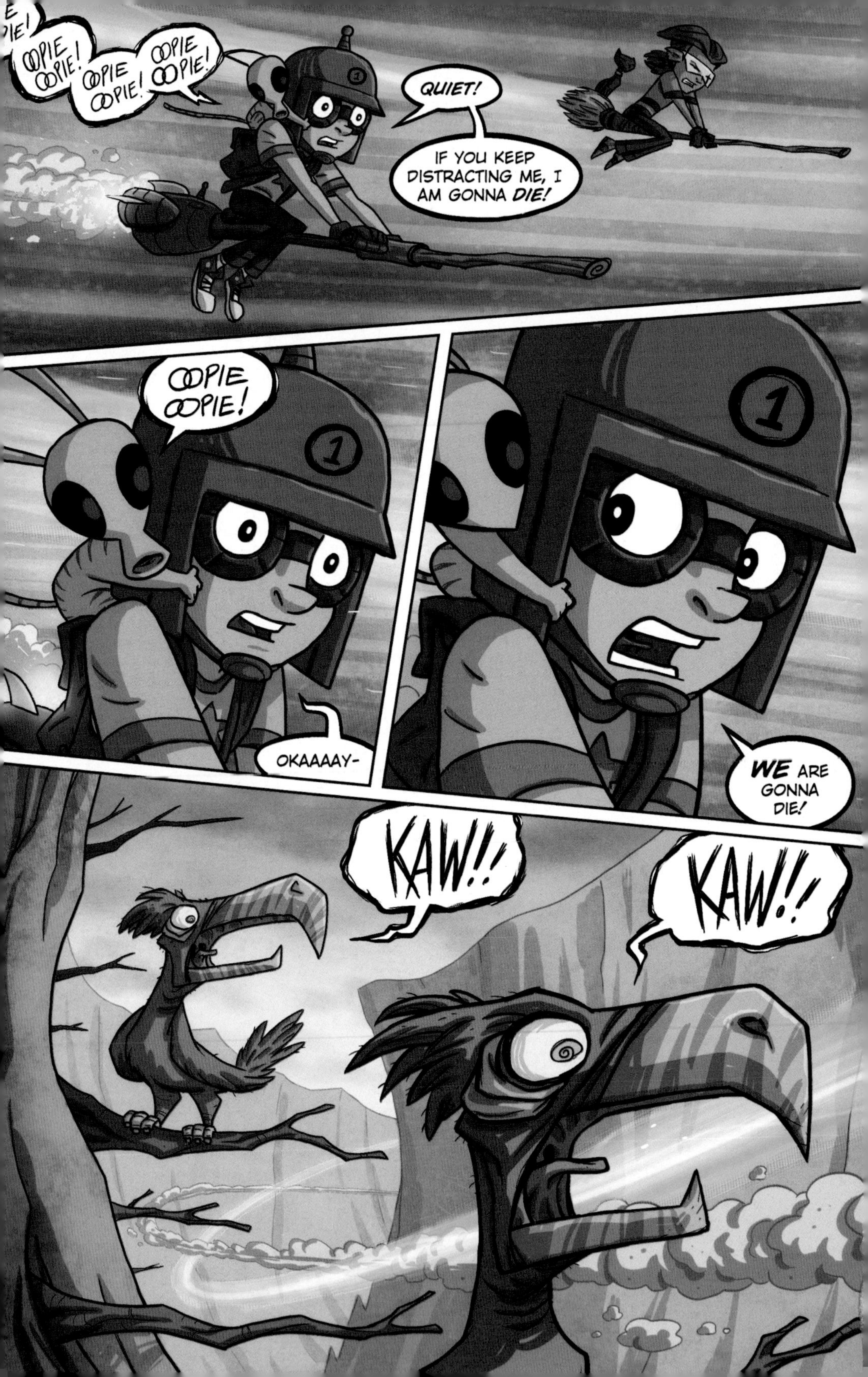

OOPIE OOPIE!
OOPIE OOPIE!
OOPIE OOPIE!
QUIET!
IF YOU KEEP DISTRACTING ME, I AM GONNA DIE!
OOPIE OOPIE!
OKAAAAY-
WE ARE GONNA DIE!
KAW!!
KAW!!

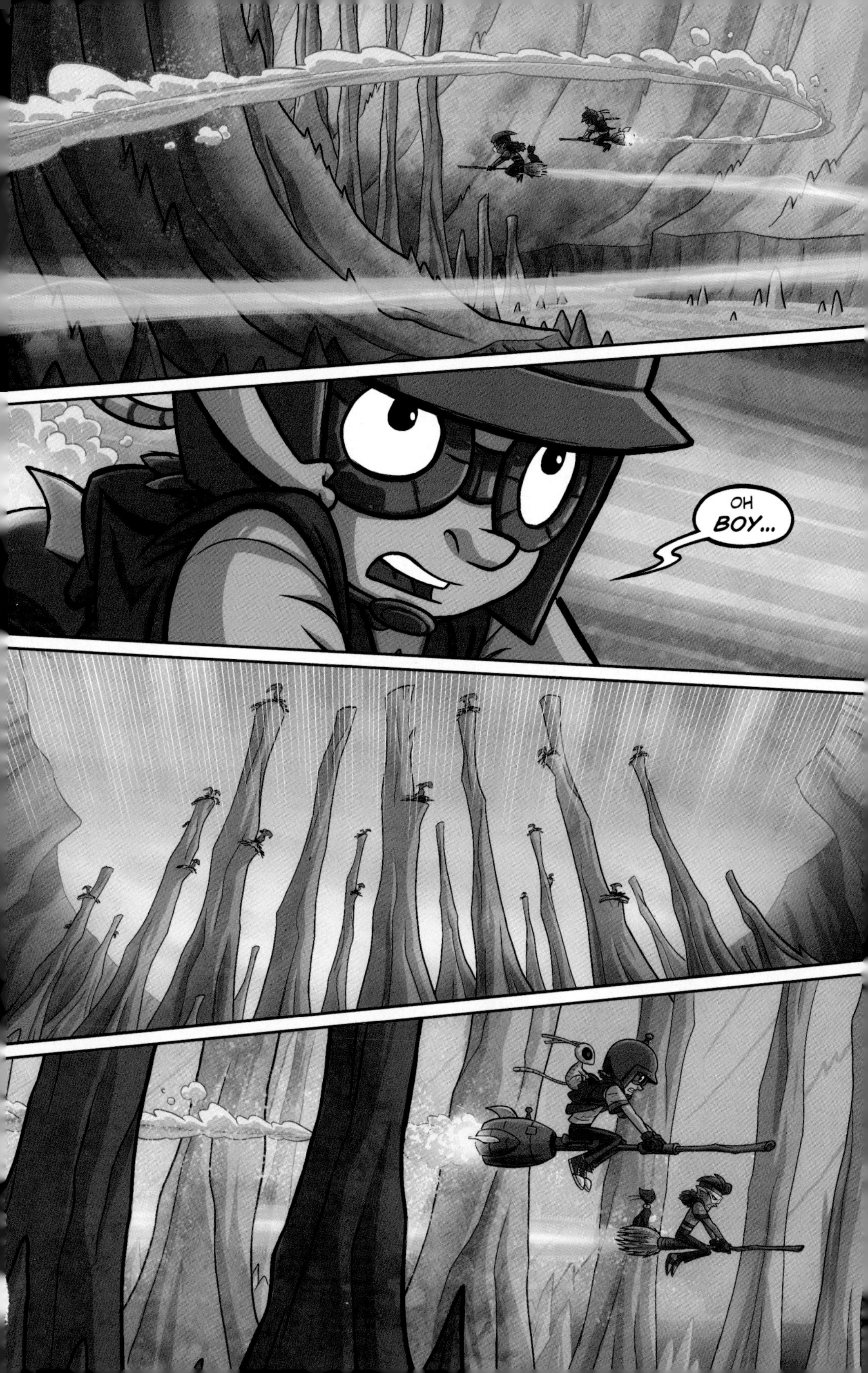
OH BOY...

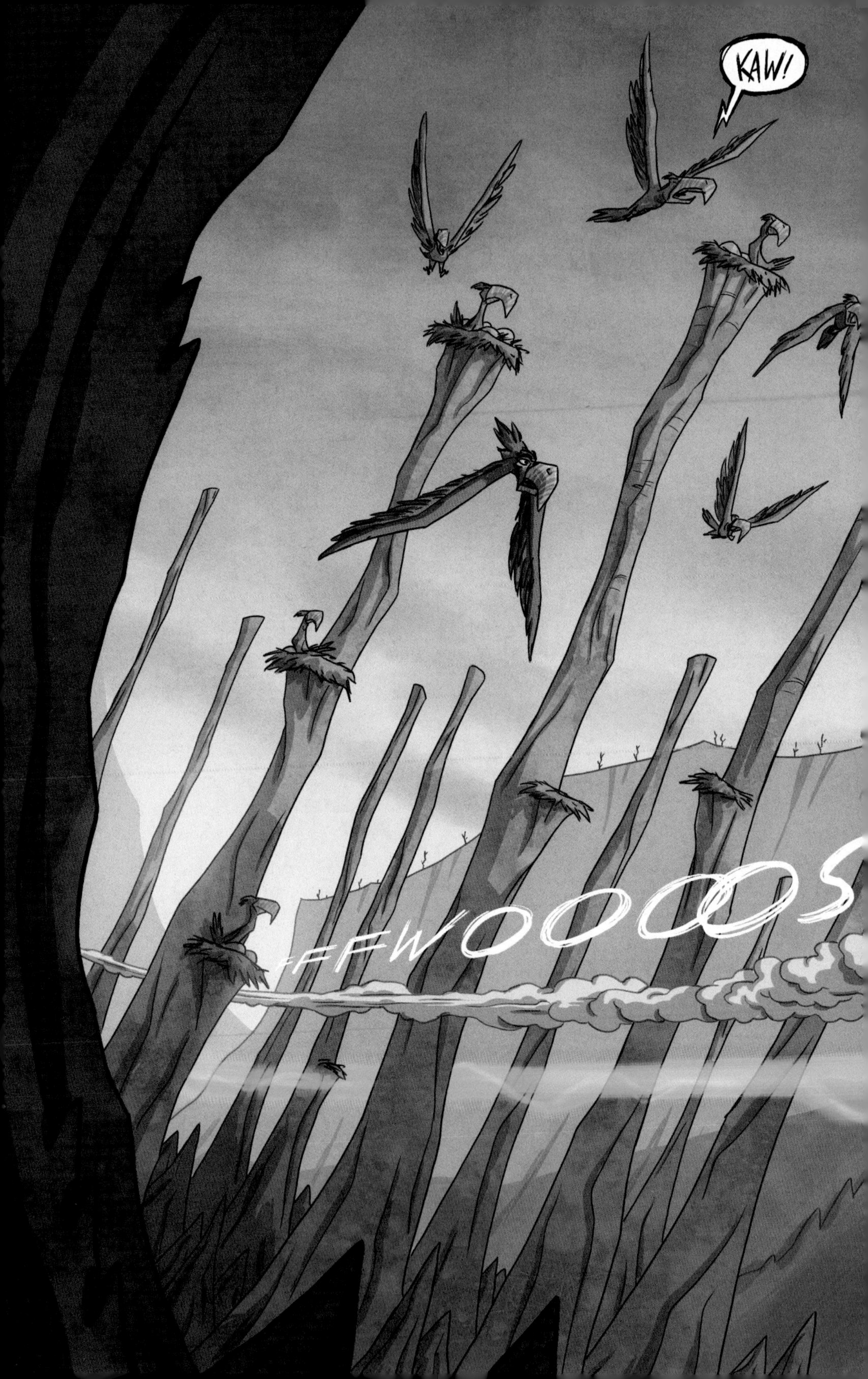
KAW!
FFFWOOOOOS

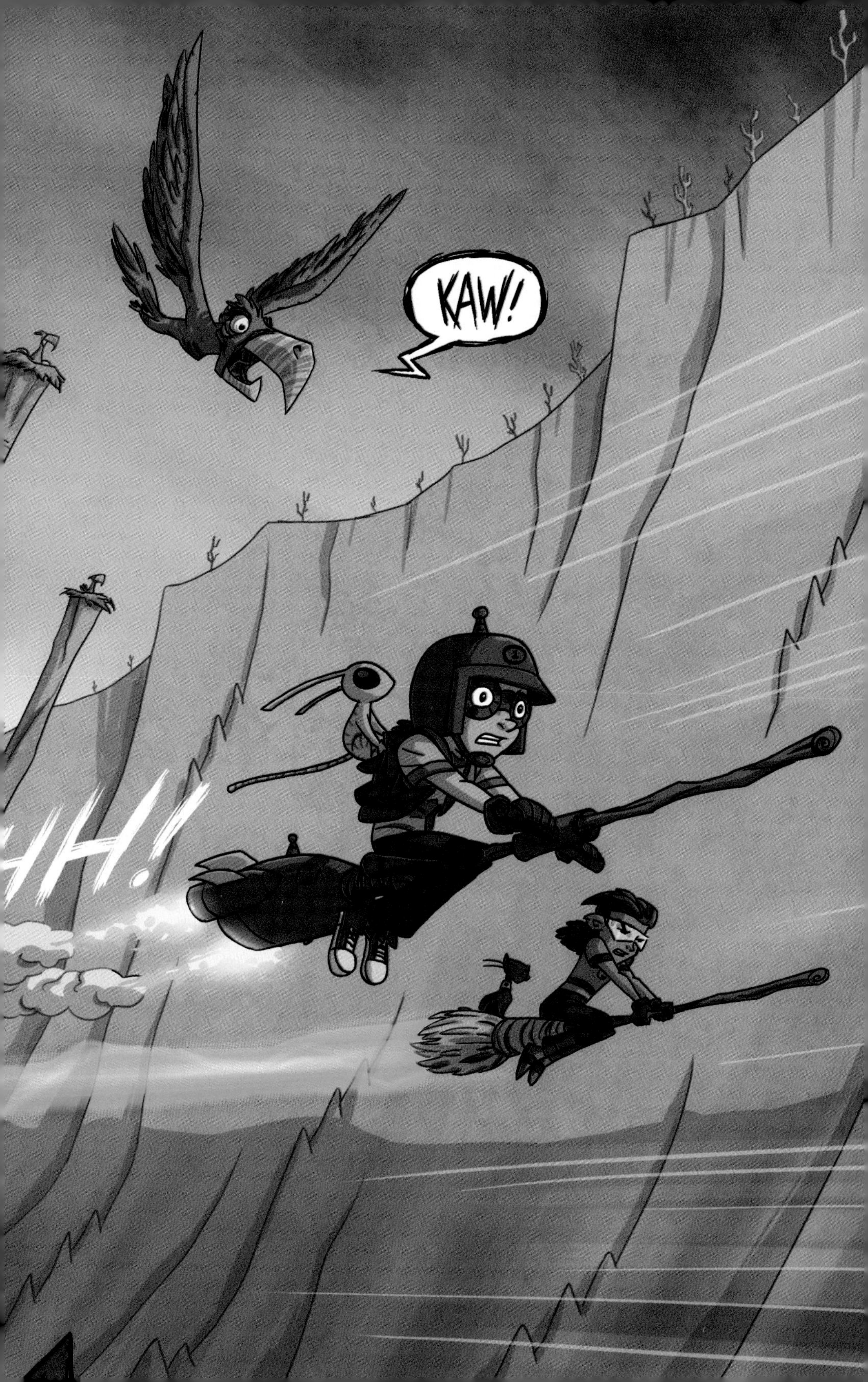
KAW!
HH!!

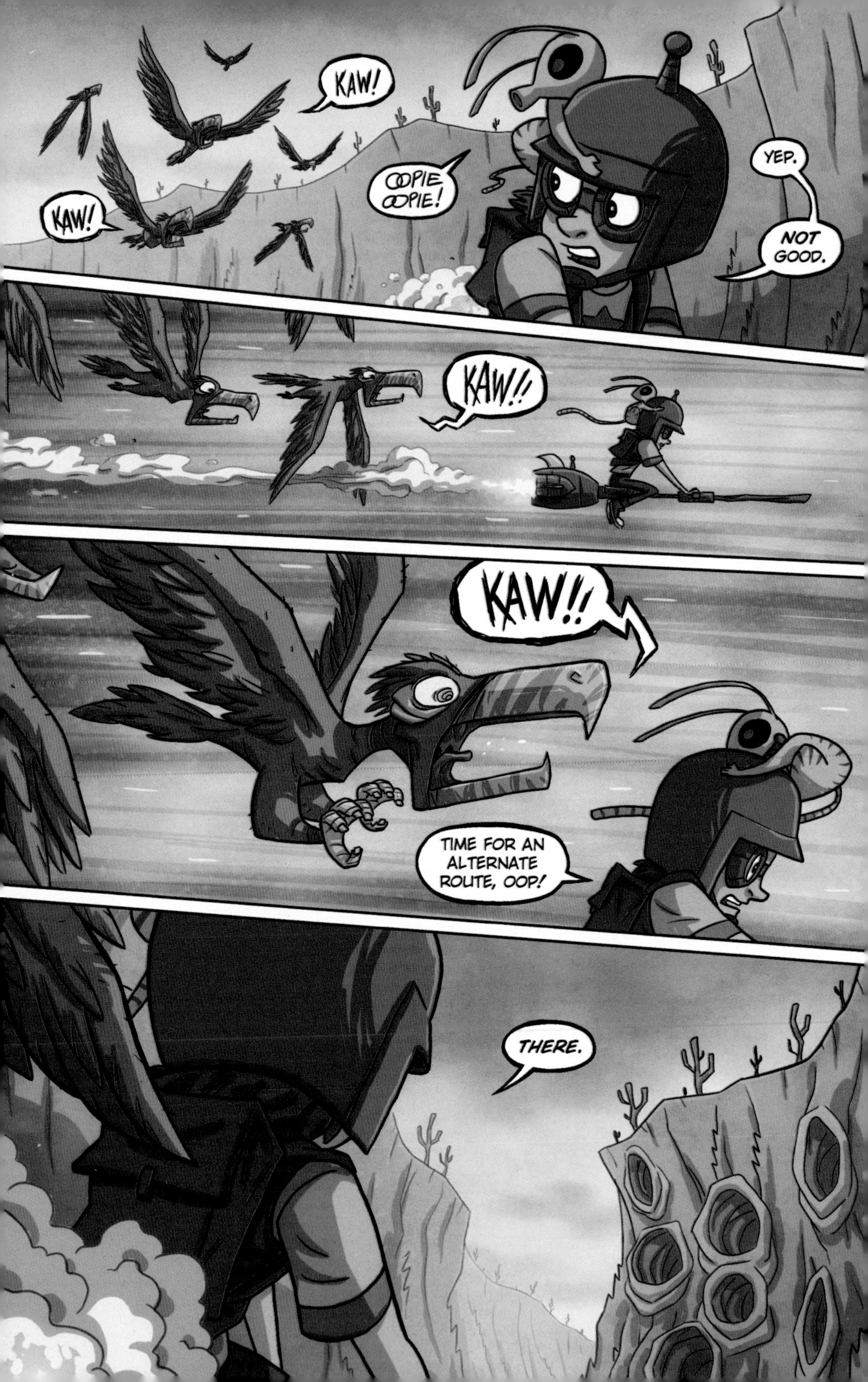
KAW!
KAW!
OOPIE OOPIE!
YEP.
NOT GOOD.
KAW!!
KAW!!
TIME FOR AN ALTERNATE ROUTE, OOP!
THERE.

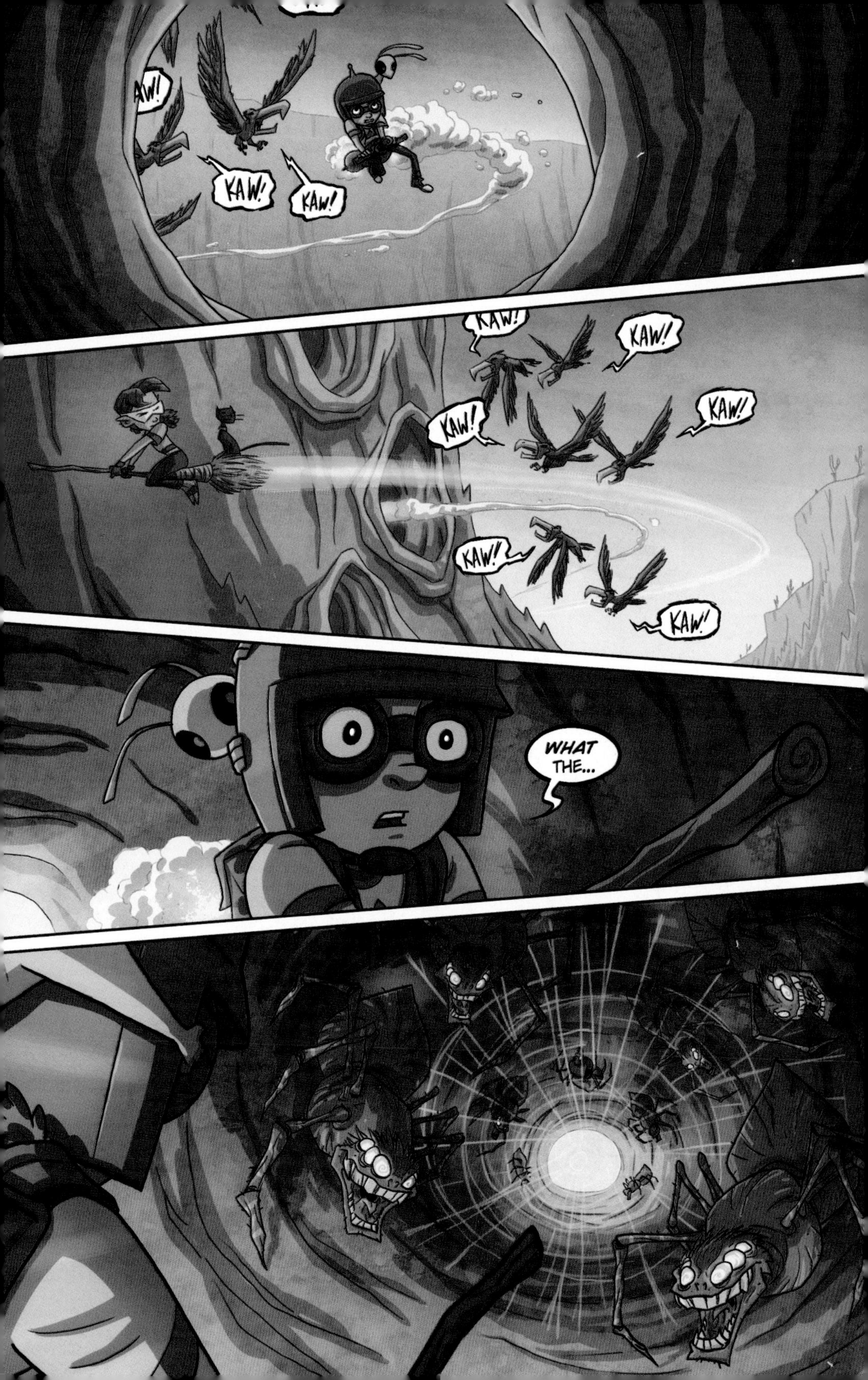
KAW!
KAW!
KAW!
KAW!
KAW!
KAW!
KAW!
KAW!
KAW!
WHAT THE...

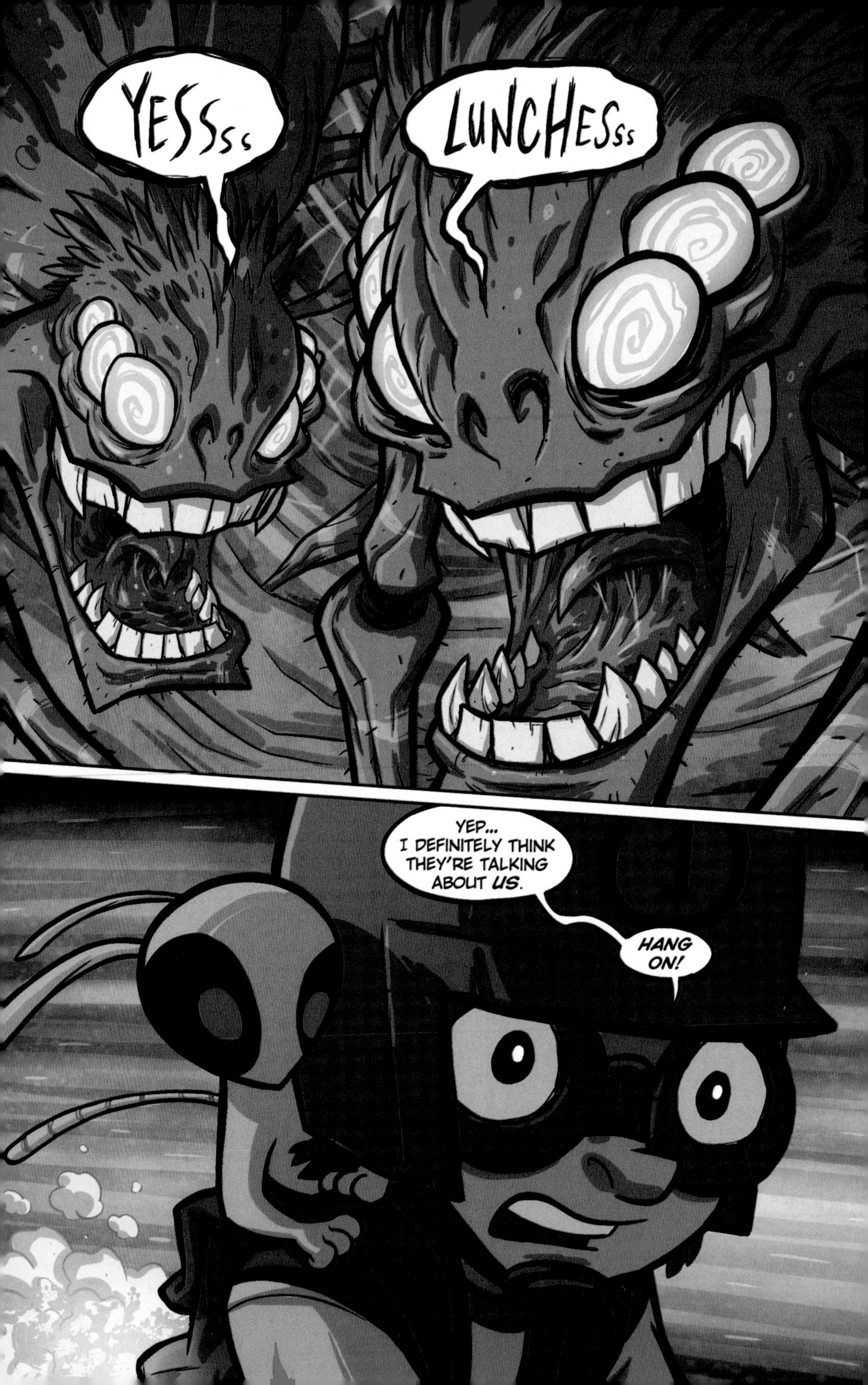
YESSss
LUNCHESss
YEP... I DEFINITELY THINK THEY'RE TALKING ABOUT *US*.
HANG ON!

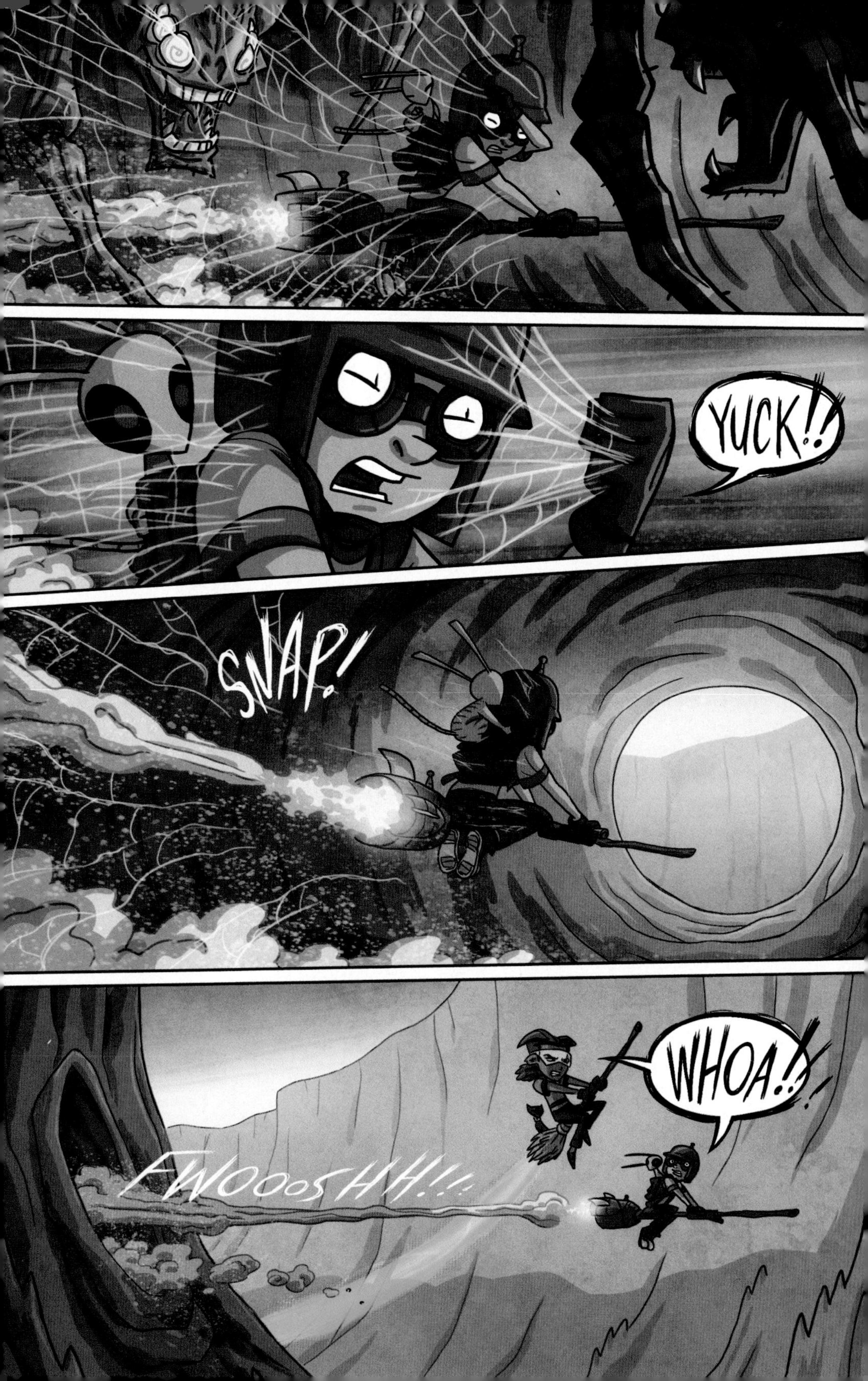
YUCK!!
SNAP!
WHOA!!
FWOOOSHH!!!

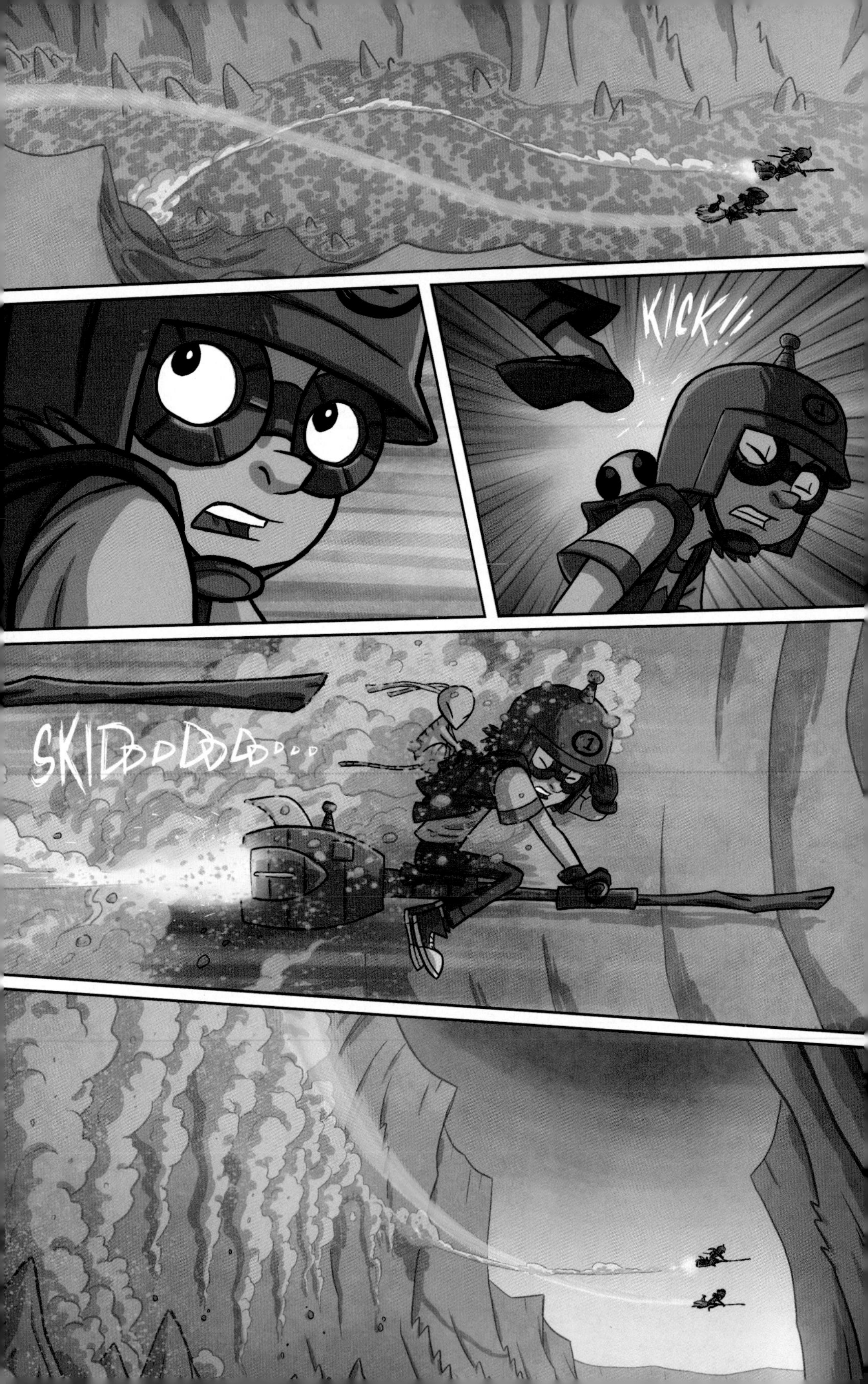
KICK!!
SKIDDDDDDDDD

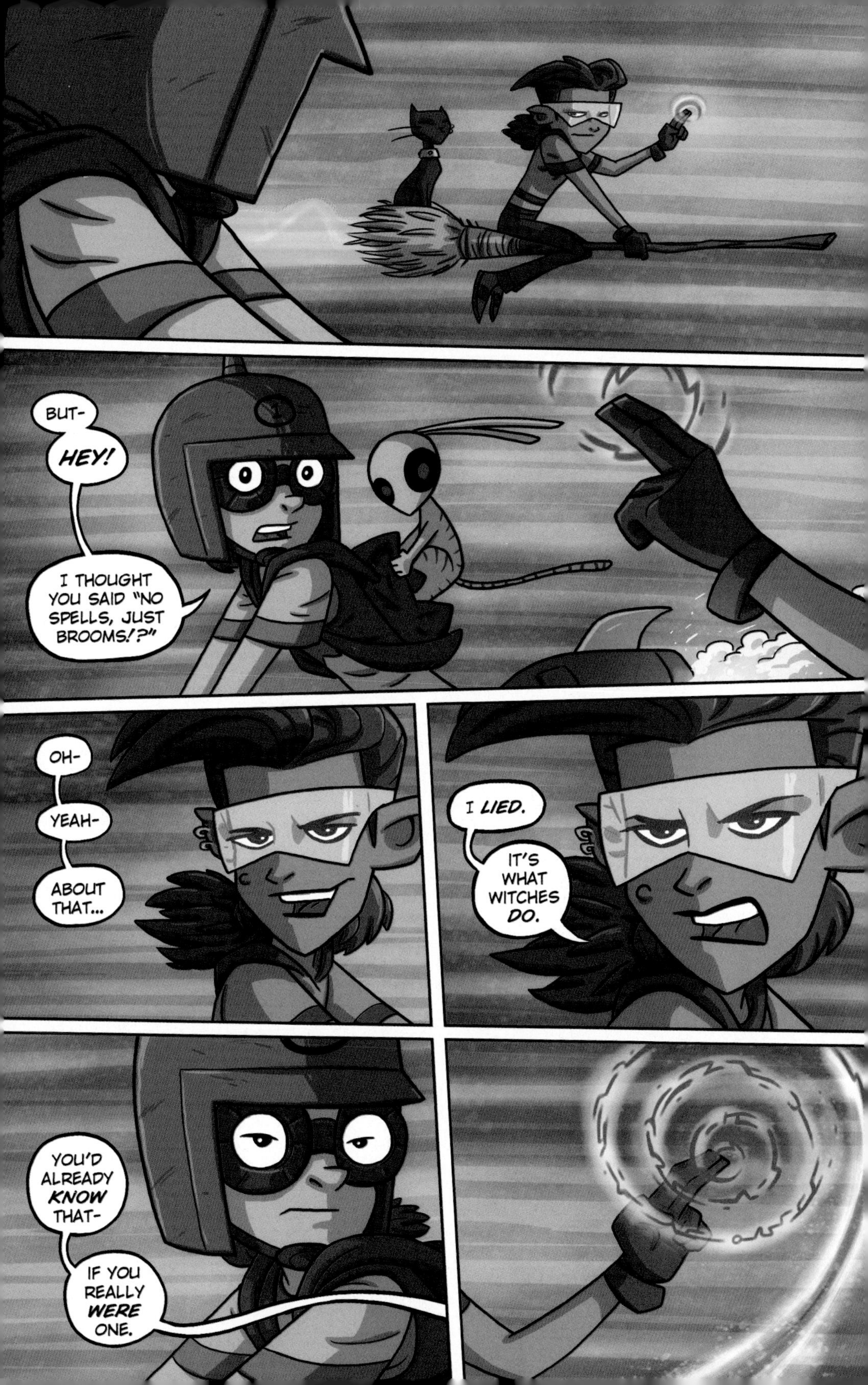
BUT-
HEY!
I THOUGHT YOU SAID "NO SPELLS, JUST BROOMS!?"
OH-
YEAH-
ABOUT THAT...
I LIED.
IT'S WHAT WITCHES DO.
YOU'D ALREADY KNOW THAT-
IF YOU REALLY WERE ONE.

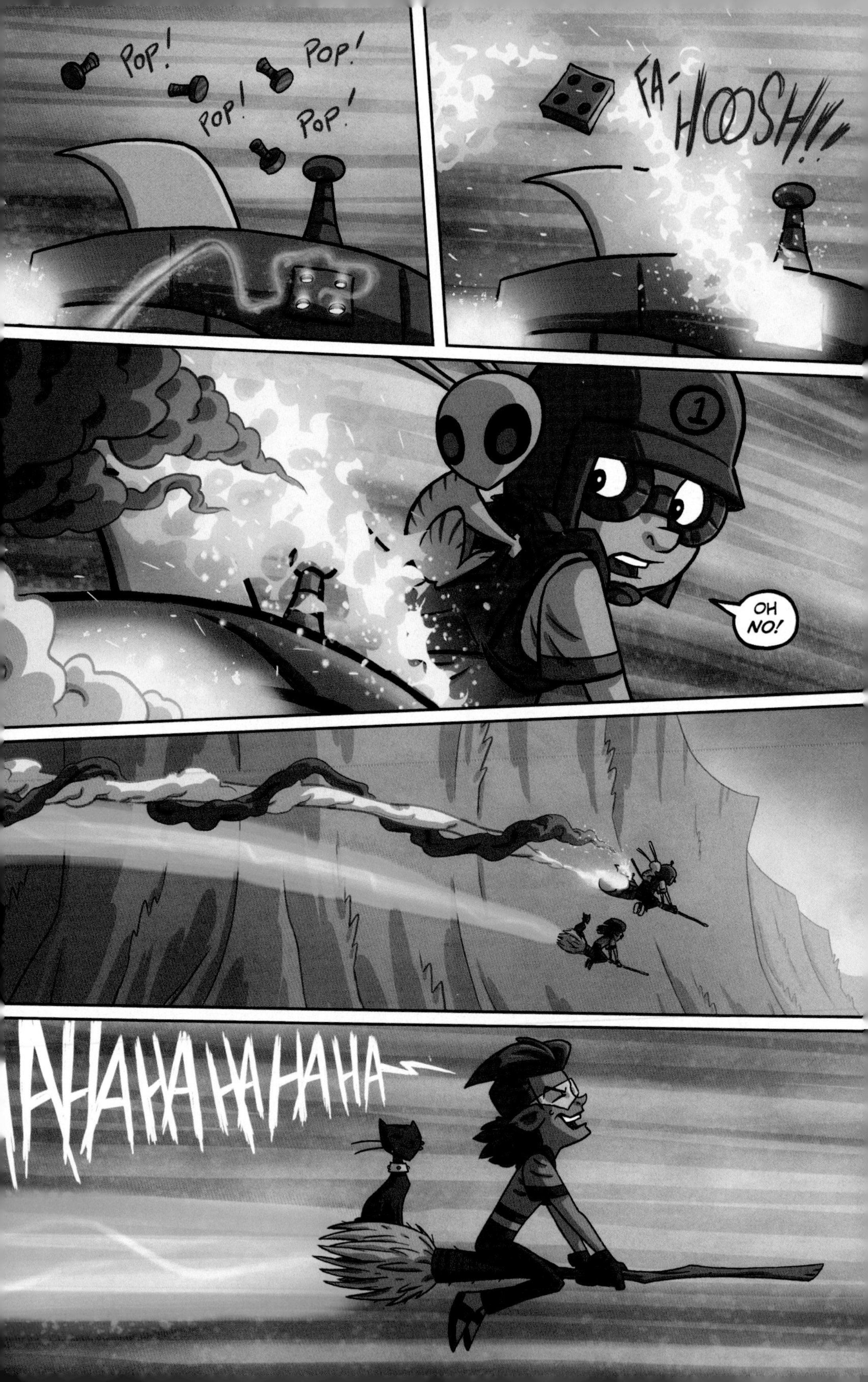
POP!
POP!
POP!
POP!
FA-HOOSH!!
OH NO!
HAHAHAHAHAHAHA

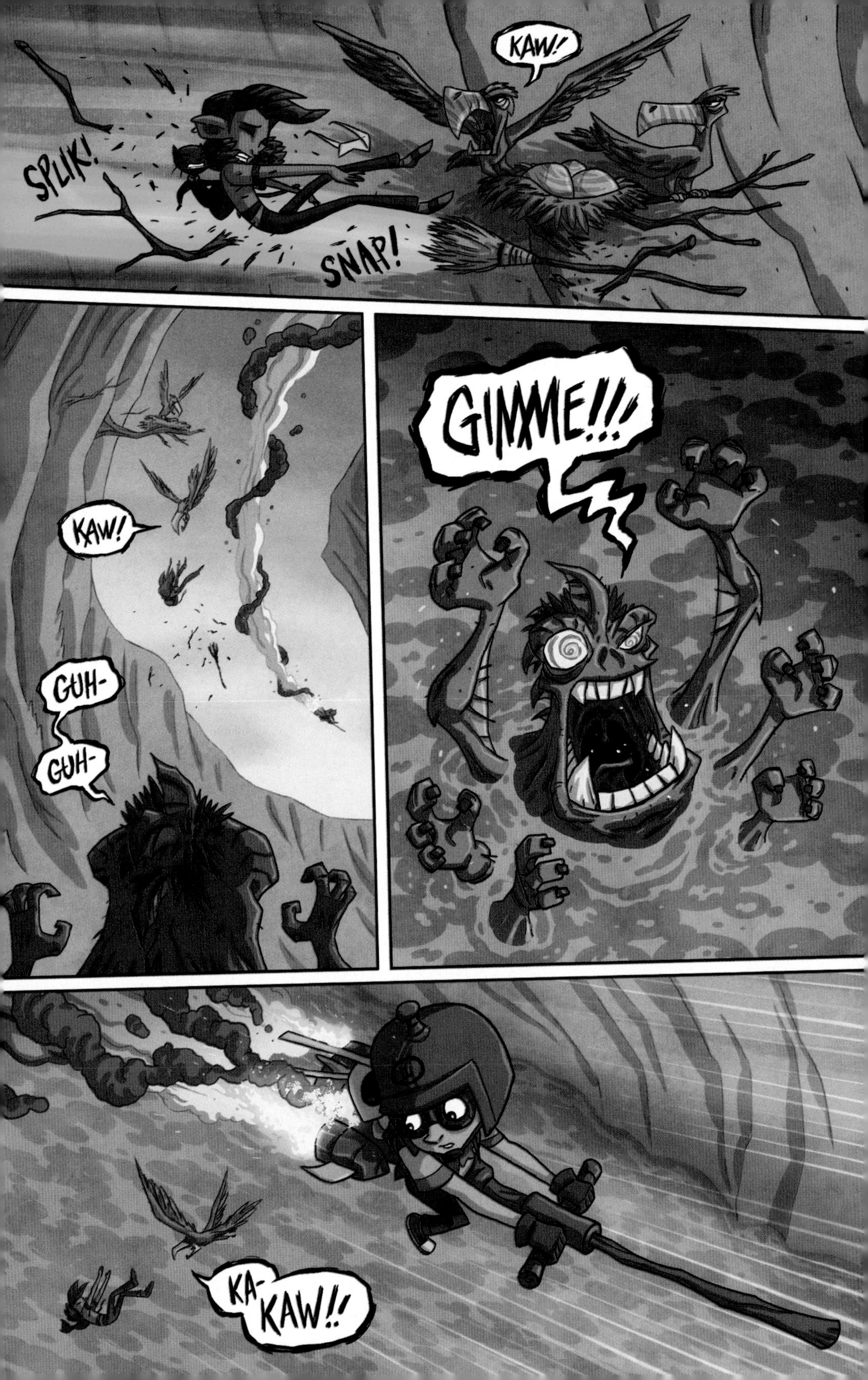
KAW!
SPLIK!
SNAP!
KAW!
GUH-
GUH-
GIMME!!!
KA-
KAW!!

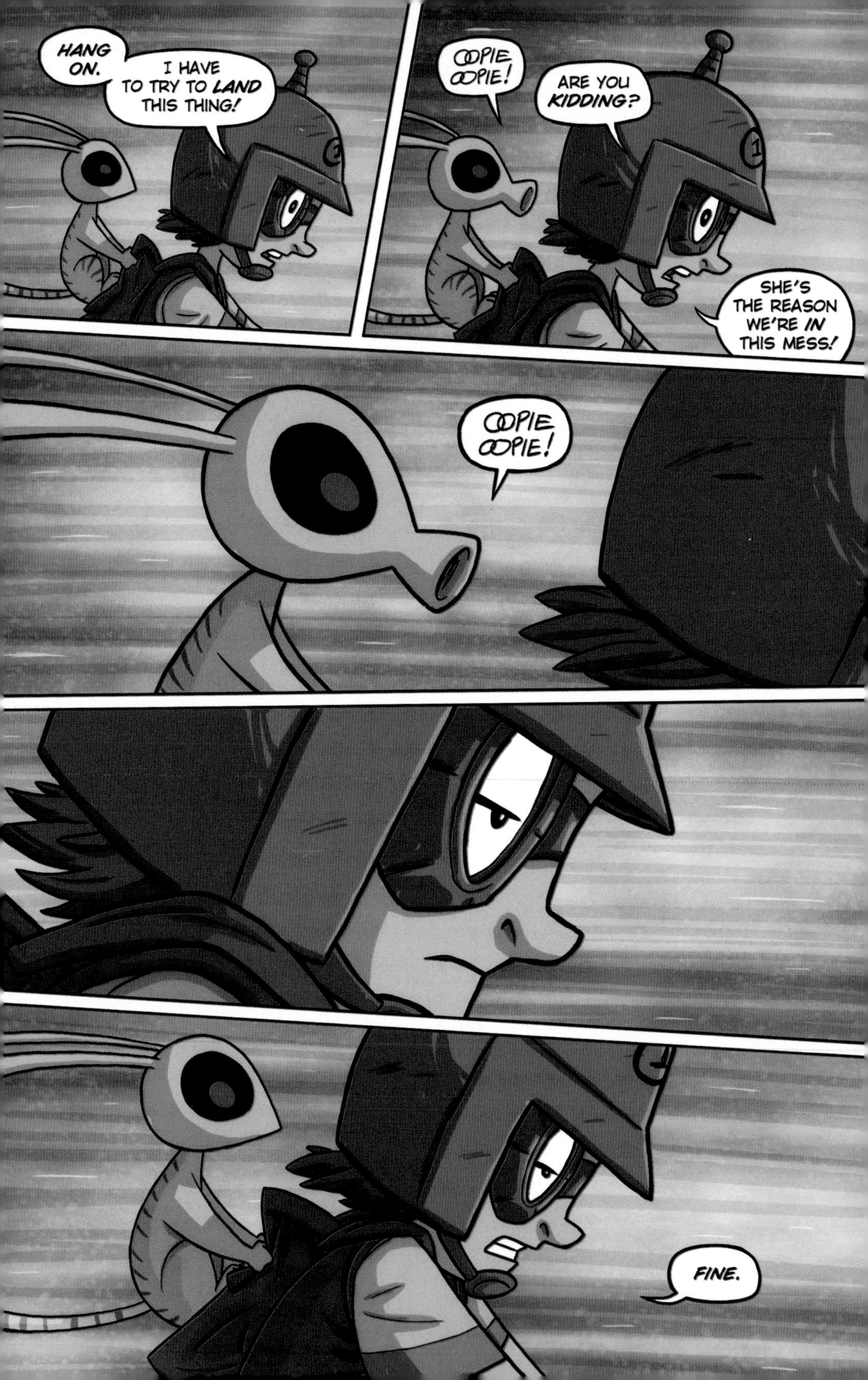
HANG ON.
I HAVE TO TRY TO LAND THIS THING!
OOPIE OOPIE!
ARE YOU KIDDING?
SHE'S THE REASON WE'RE IN THIS MESS!
OOPIE OOPIE!
FINE.

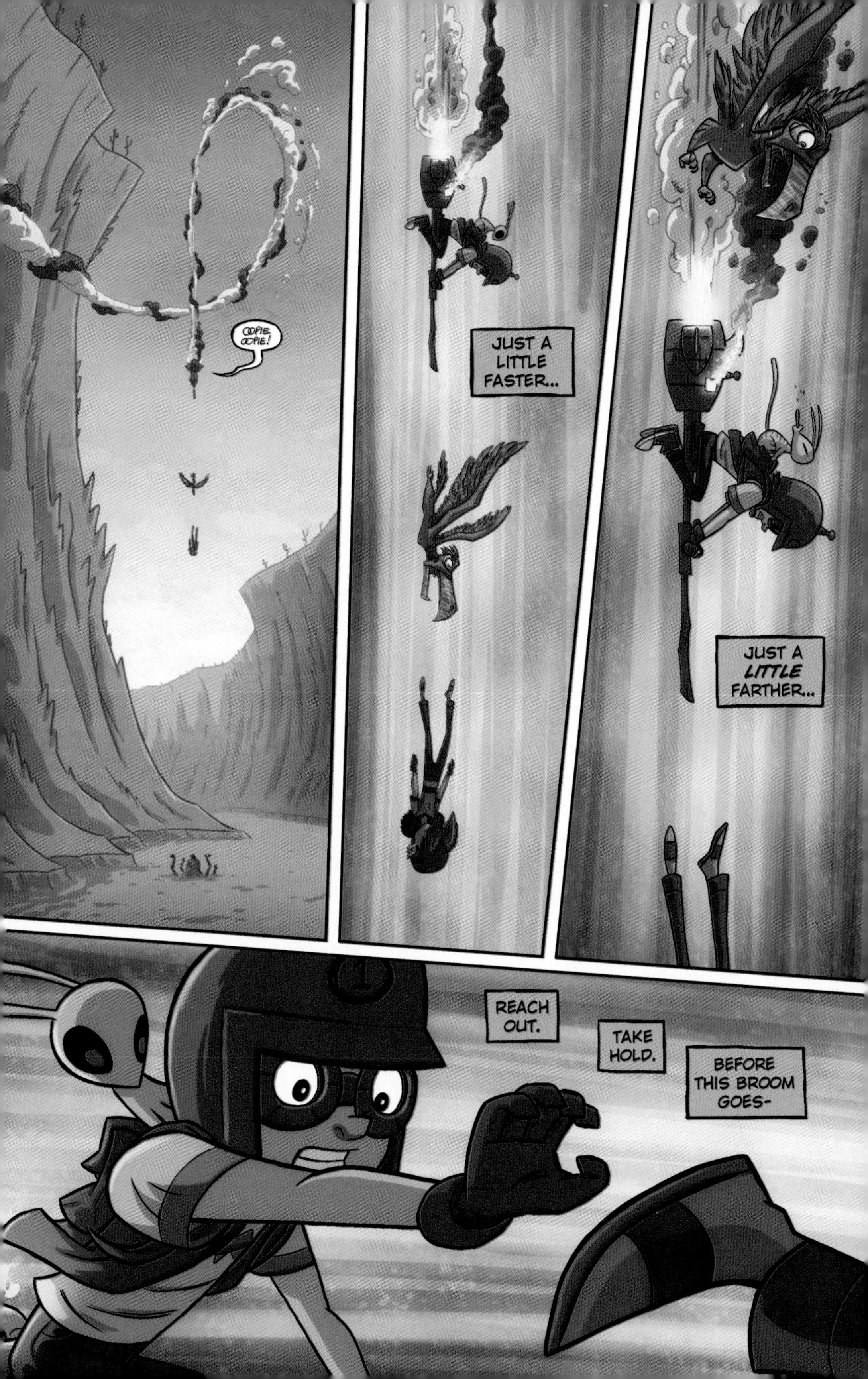
OOPIE OOPIE!
JUST A LITTLE FASTER...
JUST A LITTLE FARTHER...
REACH OUT.
TAKE HOLD.
BEFORE THIS BROOM GOES-

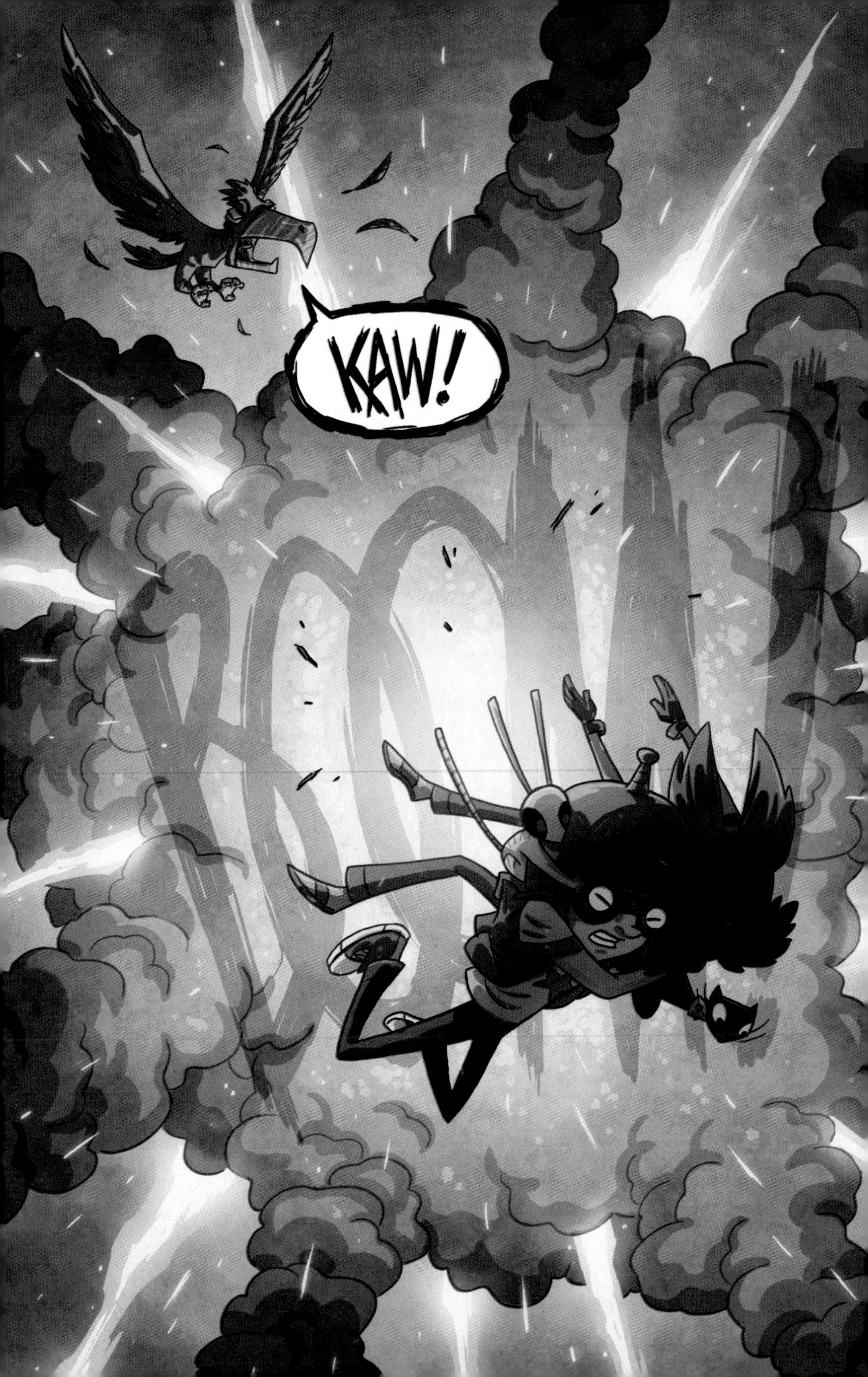
KAW!

Chapter 13
Mother's Ilk

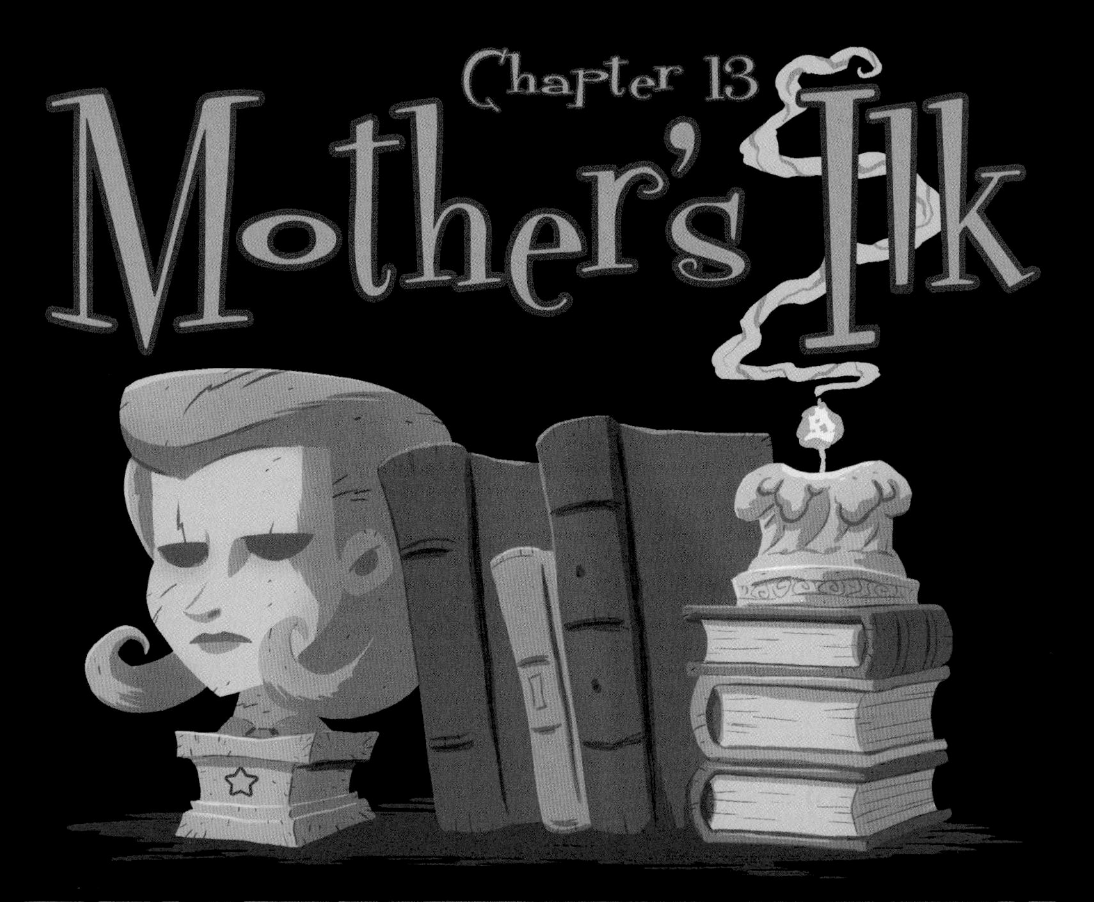

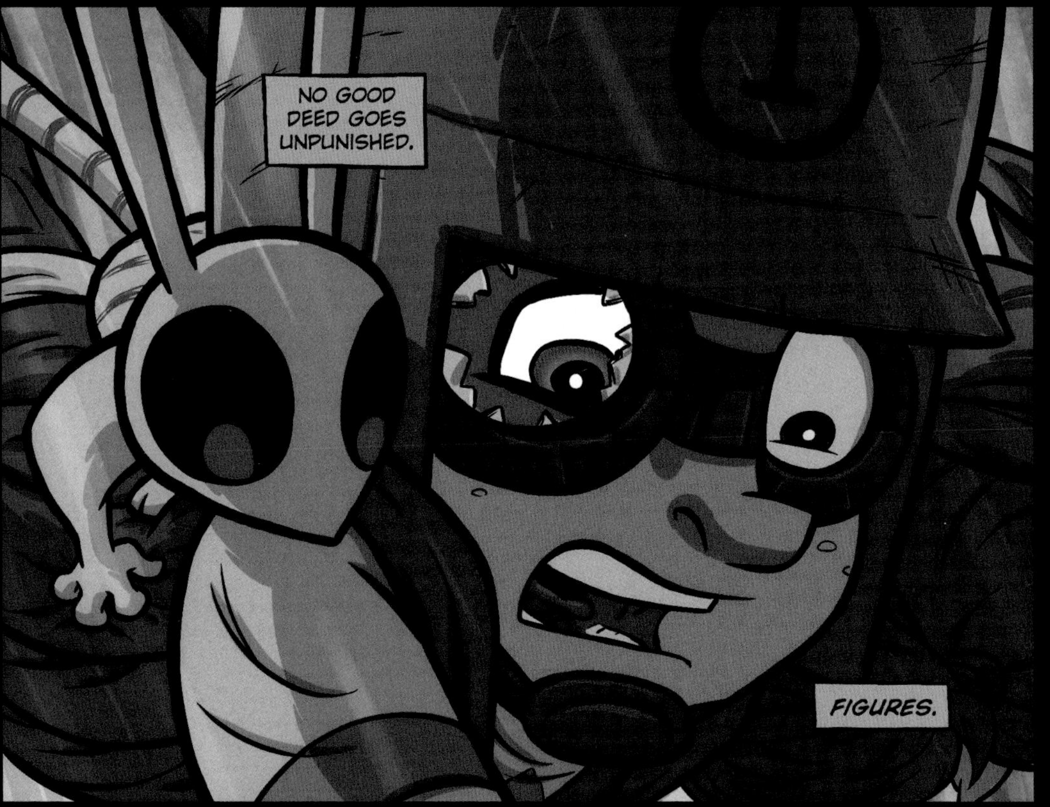
NO GOOD DEED GOES UNPUNISHED.
FIGURES.

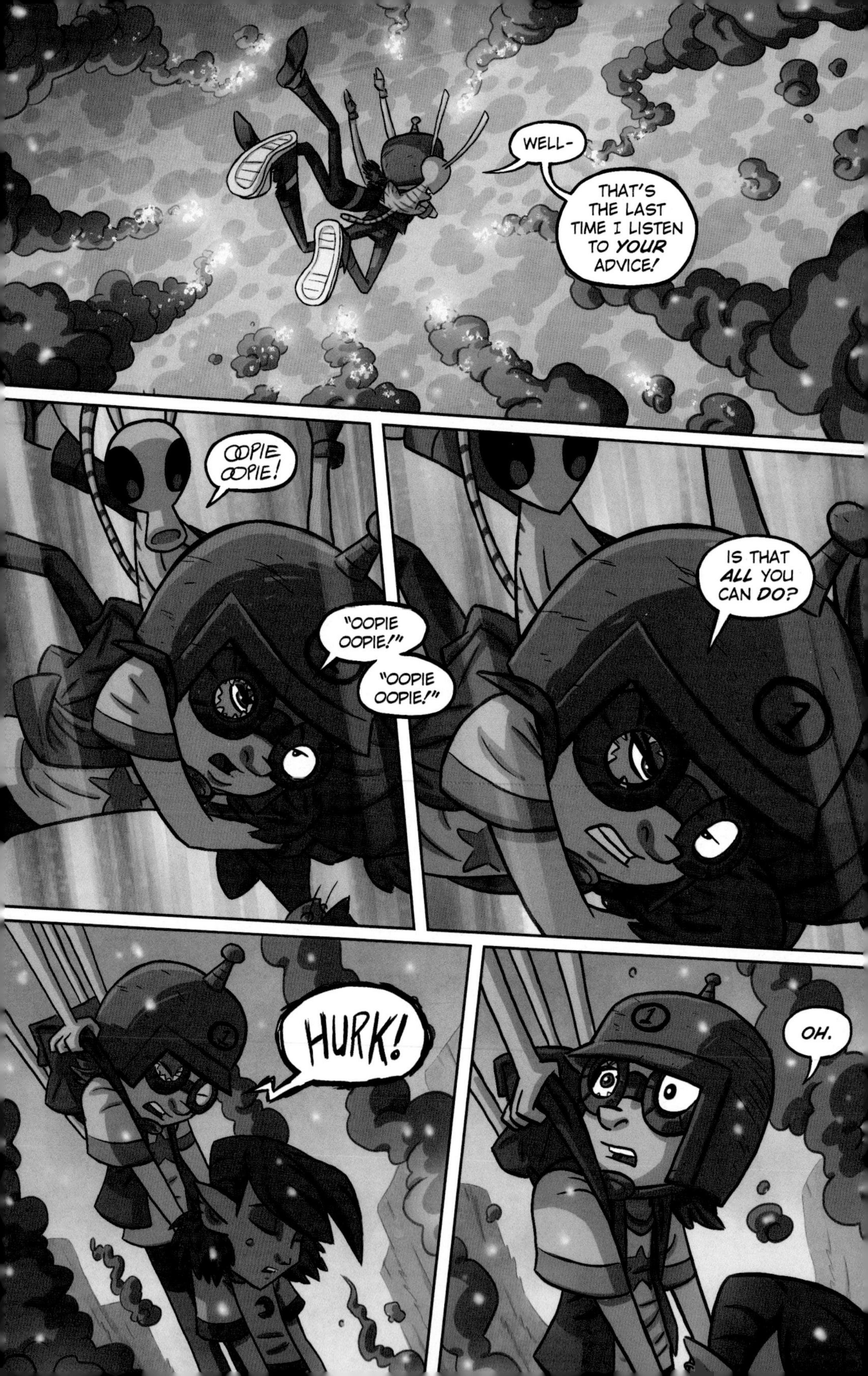
WELL-
THAT'S THE LAST TIME I LISTEN TO *YOUR* ADVICE!
OOPIE OOPIE!
"OOPIE OOPIE!"
"OOPIE OOPIE!"
IS THAT *ALL* YOU CAN *DO*?
HURK!
OH.

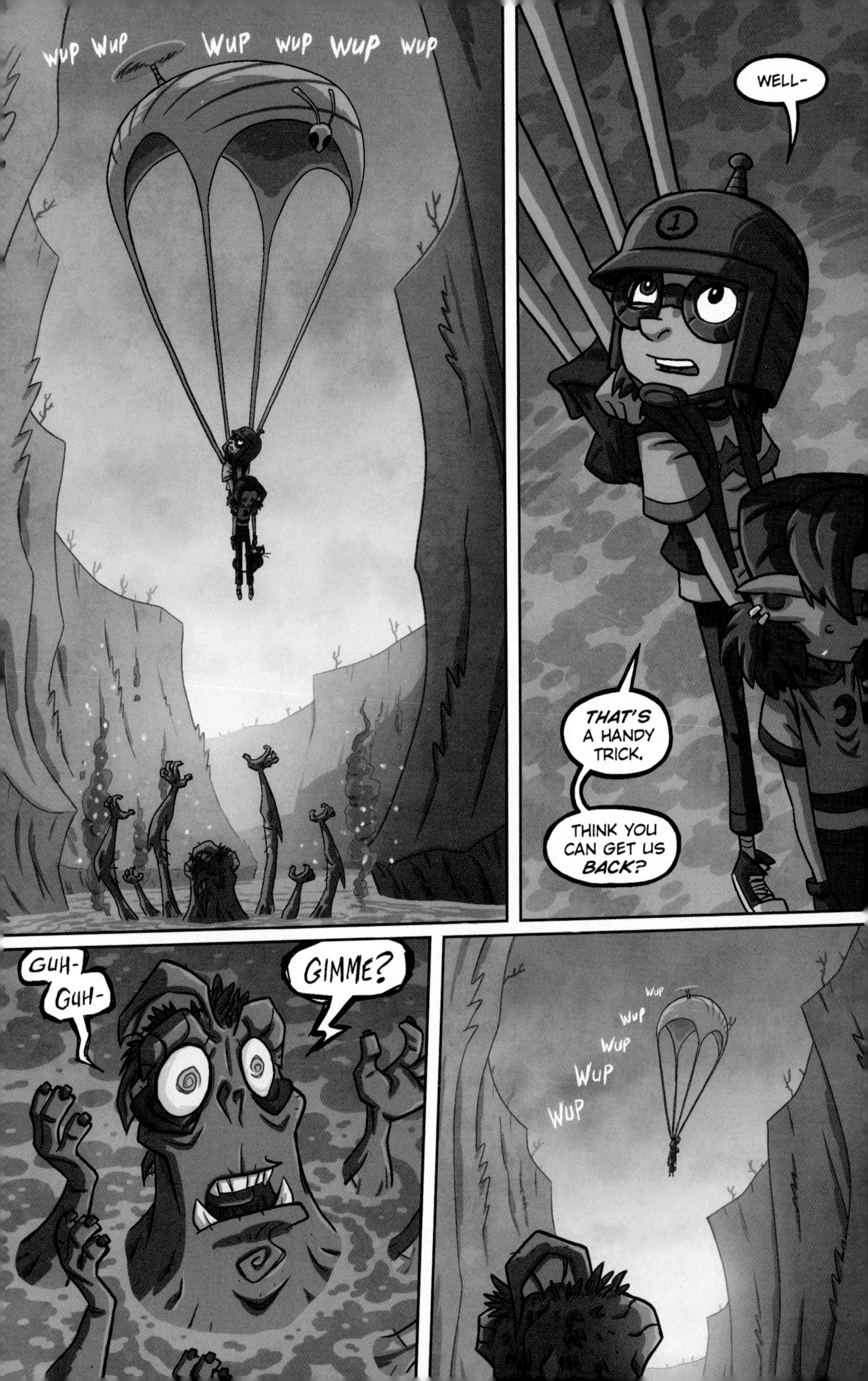
WUP WUP WUP WUP WUP WUP
WELL-
THAT'S A HANDY TRICK.
THINK YOU CAN GET US BACK?
GUH- GUH-
GIMME?
WUP WUP WUP WUP WUP

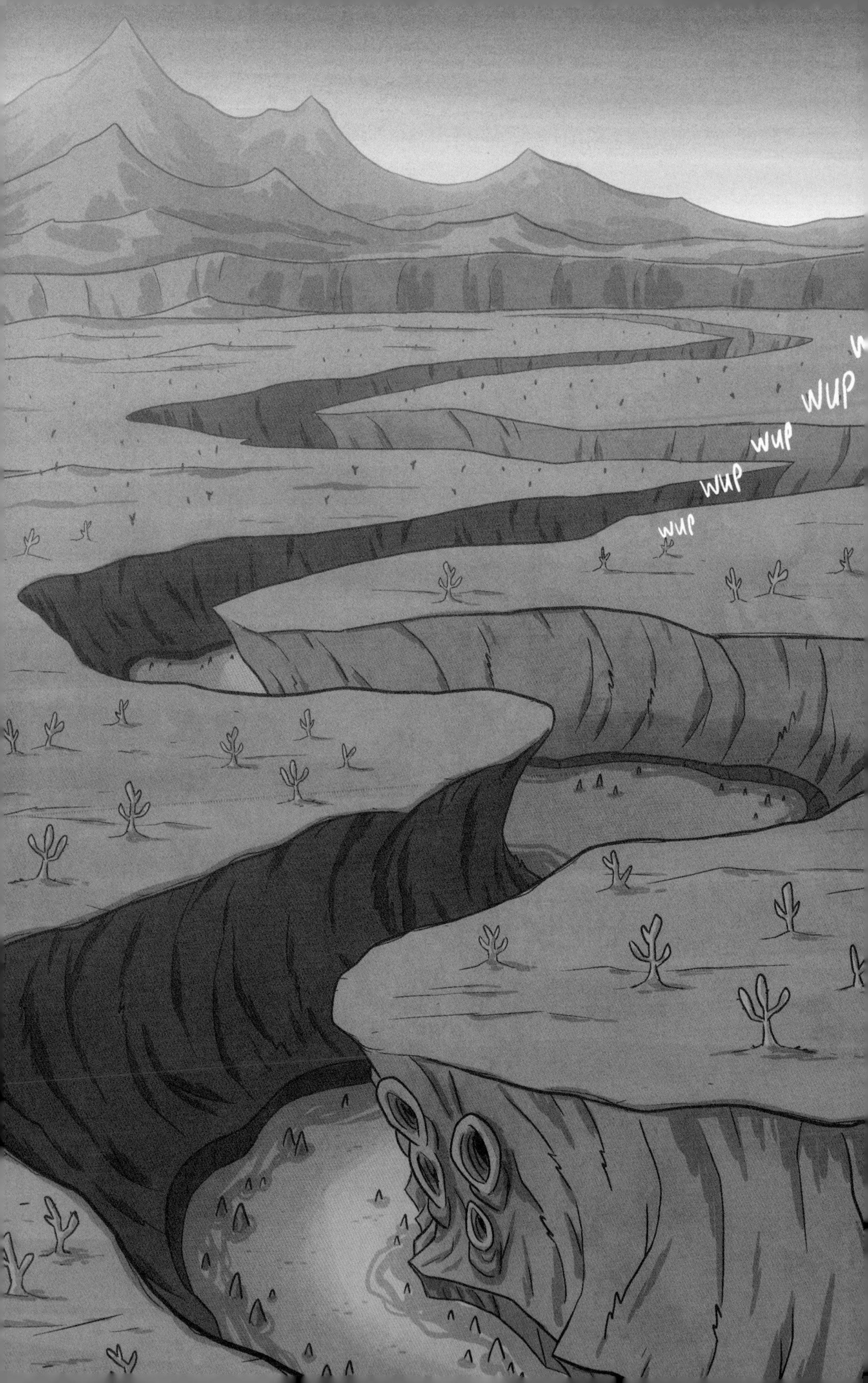
wup
wup
wup
WUP

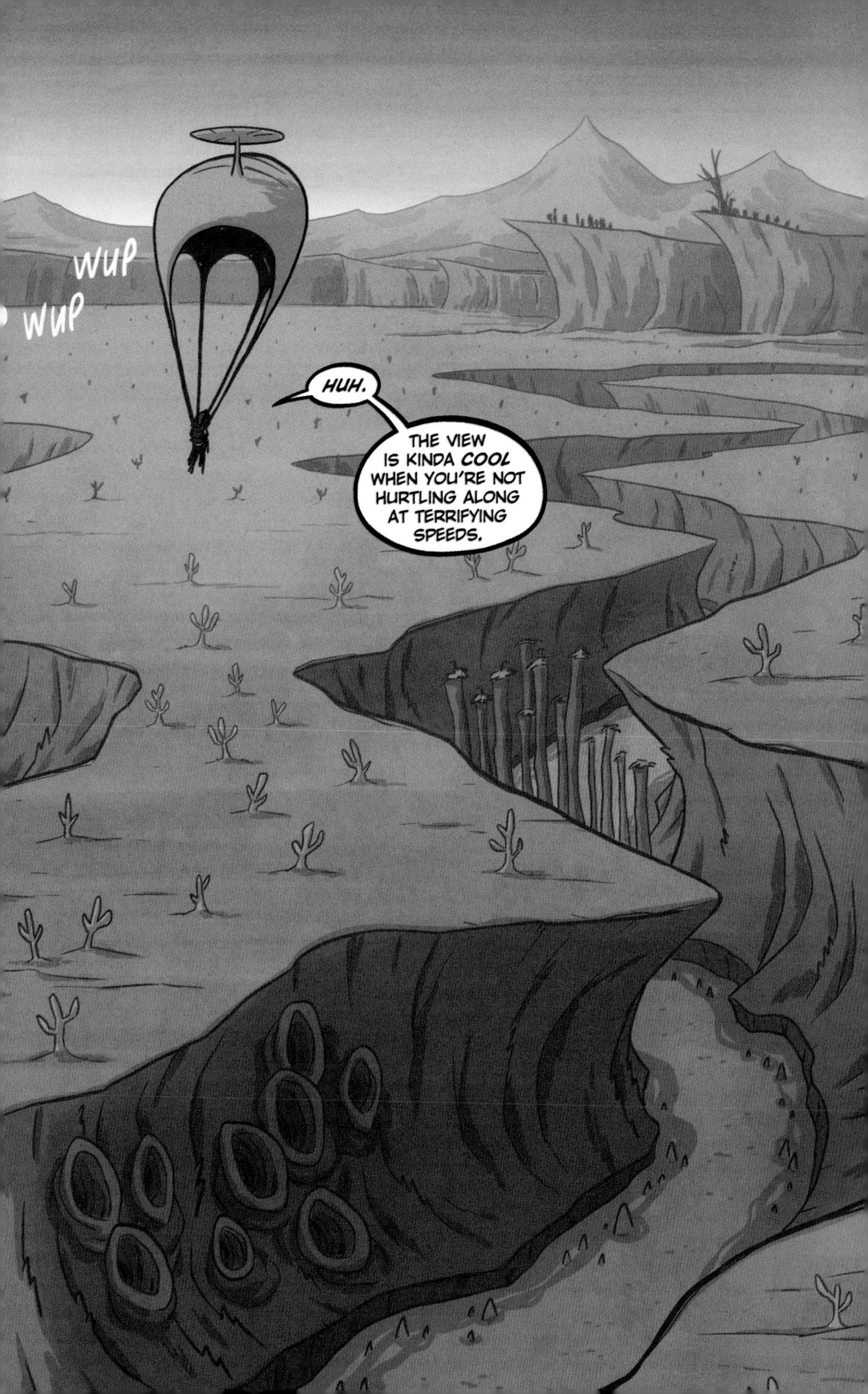
WUP
WUP
HUH.
THE VIEW IS KINDA COOL WHEN YOU'RE NOT HURTLING ALONG AT TERRIFYING SPEEDS.

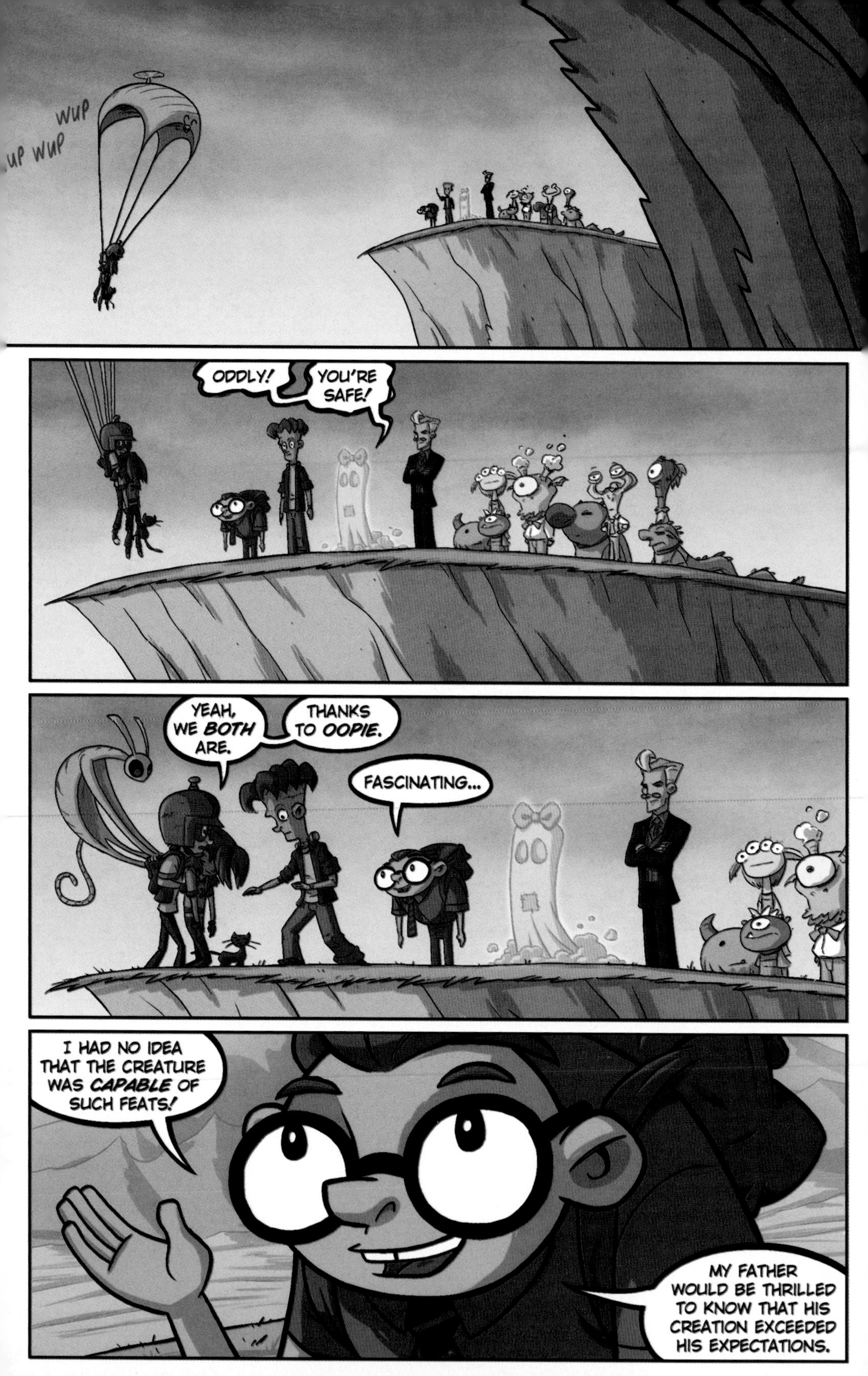
WUP
UP WUP
ODDLY!
YOU'RE SAFE!
YEAH, WE *BOTH* ARE.
THANKS TO *OOPIE*.
FASCINATING...
I HAD NO IDEA THAT THE CREATURE WAS *CAPABLE* OF SUCH FEATS!
MY FATHER WOULD BE THRILLED TO KNOW THAT HIS CREATION EXCEEDED HIS EXPECTATIONS.

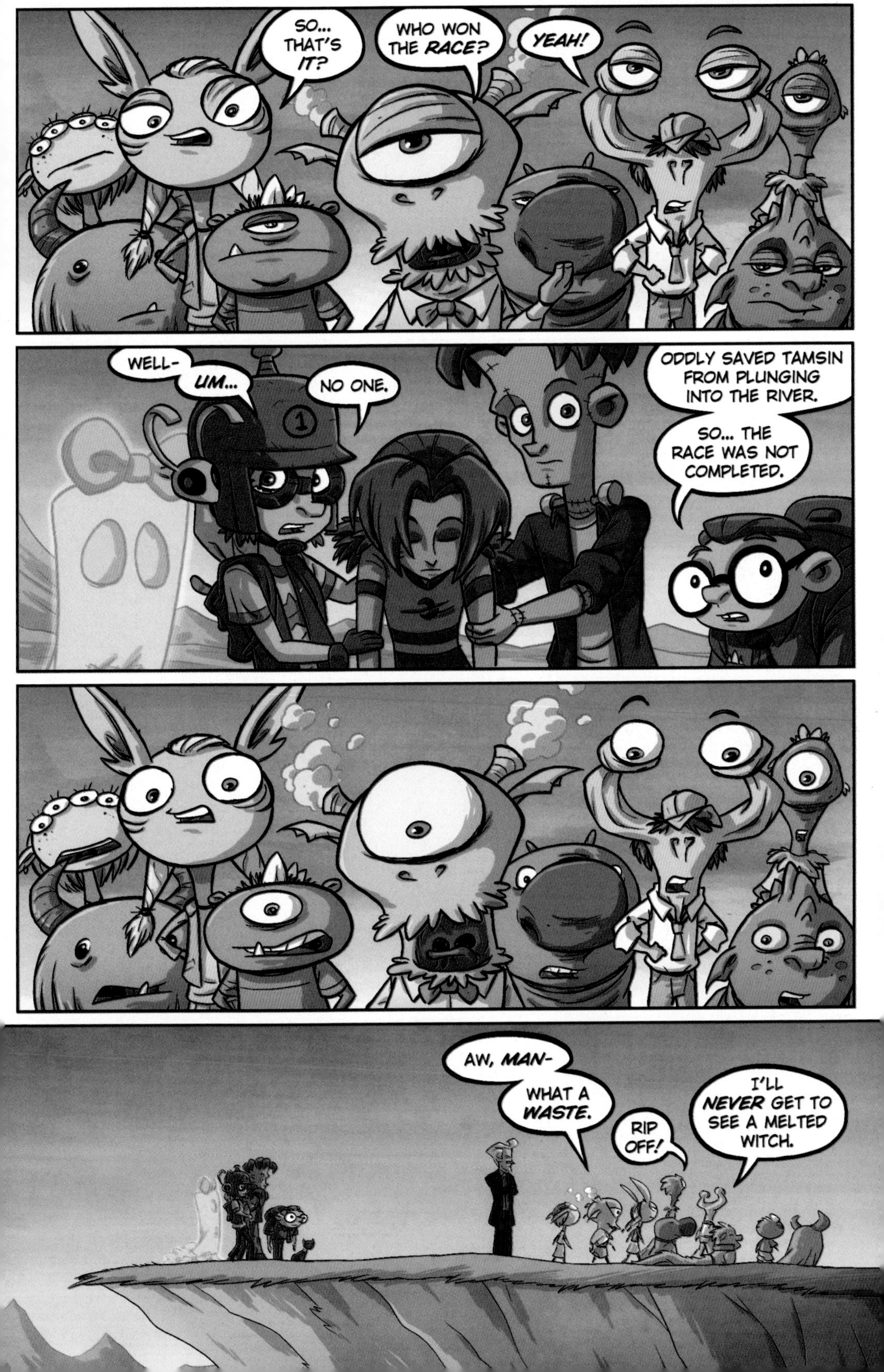
SO... THAT'S IT?
WHO WON THE RACE?
YEAH!
WELL- UM...
NO ONE.
ODDLY SAVED TAMSIN FROM PLUNGING INTO THE RIVER.
SO... THE RACE WAS NOT COMPLETED.
AW, MAN-
WHAT A WASTE.
RIP OFF!
I'LL NEVER GET TO SEE A MELTED WITCH.

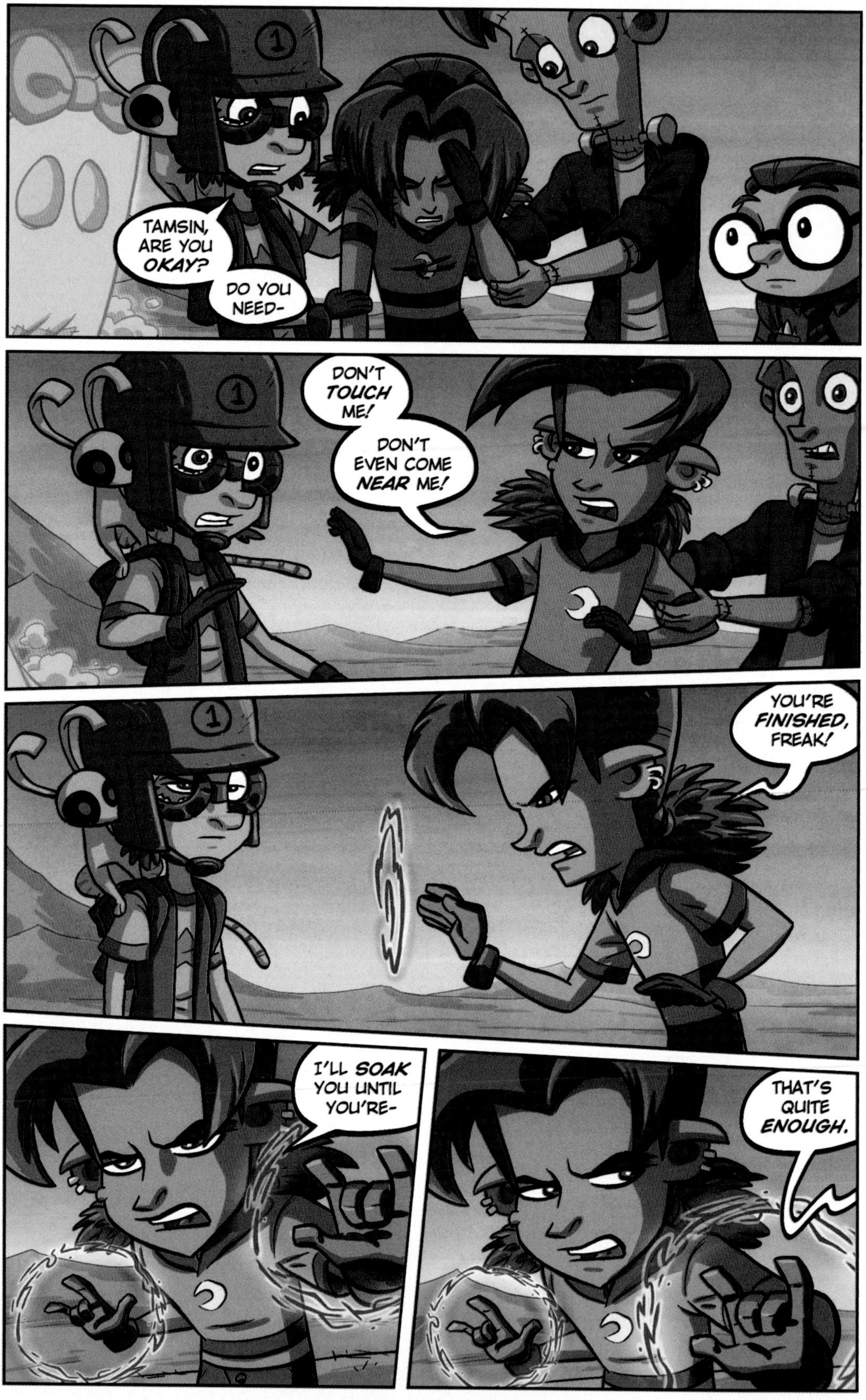
TAMSIN, ARE YOU OKAY?
DO YOU NEED-
DON'T TOUCH ME!
DON'T EVEN COME NEAR ME!
YOU'RE FINISHED, FREAK!
I'LL SOAK YOU UNTIL YOU'RE-
THAT'S QUITE ENOUGH.

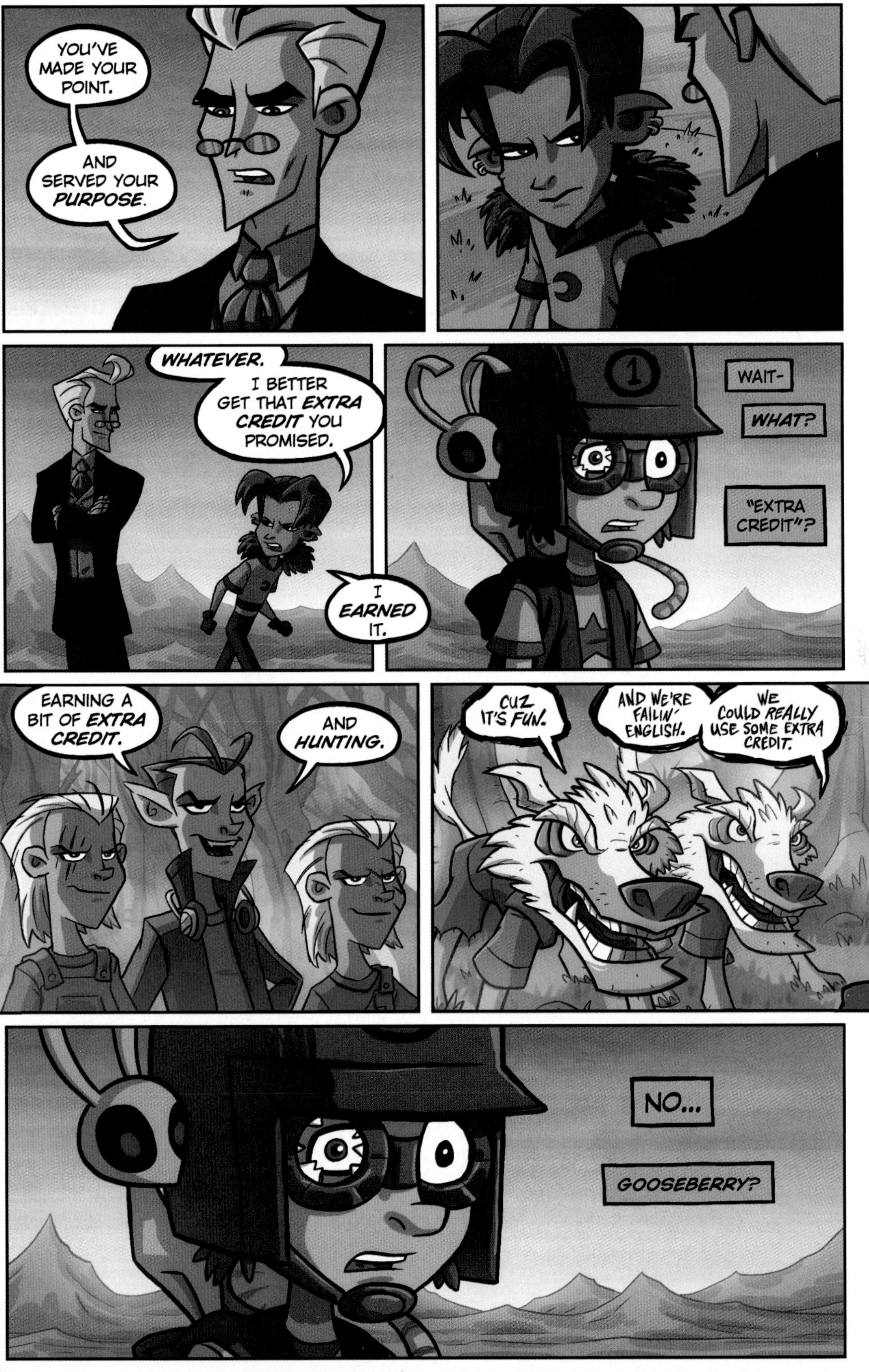
YOU'VE MADE YOUR POINT.
AND SERVED YOUR *PURPOSE*.
WHATEVER.
I BETTER GET THAT *EXTRA CREDIT* YOU PROMISED.
I *EARNED* IT.
WAIT-
WHAT?
"EXTRA CREDIT"?
EARNING A BIT OF *EXTRA CREDIT*.
AND *HUNTING*.
CUZ IT'S *FUN*.
AND WE'RE FAILIN' ENGLISH.
WE COULD *REALLY* USE SOME EXTRA CREDIT.
NO...
GOOSEBERRY?

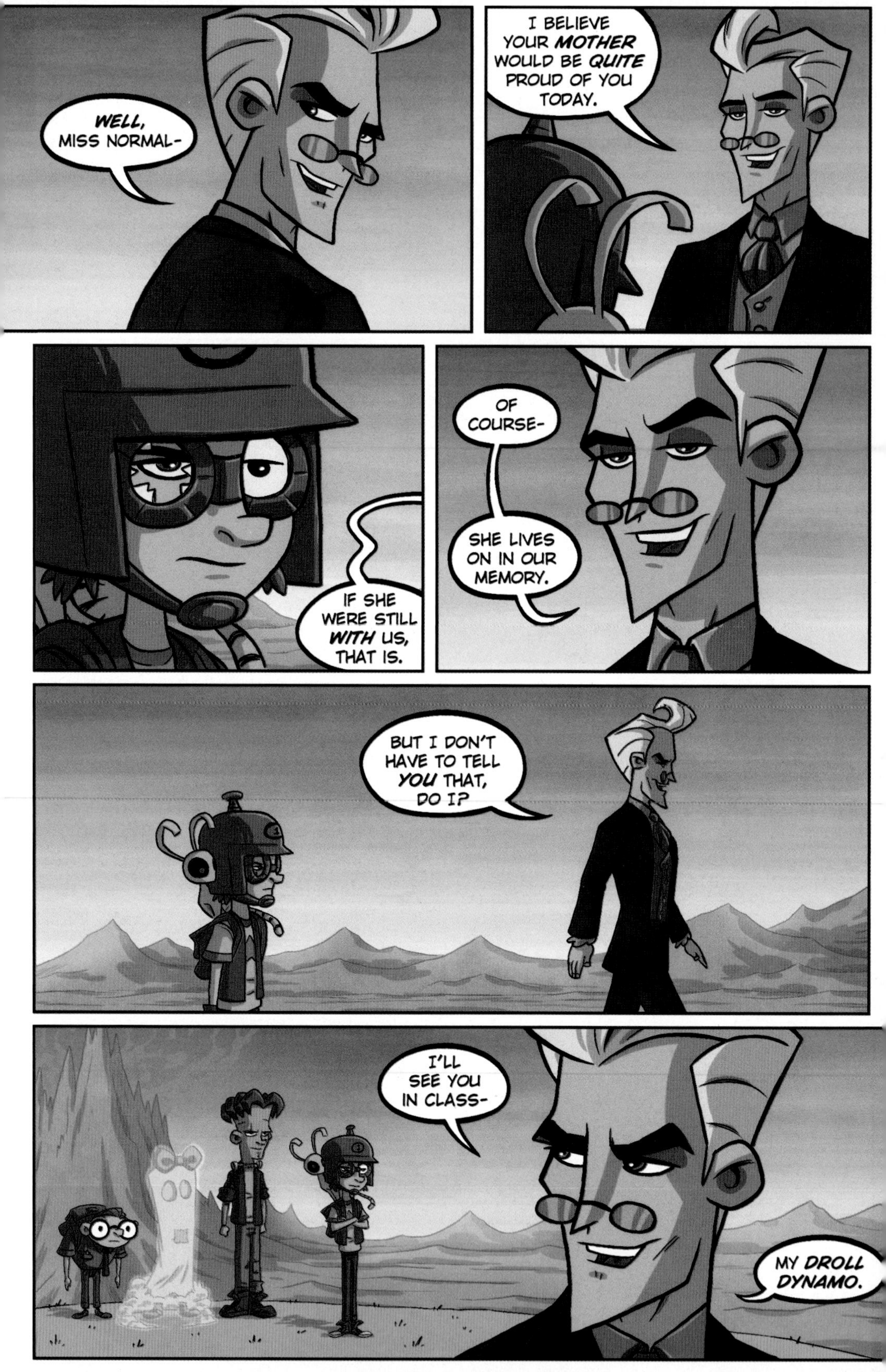

WELL, MISS NORMAL-
I BELIEVE YOUR **MOTHER** WOULD BE **QUITE** PROUD OF YOU TODAY.
IF SHE WERE STILL **WITH** US, THAT IS.
OF COURSE-
SHE LIVES ON IN OUR MEMORY.
BUT I DON'T HAVE TO TELL **YOU** THAT, DO I?
I'LL SEE YOU IN CLASS-
MY **DROLL DYNAMO.**

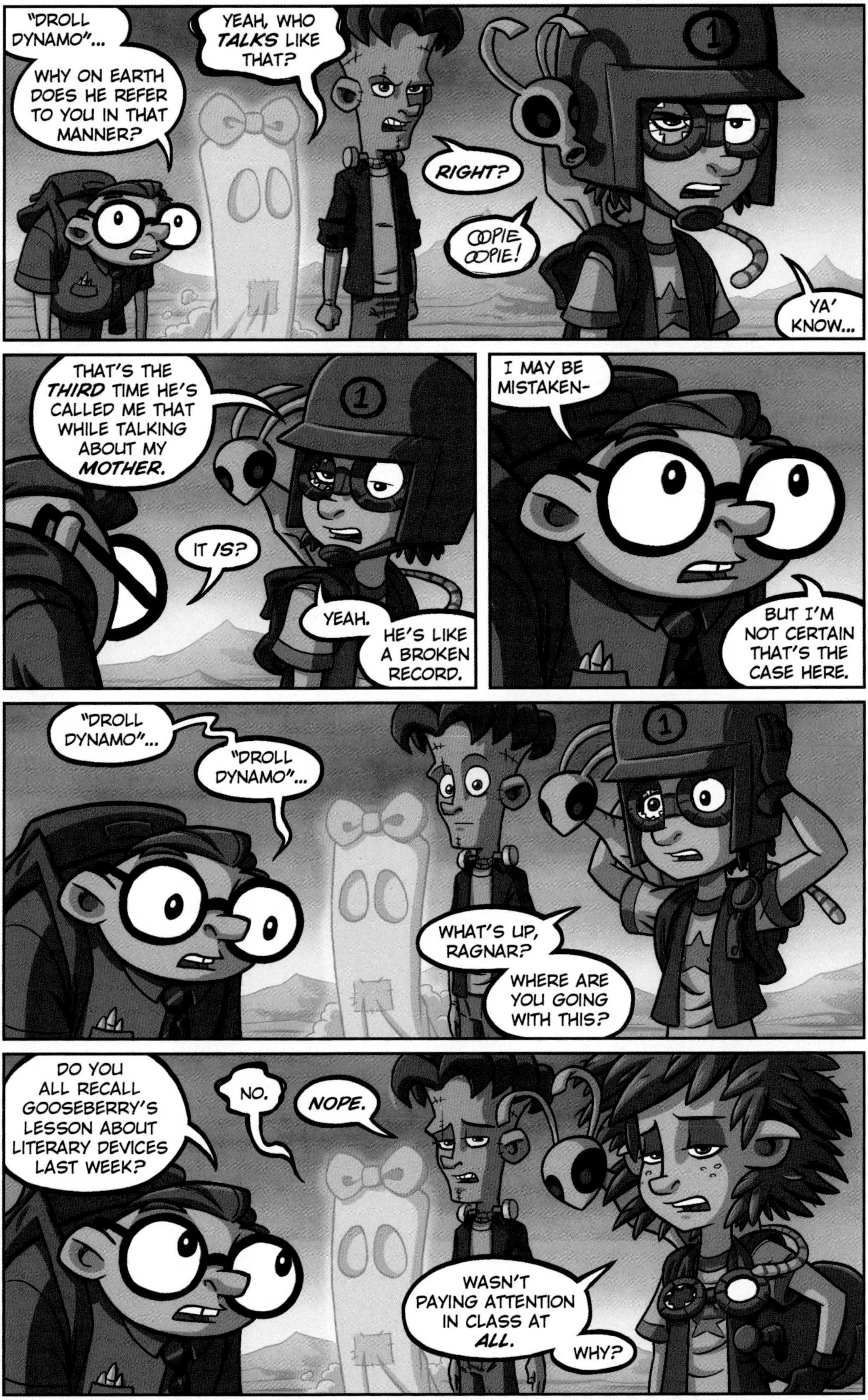
"DROLL DYNAMO"...
WHY ON EARTH DOES HE REFER TO YOU IN THAT MANNER?
YEAH, WHO TALKS LIKE THAT?
RIGHT?
OOPIE OOPIE!
YA' KNOW...
THAT'S THE THIRD TIME HE'S CALLED ME THAT WHILE TALKING ABOUT MY MOTHER.
IT IS?
YEAH.
HE'S LIKE A BROKEN RECORD.
I MAY BE MISTAKEN-
BUT I'M NOT CERTAIN THAT'S THE CASE HERE.
"DROLL DYNAMO"...
"DROLL DYNAMO"...
WHAT'S UP, RAGNAR?
WHERE ARE YOU GOING WITH THIS?
DO YOU ALL RECALL GOOSEBERRY'S LESSON ABOUT LITERARY DEVICES LAST WEEK?
NO.
NOPE.
WASN'T PAYING ATTENTION IN CLASS AT ALL.
WHY?

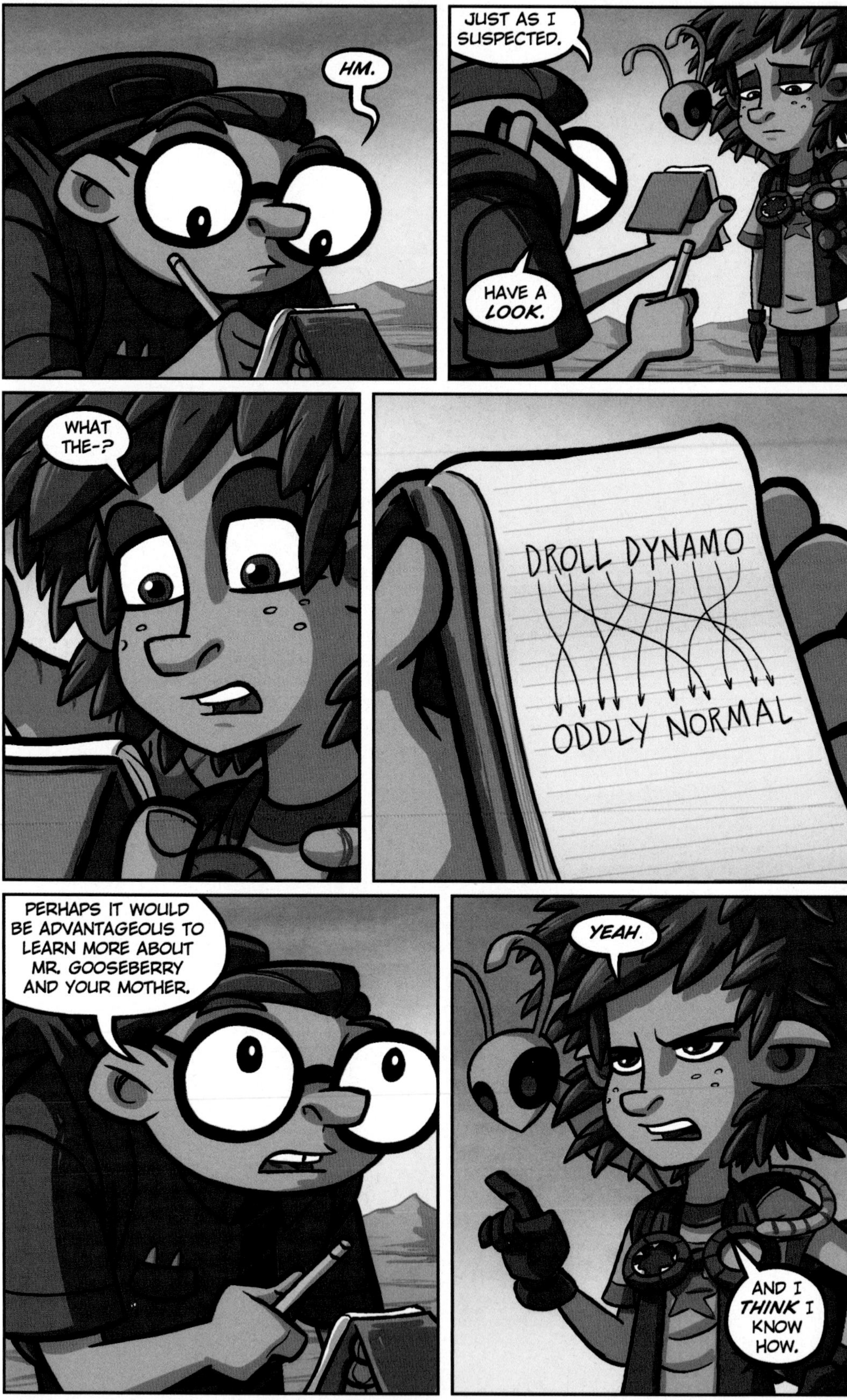
HM.
JUST AS I SUSPECTED.
HAVE A LOOK.
WHAT THE-?
DROLL DYNAMO
ODDLY NORMAL
PERHAPS IT WOULD BE ADVANTAGEOUS TO LEARN MORE ABOUT MR. GOOSEBERRY AND YOUR MOTHER.
YEAH.
AND I THINK I KNOW HOW.

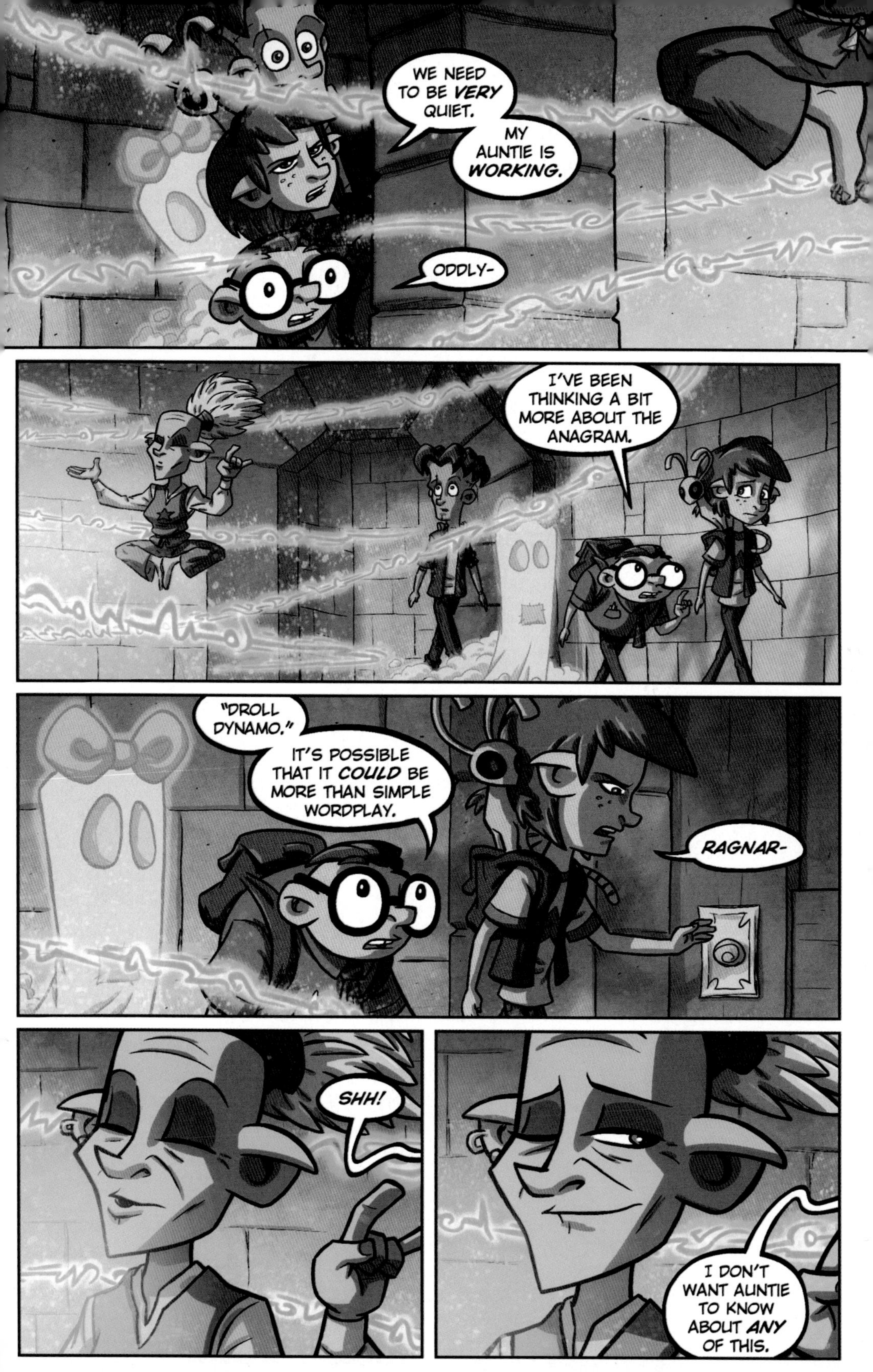
WE NEED TO BE VERY QUIET.
MY AUNTIE IS WORKING.
ODDLY-
I'VE BEEN THINKING A BIT MORE ABOUT THE ANAGRAM.
"DROLL DYNAMO."
IT'S POSSIBLE THAT IT COULD BE MORE THAN SIMPLE WORDPLAY.
RAGNAR-
SHH!
I DON'T WANT AUNTIE TO KNOW ABOUT ANY OF THIS.

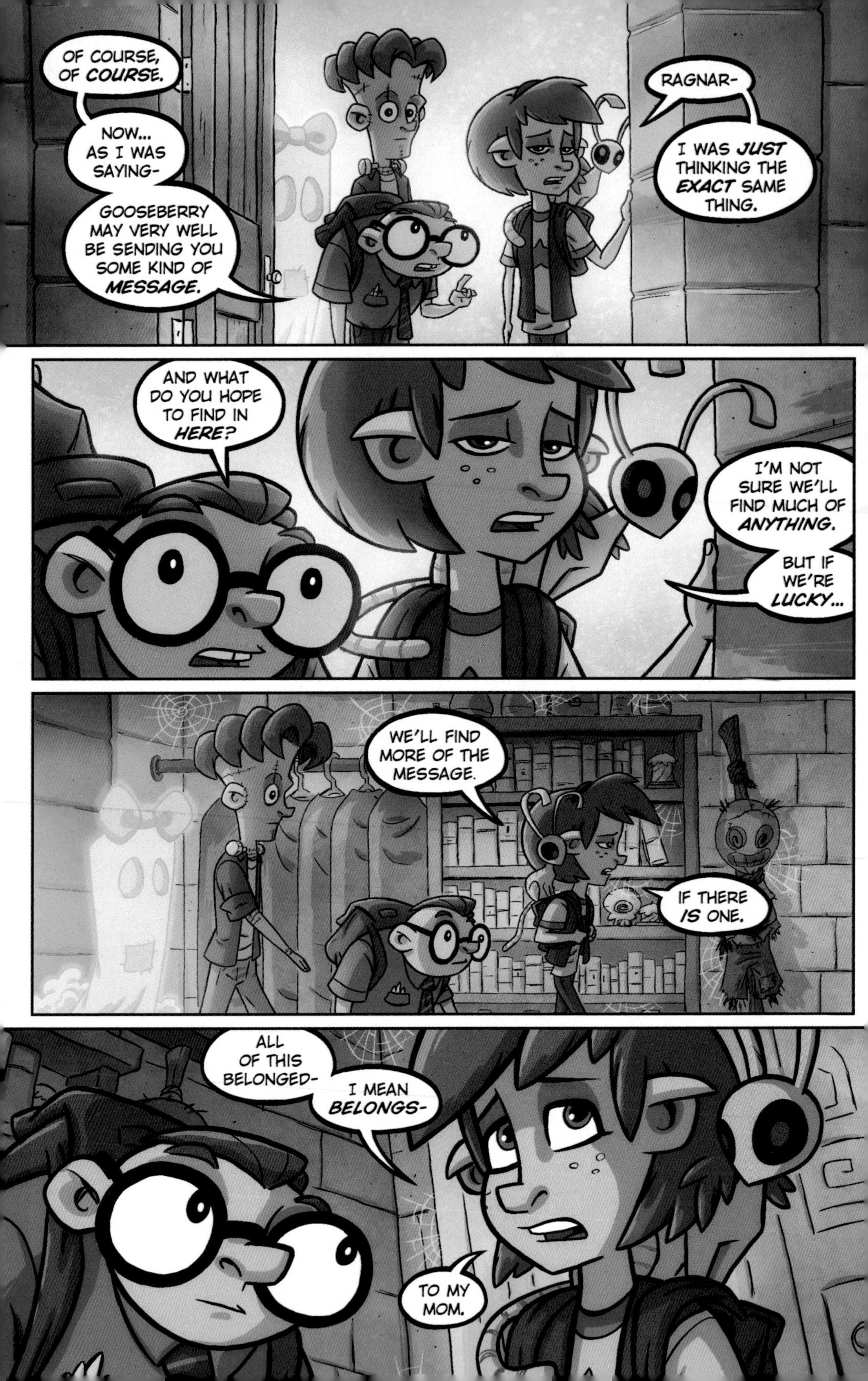
OF COURSE, OF COURSE.
NOW... AS I WAS SAYING-
GOOSEBERRY MAY VERY WELL BE SENDING YOU SOME KIND OF MESSAGE.
RAGNAR-
I WAS JUST THINKING THE EXACT SAME THING.
AND WHAT DO YOU HOPE TO FIND IN HERE?
I'M NOT SURE WE'LL FIND MUCH OF ANYTHING.
BUT IF WE'RE LUCKY...
WE'LL FIND MORE OF THE MESSAGE.
IF THERE IS ONE.
ALL OF THIS BELONGED-
I MEAN BELONGS-
TO MY MOM.

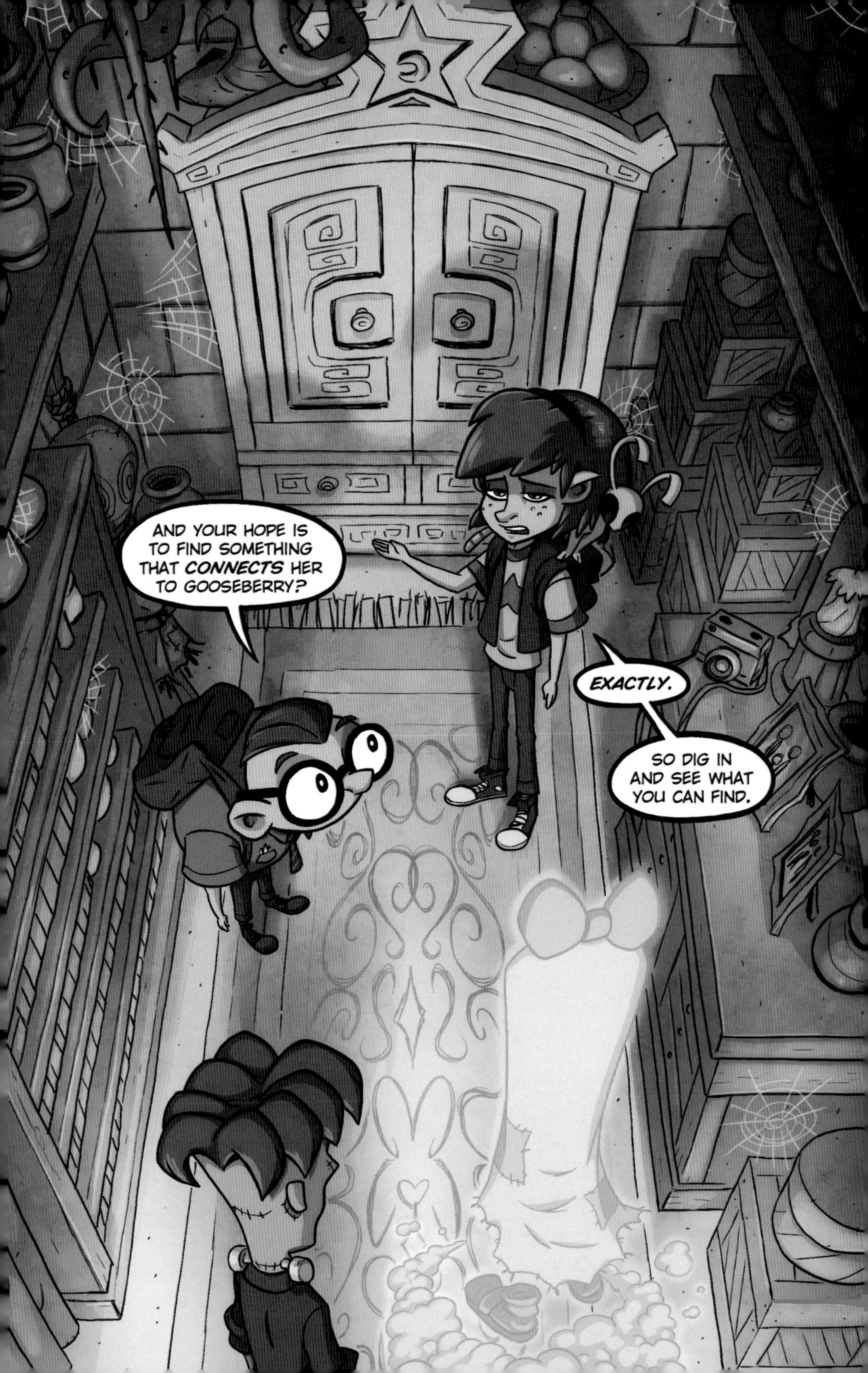
AND YOUR HOPE IS TO FIND SOMETHING THAT *CONNECTS* HER TO GOOSEBERRY?
EXACTLY.
SO DIG IN AND SEE WHAT YOU CAN FIND.

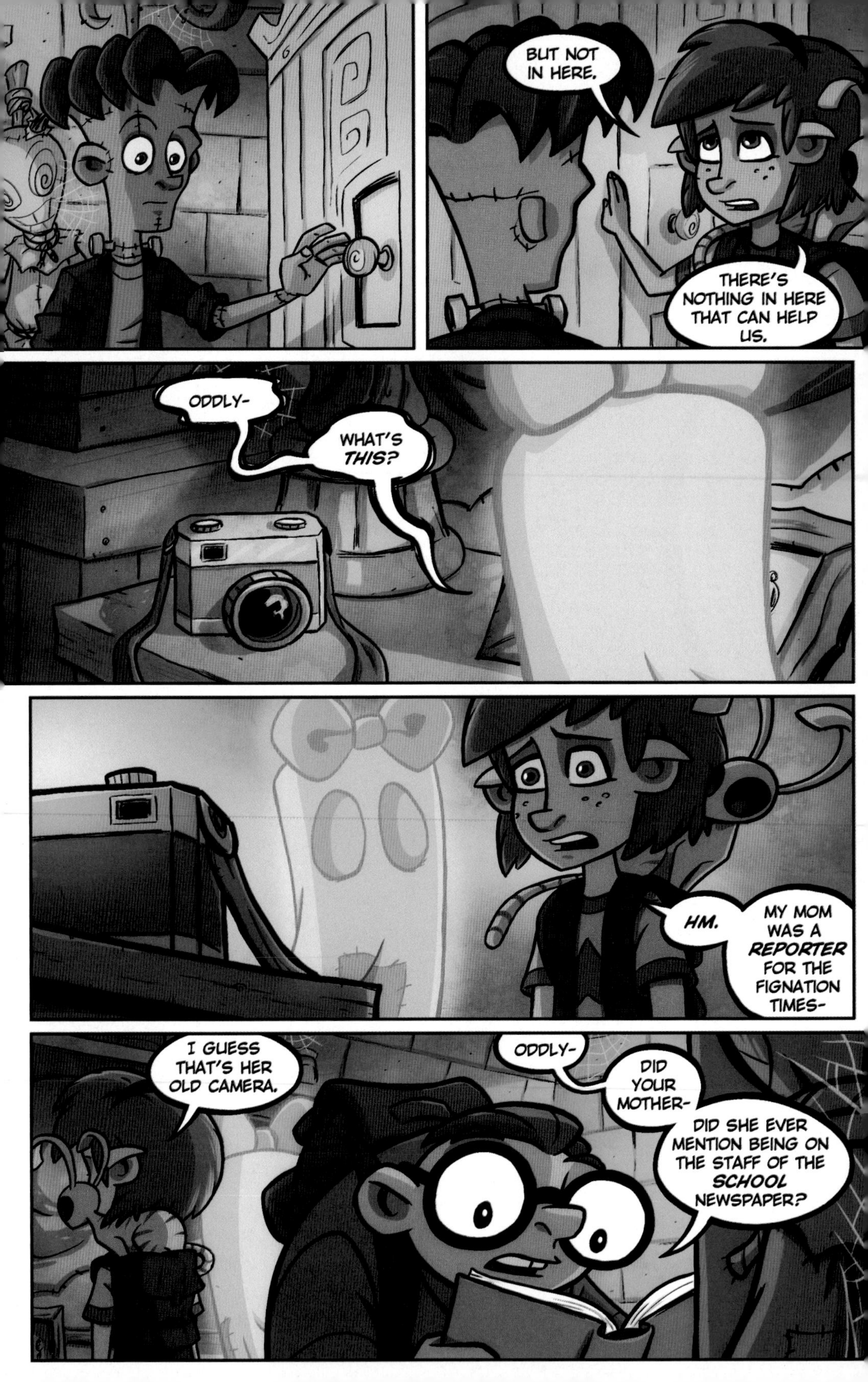

BUT NOT IN HERE.
THERE'S NOTHING IN HERE THAT CAN HELP US.
ODDLY-
WHAT'S *THIS?*
HM.
MY MOM WAS A *REPORTER* FOR THE FIGNATION TIMES-
I GUESS THAT'S HER OLD CAMERA.
ODDLY-
DID YOUR MOTHER-
DID SHE EVER MENTION BEING ON THE STAFF OF THE *SCHOOL* NEWSPAPER?

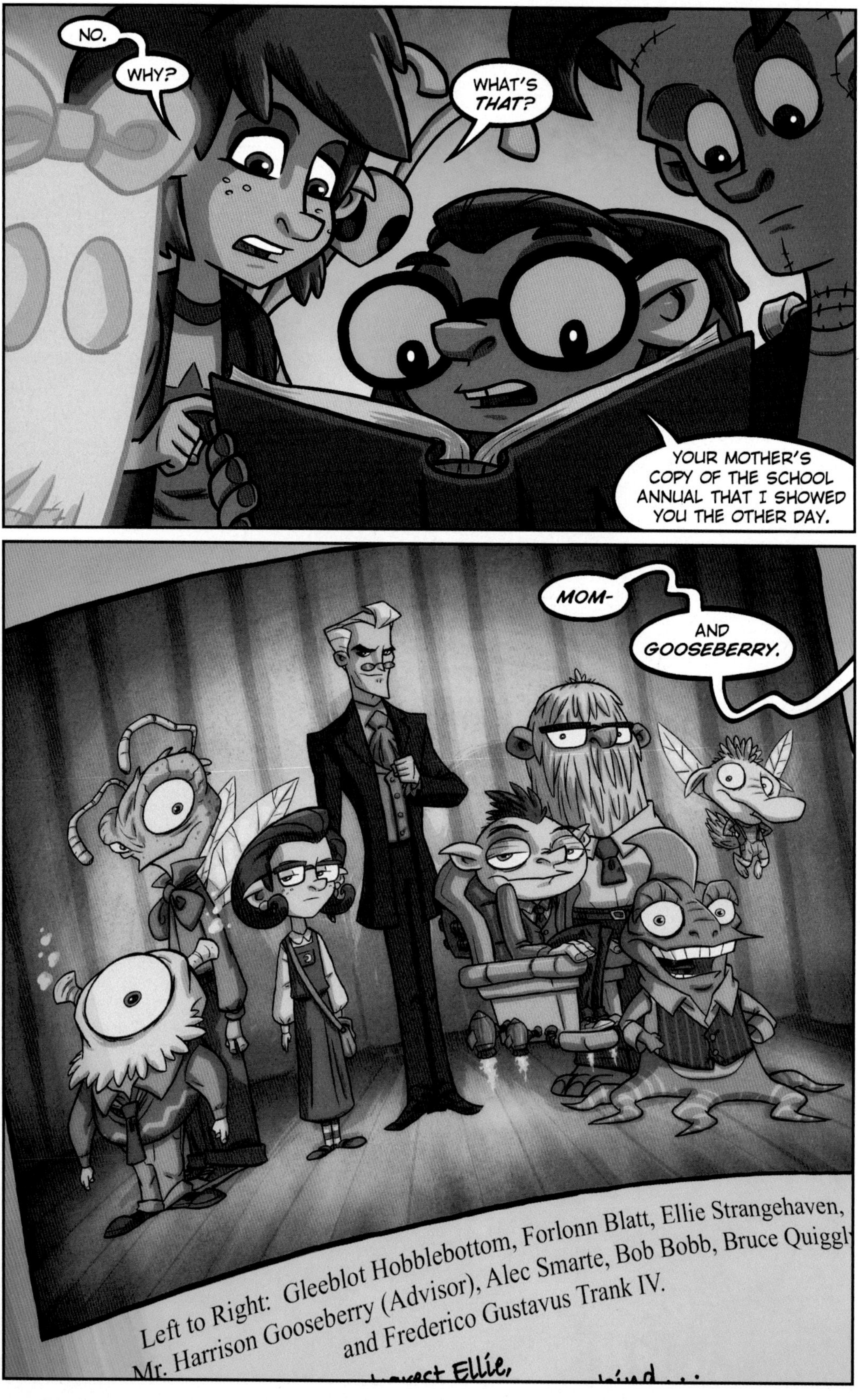
NO.
WHY?
WHAT'S *THAT?*
YOUR MOTHER'S COPY OF THE SCHOOL ANNUAL THAT I SHOWED YOU THE OTHER DAY.
MOM-
AND *GOOSEBERRY.*
Left to Right: Gleeblot Hobblebottom, Forlonn Blatt, Ellie Strangehaven,
Mr. Harrison Gooseberry (Advisor), Alec Smarte, Bob Bobb, Bruce Quiggl
and Frederico Gustavus Trank IV.

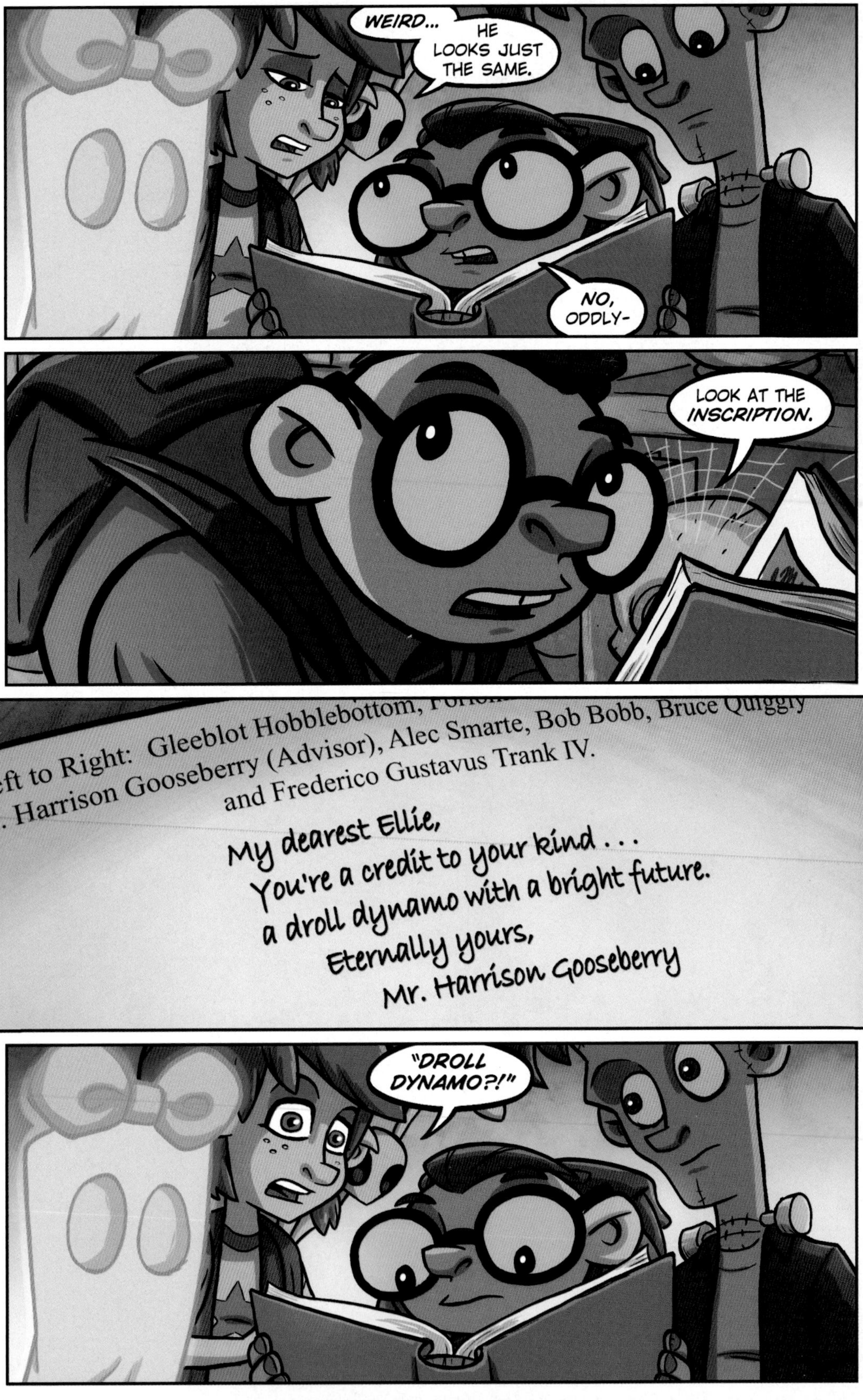
WEIRD...
HE LOOKS JUST THE SAME.
NO, ODDLY-
LOOK AT THE INSCRIPTION.
Left to Right: Gleeblot Hobblebottom,
Mr. Harrison Gooseberry (Advisor), Alec Smarte, Bob Bobb, Bruce Quiggly
and Frederico Gustavus Trank IV.
My dearest Ellie,
You're a credit to your kind . . .
a droll dynamo with a bright future.
Eternally yours,
Mr. Harrison Gooseberry
"DROLL DYNAMO?!"

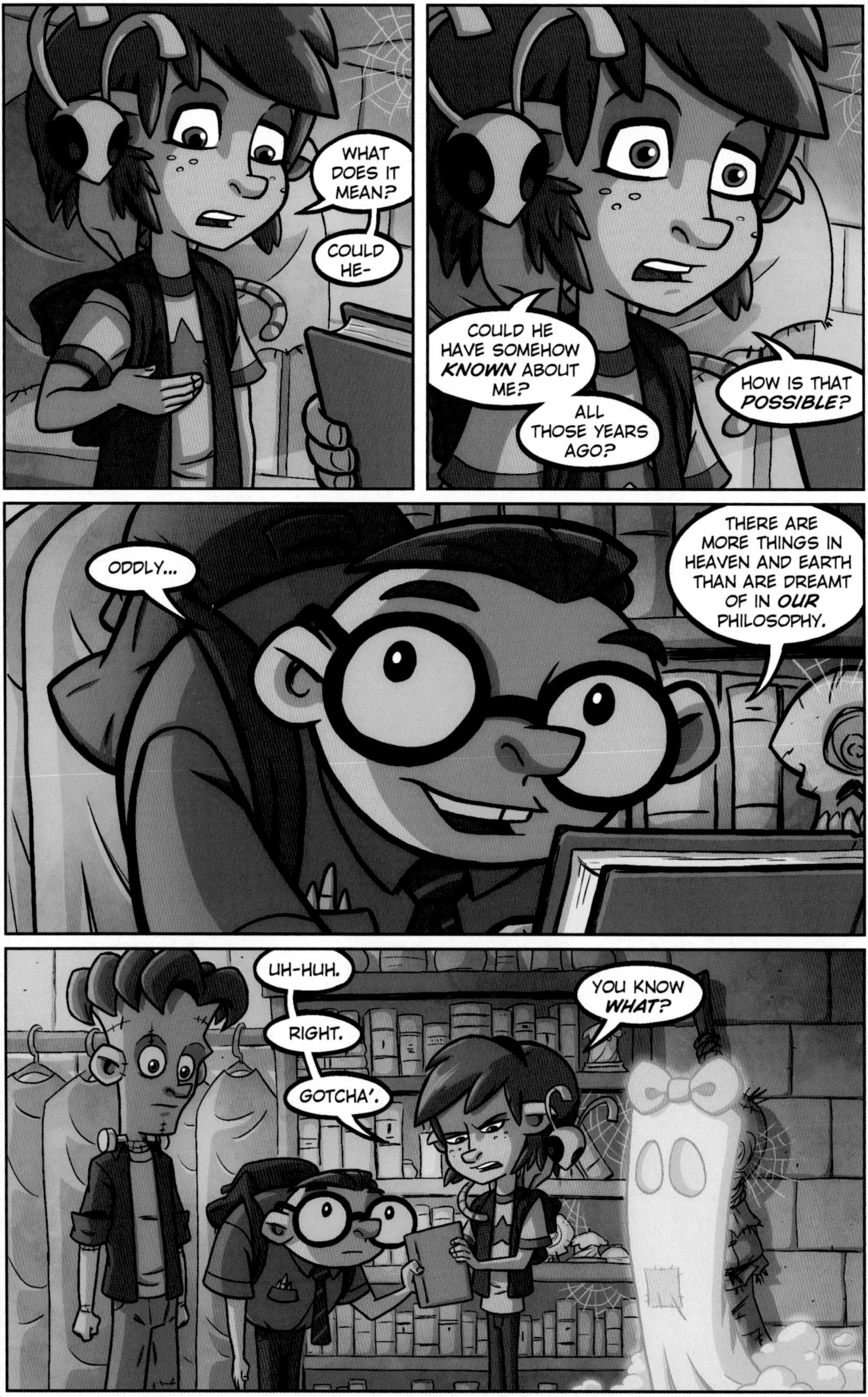
WHAT DOES IT MEAN?
COULD HE-
COULD HE HAVE SOMEHOW *KNOWN* ABOUT ME?
ALL THOSE YEARS AGO?
HOW IS THAT *POSSIBLE?*
ODDLY...
THERE ARE MORE THINGS IN HEAVEN AND EARTH THAN ARE DREAMT OF IN *OUR* PHILOSOPHY.
UH-HUH.
RIGHT.
GOTCHA'.
YOU KNOW *WHAT?*

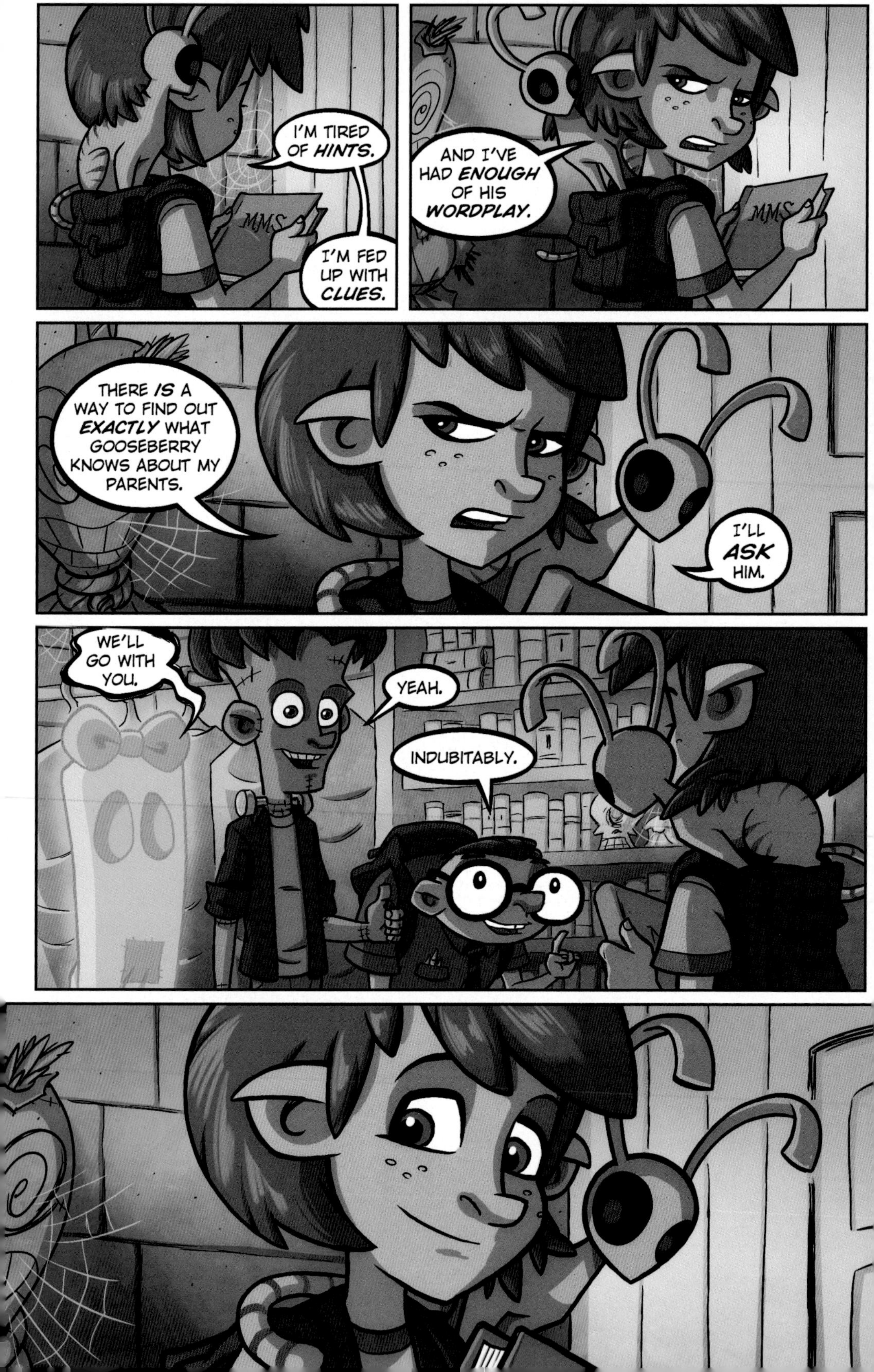
I'M TIRED OF HINTS.
I'M FED UP WITH CLUES.
AND I'VE HAD ENOUGH OF HIS WORDPLAY.
THERE IS A WAY TO FIND OUT EXACTLY WHAT GOOSEBERRY KNOWS ABOUT MY PARENTS.
I'LL ASK HIM.
WE'LL GO WITH YOU.
YEAH.
INDUBITABLY.

Chapter 14
The Angel of the Bottomless Pit

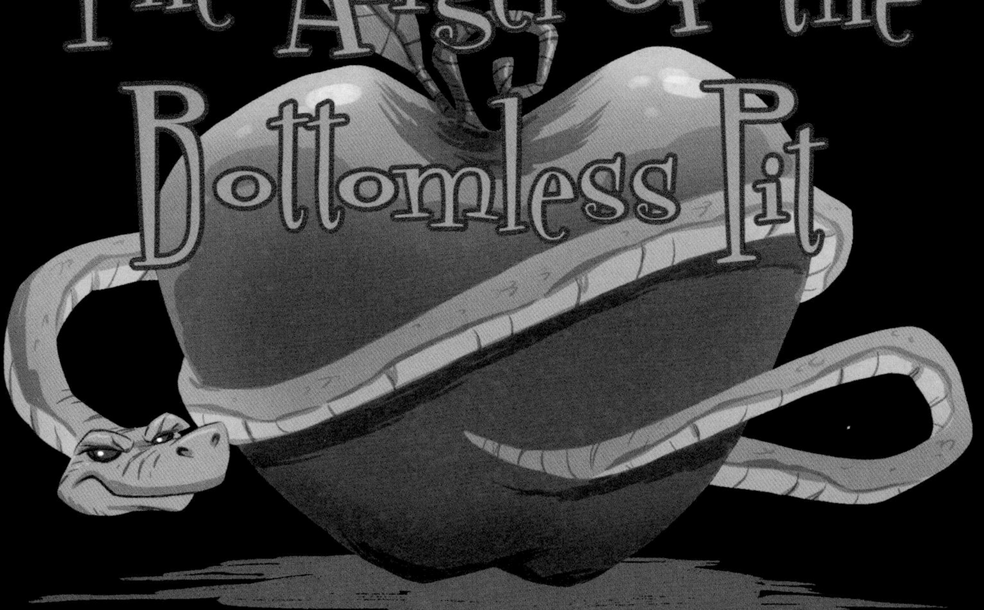

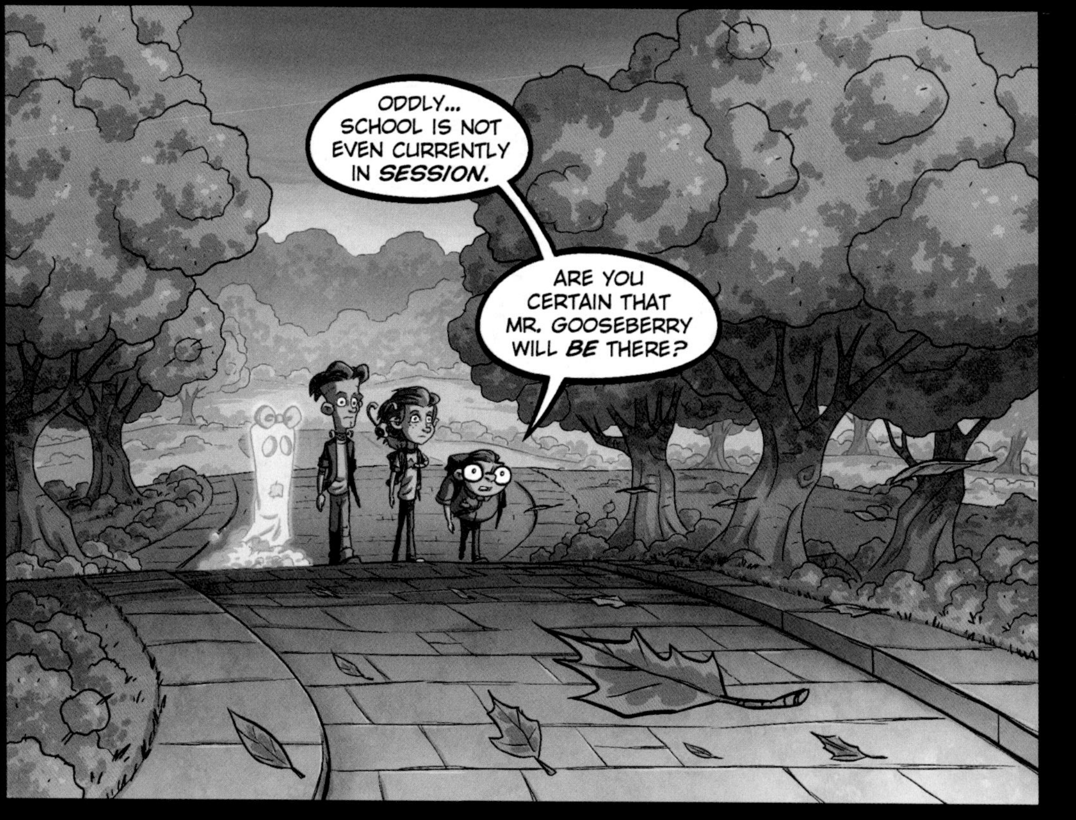
ODDLY... SCHOOL IS NOT EVEN CURRENTLY IN *SESSION.*
ARE YOU CERTAIN THAT MR. GOOSEBERRY WILL *BE* THERE?

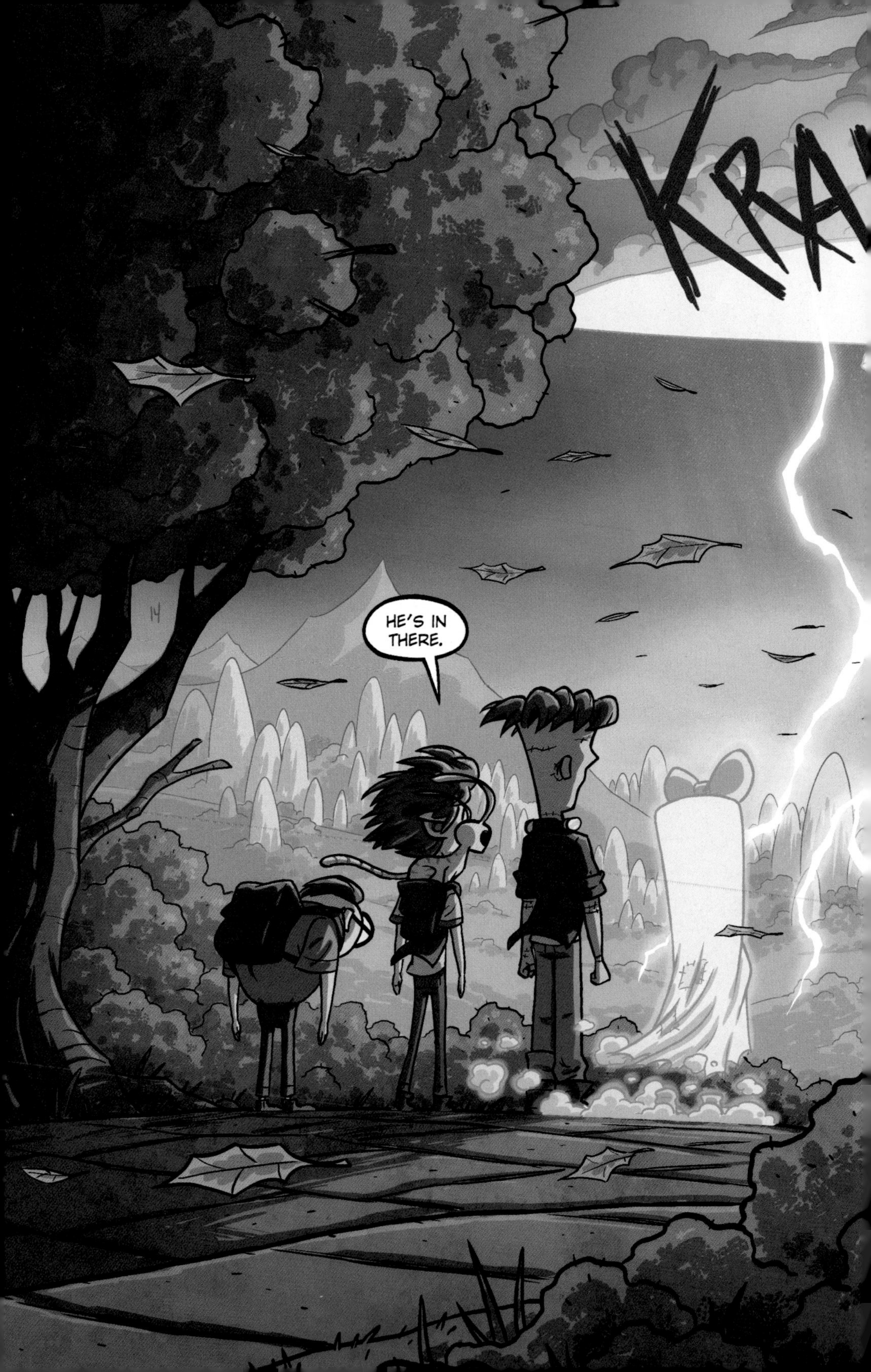
KRA
HE'S IN THERE.

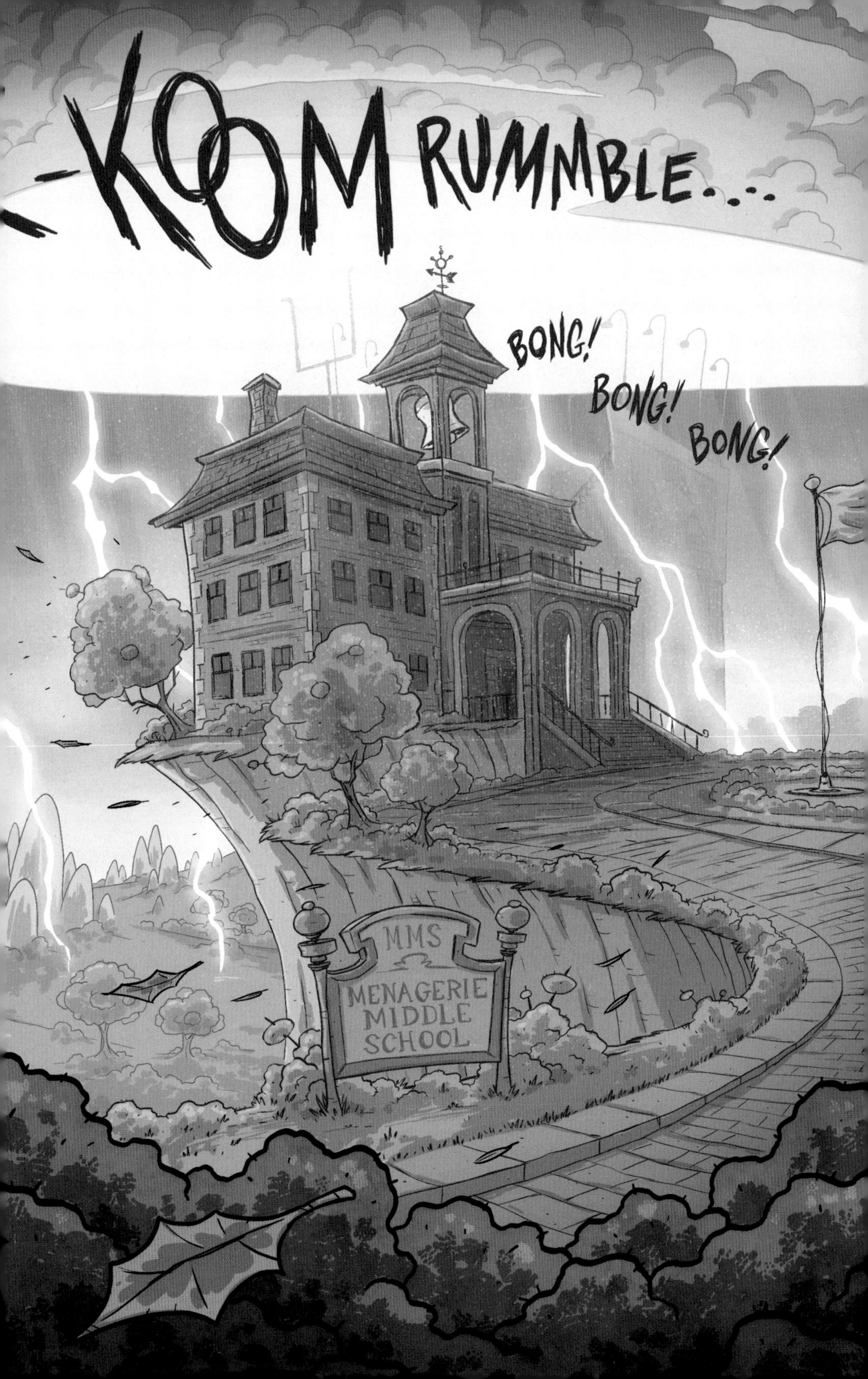
-KOOM RUMMBLE...
BONG!
BONG!
BONG!
MMS
MENAGERIE
MIDDLE
SCHOOL

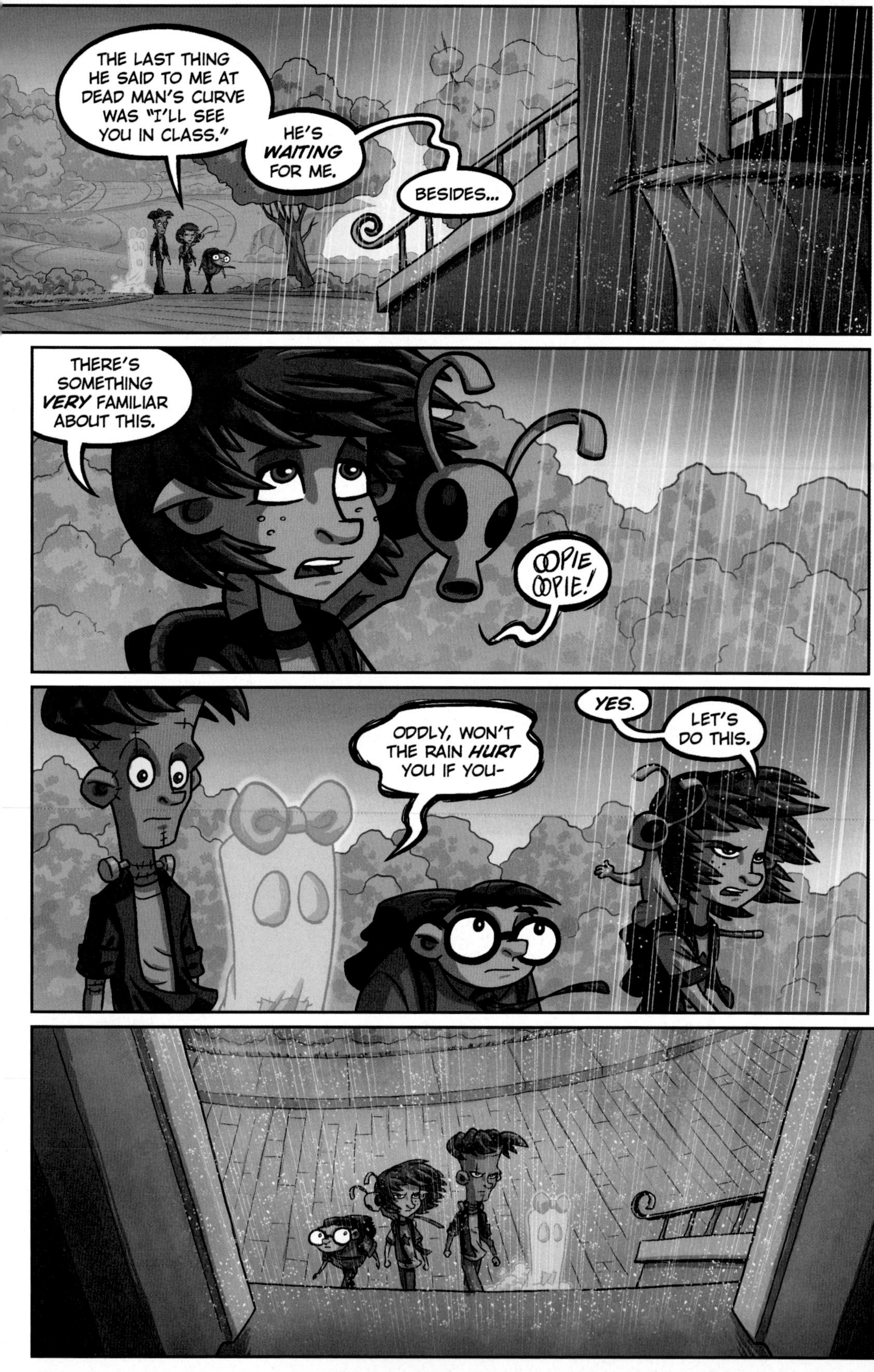
THE LAST THING HE SAID TO ME AT DEAD MAN'S CURVE WAS "I'LL SEE YOU IN CLASS."
HE'S *WAITING* FOR ME.
BESIDES...
THERE'S SOMETHING *VERY* FAMILIAR ABOUT THIS.
OOPIE OOPIE!
ODDLY, WON'T THE RAIN *HURT* YOU IF YOU-
YES.
LET'S DO THIS.

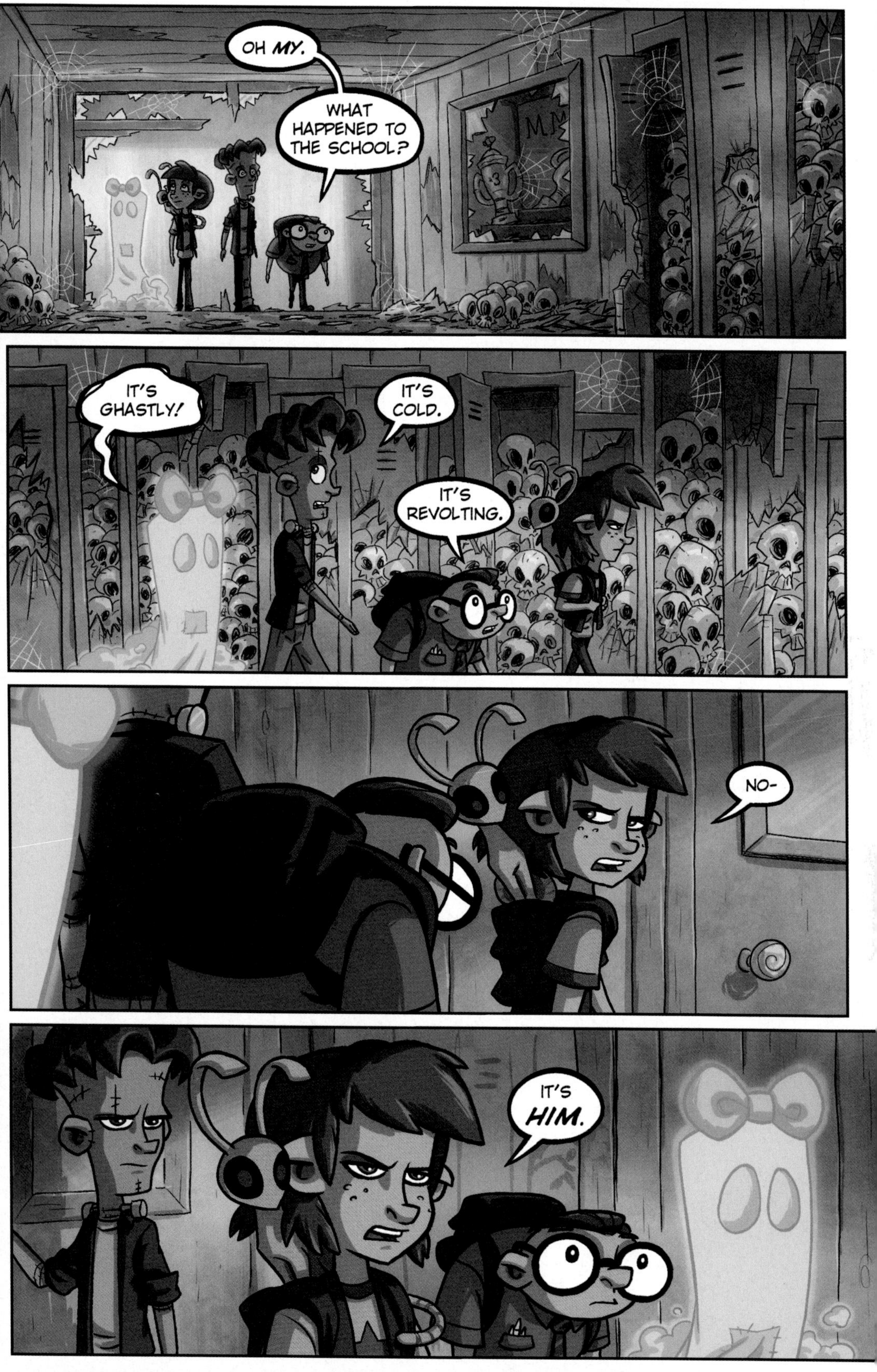
OH MY.
WHAT HAPPENED TO THE SCHOOL?
IT'S GHASTLY!
IT'S COLD.
IT'S REVOLTING.
NO-
IT'S HIM.

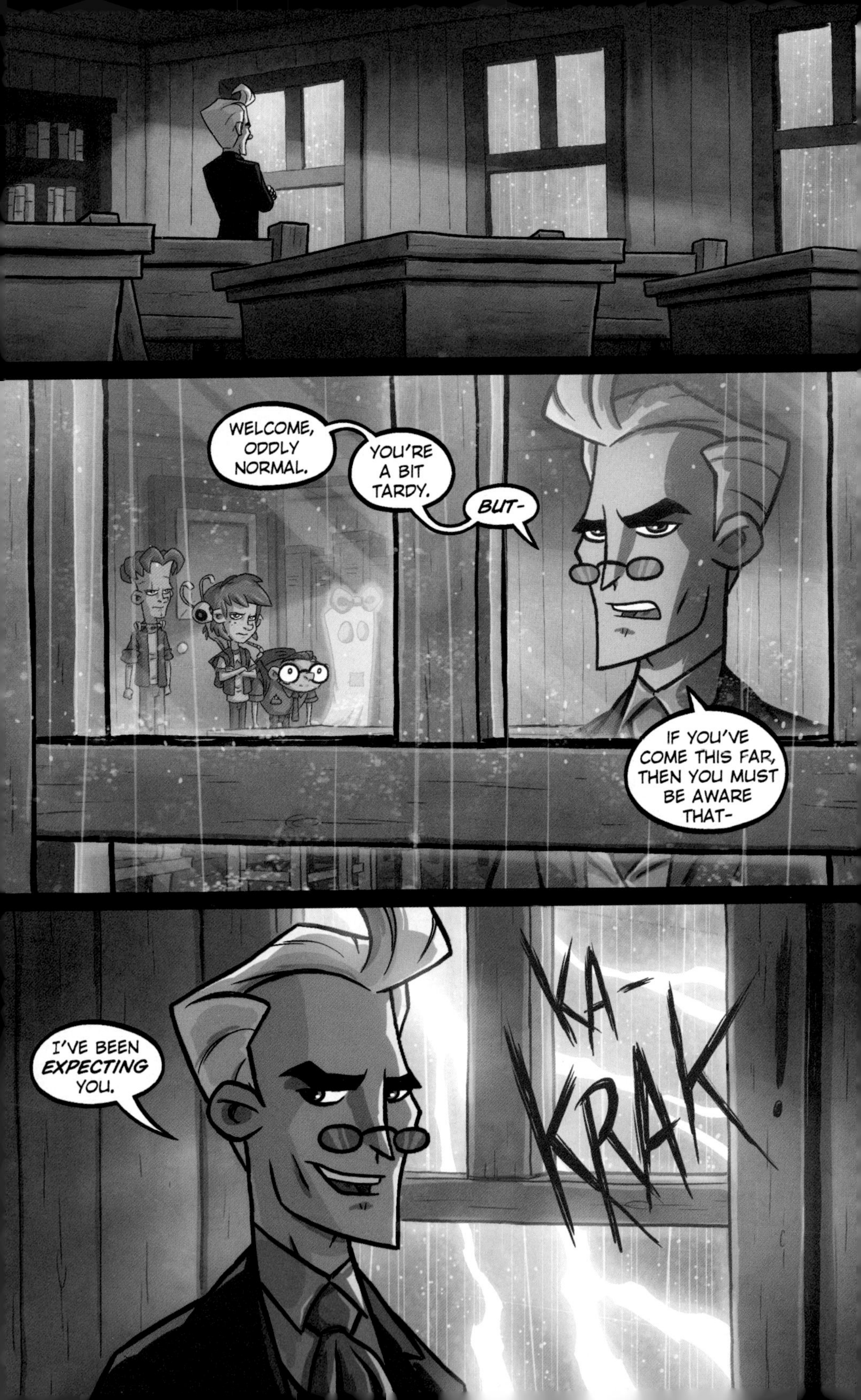
WELCOME, ODDLY NORMAL.
YOU'RE A BIT TARDY.
BUT-
IF YOU'VE COME THIS FAR, THEN YOU MUST BE AWARE THAT-
I'VE BEEN *EXPECTING* YOU.
KA-KRAK

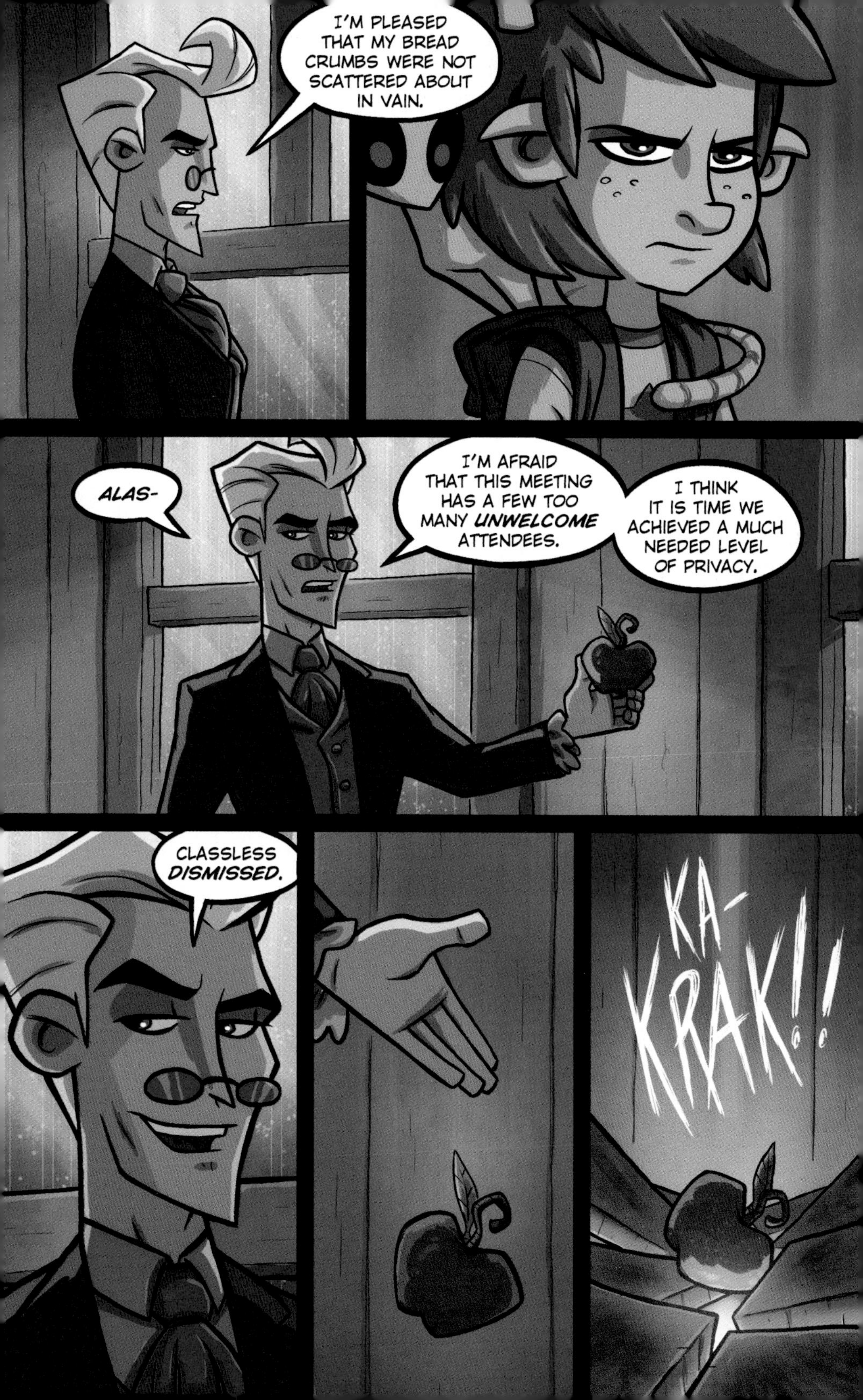
I'M PLEASED THAT MY BREAD CRUMBS WERE NOT SCATTERED ABOUT IN VAIN.
ALAS-
I'M AFRAID THAT THIS MEETING HAS A FEW TOO MANY UNWELCOME ATTENDEES.
I THINK IT IS TIME WE ACHIEVED A MUCH NEEDED LEVEL OF PRIVACY.
CLASSLESS DISMISSED.
KA-KRAK!!

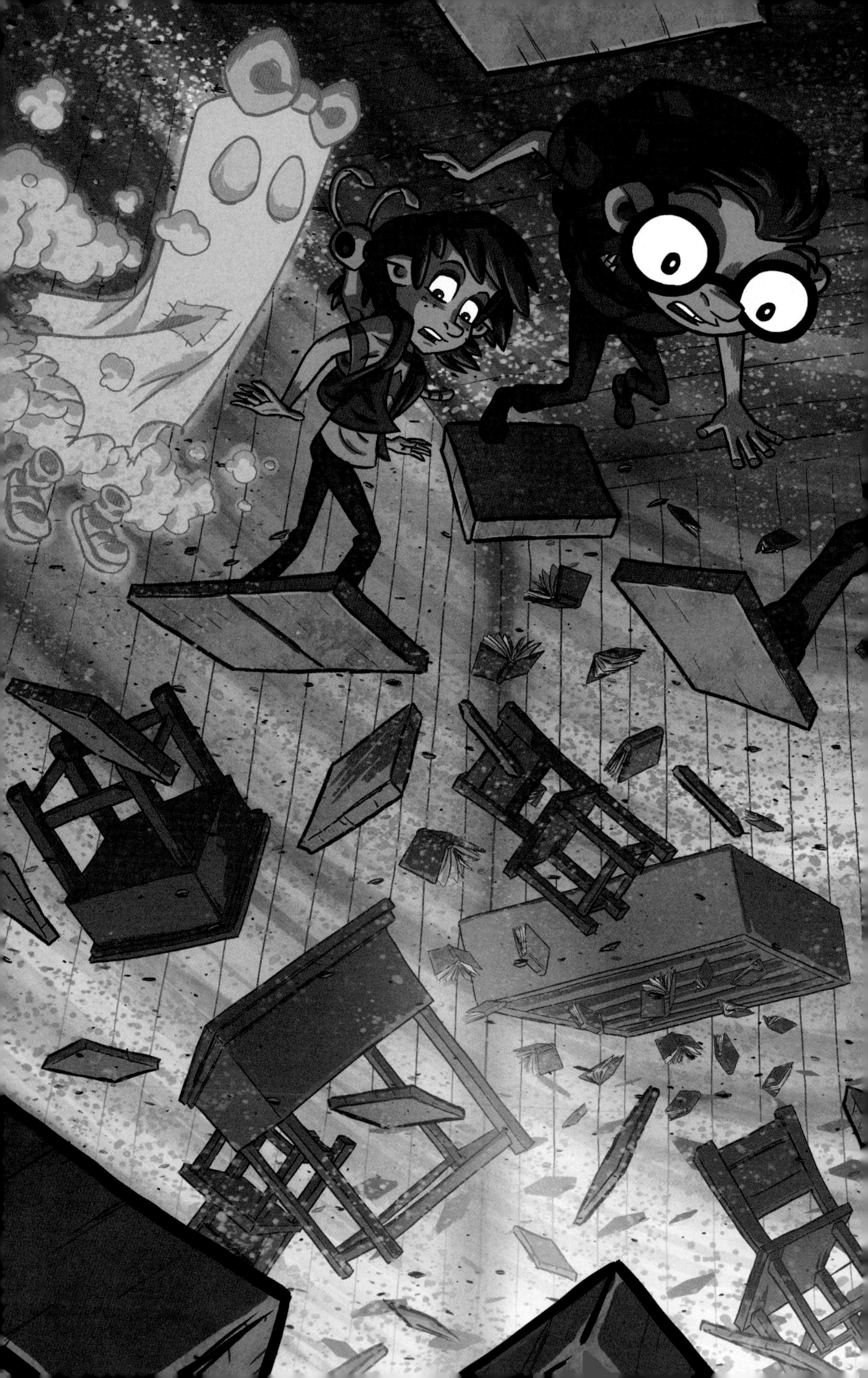

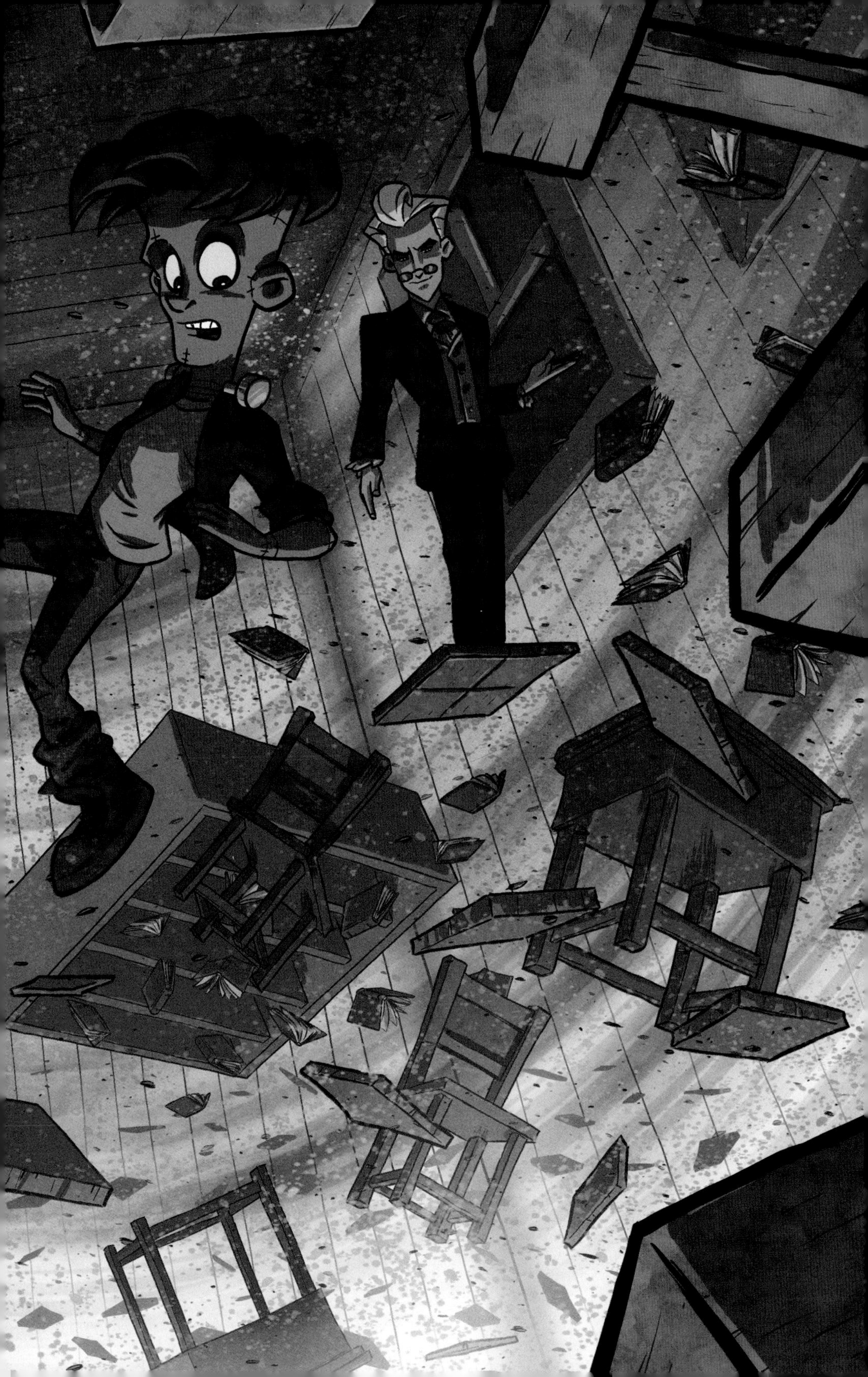

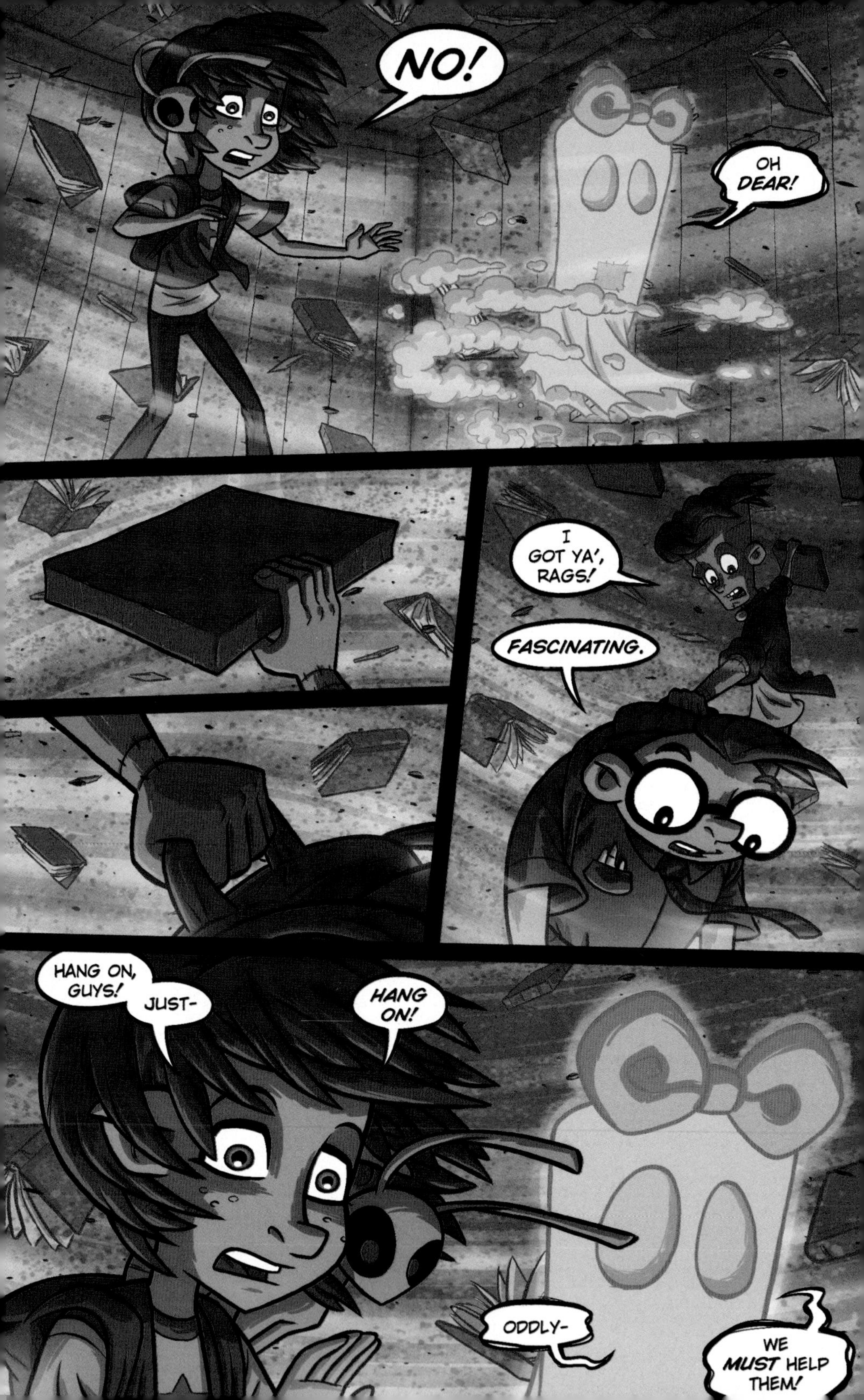
NO!
OH DEAR!
I GOT YA', RAGS!
FASCINATING.
HANG ON, GUYS!
JUST-
HANG ON!
ODDLY-
WE MUST HELP THEM!

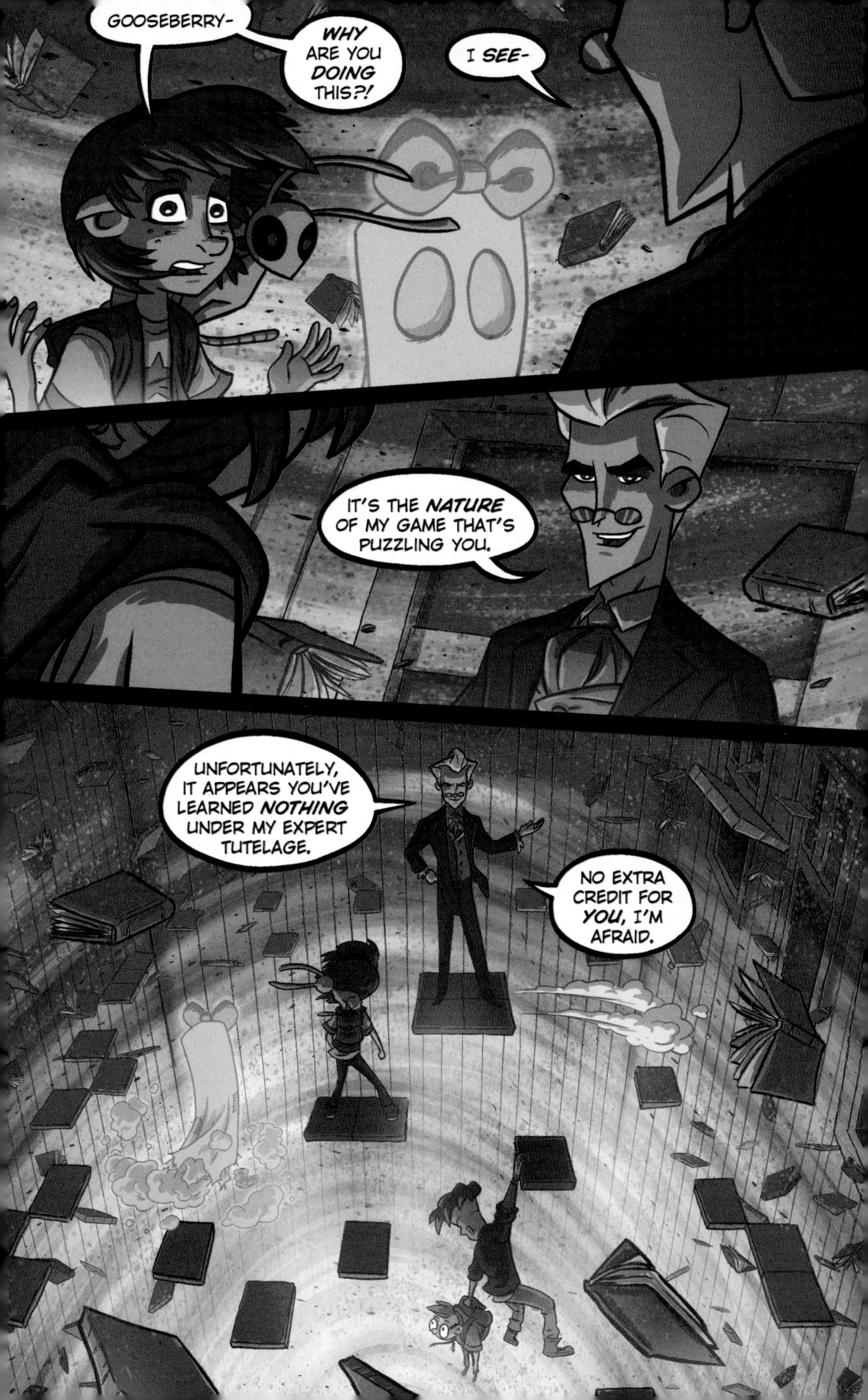
GOOSEBERRY-
WHY ARE YOU DOING THIS?!
I SEE-
IT'S THE NATURE OF MY GAME THAT'S PUZZLING YOU.
UNFORTUNATELY, IT APPEARS YOU'VE LEARNED NOTHING UNDER MY EXPERT TUTELAGE.
NO EXTRA CREDIT FOR YOU, I'M AFRAID.

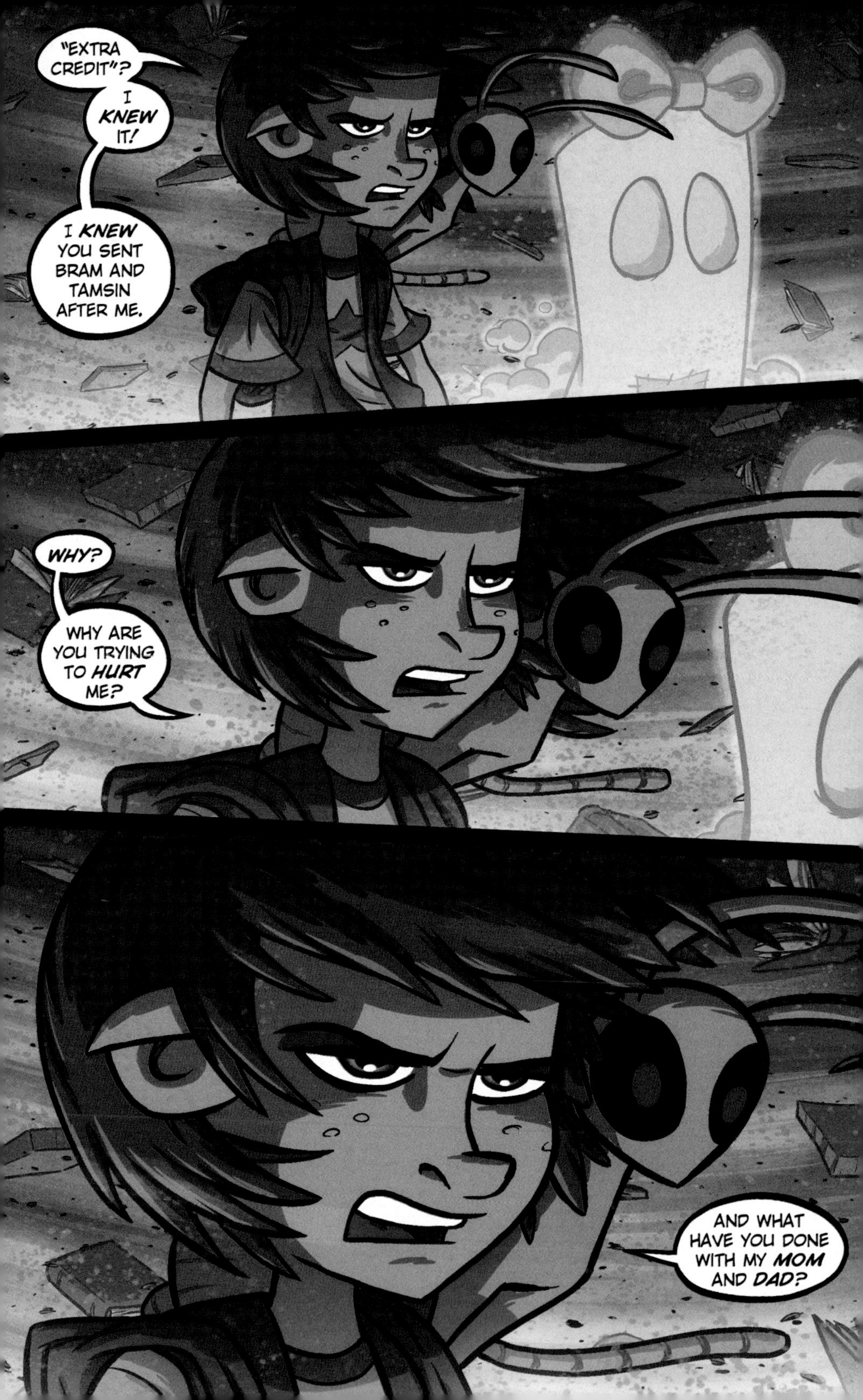
"EXTRA CREDIT"?
I *KNEW* IT!
I *KNEW* YOU SENT BRAM AND TAMSIN AFTER ME.
WHY?
WHY ARE YOU TRYING TO *HURT* ME?
AND WHAT HAVE YOU DONE WITH MY *MOM* AND *DAD?*

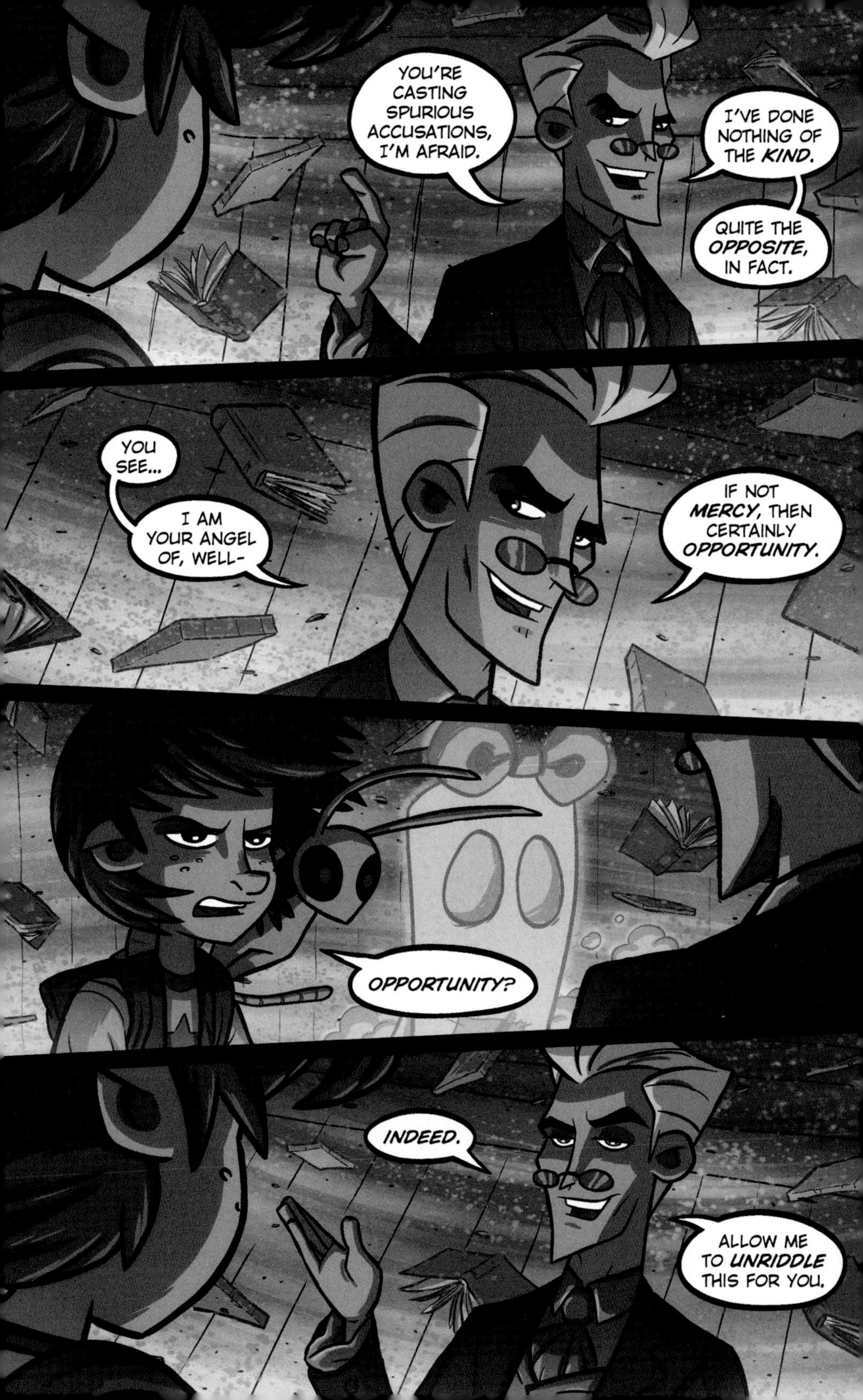
YOU'RE CASTING SPURIOUS ACCUSATIONS, I'M AFRAID.
I'VE DONE NOTHING OF THE KIND.
QUITE THE OPPOSITE, IN FACT.
YOU SEE...
I AM YOUR ANGEL OF, WELL-
IF NOT MERCY, THEN CERTAINLY OPPORTUNITY.
OPPORTUNITY?
INDEED.
ALLOW ME TO UNRIDDLE THIS FOR YOU.

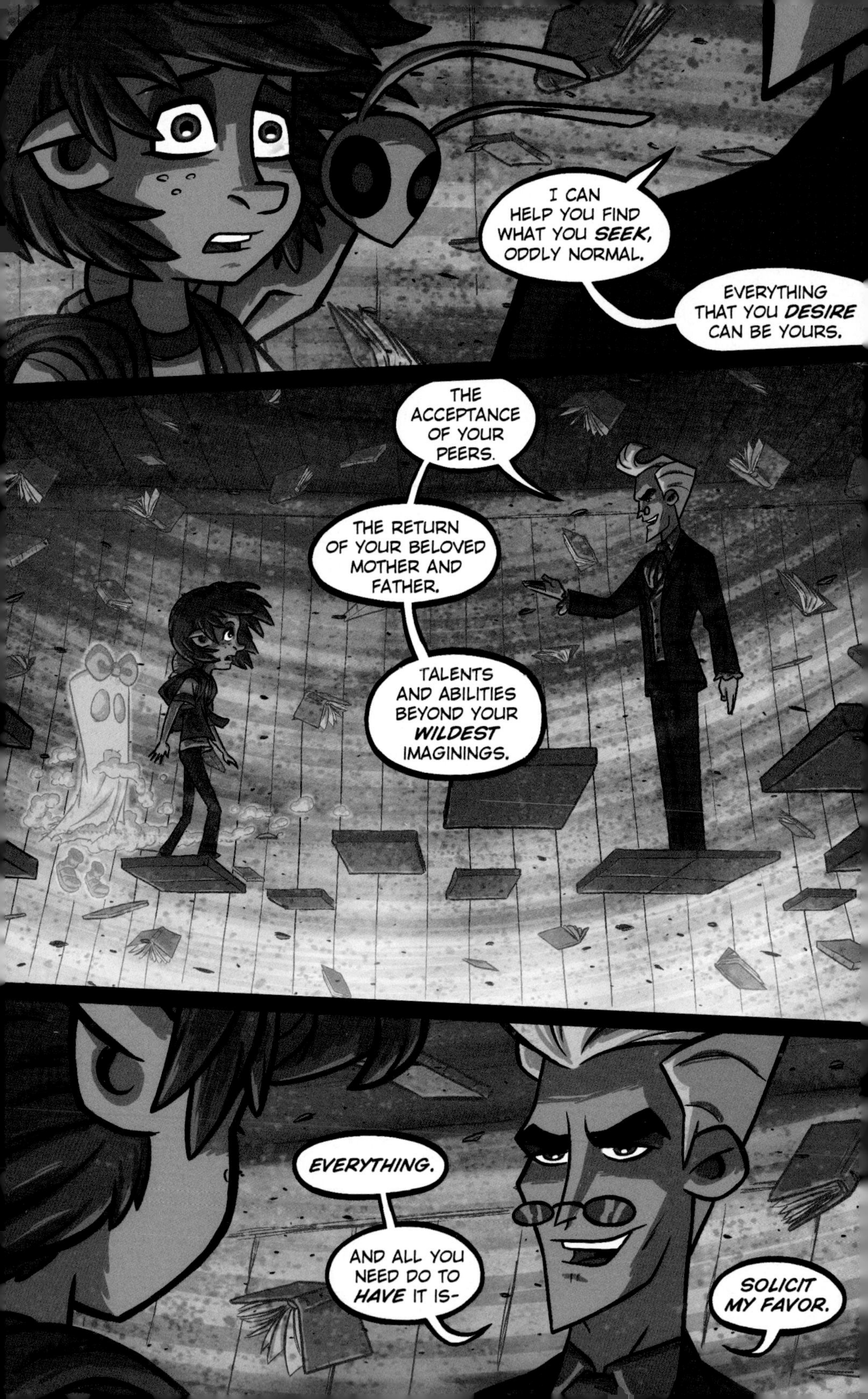
I CAN HELP YOU FIND WHAT YOU SEEK, ODDLY NORMAL.
EVERYTHING THAT YOU DESIRE CAN BE YOURS.
THE ACCEPTANCE OF YOUR PEERS.
THE RETURN OF YOUR BELOVED MOTHER AND FATHER.
TALENTS AND ABILITIES BEYOND YOUR WILDEST IMAGININGS.
EVERYTHING.
AND ALL YOU NEED DO TO HAVE IT IS-
SOLICIT MY FAVOR.

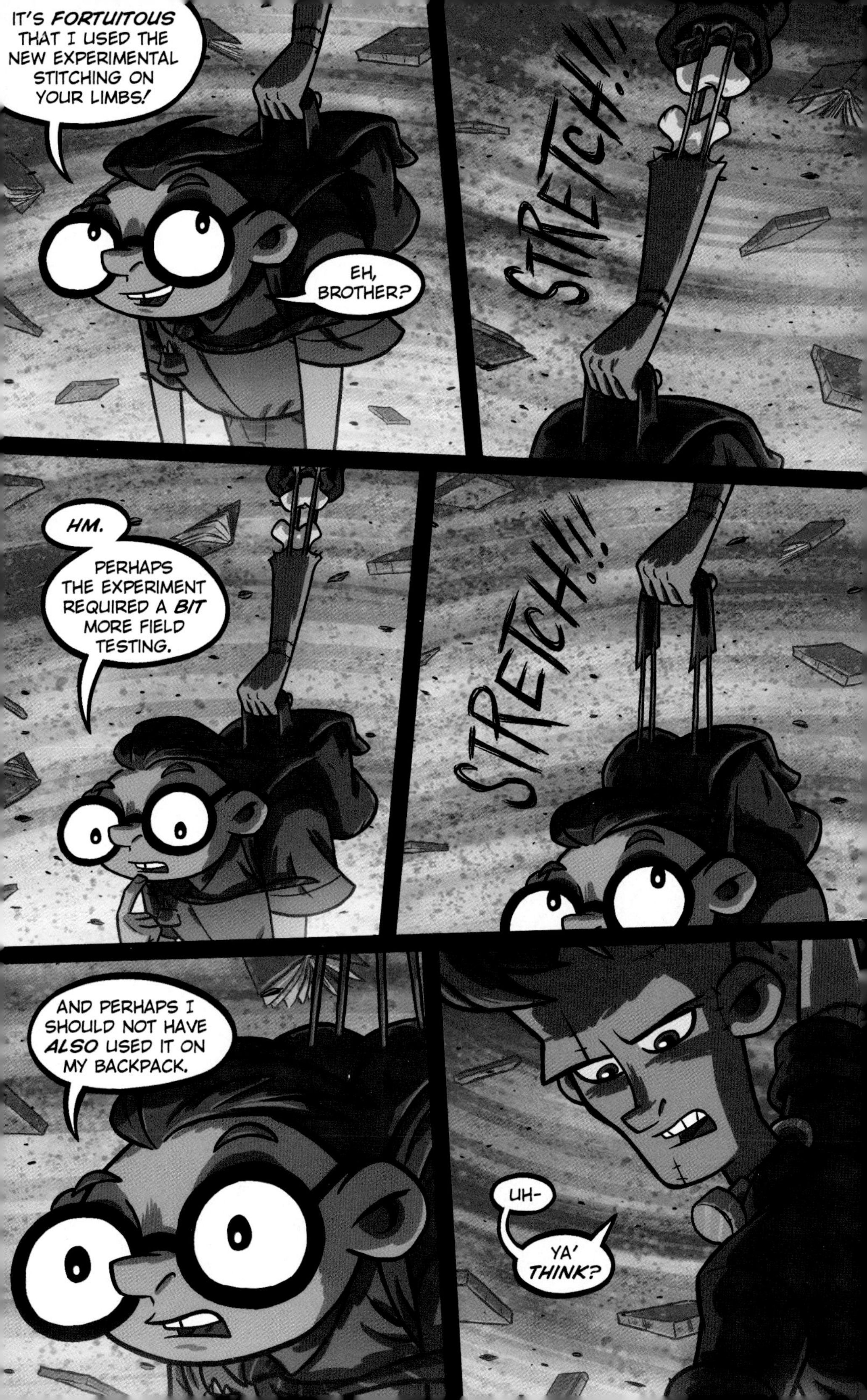

IT'S *FORTUITOUS* THAT I USED THE NEW EXPERIMENTAL STITCHING ON YOUR LIMBS!
EH, BROTHER?
STRETCH!!!
HM.
PERHAPS THE EXPERIMENT REQUIRED A *BIT* MORE FIELD TESTING.
STRETCH!!!
AND PERHAPS I SHOULD NOT HAVE *ALSO* USED IT ON MY BACKPACK.
UH-
YA' *THINK?*

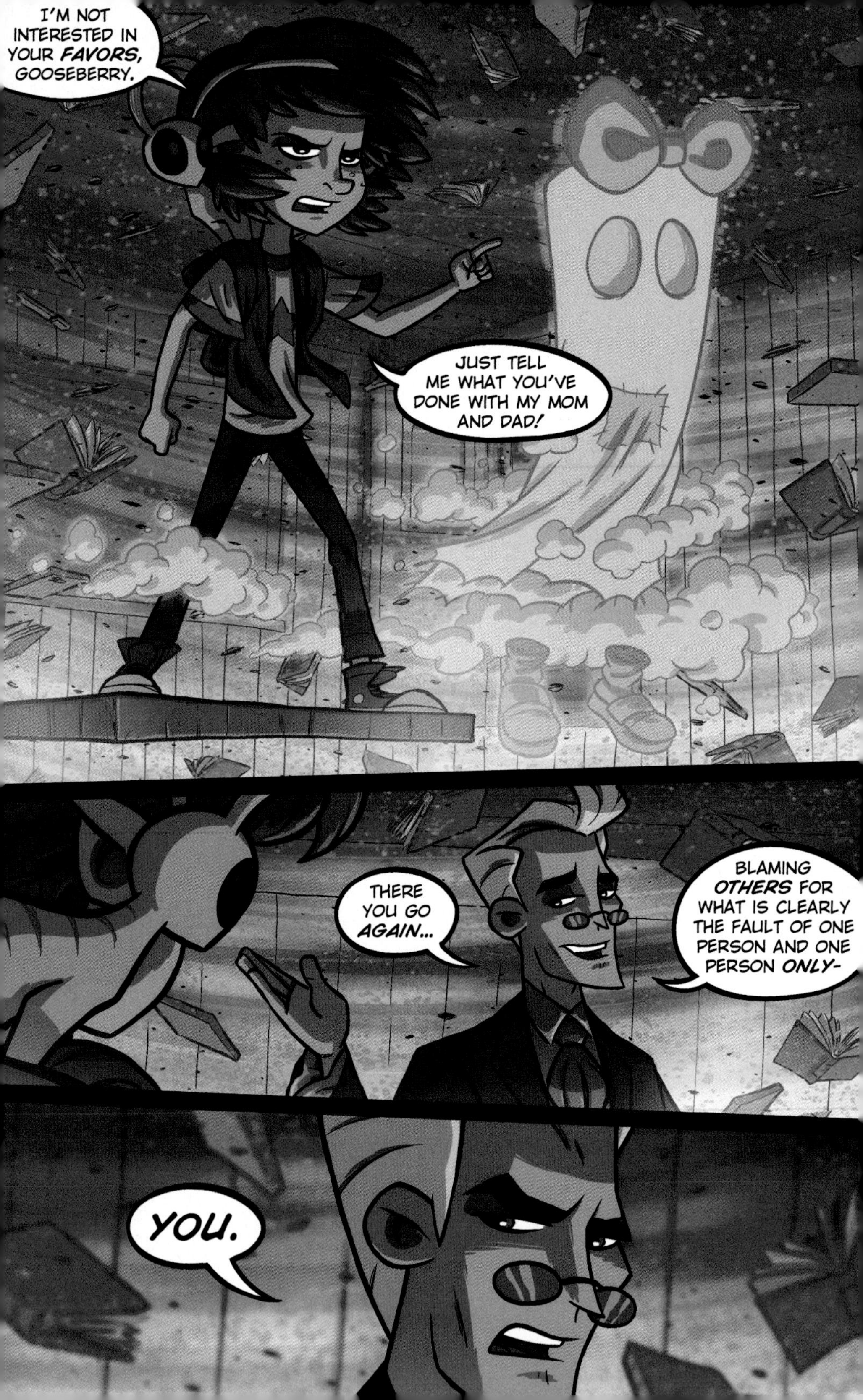
I'M NOT INTERESTED IN YOUR FAVORS, GOOSEBERRY.
JUST TELL ME WHAT YOU'VE DONE WITH MY MOM AND DAD!
THERE YOU GO AGAIN...
BLAMING OTHERS FOR WHAT IS CLEARLY THE FAULT OF ONE PERSON AND ONE PERSON ONLY-
YOU.

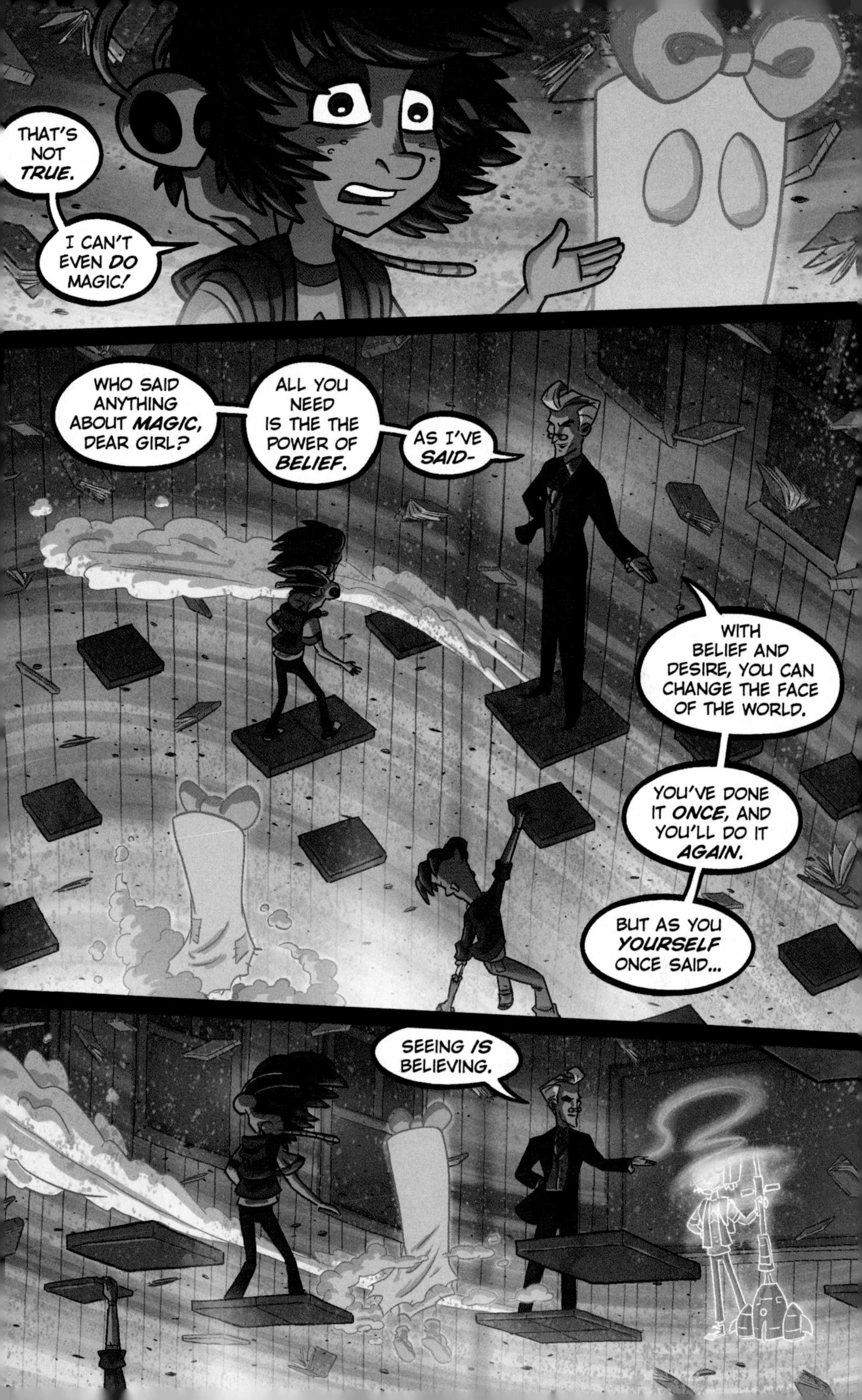
THAT'S NOT TRUE.
I CAN'T EVEN DO MAGIC!
WHO SAID ANYTHING ABOUT MAGIC, DEAR GIRL?
ALL YOU NEED IS THE THE POWER OF BELIEF.
AS I'VE SAID-
WITH BELIEF AND DESIRE, YOU CAN CHANGE THE FACE OF THE WORLD.
YOU'VE DONE IT ONCE, AND YOU'LL DO IT AGAIN.
BUT AS YOU YOURSELF ONCE SAID...
SEEING IS BELIEVING.

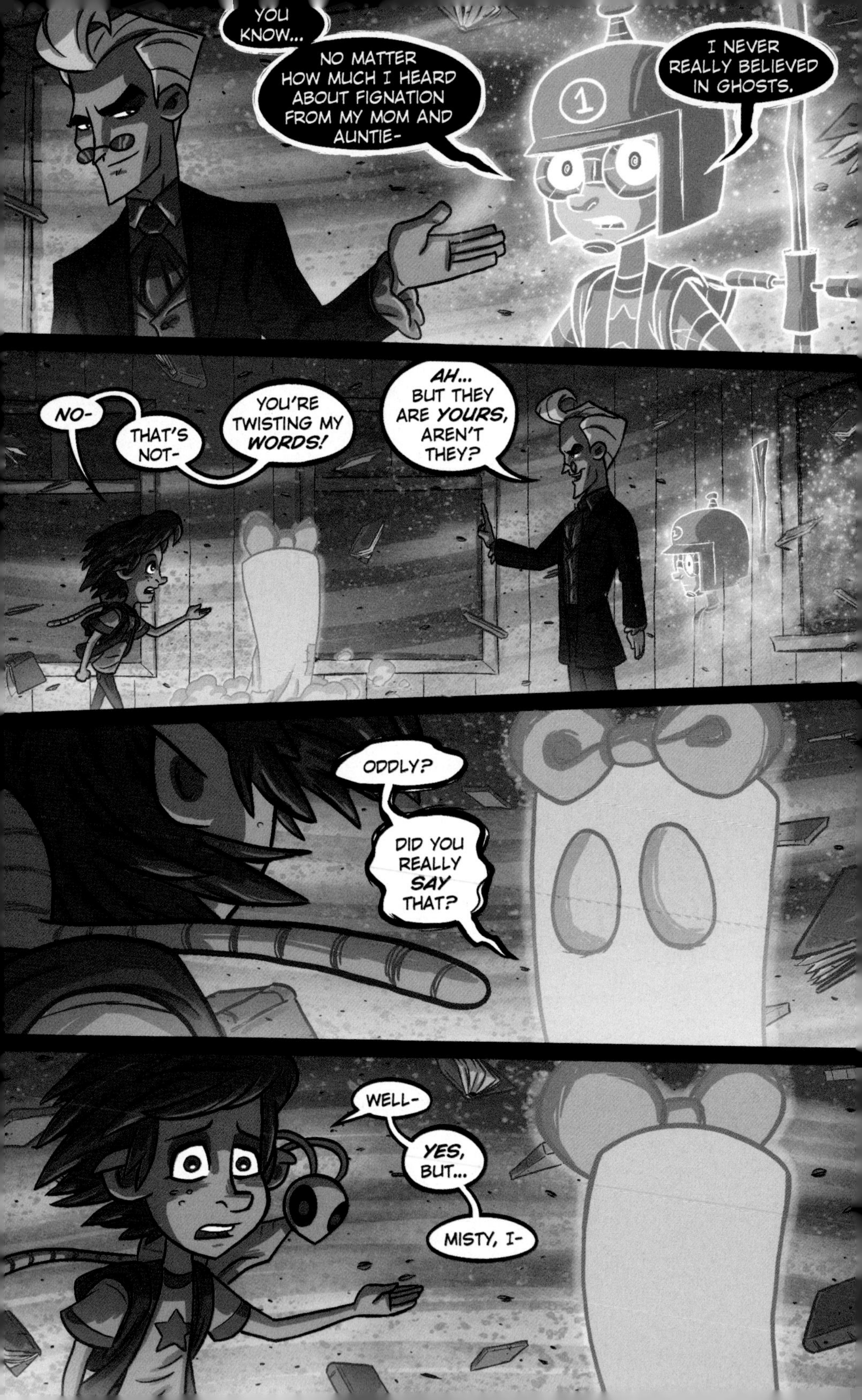
YOU KNOW...
NO MATTER HOW MUCH I HEARD ABOUT FIGNATION FROM MY MOM AND AUNTIE-
I NEVER REALLY BELIEVED IN GHOSTS.
NO-
THAT'S NOT-
YOU'RE TWISTING MY WORDS!
AH... BUT THEY ARE YOURS, AREN'T THEY?
ODDLY?
DID YOU REALLY SAY THAT?
WELL-
YES, BUT...
MISTY, I-

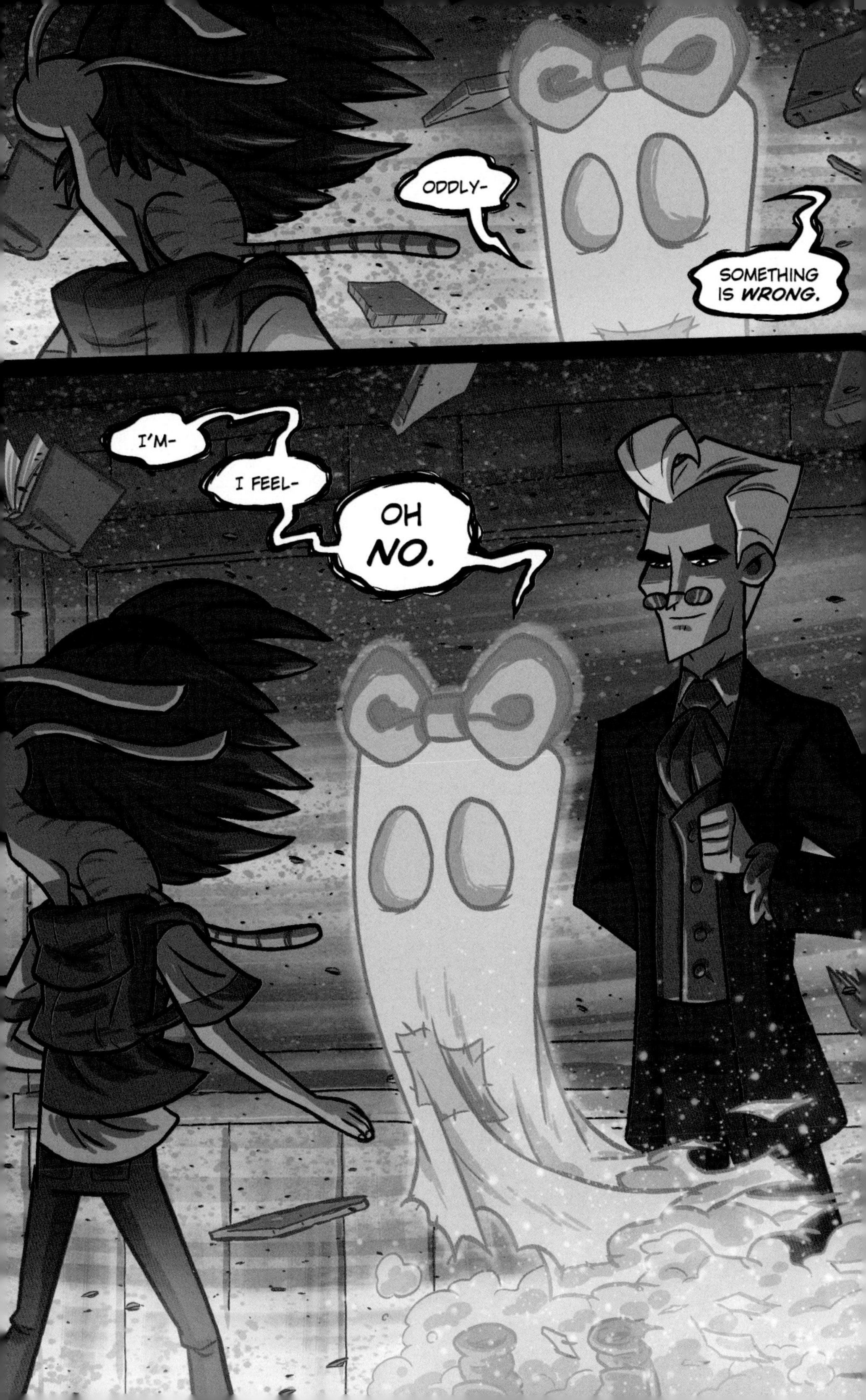
ODDLY-
SOMETHING IS WRONG.
I'M-
I FEEL-
OH NO.

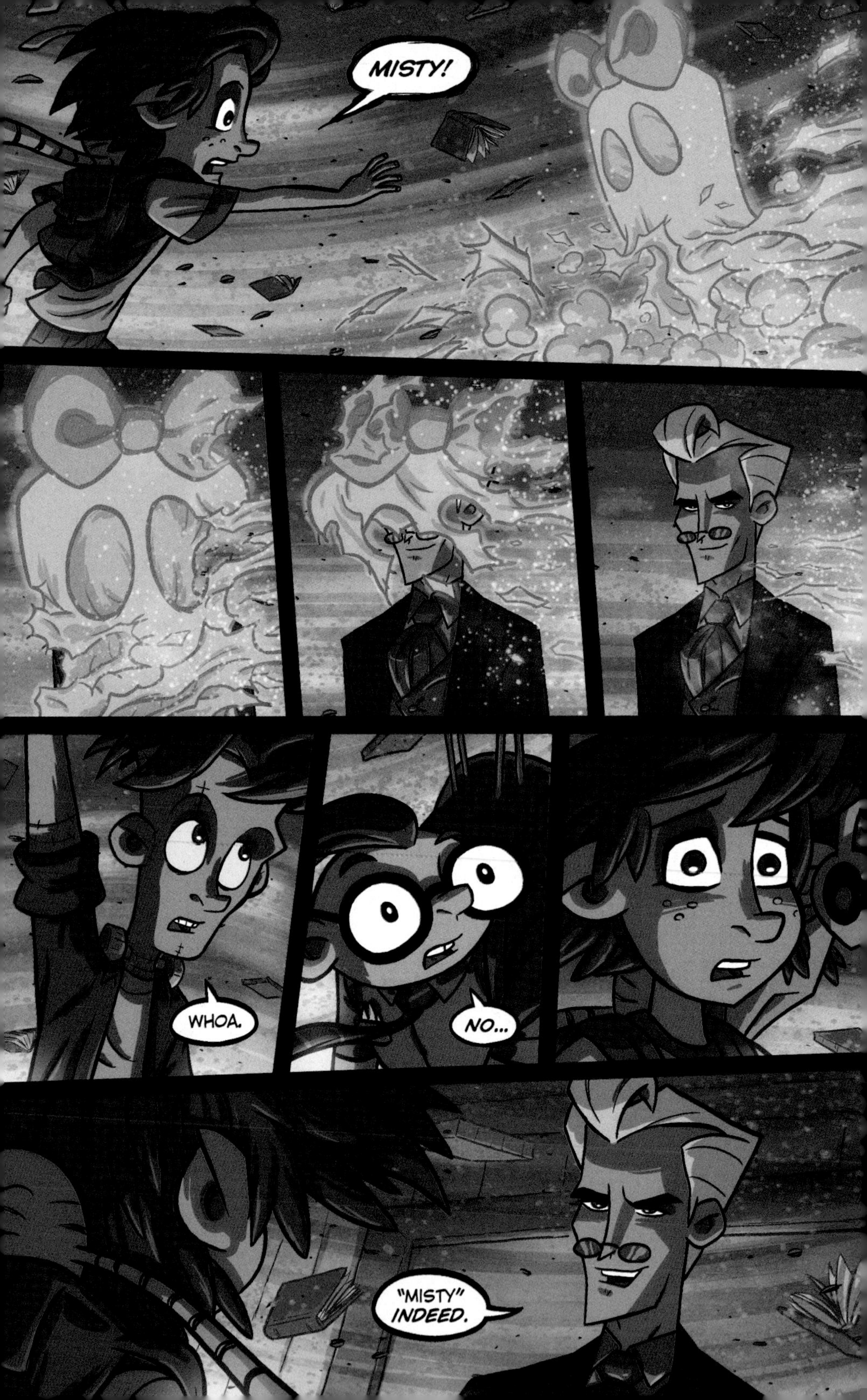
MISTY!
WHOA.
NO...
"MISTY" INDEED.

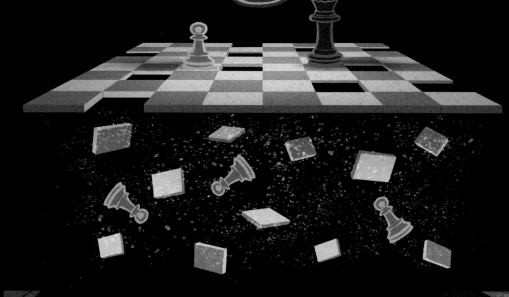

Chapter 15
Endgame

WHERE IS SHE?

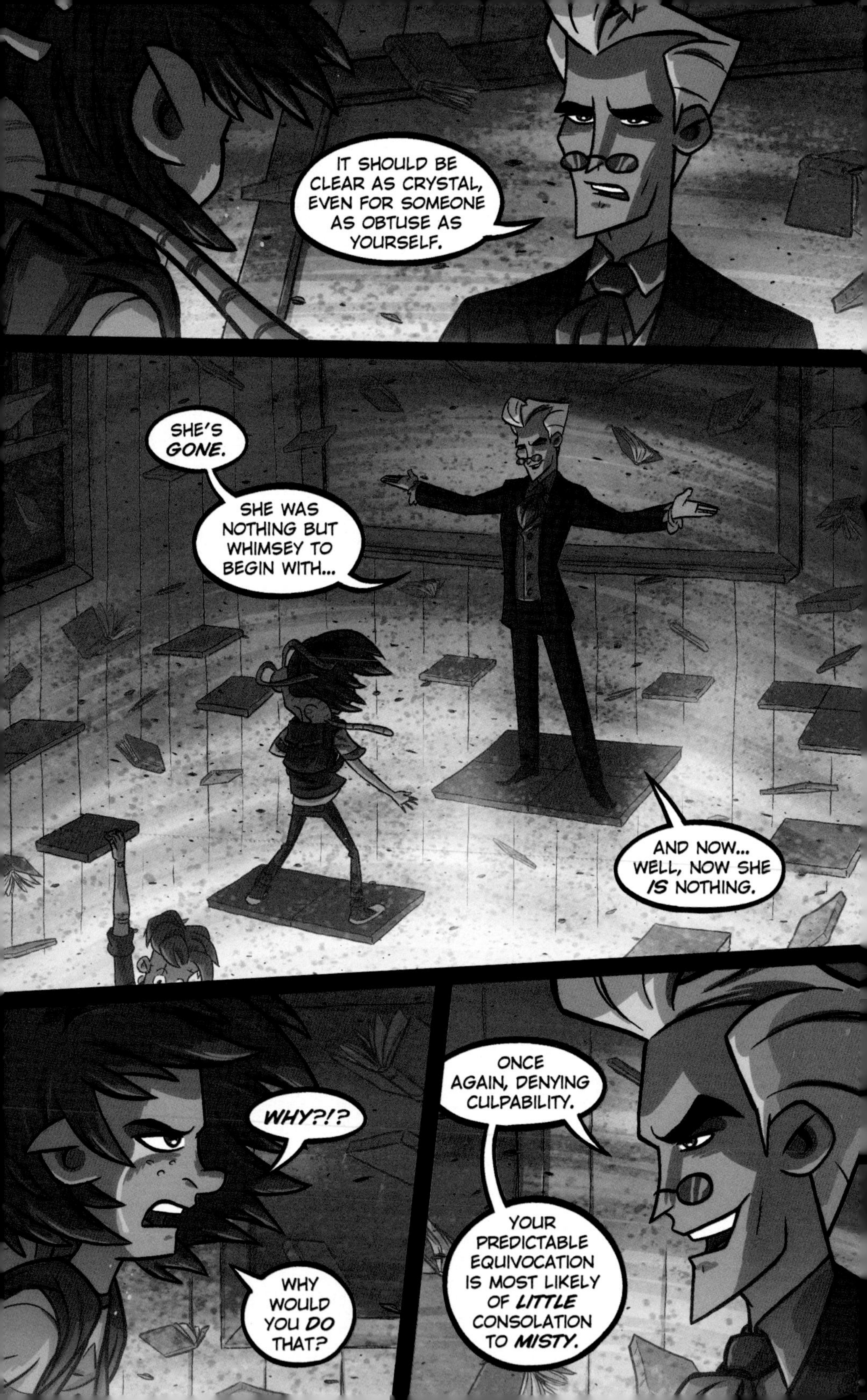
IT SHOULD BE CLEAR AS CRYSTAL, EVEN FOR SOMEONE AS OBTUSE AS YOURSELF.
SHE'S *GONE.*
SHE WAS NOTHING BUT WHIMSEY TO BEGIN WITH...
AND NOW... WELL, NOW SHE *IS* NOTHING.
WHY?!?
WHY WOULD YOU *DO* THAT?
ONCE AGAIN, DENYING CULPABILITY.
YOUR PREDICTABLE EQUIVOCATION IS MOST LIKELY OF *LITTLE* CONSOLATION TO *MISTY.*

YOU'RE- YOU'RE JUST-

YOU'RE *EVIL!*

RIGHT THE FIRST TIME.

WELL DONE.

A-PLUS.

ONE OF THE *OLDEST* WORDS IN ANY LANGUAGE.

SO *NICE* TO BE IDENTIFIED RIGHT OUT OF THE GATE.

BUT IT'S UNFORTUNATE THAT YOUR KIND HAS BEEN SO *NEGLECTFUL* OF ME AS OF LATE.

n.
the quality of being morally bad or wrong; wickedness.
that which causes harm, misfortune, or destruction.
an evil force, power, or

THE LAST TIME YOU FLESH-BAGS TOOK ANY *REAL* NOTICE WAS WHEN THAT AUSTRIAN FELLOW STIRRED UP ALL THAT TROUBLE IN EUROPE.

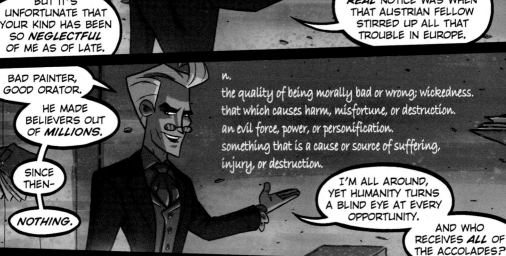

BAD PAINTER, GOOD ORATOR.

HE MADE BELIEVERS OUT OF *MILLIONS.*

SINCE THEN-

NOTHING.

n.
the quality of being morally bad or wrong; wickedness.
that which causes harm, misfortune, or destruction.
an evil force, power, or personification.
something that is a cause or source of suffering, injury, or destruction.

I'M ALL AROUND, YET HUMANITY TURNS A BLIND EYE AT EVERY OPPORTUNITY.

AND WHO RECEIVES *ALL* OF THE ACCOLADES?

"IDEOLOGY."

n.
the q
that
an e
som
inju

"TROUBLED CHILDHOODS."

n.
the
that
an

n.
th
th
a
sc
in

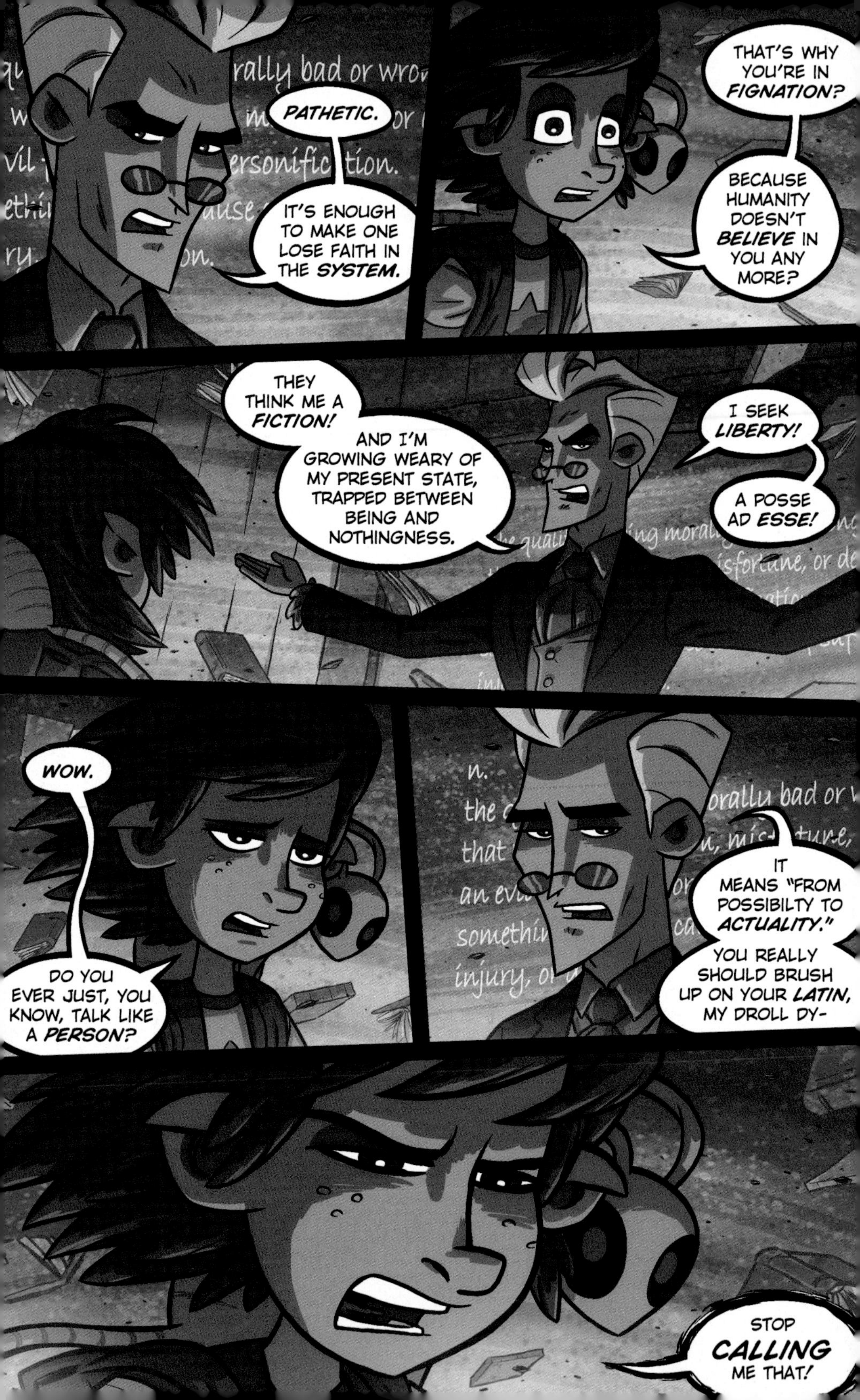
PATHETIC.
IT'S ENOUGH TO MAKE ONE LOSE FAITH IN THE SYSTEM.
THAT'S WHY YOU'RE IN FIGNATION?
BECAUSE HUMANITY DOESN'T BELIEVE IN YOU ANY MORE?
THEY THINK ME A FICTION!
AND I'M GROWING WEARY OF MY PRESENT STATE, TRAPPED BETWEEN BEING AND NOTHINGNESS.
I SEEK LIBERTY!
A POSSE AD ESSE!
WOW.
DO YOU EVER JUST, YOU KNOW, TALK LIKE A PERSON?
IT MEANS "FROM POSSIBILTY TO ACTUALITY."
YOU REALLY SHOULD BRUSH UP ON YOUR LATIN, MY DROLL DY-
STOP CALLING ME THAT!

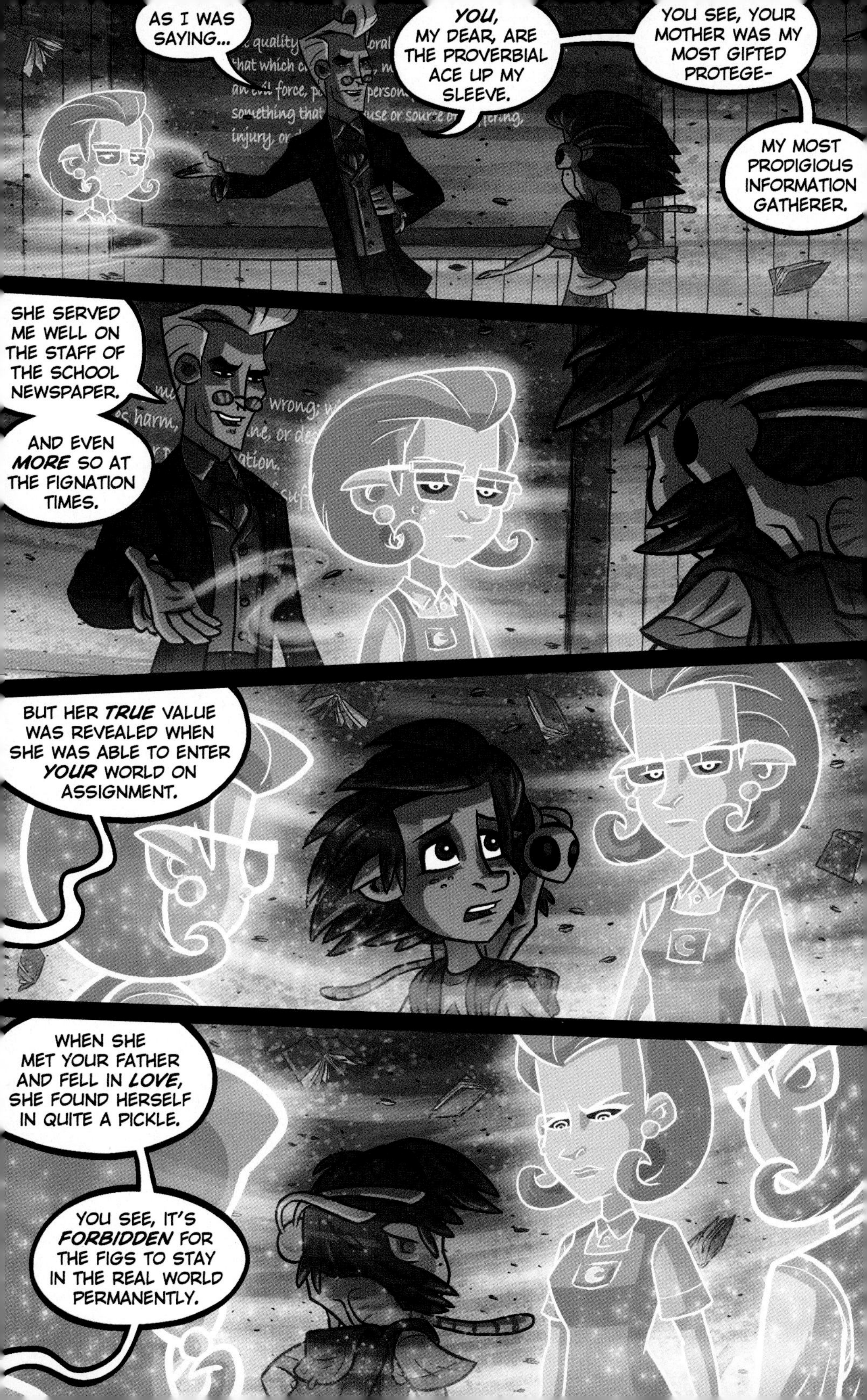
AS I WAS SAYING...
YOU, MY DEAR, ARE THE PROVERBIAL ACE UP MY SLEEVE.
YOU SEE, YOUR MOTHER WAS MY MOST GIFTED PROTEGE-
MY MOST PRODIGIOUS INFORMATION GATHERER.
SHE SERVED ME WELL ON THE STAFF OF THE SCHOOL NEWSPAPER.
AND EVEN MORE SO AT THE FIGNATION TIMES.
BUT HER TRUE VALUE WAS REVEALED WHEN SHE WAS ABLE TO ENTER YOUR WORLD ON ASSIGNMENT.
WHEN SHE MET YOUR FATHER AND FELL IN LOVE, SHE FOUND HERSELF IN QUITE A PICKLE.
YOU SEE, IT'S FORBIDDEN FOR THE FIGS TO STAY IN THE REAL WORLD PERMANENTLY.

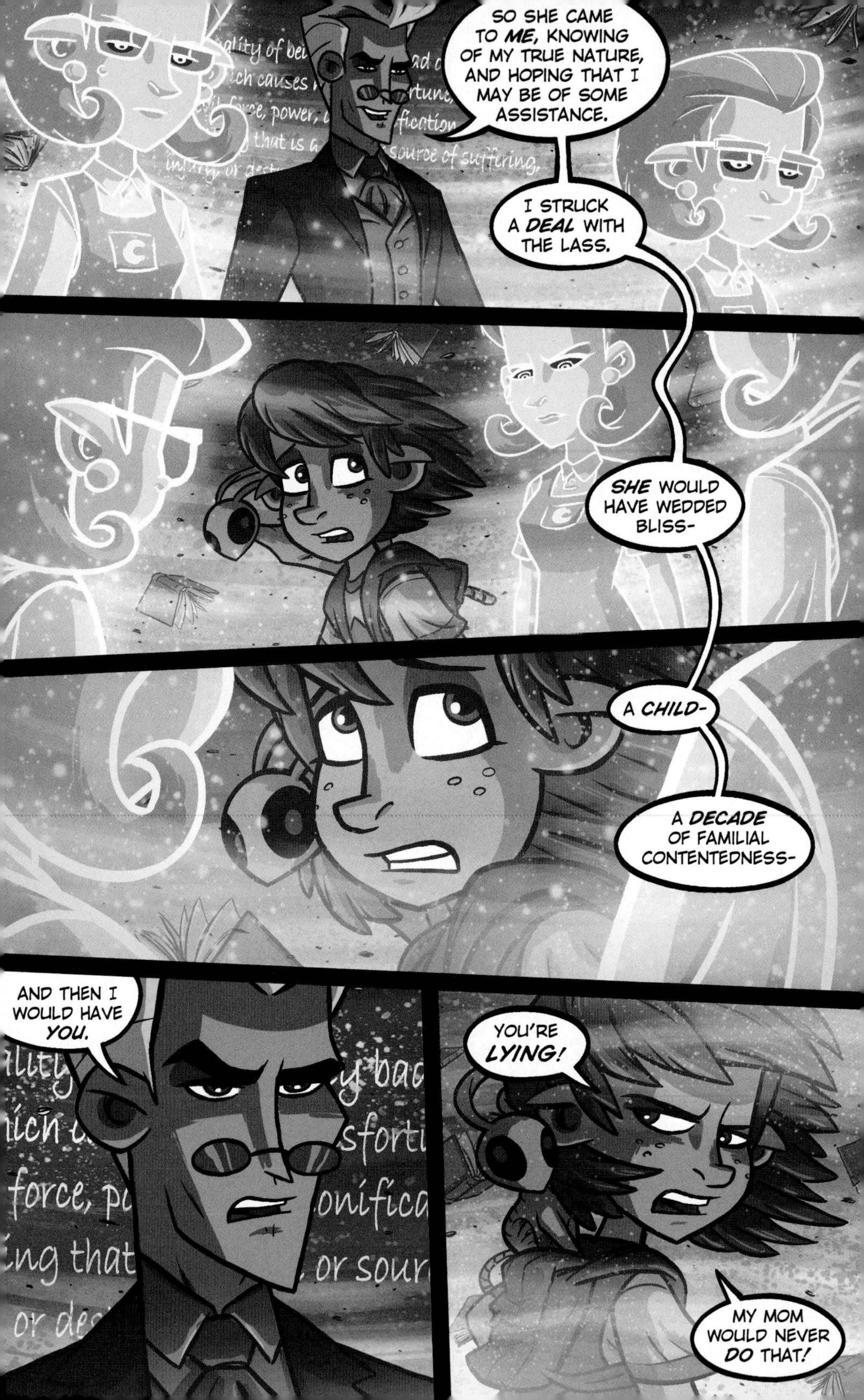
SO SHE CAME TO *ME,* KNOWING OF MY TRUE NATURE, AND HOPING THAT I MAY BE OF SOME ASSISTANCE.
I STRUCK A *DEAL* WITH THE LASS.
SHE WOULD HAVE WEDDED BLISS-
A *CHILD-*
A *DECADE* OF FAMILIAL CONTENTEDNESS-
AND THEN I WOULD HAVE *YOU.*
YOU'RE *LYING!*
MY MOM WOULD NEVER *DO* THAT!

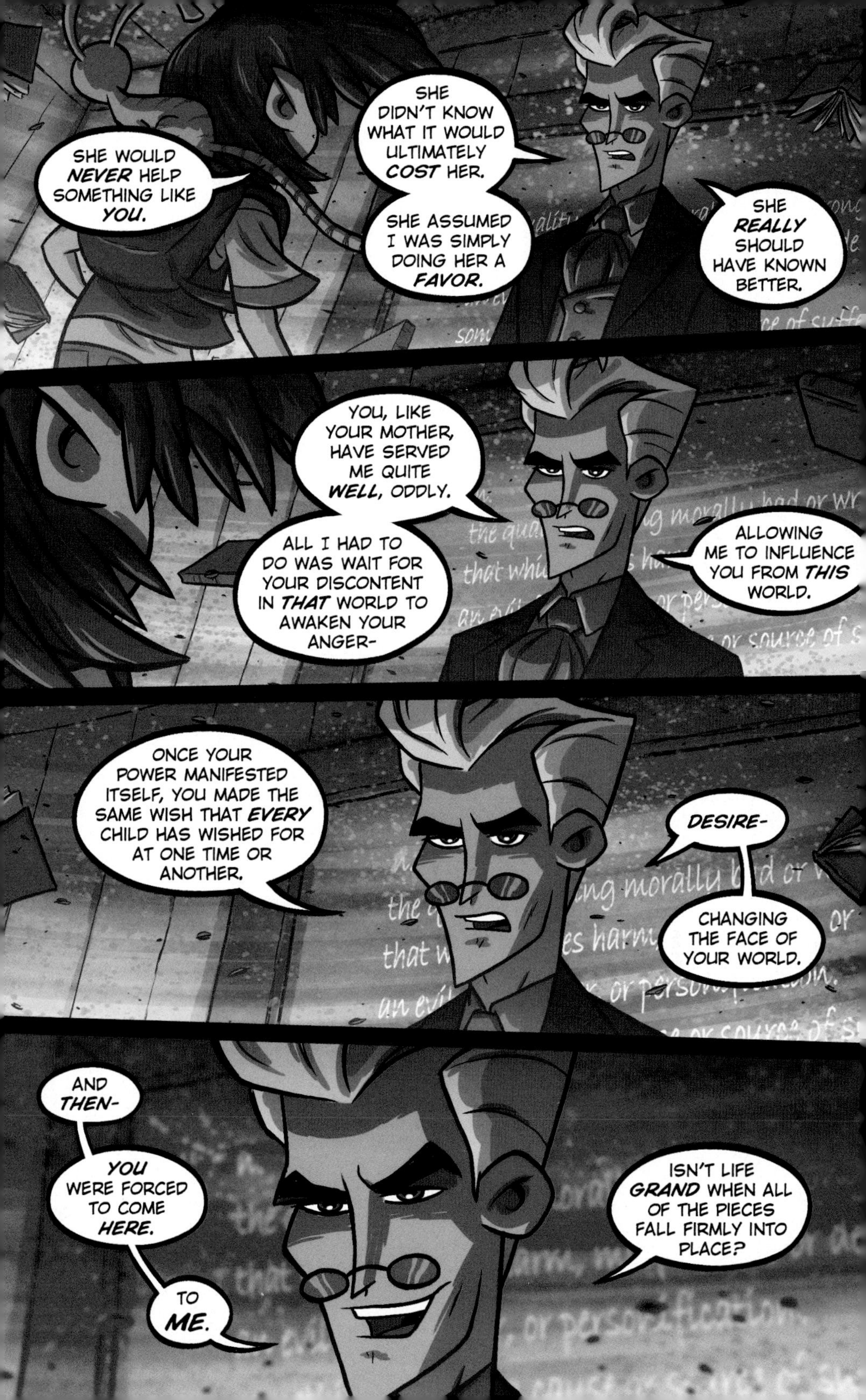
SHE WOULD NEVER HELP SOMETHING LIKE YOU.
SHE DIDN'T KNOW WHAT IT WOULD ULTIMATELY COST HER.
SHE ASSUMED I WAS SIMPLY DOING HER A FAVOR.
SHE REALLY SHOULD HAVE KNOWN BETTER.
YOU, LIKE YOUR MOTHER, HAVE SERVED ME QUITE WELL, ODDLY.
ALL I HAD TO DO WAS WAIT FOR YOUR DISCONTENT IN THAT WORLD TO AWAKEN YOUR ANGER-
ALLOWING ME TO INFLUENCE YOU FROM THIS WORLD.
ONCE YOUR POWER MANIFESTED ITSELF, YOU MADE THE SAME WISH THAT EVERY CHILD HAS WISHED FOR AT ONE TIME OR ANOTHER.
DESIRE-
CHANGING THE FACE OF YOUR WORLD.
AND THEN-
YOU WERE FORCED TO COME HERE.
TO ME.
ISN'T LIFE GRAND WHEN ALL OF THE PIECES FALL FIRMLY INTO PLACE?

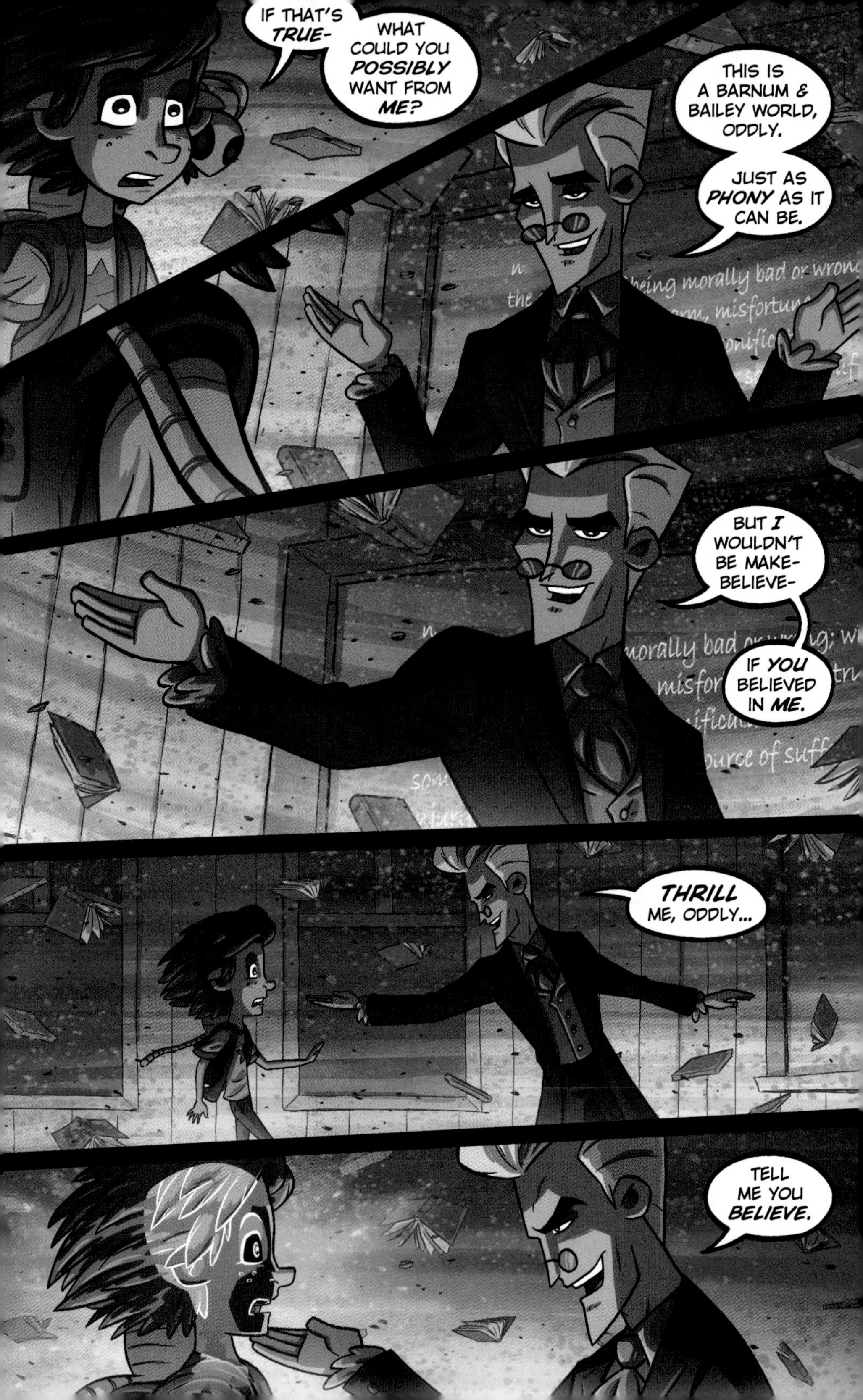
IF THAT'S TRUE-
WHAT COULD YOU POSSIBLY WANT FROM ME?
THIS IS A BARNUM & BAILEY WORLD, ODDLY.
JUST AS PHONY AS IT CAN BE.
BUT I WOULDN'T BE MAKE-BELIEVE-
IF YOU BELIEVED IN ME.
THRILL ME, ODDLY...
TELL ME YOU BELIEVE.

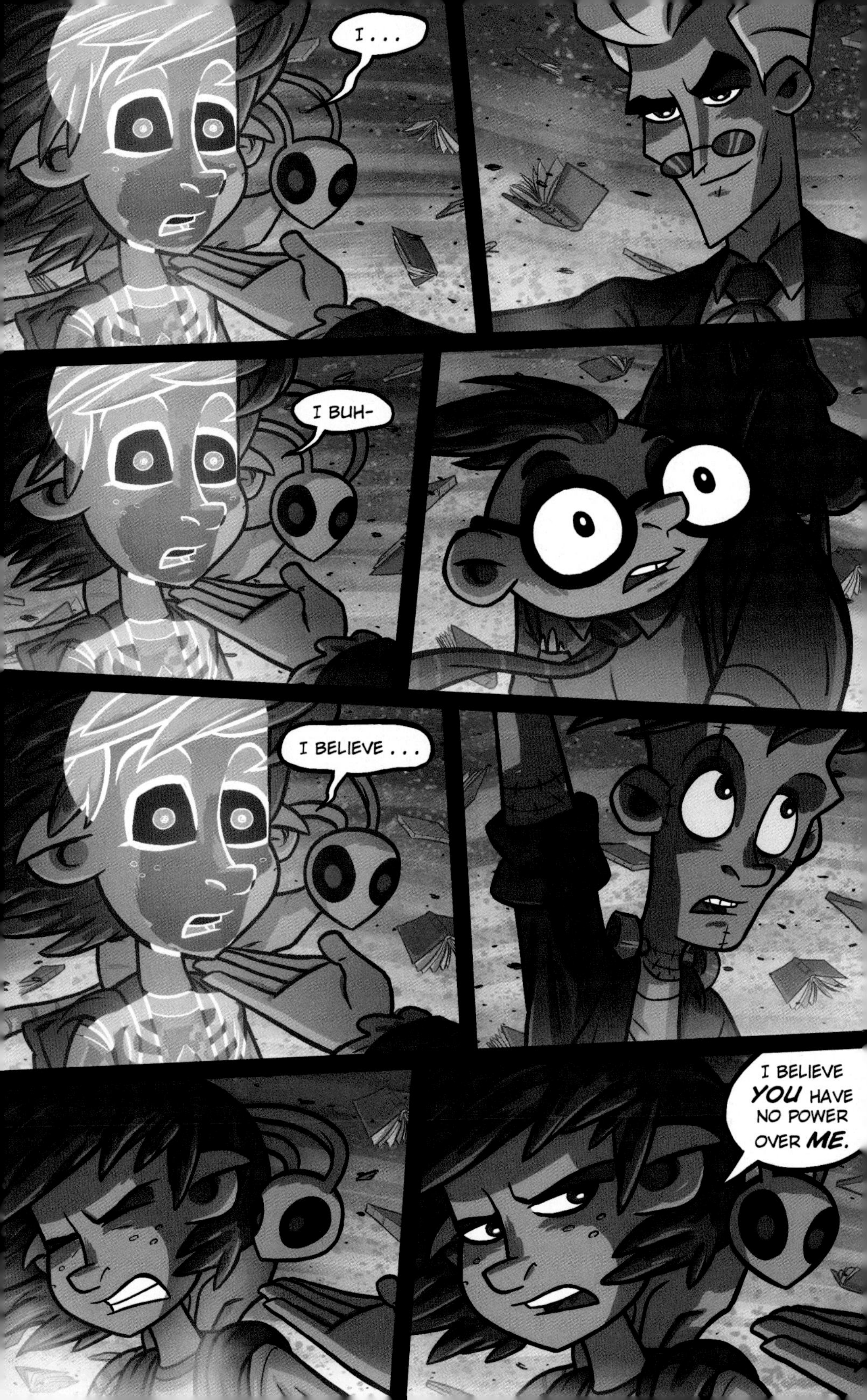
I...
I BUH-
I BELIEVE...
I BELIEVE YOU HAVE NO POWER OVER ME.

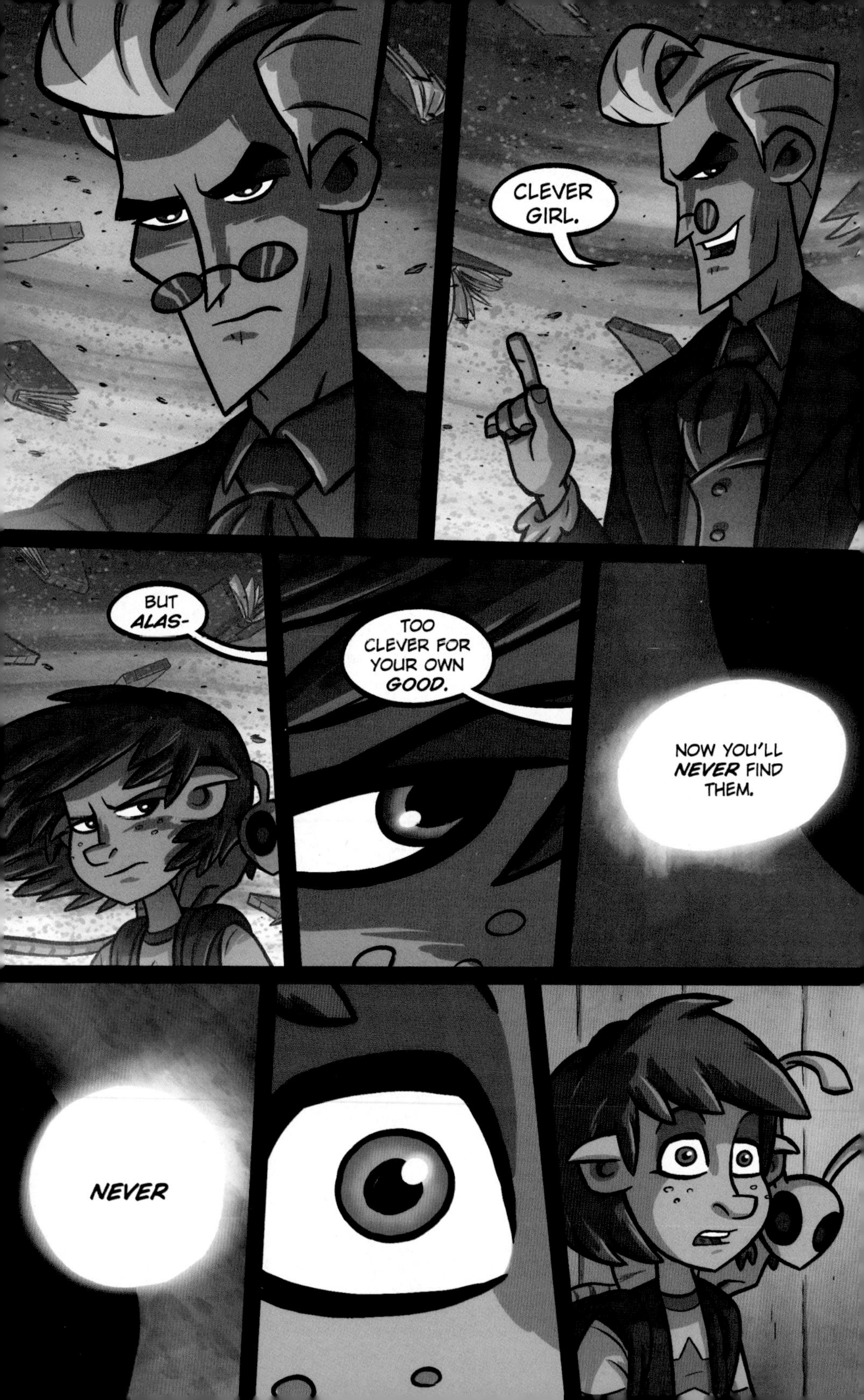
CLEVER GIRL.
BUT ALAS-
TOO CLEVER FOR YOUR OWN GOOD.
NOW YOU'LL NEVER FIND THEM.
NEVER

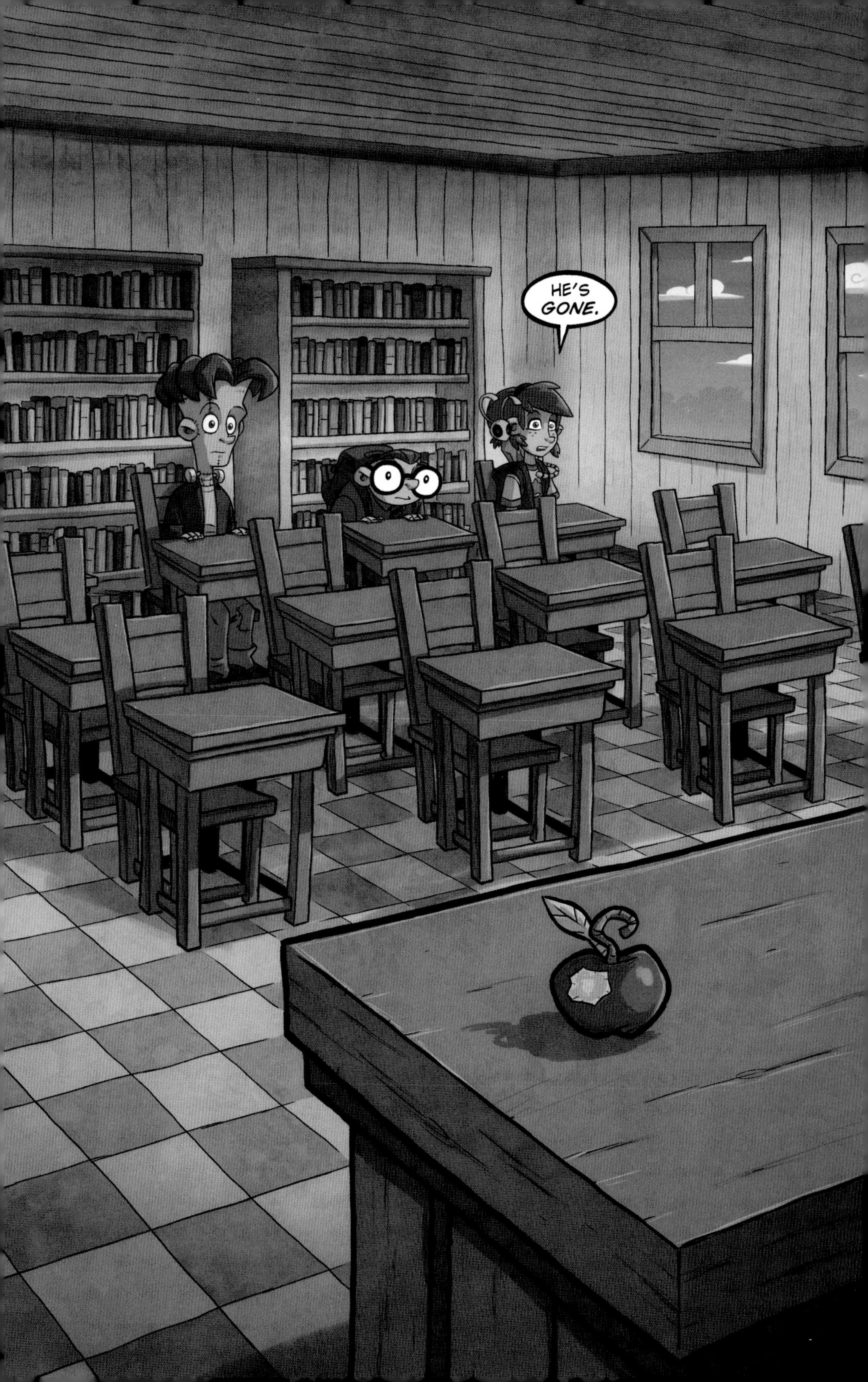
HE'S GONE.

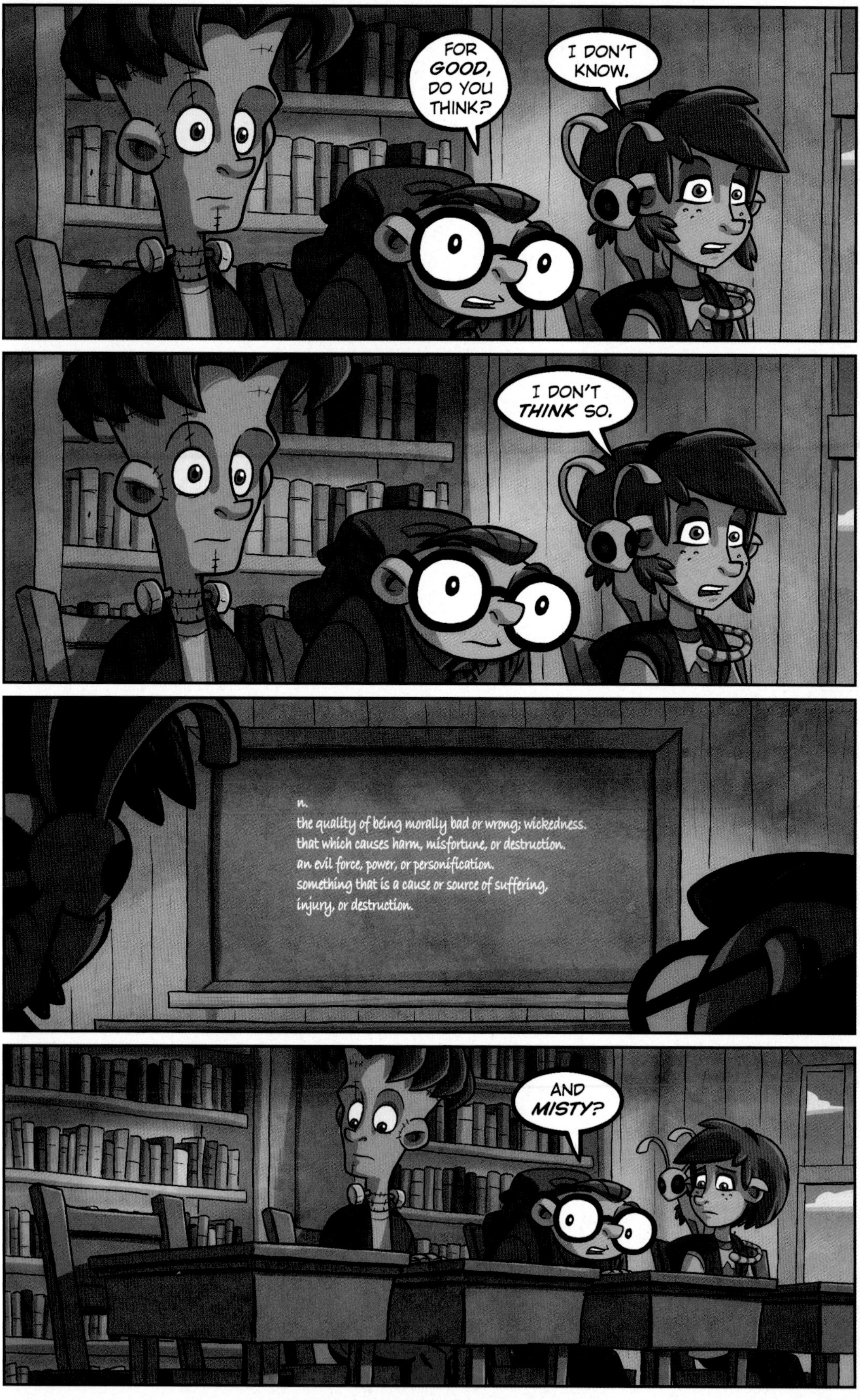
FOR GOOD, DO YOU THINK?
I DON'T KNOW.
I DON'T THINK SO.
n.
the quality of being morally bad or wrong; wickedness.
that which causes harm, misfortune, or destruction.
an evil force, power, or personification.
something that is a cause or source of suffering, injury, or destruction.
AND MISTY?

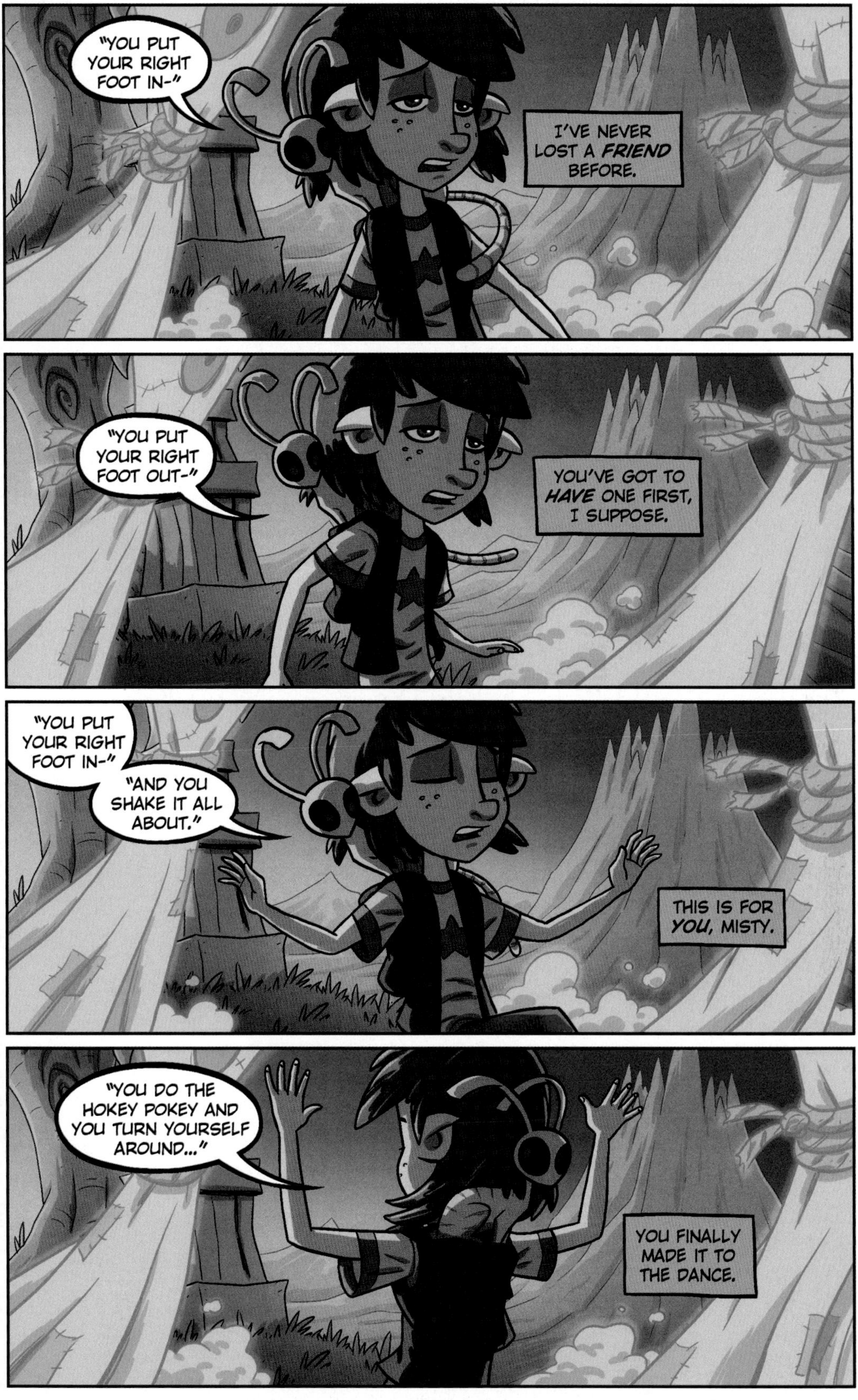
"YOU PUT YOUR RIGHT FOOT IN-"
I'VE NEVER LOST A *FRIEND* BEFORE.
"YOU PUT YOUR RIGHT FOOT OUT-"
YOU'VE GOT TO *HAVE* ONE FIRST, I SUPPOSE.
"YOU PUT YOUR RIGHT FOOT IN-"
"AND YOU SHAKE IT ALL ABOUT."
THIS IS FOR *YOU*, MISTY.
"YOU DO THE HOKEY POKEY AND YOU TURN YOURSELF AROUND..."
YOU FINALLY MADE IT TO THE DANCE.

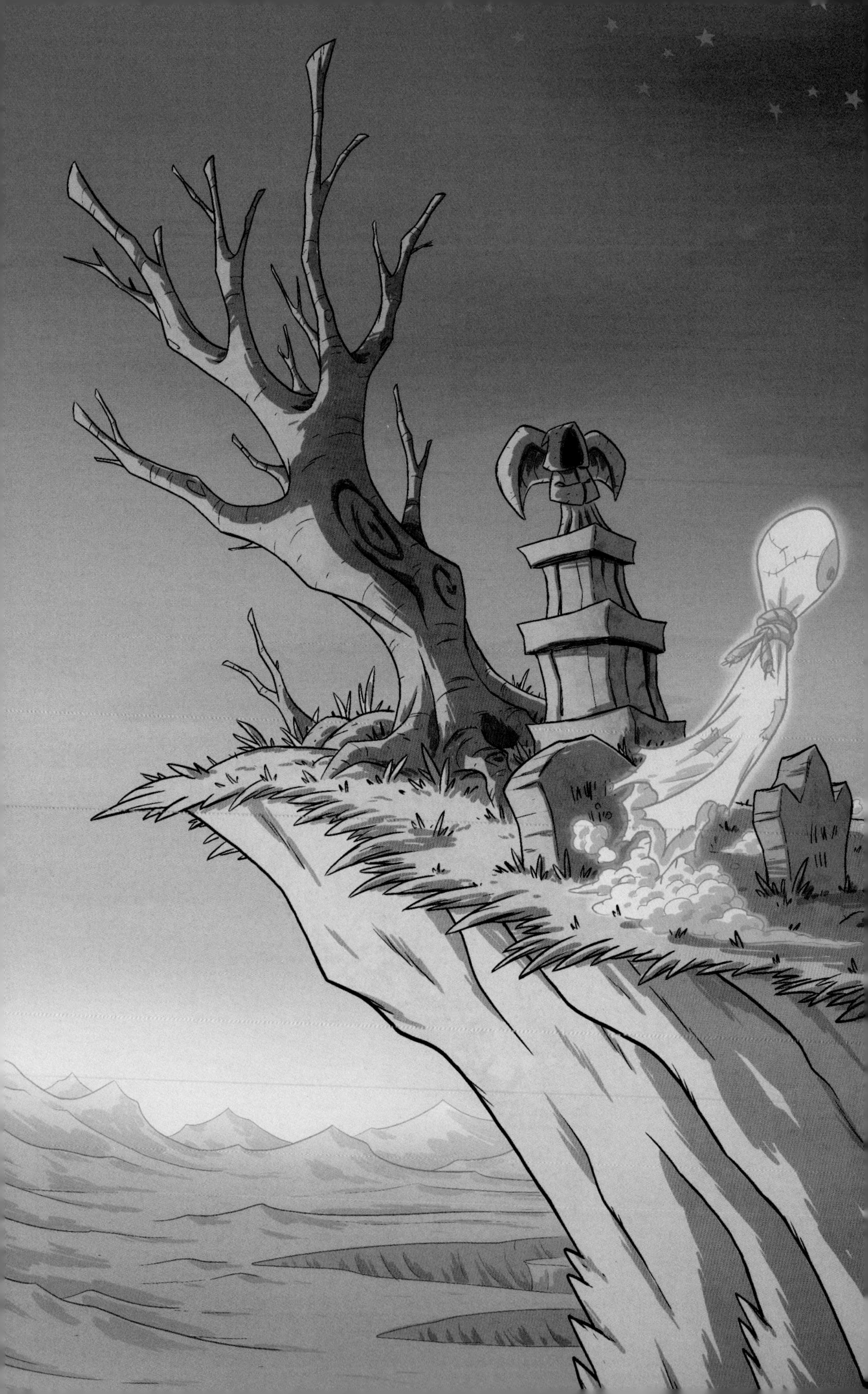

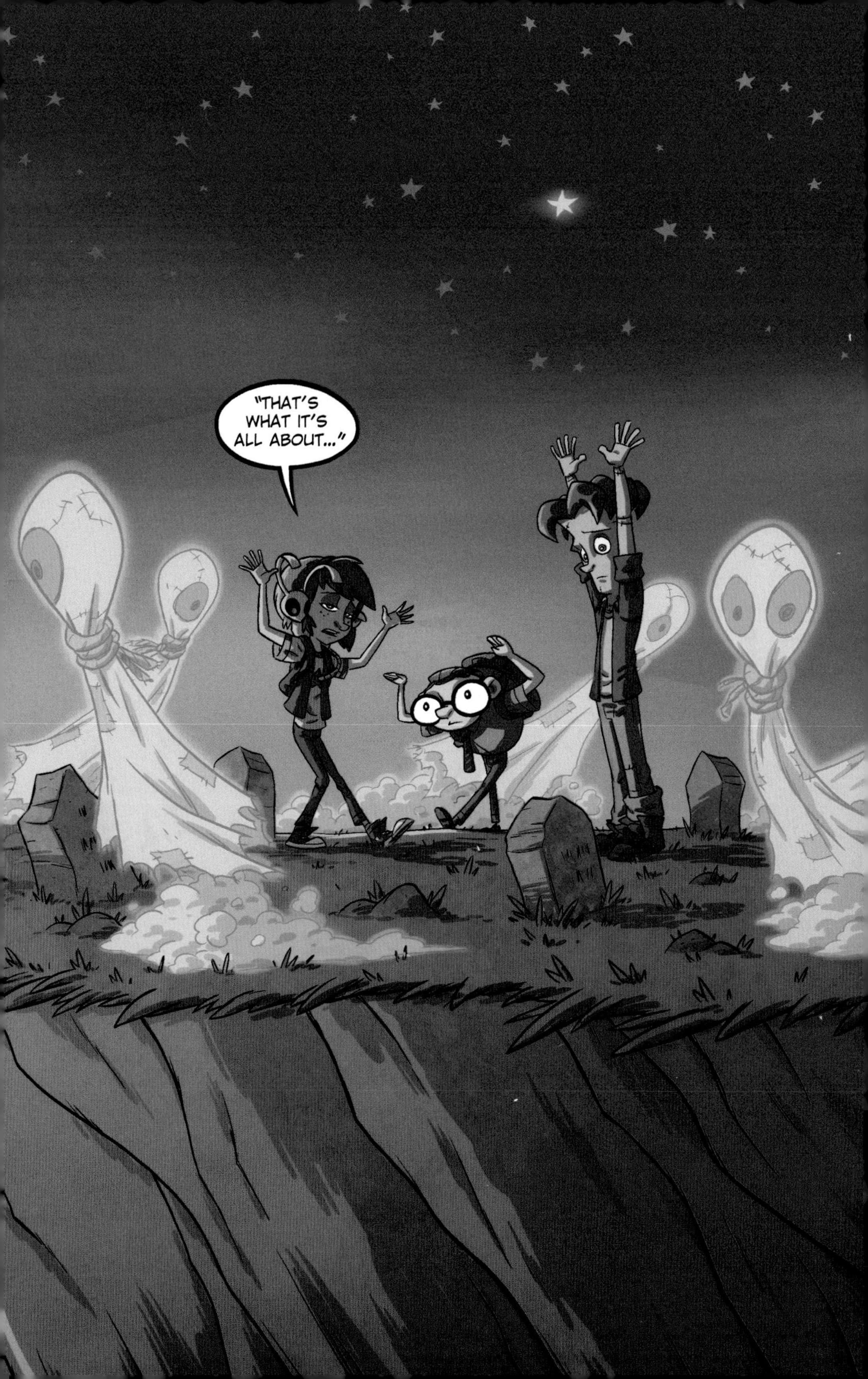
"THAT'S WHAT IT'S ALL ABOUT..."

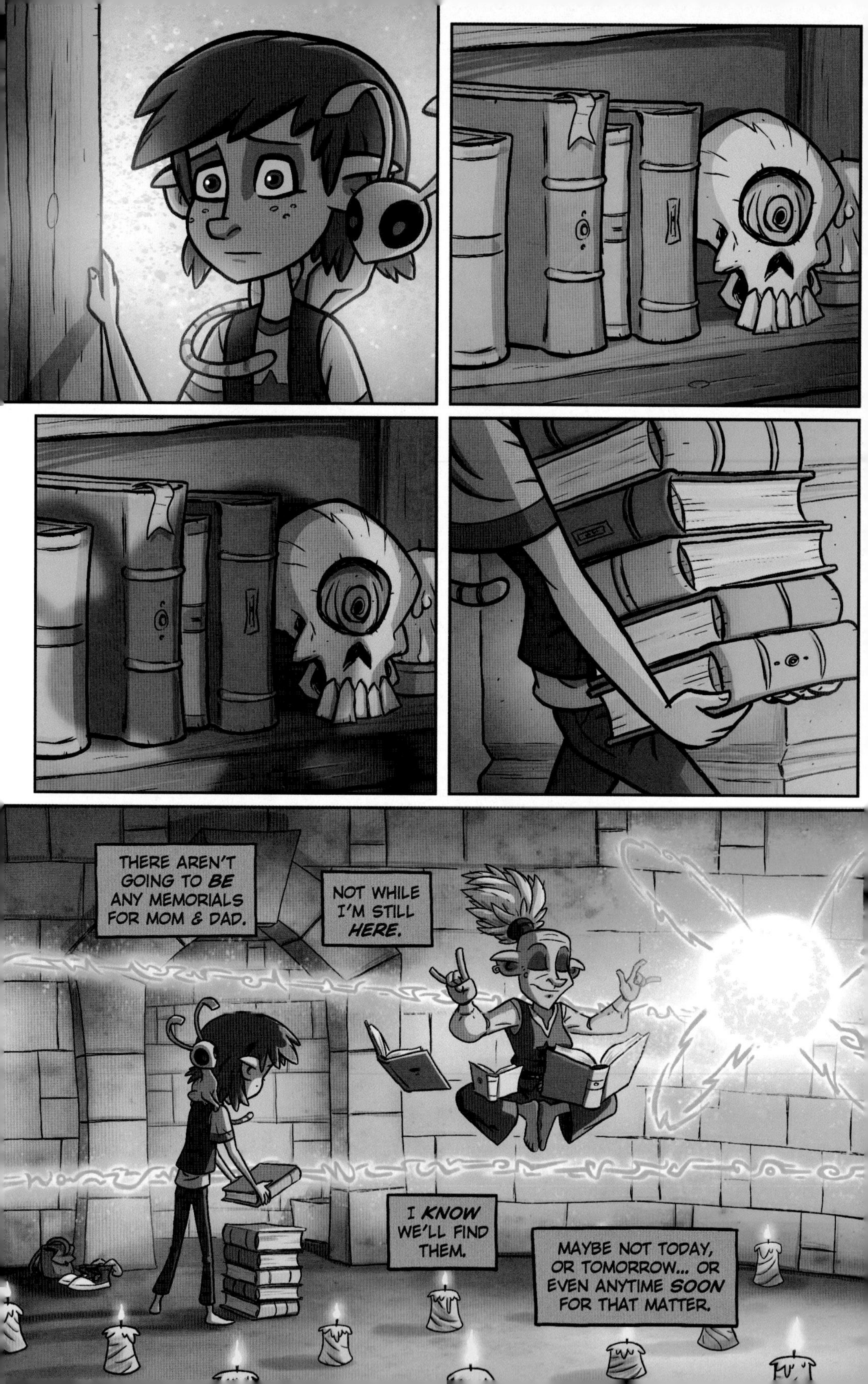
THERE AREN'T GOING TO *BE* ANY MEMORIALS FOR MOM & DAD.
NOT WHILE I'M STILL *HERE*.
I *KNOW* WE'LL FIND THEM.
MAYBE NOT TODAY, OR TOMORROW... OR EVEN ANYTIME *SOON* FOR THAT MATTER.

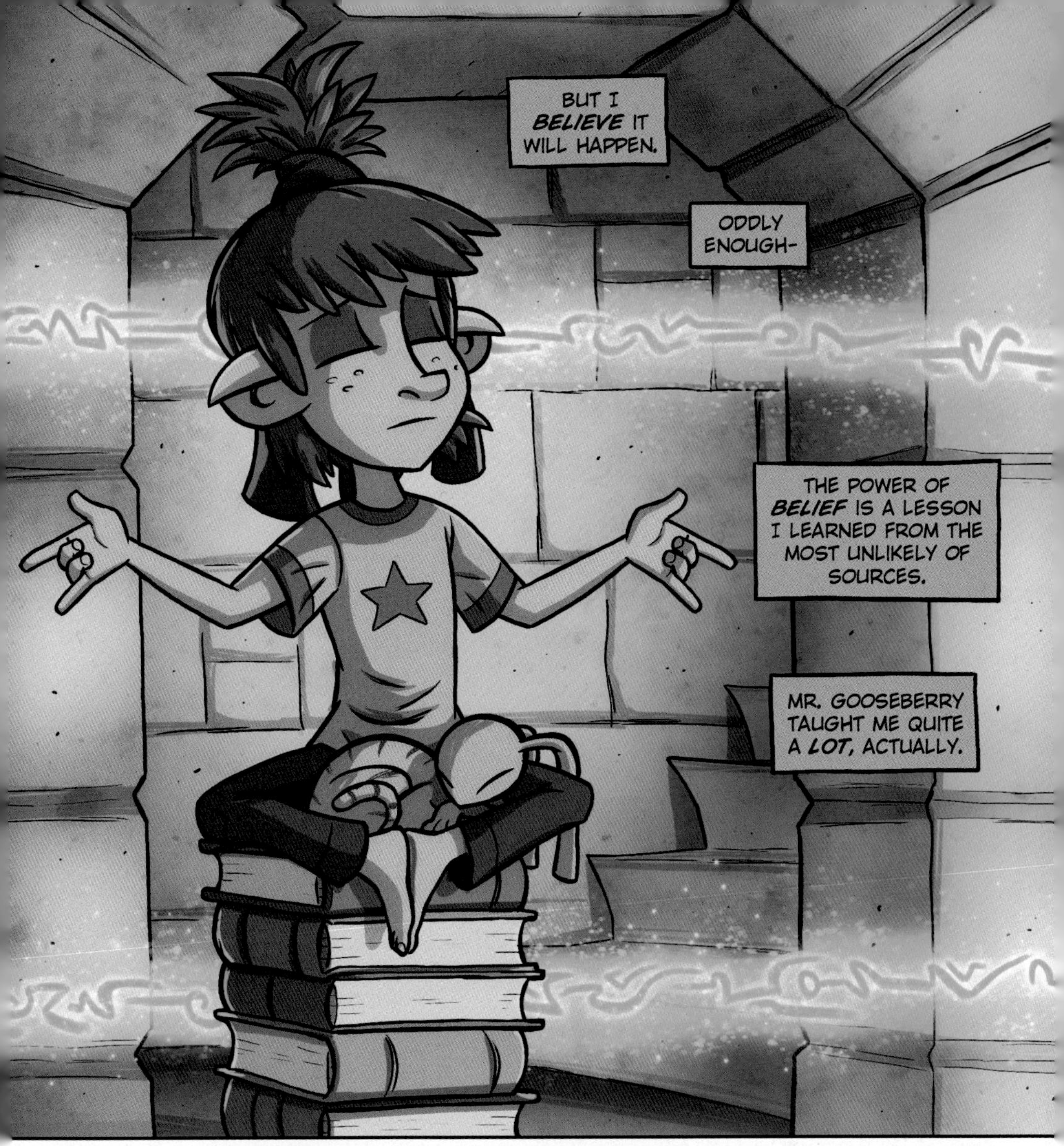
BUT I BELIEVE IT WILL HAPPEN.
ODDLY ENOUGH-
THE POWER OF BELIEF IS A LESSON I LEARNED FROM THE MOST UNLIKELY OF SOURCES.
MR. GOOSEBERRY TAUGHT ME QUITE A LOT, ACTUALLY.
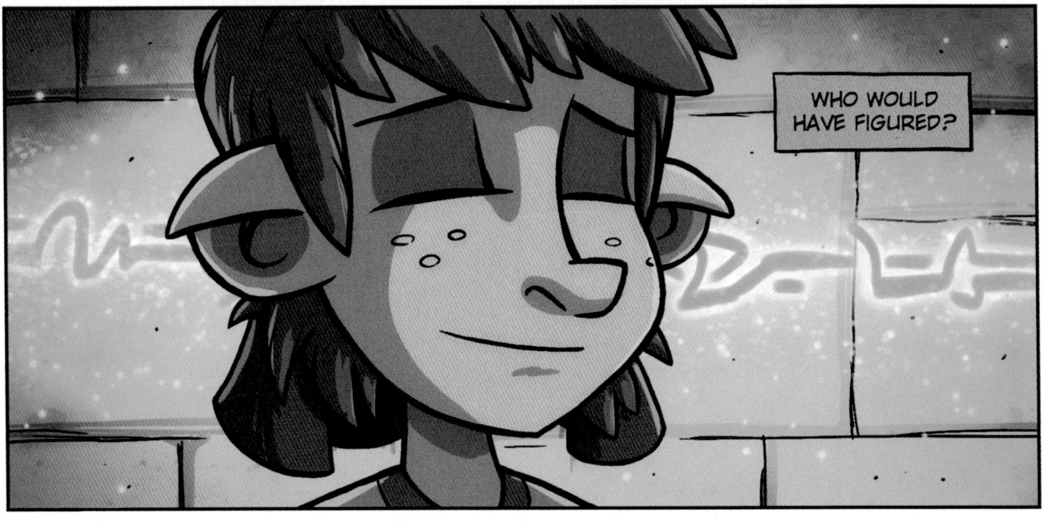
WHO WOULD HAVE FIGURED?

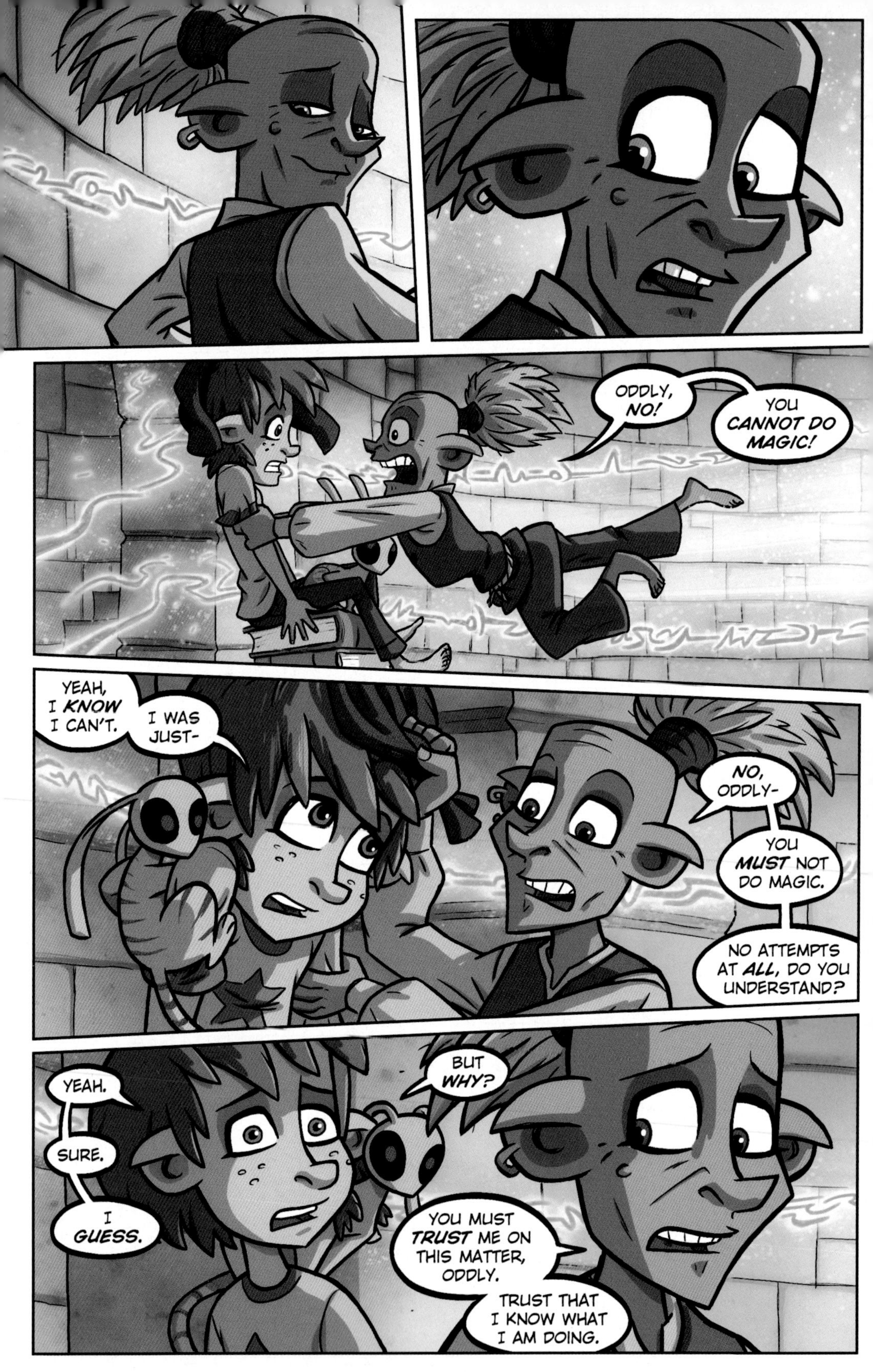
ODDLY, NO!
YOU CANNOT DO MAGIC!
YEAH, I KNOW I CAN'T.
I WAS JUST-
NO, ODDLY-
YOU MUST NOT DO MAGIC.
NO ATTEMPTS AT ALL, DO YOU UNDERSTAND?
YEAH.
SURE.
I GUESS.
BUT WHY?
YOU MUST TRUST ME ON THIS MATTER, ODDLY.
TRUST THAT I KNOW WHAT I AM DOING.

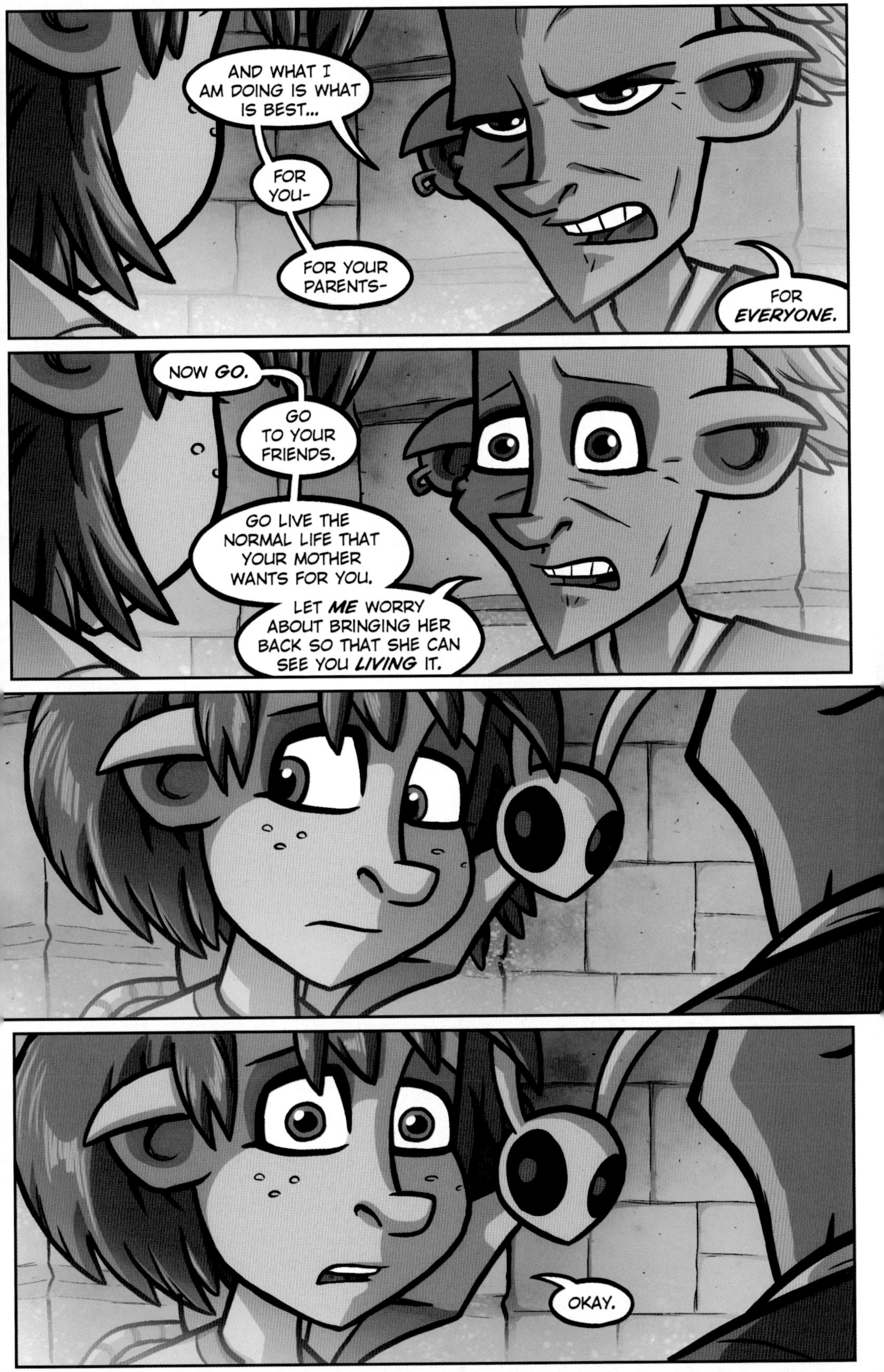
AND WHAT I AM DOING IS WHAT IS BEST...
FOR YOU-
FOR YOUR PARENTS-
FOR *EVERYONE.*
NOW *GO.*
GO TO YOUR FRIENDS.
GO LIVE THE NORMAL LIFE THAT YOUR MOTHER WANTS FOR YOU.
LET *ME* WORRY ABOUT BRINGING HER BACK SO THAT SHE CAN SEE YOU *LIVING* IT.
OKAY.

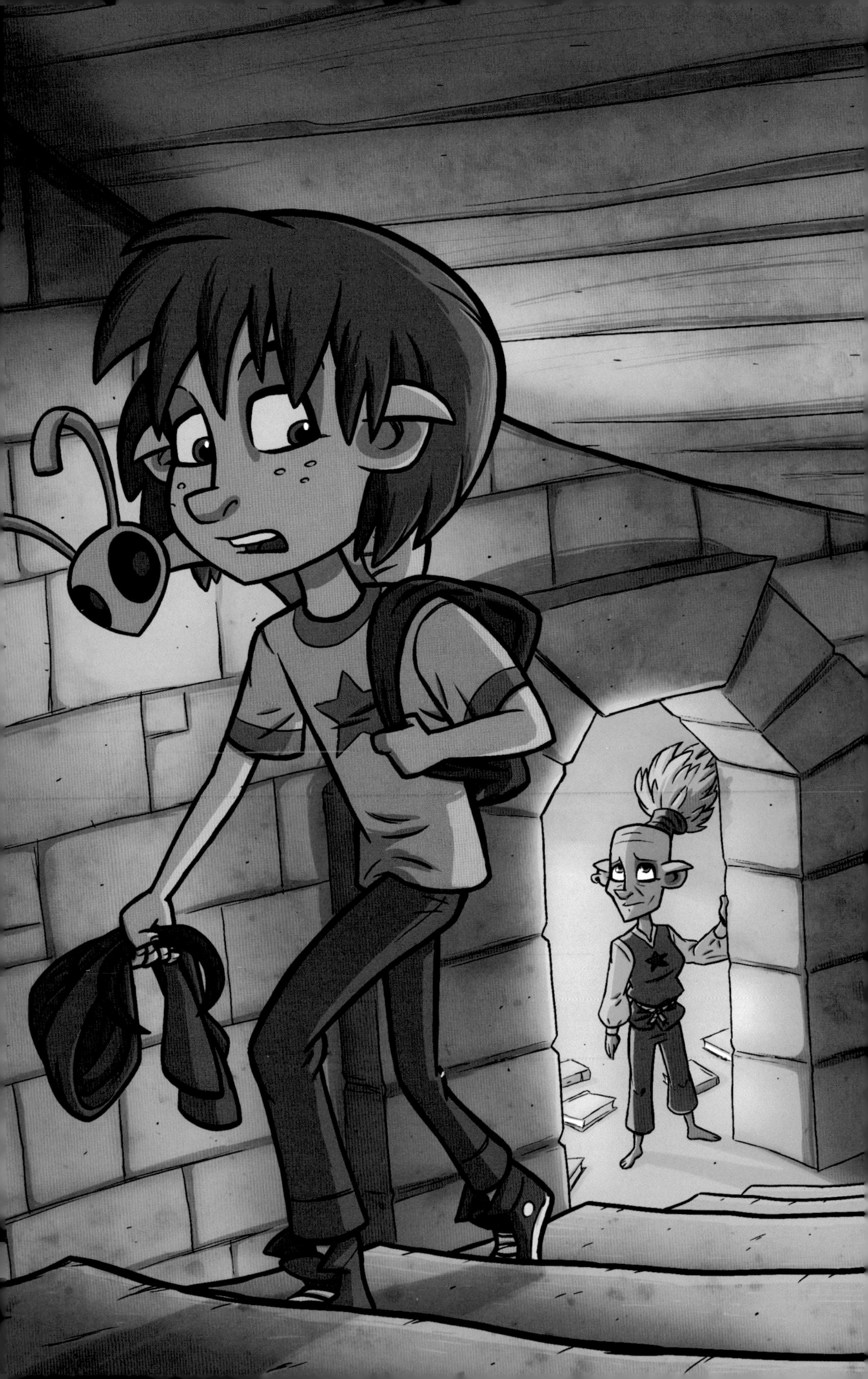

Oddly ★ Normal

WILL RETURN IN

BOOK
④

Oddly ★ Normal

BOOK
③

WRITTEN, ILLUSTRATED & LETTERED BY

OTIS FRAMPTON

COLORED BY

OTIS FRAMPTON

&

TRACY BAILEY

**COLOR FLATS BY
DANIEL MEAD, TRACY BAILEY,
SHELBY EDMUNDS, OTIS FRAMPTON
AND THOMAS BOATWRIGHT**

ABOUT THE AUTHOR

Otis Frampton is a comic book writer/artist, freelance illustrator and animator. He is the creator of the webcomic and animated series "ABCDEFGeek." He is also one of the artists on the popular animated web series "How It Should Have Ended."

You can visit Otis on the web at: www.otisframpton.com

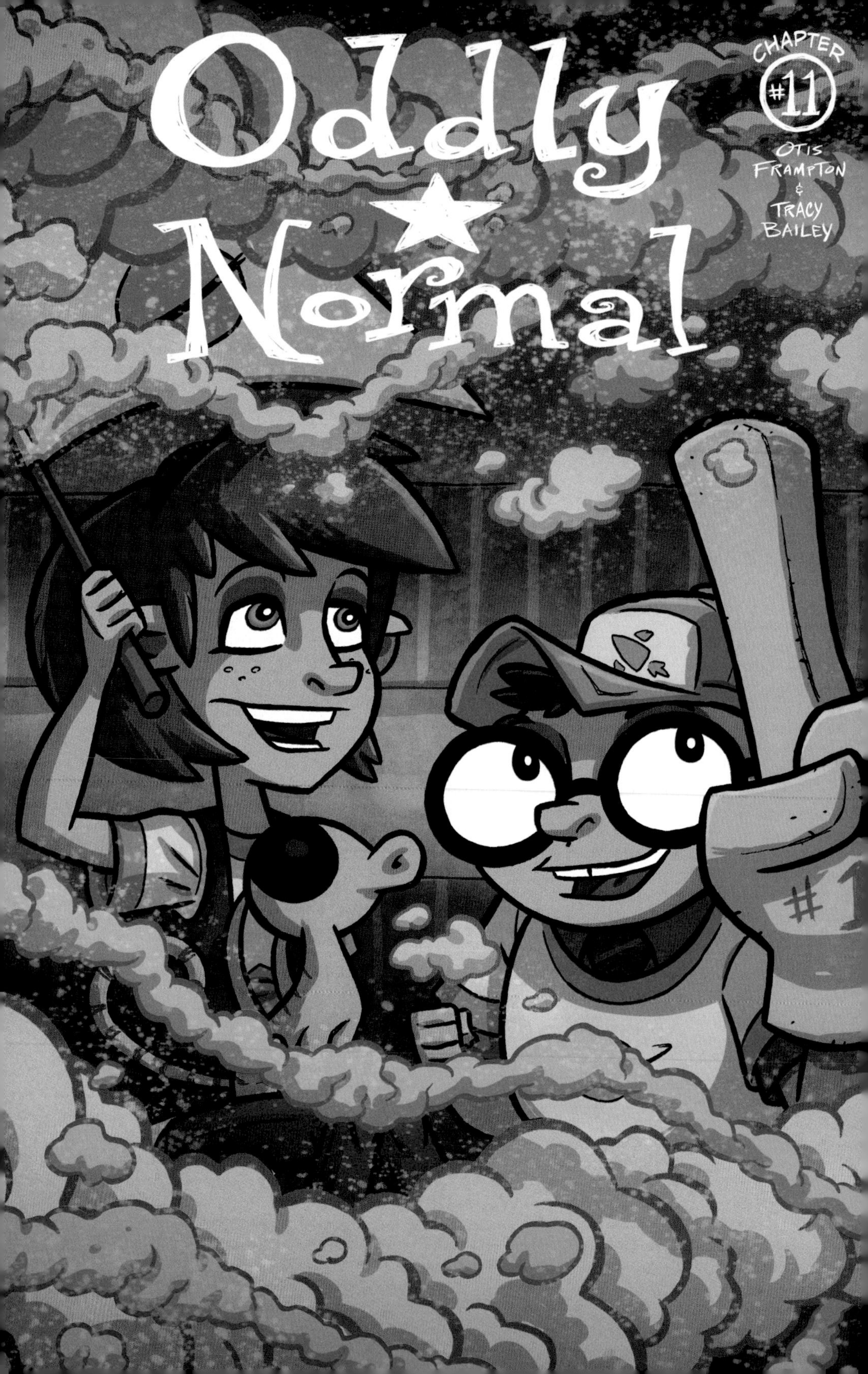
Oddly Normal
CHAPTER #11
OTIS FRAMPTON & TRACY BAILEY
#1

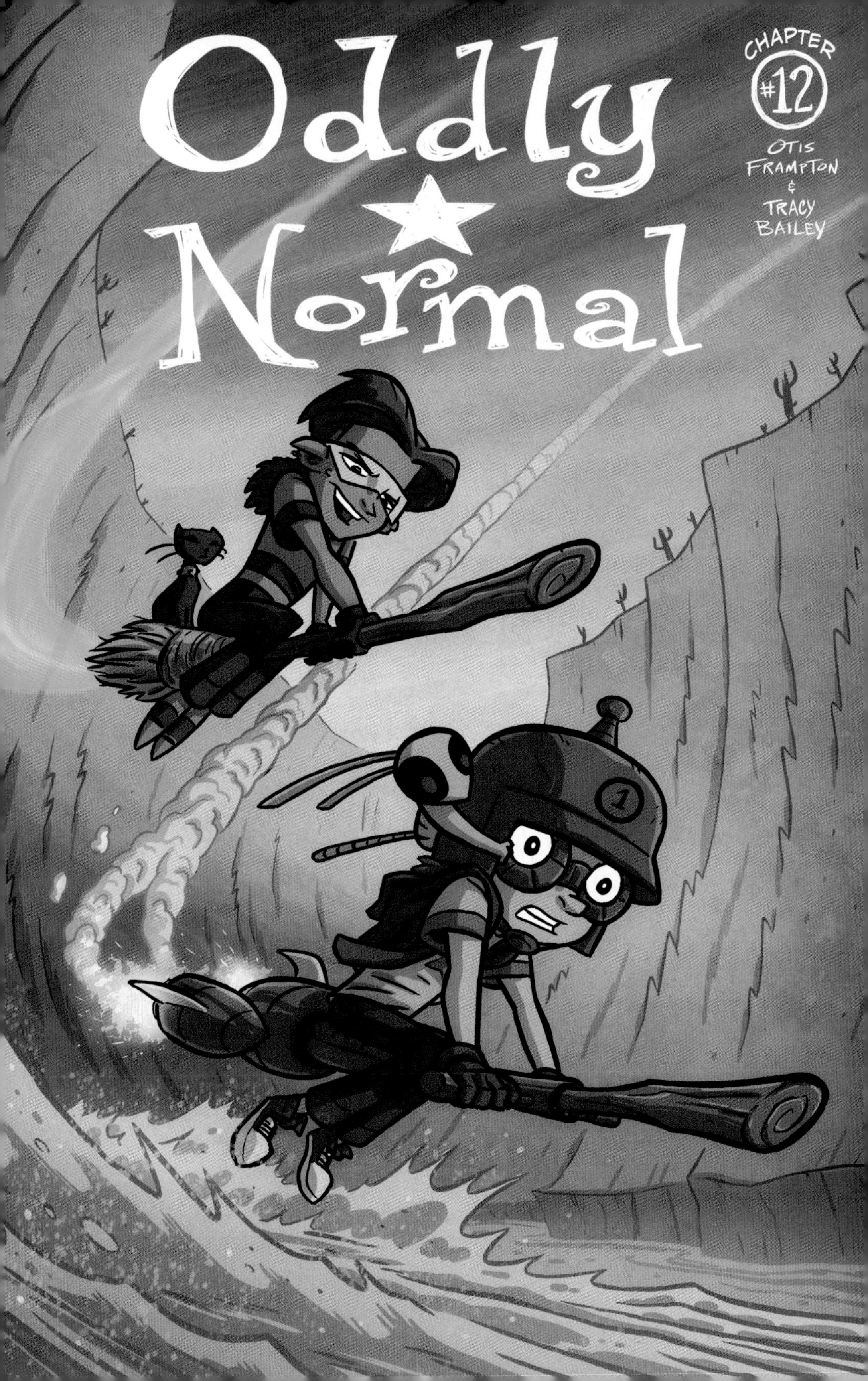
Oddly Normal
CHAPTER #12
OTIS FRAMPTON & TRACY BAILEY

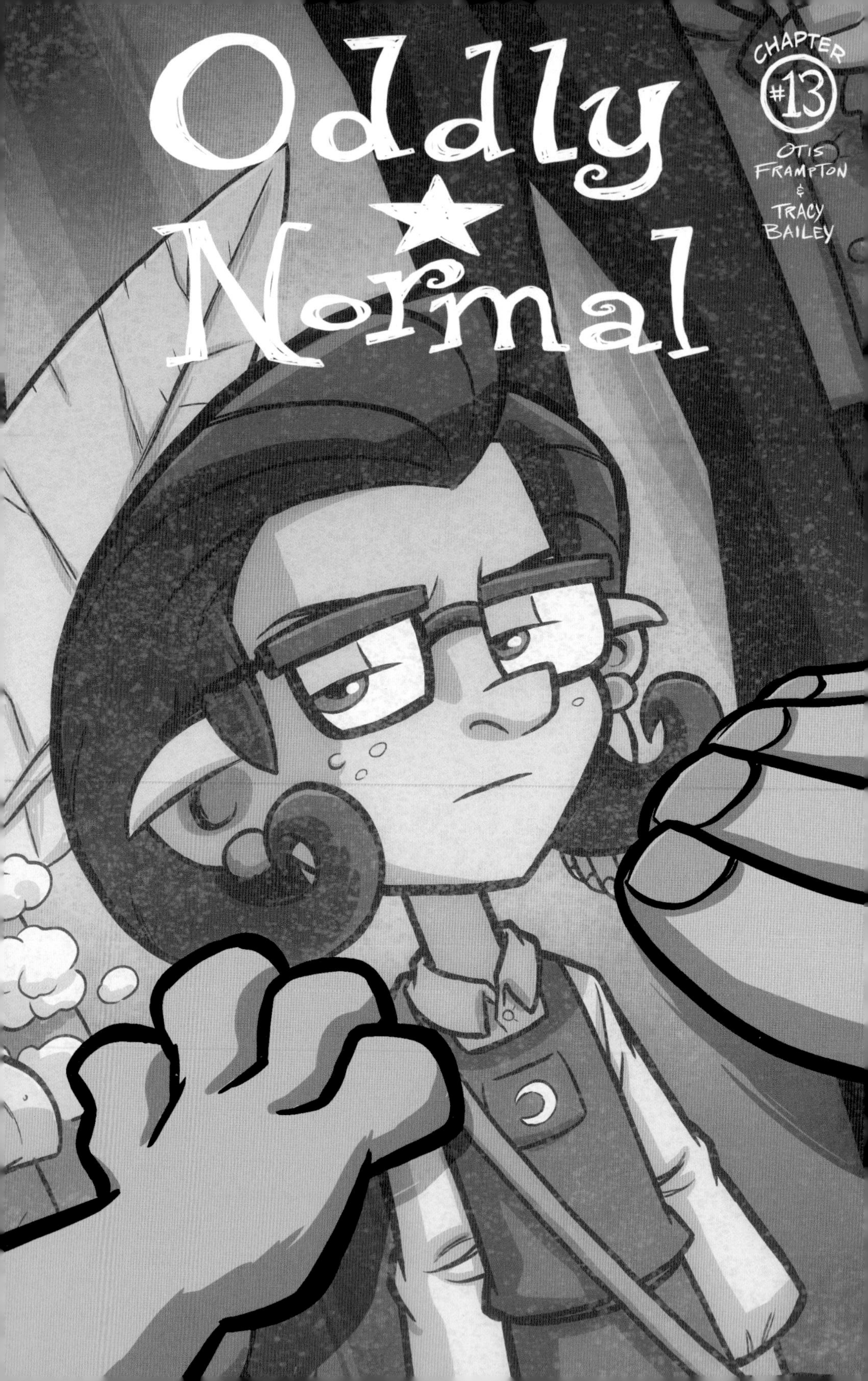

Oddly ★ Normal
CHAPTER #13
OTIS FRAMPTON & TRACY BAILEY

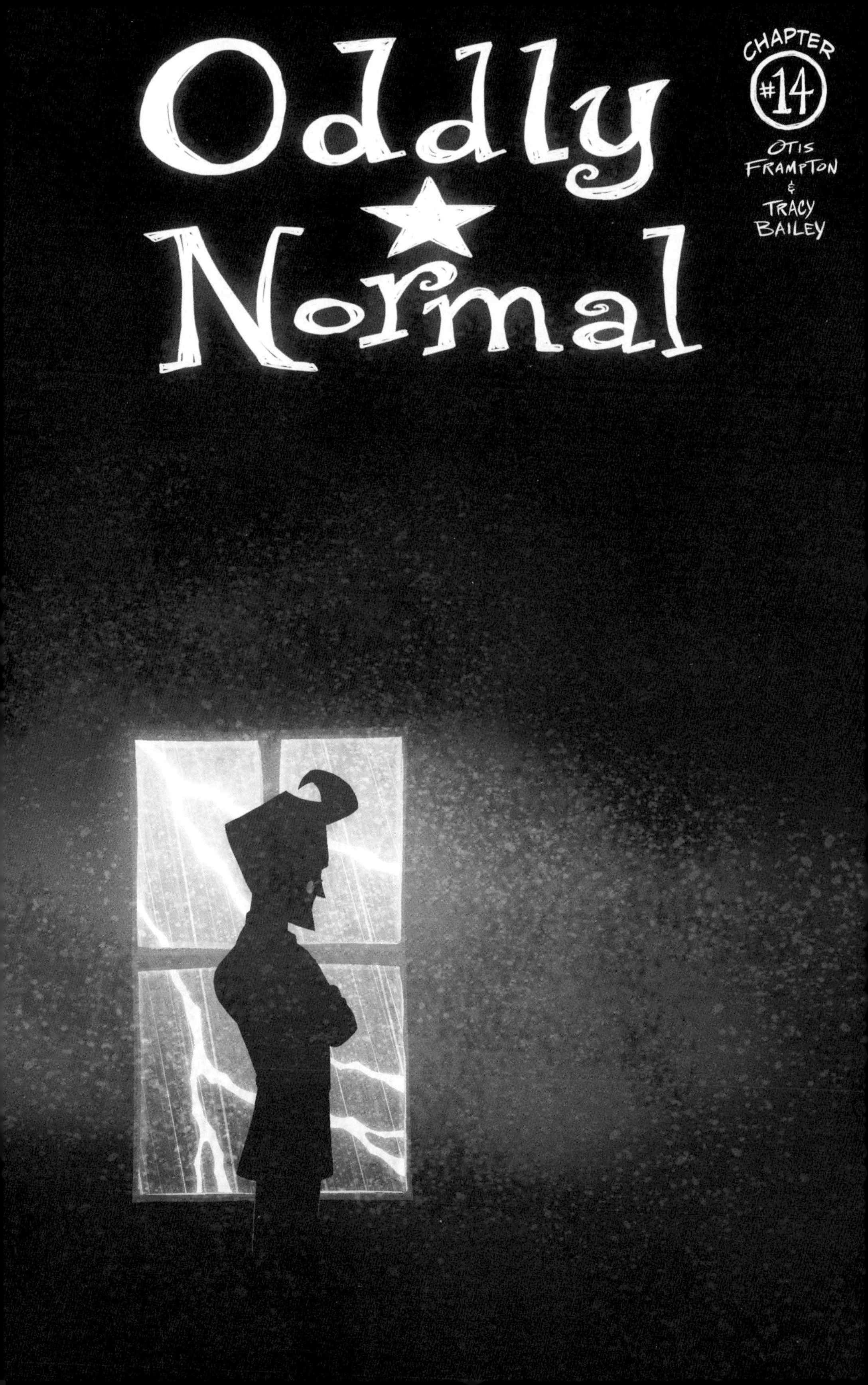
Oddly Normal
CHAPTER #14
OTIS FRAMPTON & TRACY BAILEY

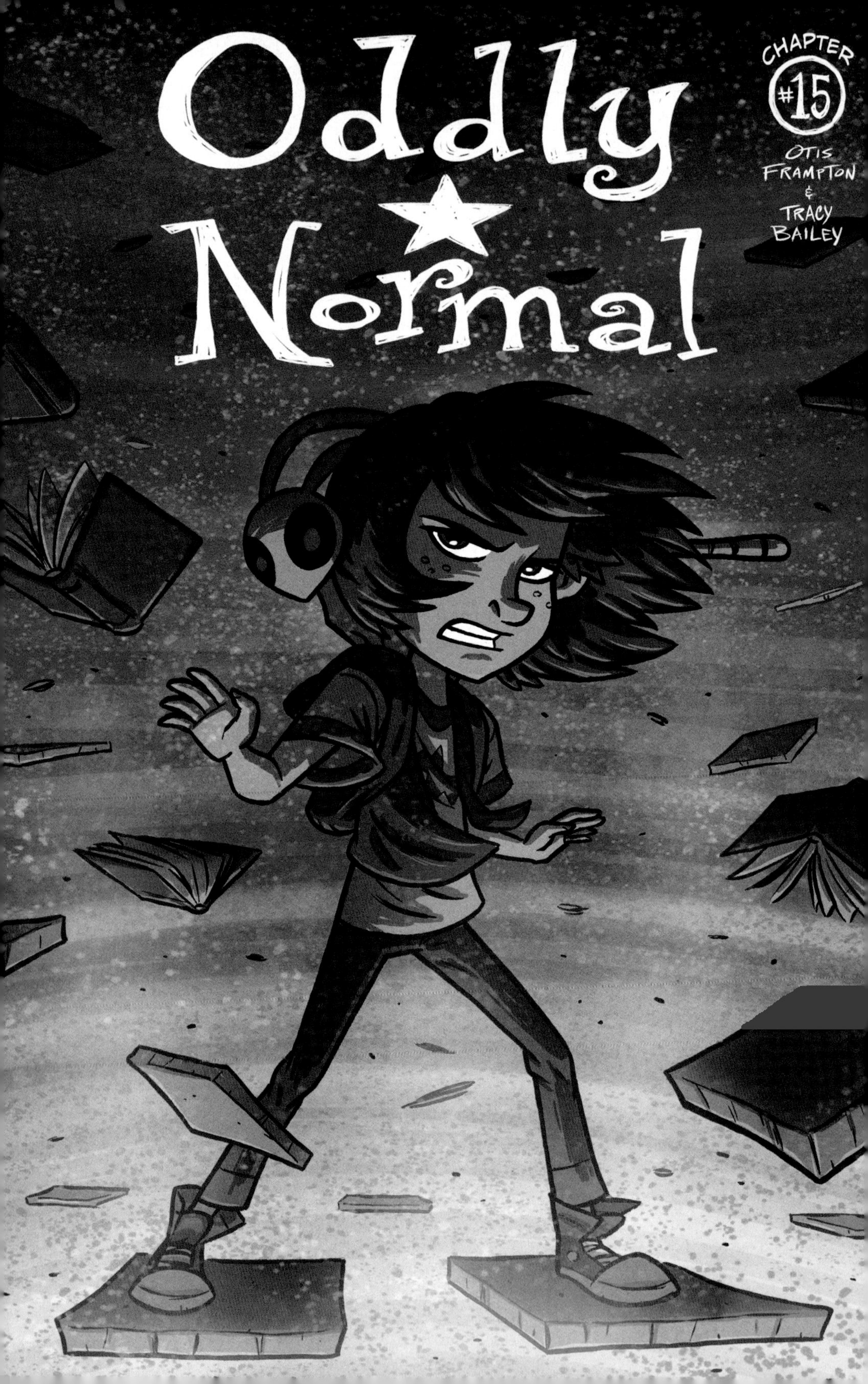
Oddly ★ Normal
CHAPTER #15
OTIS FRAMPTON & TRACY BAILEY

GALLERY CREDITS:

SCOTT BROWN

SKYLAR CHANDLER

KATIE COOK

GRANT GOULD

VAL HOCHBERG

DANI JONES

CAM KENDELL

JAMES LENT

JAY MYERS

SERGIO QUIJADA

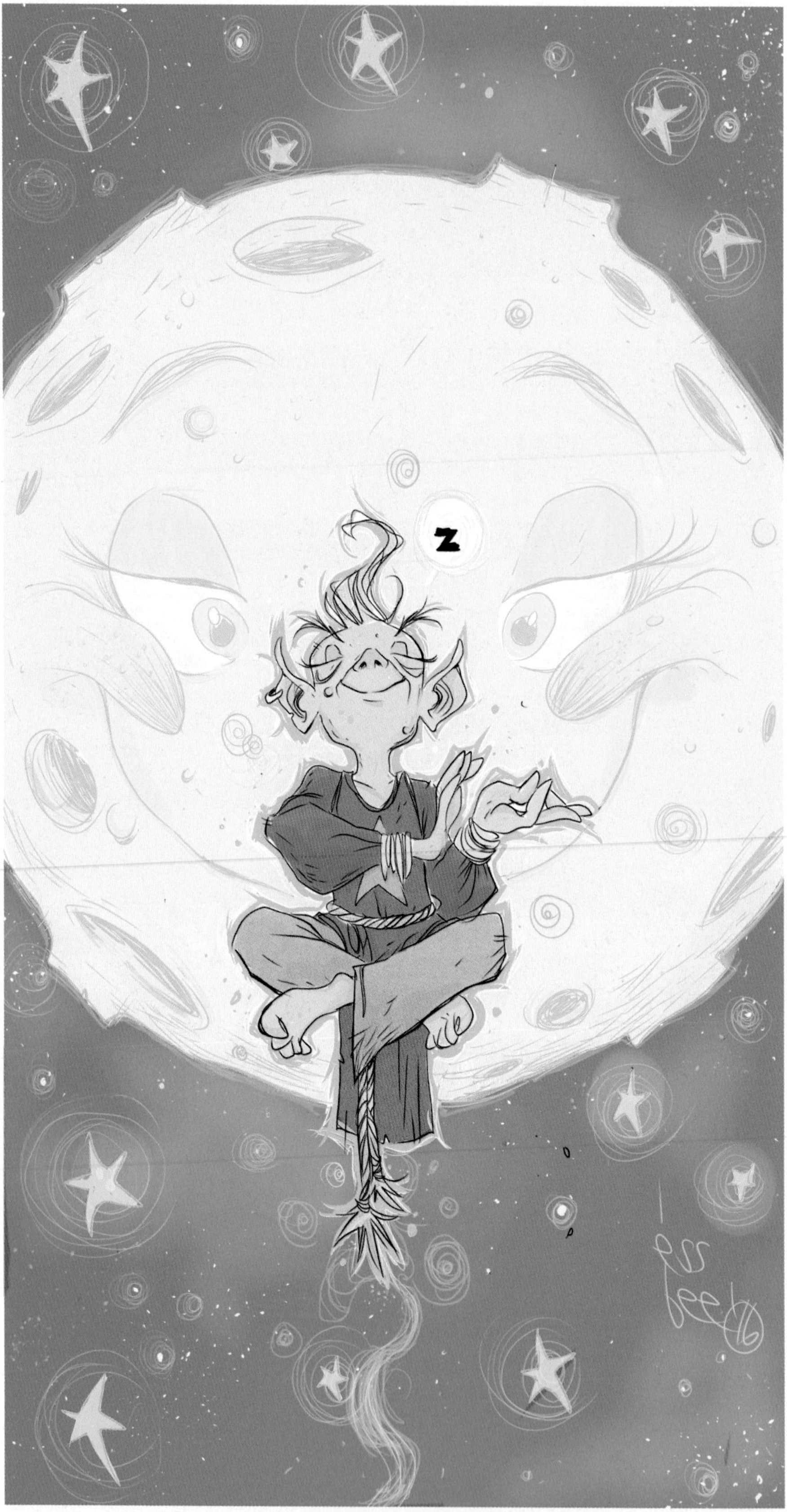
Z

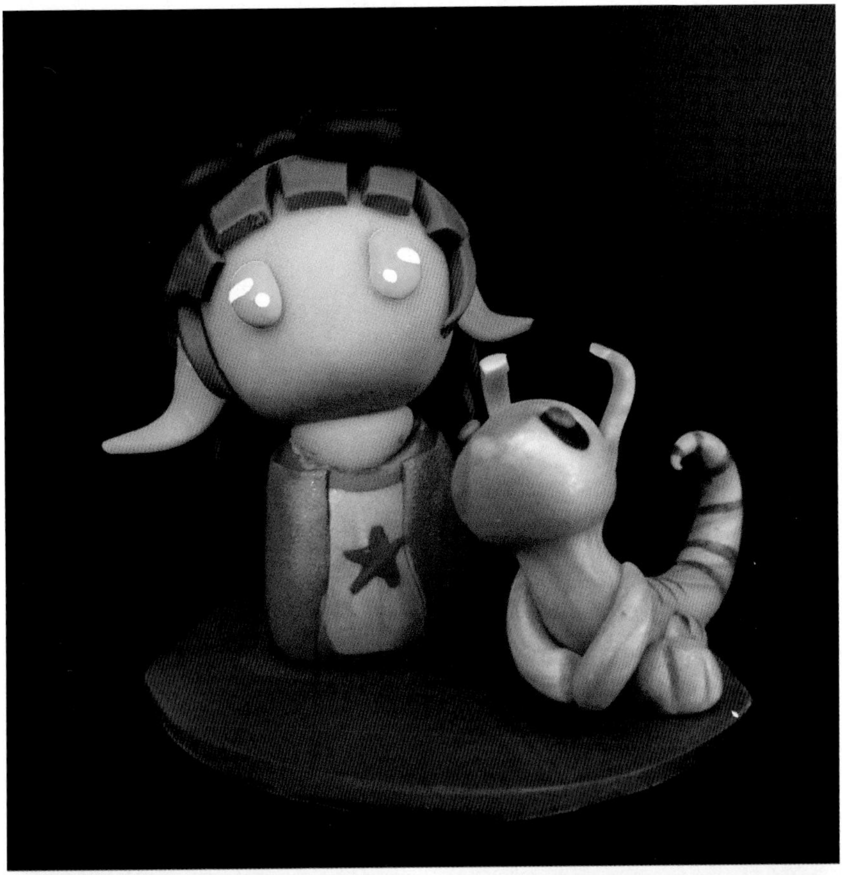

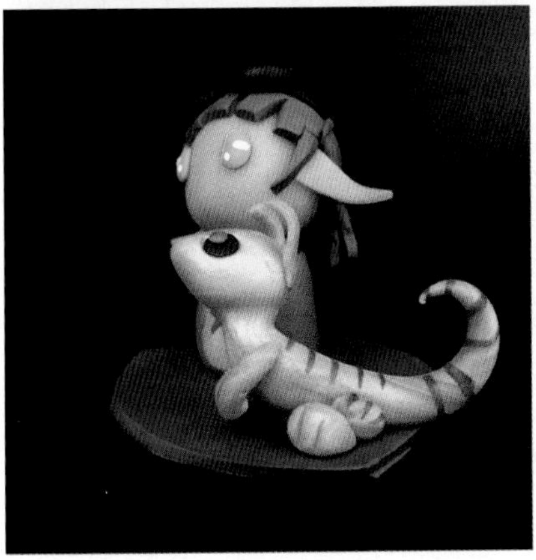

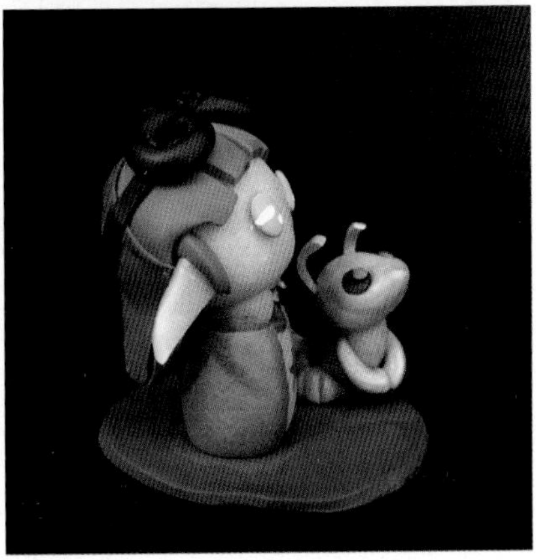

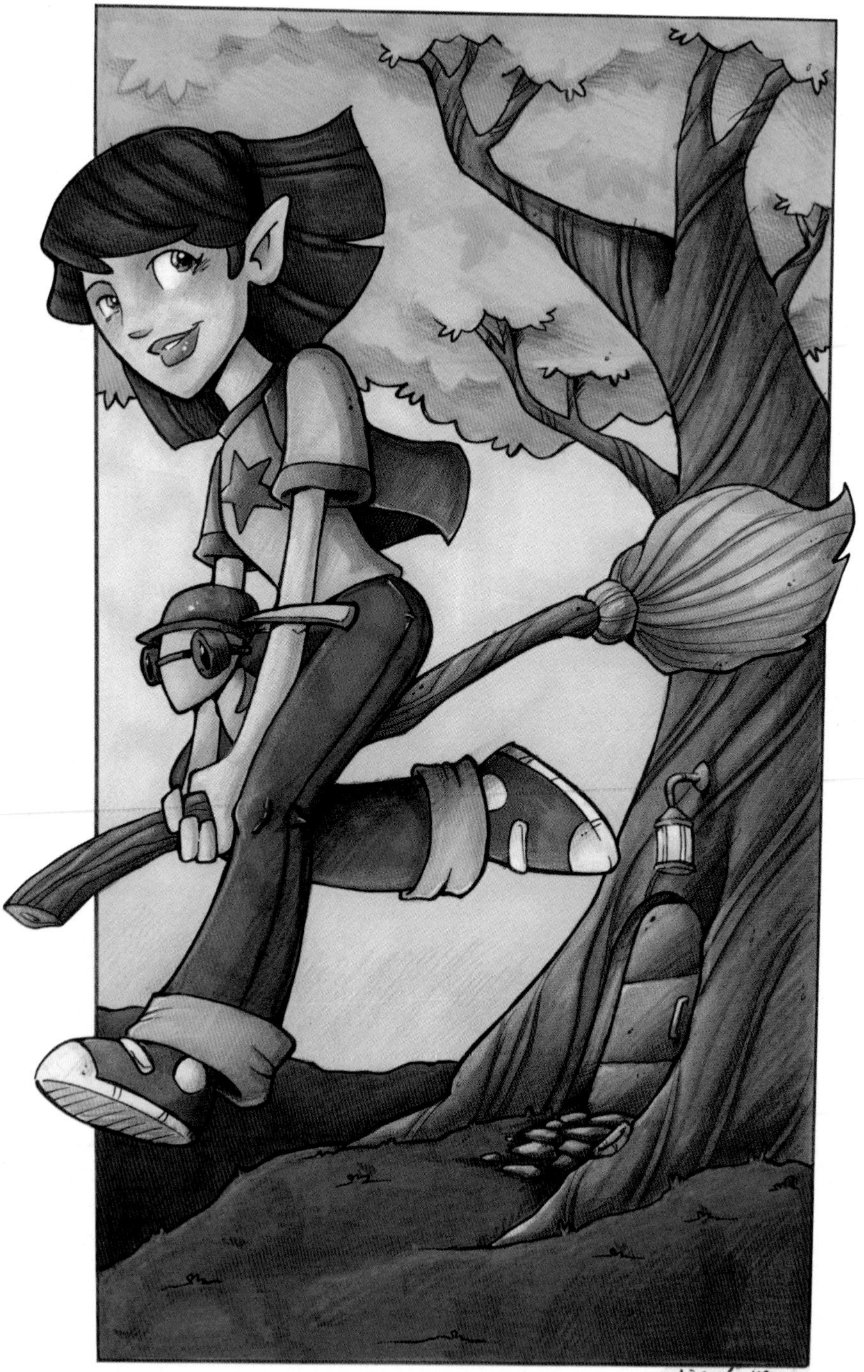

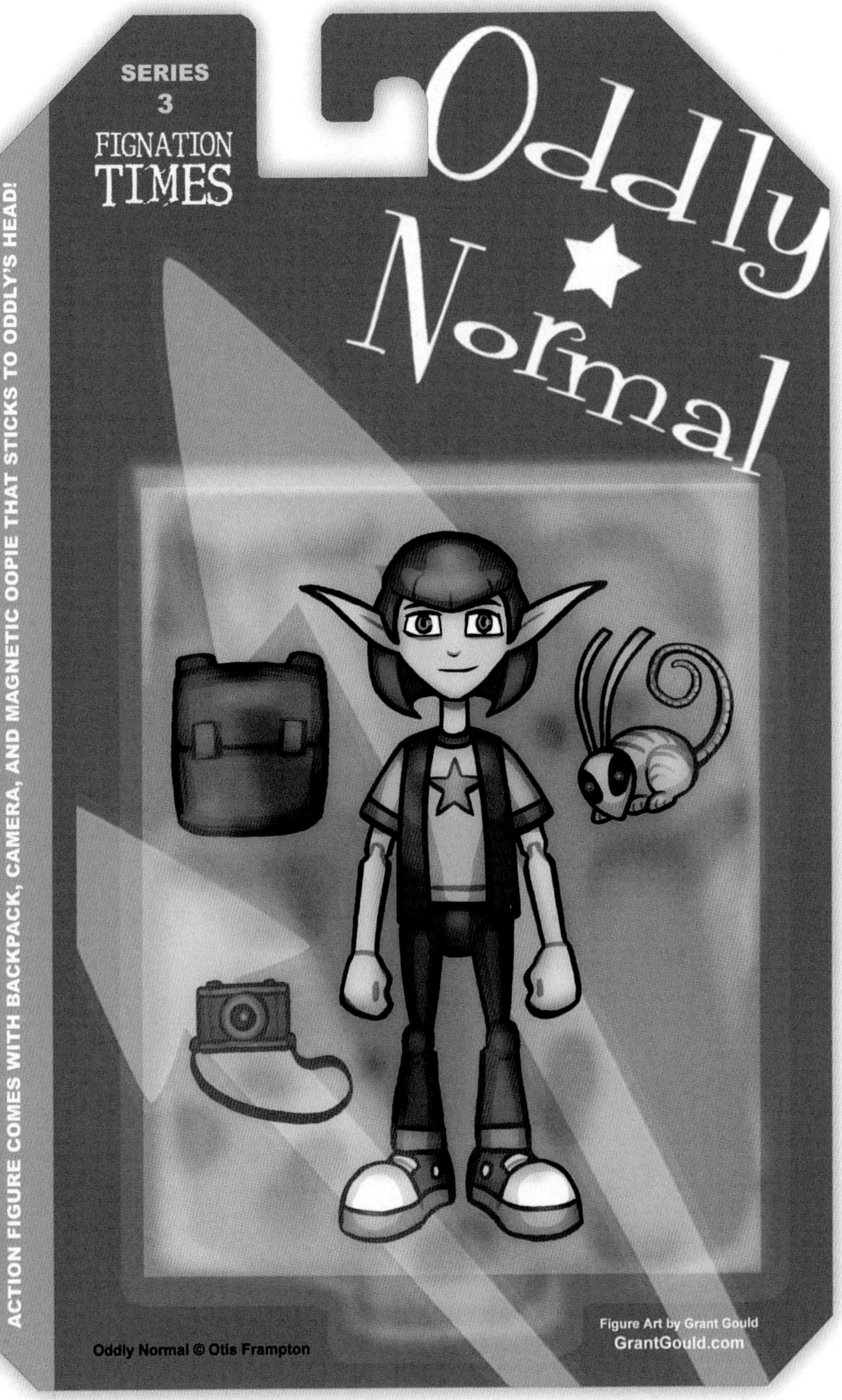
SERIES
3
FIGNATION
TIMES
Oddly ★ Normal
ACTION FIGURE COMES WITH BACKPACK, CAMERA, AND MAGNETIC OOPIE THAT STICKS TO ODDLY'S HEAD!
Oddly Normal © Otis Frampton
Figure Art by Grant Gould
GrantGould.com

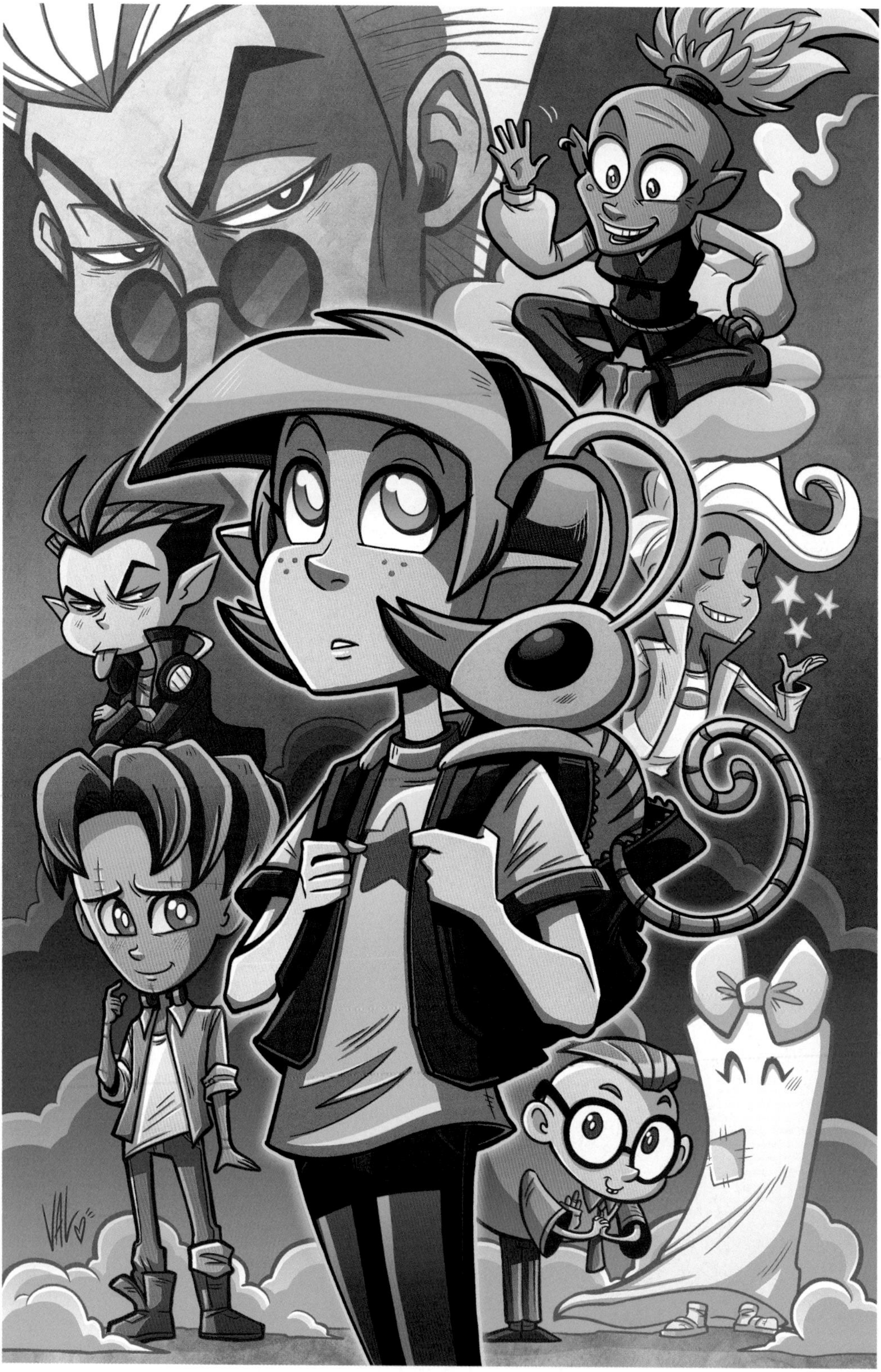

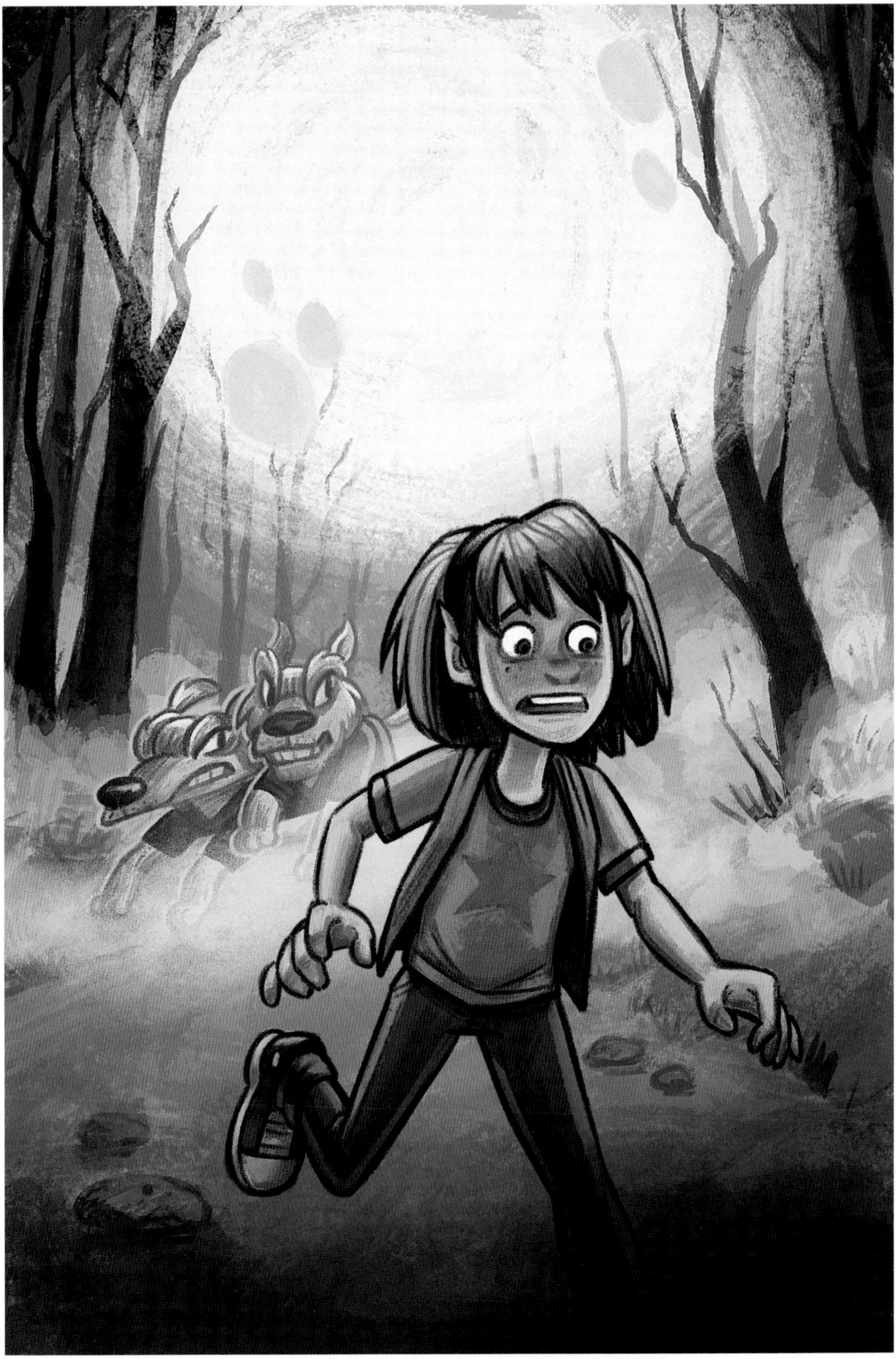

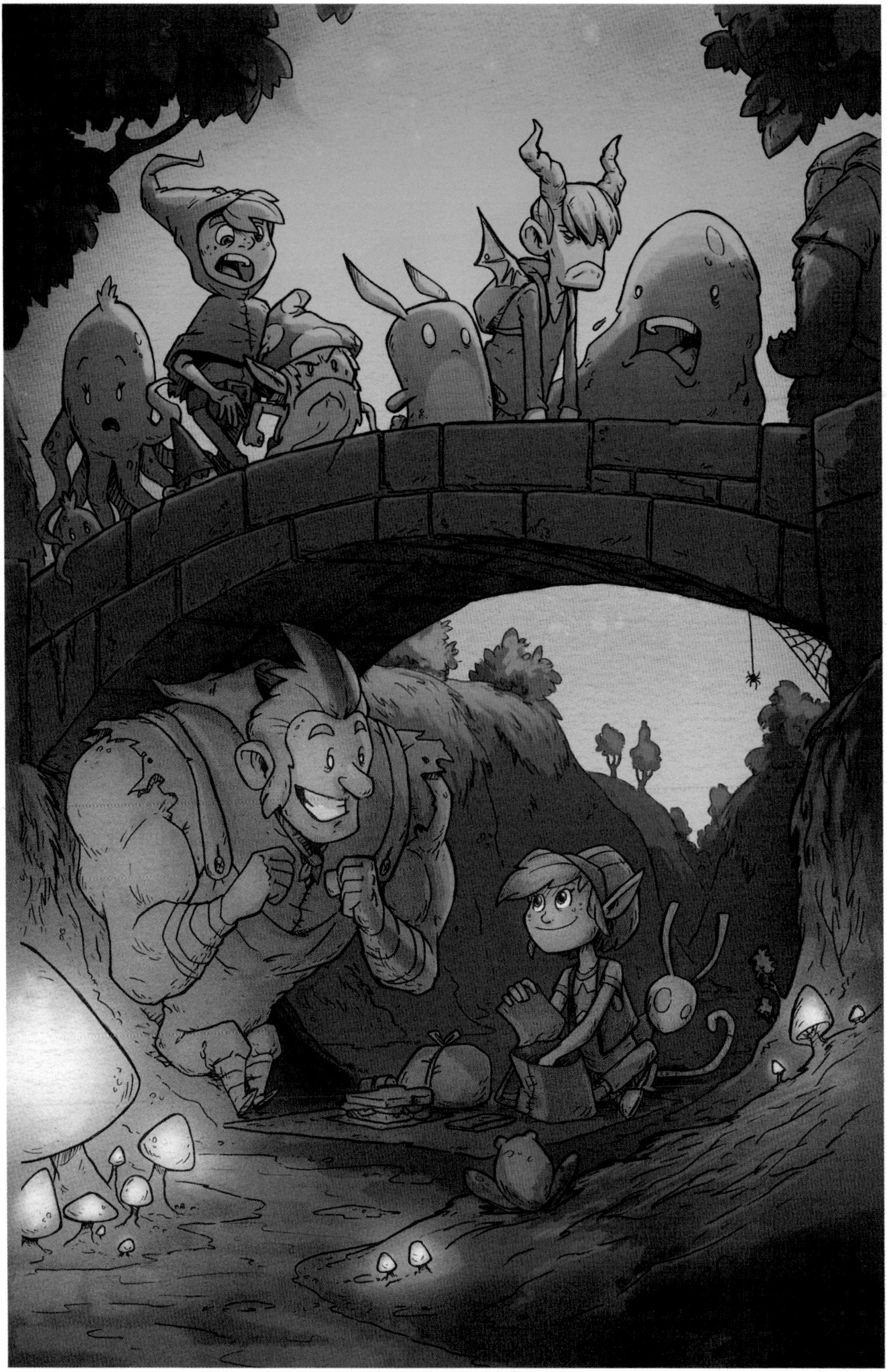

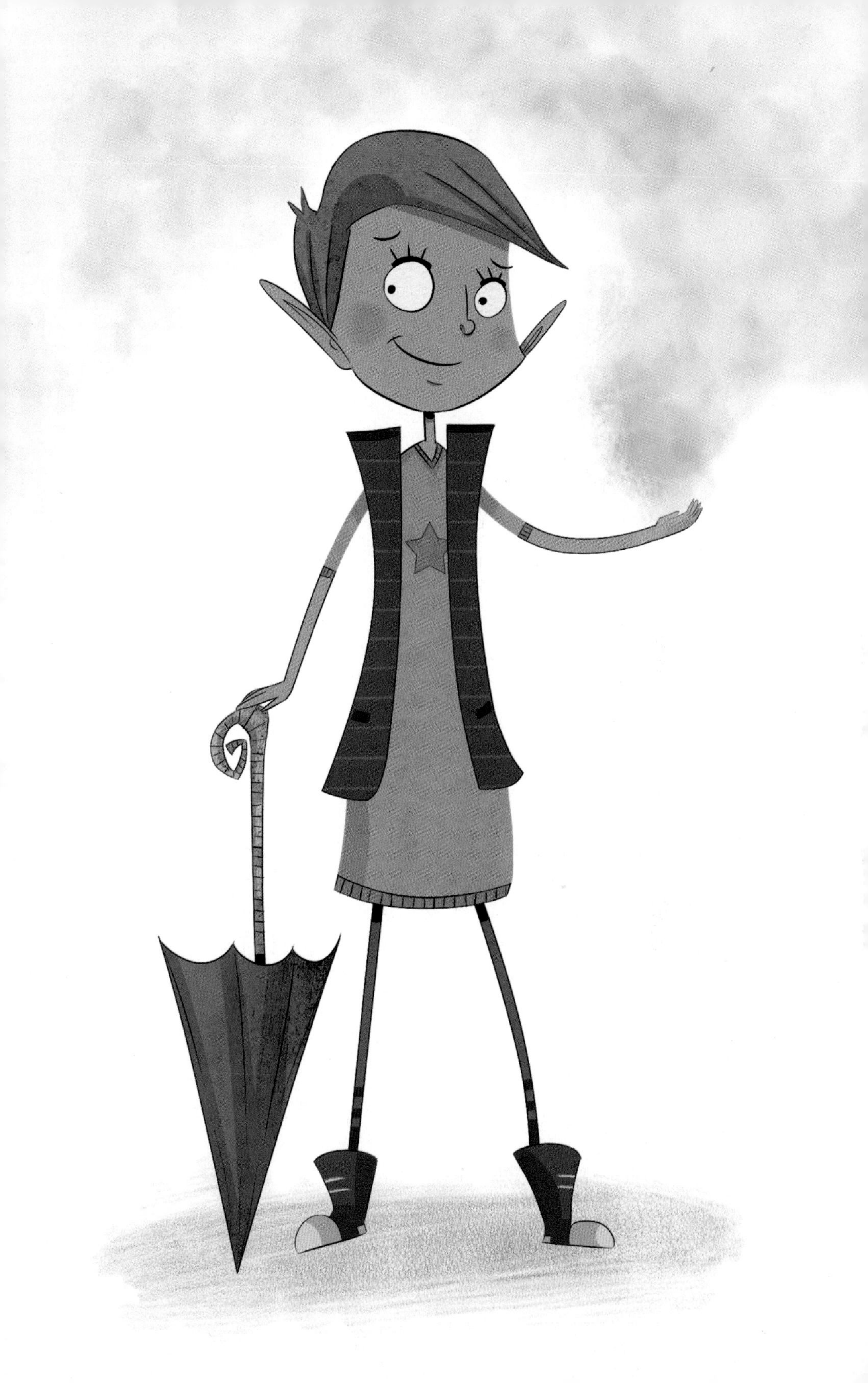

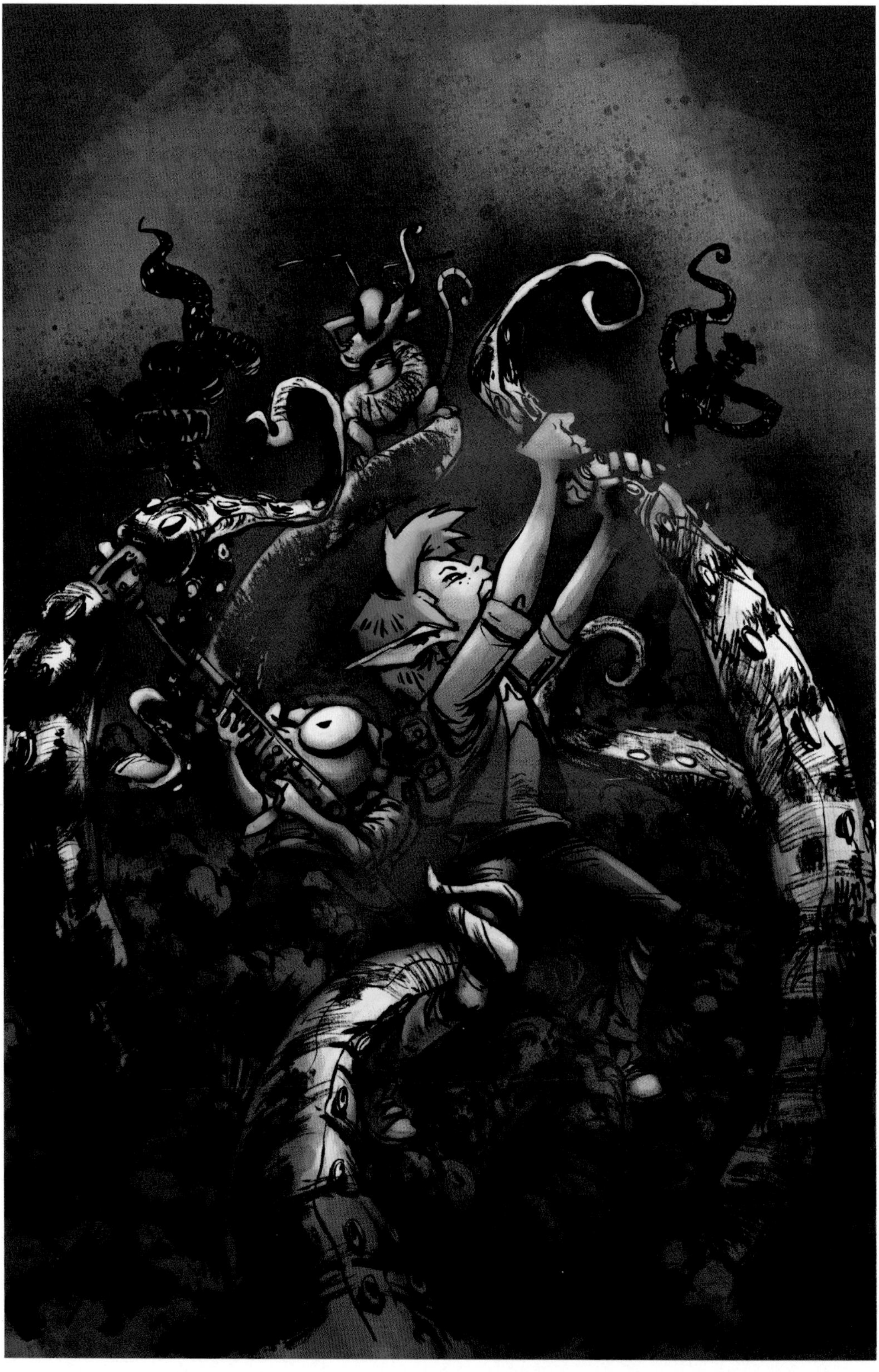

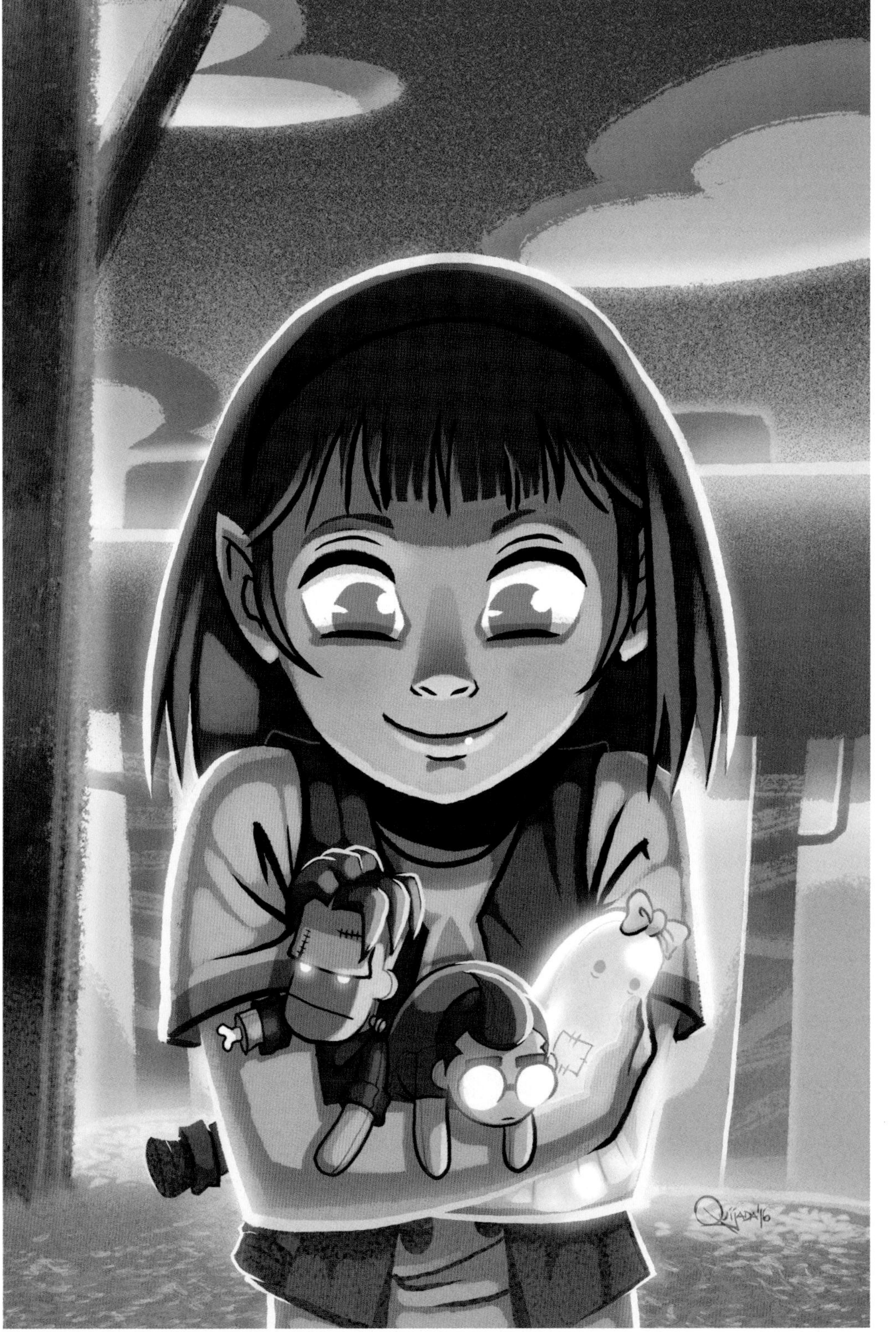
Quijada'16

ACKNOWLEDGMENTS

Thank you to everyone who helped make "Oddly Normal" a reality!

To you, dear reader. Thank you so much for your support!

To Mom and Dad... your support for me and my work has been invaluable.

To my awesome co-colorist, Tracy Bailey.

To Kate Youngdahl for the care and feeding of a graphic novelist.

To Branwyn Bigglestone, Jonathan Chan, Addison Duke, Monica Garcia, Sasha Head, Vincent Kukua, Sarah Mello, Emily Miller, Corey Murphy, Randy Okamura, Tricia Ramos, Ron Richards, Kat Salazar, Jenna Savage, Eric Stephenson, Meredith Wallace and everyone else at Image Comics for their amazing behind-the-scenes work.

To my able and speedy team of color flatters: Daniel Mead, Shelby Edmunds and Thomas Boatwright.

To the amazing and generous artists who contributed beautiful pin-ups to this book: Scott Brown, Skylar Chandler, Katie Cook, Grant Gould, Val Hochberg, Dani Jones, Cam Kendell, James Lent, Jay Myers and Sergio Quijada.

To the many friends and colleagues who have been there for me over the years, including... Leigh Boone, Pat Bussey, John Copeland, Ronn Dech, Tracy Edmunds, Adam Fellows, Brian Fies, Scott Gagain, Jessie Garza, Grant Gould, Judy Hansen, Gisela Hernandez-Rosa, Josh Howard, Doug Netter and John J. Walsh IV.

And last but not least... many thanks to my "Oddly Normal 2.0" Kickstarter supporters: Janel A, Regi Aaron, Kathryn Alice, Charles Alvis, John Anthony, Matthew Ashcraft, Ray B., David Barnett, Hudson On Bass, Bchan84, Jessie Beck, Alison Benowitz, Jennifer Berk, Daniel Blackburn, Daniel J. Blomberg IV, Leigh Boone, Brian Braatz, Sacha Brady, Michael Branham, Dominic Brennan, Mark Brenner, John Brown, Darren Calvert, Jeffrey Chandler, Michael Chapman, Chris, Chooi, Chouck, Cody Christopher, Justin Chung, Coffinail, Christopher Cole, CoolB, Cathy Cooper, Corrodias, Aaron Cullers, Julian Damy, Brad Dancer, Lara Dann, Joséantonio W. Danner, Daniel & Kanako, Ted Dastick Jr., DebraS, Ronn Dech, James DeMarco, Harald Demler, Arik Devens, Vic DiGital, Brandon Eaker, Tracy Edmunds, Jamas Enright, Susan Eisner, Leandro Garcia Estevam, Evilgeniuslady, Harry Ewasiuk, Dan Eyer, Adam Fellows, Brian Fies, Fletcher, Phil Flickinger, Thomas Forsythe, Mary Frampton, Tracey Frampton, Corey Funt, Andrea Futrelle, Gdm_online, George, Tim Goldenburg, Sara Gordon, Stuart Gorman, Ingrid K. V. Hardy, Michael Hawk, Helena S. M., Jessica Hightower, Stephen Hill, David Hopkins, Michael Hunter, Chris Inoue, Arul Isai Imran, Jayvs1, Delores Jeffrey, Jimi, JMShelledy, Wendy Johnson-Diedrich, Dani Jones, Anne K, Peter Karmanos III, Kathryn, Kelso, Thanun Khowdee, Kirsten, André Kishimoto, Veronika Knurenko, Matthew Koelbl, Laura Kokaisel, Axel 'dervideospieler' Kothe, Karen Krajenbrink, Zeus & Hera Kramer, Manuel Kroeber, Tom Kurzanski, Amber Lanagan, Patrick Larcada, Jeremie Lariviere, Linda LeClair, Matt Leitzen, Yoni Limor, Lulu Lin, Tim Lindvall, Rick Long, Lisa M. Lorelli, MageAkyla, Dan Manson, Marina, Miles Matton, Fergus Maximus, Jamie McIntyre, Tim McKnight, Jeff McRorie, Daniel Mead, Jeff Metzner, Michael and Liz, Mika, Miroatme, Riaz Skrenes Missaghi, Casey Moeller, Björn Morén, Rich Moulton, Movet, Matthew Munk, Molly Murphy, Jussi Myllyluoma, John Nacinovich, Cynthia Narcisi, Bruce Nelson, Sian Nelson, Niels, Michael "Waffles" Nguyen, Rhonda Parker, James Parris, Merrisa Patel, Shane & Marjan Patrick, C. Raymond Pechonick, Tawnly Pranger, David Recor, Rhel, Ben Rosenthal, Harrison Sayre, Ryan Schrodt, Patrick Scullin, Nick Seal, Jenny Seay, Senatorhung, Sgllama, Shervyn, Todd Shipman, Andy Shuping, Ashtara Silunar, Skraldesovs, Chazen Smith, Stephen Smoogen, Ryan Snow, Daniel Snyder, Stormy, Stu, Stephen Stutesman, Erik Taylor, Bruce Thompson, Tialessa, Kevin Tian, Tom Tinneny, Rachel Tougas, PJ Trauger, TriOmegaZero, Mai Tzimaka, Tim The Unlucky, Frankie Vanity, Martha Wald, James P. Walker, John J. Walsh IV, Shannon Wendlick, Paul Westover, A. M. White, Heath White, Kiwi Wiltshire, Daniel Winterhalter, Stephen "Switt!" Wittmaak, Christoph Wolf, Emiko Wong, Ryan Worrell, Samuel Young, Zabuni, and Matt Zollmann.

ALSO BY OTIS FRAMPTON

Oddly Normal
BOOK 1
WRITTEN & ILLUSTRATED
by OTIS FRAMPTON

ODDLY NORMAL BOOK 1

Oddly Normal
BOOK 2
WRITTEN & ILLUSTRATED
by OTIS FRAMPTON

ODDLY NORMAL BOOK 2

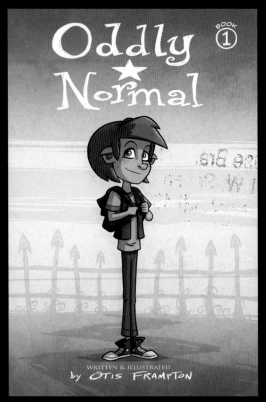

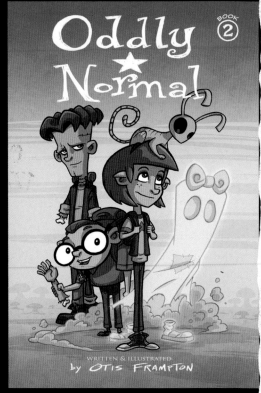